The
Face of
Sam

J.A. Ratcliffe

© 2013 Julie Ratcliffe
Published by High Sails Publications
PO Box 7575, Christchurch, BH23 9HJ
Tel: +44 (0)1202 471097
www.highsailspublications.co.uk

First published 2013 by High Sails Publications
ISBN: 978-0-9568572-1-7

British Library Cataloguing in Publication Data
A catalogue record for this book is available from the British
Library

Illustrations and cover artwork © Domini Deane
www.dominideane.com

Author photograph © Amanda Clay
www.clayphotography.co.uk

Set by www.beamreachuk.co.uk
Printed by www.beamreachuk.co.uk

Acknowledgements

I have received tremendous support from the people of Christchurch and beyond following the publication of *The Thirteenth Box*. I would like to thank in particular Eric Montague, who created the promotional video and the Penny family of Ye Olde Eight Bells shop, which was the Eight Bells alehouse at the time of the books. Thanks also to local retailers for their support.

For this book, *The Face of Sam*, I would like to thank the following people:

Judy Hall, for her expert guidance and support; Gwynneth Ashby, for her invaluable help and members of the village writers, for their constructive comments.

Thanks go to Pat Richards, Churchwarden, Christchurch Priory Church and my neighbour, Vivien Beale along with Les Hiley and Howard Adams, for their assistance in getting me into places I couldn't normally reach!

I would also like to thank author and architect, Eric Cockain, who gave the carved face in the nave of the Priory Church the name Sam and was happy for me to use this in my book title.

Also: my friend and local historian, Michael Andrews; my sisters, Susan Robertson and Wendy Edmond for their feedback, and, once again, thanks to the very talented Domini Deane for the beautiful illustrations.

Last, but not least, thanks to my husband, Michael for his continued support, especially as he thought I was writing only one book!

For all those who in the past, present and future,
cherish and care for the Priory Church, Christchurch

Contents

Cast of Characters

Cliff House

Sir Charles Tarrant
Lady Elizabeth Tarrant
Edmund Tarrant (their son, currently away at school)
Jane Menniere, cousin to Sir Charles
Yves Menniere, Jane's husband – away on business
Perinne Menniere (their daughter)

Household

Joseph – butler
Susan – cook
Lucy Scott – maid to Perinne
John Scott – stableman, coachman – Lucy's father
Ben – stable boy
Miss Foster – Perinne's tutor

Townsfolk of Christchurch

The Reverend William Jackson – Vicar of Christchurch
Adam Jackson (his son)
Will Gibbs
Meg Gibbs, Will's mother
Beth Gibbs, Will's sister
Nathan, Will's friend
Sam the dog
Isaac Hooper, the Gibbs' neighbour – smuggler
Adam Litty, brewery worker – smuggler
Caleb Brown, blacksmith – smuggler
Bessie Brown, Caleb's wife
Guy Cox, fisherman – smuggler
Joseph Martin, landlord of the George Inn
David Preston, Poor House Master – smuggler
Judith Preston, Poor House Mistress
Henry Lane – smuggler
Thomas Walton, the new schoolmaster, originally from Bristol
Joshua Stevens – Chief Revenue Officer
Captain Palmer – dragoons' captain

Burton Village

James Clarke, right-hand-man to Sir Charles Tarrant
Hannah Clarke, his wife
Jack Clarke, their son

Danny Clarke, their son
Sarah Clarke, their daughter
Grandpa Hopkins

Burton Hall
Philip Stone, plantation owner, main residence Gloucestershire
Isobel Stone, his wife
Patience Stone, their daughter
Malvina Stone, their daughter
Benjamin Kelly, butler to the Stones
Mary Maunder, maid

Hinton
John Hewitt, former sailor – smuggler
Mary Hewitt, John's wife, sister to Hannah Clarke
(Danny Clarke's Aunt and Uncle)

Ringwood
Meekwick Ginn, venturer

Kent – Conyer
Rowland Blackbourne, blacksmith – smuggler
Susannah Blackbourne, Rowland's wife
Josh Blackbourne, their son
Henry Cotton, baker – smuggler
Tabitha Cotton, his wife
Peter Graves – smuggler

Other Kent smugglers
Levi Bird, fruit grower – smuggler
Saul Bird, smuggler – in Maidstone gaol facing trial
Pip, Levi's friend – smuggler
Thomas Slaughter, deceased – smuggler

The Woolsey Family, formerly of Faversham
Francis Woolsey, dragoon captain
Amelia Woolsey, Francis's wife, lost at sea
Rosamund Woolsey, their daughter
Samuel Pascoe, of Sidmouth – Amelia Woolsey's brother

London
Sir George Cook, scientist and Member of the Royal Society
Various incidental characters.

See not the priest,
nor he spy thee

Prologue – Hampshire 1723

Richard Redcliffe bent, hands on his knees, panting and huffing from his wide-open mouth until he gradually regained his breath. One hand clung on to a small brown leather sack. His thin shirt stuck to his sweat-covered back, his long, dark coat a heavy burden when running. He looked back across the river towards the shadowy heath, mist clinging to the pale purple heather like ghosts of the dawn. Had he lost them? Over to the west the early autumn sun, casting gold and grey hues across the sky, was nearing its time to wake up the tiny town of Christchurch, insignificant but for the large church and the castle keep, both standing high above the thatched cottages nearby.

He had no time to lose. Wet from crossing the river he made his way beside the quomp, past the old mill and towards the south of the Priory Church. Centuries had passed since Henry VIII had spared the ancient building. Inching his way around the walls he found a small door and crept into the building, its musty chill eerily whispering around his legs. It had been many years since he'd been here, but it would always be as it was. No one was about. He moved quietly down the south nave aisle keeping close to the tall arches lest he needed to hide quickly, looking about as he made his way deep into the building. Somewhere a door creaked. He grasped the sack and crouched, but no footsteps followed. He moved into the nave and gazed up at the magnificent triforiums at either side. Then something caught his eye. A face, not a gargoyle or a man of the cloth, just a simple, carved face. But he shouldn't linger, he needed to find a hiding place.

He stepped back underneath the arch and continued on to the steps of the great quire. He looked at the sack. This was his new life, one of comfort and wealth. Treasure of gold and brilliant jewels, he'd all to gain. It had to be safe until he could return. He gazed around; amongst the ancient columns and chantries he saw what he was looking for. The space was small though enough to fit the sack, but he'd need to enclose it somehow. His task was almost done. All he needed was to draw some clues, lest it wasn't he who came to retrieve his treasure.

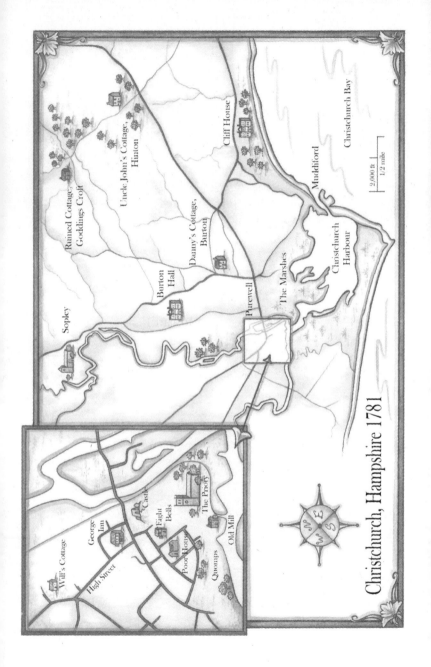

Christchurch, Hampshire 1781

Chapter 1

Shipwreck!

Christchurch, Tuesday 12th June 1781

'The coat, get the coat!'

The little girl turned her face towards the sound of a gruff voice. The sky was black. The rain had stopped but the wind still lashed and waves were crashing like thunder onto the shore around her. She could feel the water rolling over her legs and back again. Sand stuck to her cheeks and her lips were dry and salty. Shouts bellowed amongst the sound of the sea as a large shadowy figure loomed towards her. She lay, motionless, opening her mouth to shout 'help', though nothing came out.

'C'mon!'

The girl watched, helpless as the huge figure bent towards her and began to unbutton the sodden, woollen garment. She had no strength to fight off the man.

'Be ye alive?'

The girl opened her eyes and tried to speak, but the wind blew her words away.

'Tis only a girl,' the man whispered under his breath.

'Get the coat.'

'Be still as ye can girl, fer ye life, don't speak a word,'

1

the stranger whispered, as he scooped her up from the sands and threw her over his broad shoulder. She stayed limp, her arms dangling down the man's back like she were a deer he'd poached. His wet leather jacket smelled of fire and animal. The beach seemed full of the shadows of people and ponies and noise.

'Where's mother?' she wanted to ask.

The man carried her across the sands and lifted her onto a waiting cart; her legs, cold, wet and unsteady could barely hold her. The moon peeked from behind a break in the cloud lighting up the man's bearded face. He lifted his finger to his lips then he pushed some small barrels to one side.

'Lay thee down girl, quickly now.'

She curled herself beside the barrels terrified but helpless as he covered her with some sacks. She could still hear shouting and felt the cart jolt as if other items were thrown in. The cart set off. The wheels struggled in the sand until finally they crunched onto gravel.

'Caleb, wait!' It was a woman's voice. Rosamund peered over the cover. The woman was carrying a huge sack which weighed her down on one side. Her coat and hat were soaked, her weather-worn face barely visible in the stormy gloom as she hurried after the cart.

'Climb up our Bessie,' Caleb replied. 'What did ye get?'

'The Lord 'ave mercy on us, what a night. But I got a couple o' small ankers and a bag o' small parcels wrapped in sackin', not sure what's inside, some decent silk would be good. Twas 'ard to see anythin' other than what the light'nin' showed up. Adam Litty said to keep the lamps low, get as much as we're able before the controller gets o'er from Poole. But I c'n go back later and see. The cart looks goodly full. What did ye find?'

He gave his wife a long look and shook his head from side to side. 'Well, Bessie, a bit more than I expected.'

Danny Clarke's shoulders jolted as the latest crash of thunder followed the lightning's flash. In all his thirteen years, Danny had never known a wilder night. He hadn't been able to sleep for fear and had crept down the stairs of the little cottage in Burton to sit in the gloom with Grandpa Hopkins, who hadn't been well and preferred to sleep in his chair by the fire.

'Aint seen storms like these since I were a boy,' Grandpa said, as he began to cough.

The bad weather had lashed the coast for the past week and some people were saying it was the end of the world. But Danny knew better. His Uncle John often told stories about storms at sea, but still he didn't like this. There'd been a storm last summer when lightning had hit a cottage in nearby Christchurch. The thatched roof caught fire and it had burned down. The family who'd lived there had to go and live in the Poor House. A chilly shudder ran through his body at the thought. His parents, his brother Jack and sister, Sarah were all upstairs in bed. Danny couldn't bear the thought of a similar horror befalling his family.

He thought about Will, the boy he'd met over a year ago and with whom he'd shared a fantastic adventure. Will was on an adventure of his own. He'd left Poole to sail across the Atlantic Ocean to Newfoundland, taking an exciting newly invented machine to America. Danny hadn't heard from Will, but a letter had been received at Cliff House where his father worked for local landowner, Sir Charles Tarrant. The letter said that Will's ship, the *Majesty*, had arrived in St John's and that Will had chosen to continue onward to Boston to the machine's final destination, where a man called Simon Dufaut hoped to get it to work.

Suddenly the room lit up like daylight. Danny could hear Sarah's startled cries through the ceiling. A crack was quickly followed by a blast of thunder which shook the walls, Danny's heart drummed. Is this what cannon fire sounded like? Would Will become trapped by the war raging between Britain and America, he shuddered at the thought. Why had Will been allowed to travel with the machine that they, along with their friend, Perinne Menniere, had found? Would he be safe?

Danny counted the seconds between the flashes and the thunder. Uncle John told him that the more seconds, the further the storm was moving away. At last the thunder dulled to a distant grumble. It would soon be daylight and Danny would have to make his way to the Priory Church and his school. He peered out of the window and saw that the almost full moon was trying to break through the clouds. He'd been back at the free grammar school since last Easter, having been to a boarding school near Dorchester for just under a year. He hadn't liked it and was quietly pleased when his father had told him Sir Charles Tarrant would no longer be paying the fees given as a reward for a daring rescue and finding the machine. Grandpa had fallen asleep, hardly stirring but for the wheezing of his chest. Danny made his way up the stairs to try and catch a couple of hours sleep.

'But Caleb, we can't keep the little mite. Shall we take 'er to the Poor House?' Bessie spoke as the cart turned into the blacksmith's yard.

'They'll ask too many questions. Revenue'd want the goods returned.'

'Then what'll we do?'

'I've an idea, c'me on, let's unpack an' I'll move 'er on

just afore daybreak. But we keep this to ourselves. We tell no one Bessie, no one.'

Rosamund had woken from an exhausted sleep when the cart stopped and was watching the two strangers working in the shadows. The huge man who'd carried her from the beach was making an easy job of heaving barrels from the cart and storing them under hay at the back of the building. The woman, sturdily built and with a round face, had been lifting packages and setting them aside on a table. Rosamund crouched as they approached her.

'You awake little miss?' Bessie whispered. 'Come wi' me, let's get ye some small beer an' I'll get a dry blanket to warm ye up.'

Rosamund froze. She didn't know these people, where was her mother? All she could remember was a huge boom followed by ear-splitting banging. It felt as though someone had picked her up and thrown her and she was suddenly being thrashed around in the chilly water. She climbed down from the cart. She felt the woman's hand press gently on her shoulder and encourage her towards a small cottage beside the stable. After unhitching the horse and closing it into its stall, the man followed them.

'Come on, we shan't hurt thee,' Caleb said. He towered beside her like a giant, yet he didn't seem threatening.

She allowed herself to be led into a small, dim parlour. The man took a wooden spill and set it glowing using flint and tinder. Soon the smell of a candle, with a mix of tallow and beeswax, filled the air. The same spill was used to set light to twigs that the woman had placed onto the ashes in a grate. Before long the flames were strong enough for Caleb to place a log on top. It gave the tiny room a ghostly glow.

'Now then, miss, we can't keep ye 'ere,' he looked down at the bedraggled child and smiled through his whiskery face. 'Once ye've 'ad somthin' to eat, an' a drink, an' warmed up, I'll take ye somewhere where ye'll be safe

5

an' sure to be found soon. Don't be afraid.'

Bessie moved to take off Rosamund's coat, but she clasped the collar tightly. 'C',mon, miss, it be wet, let me dry it fer ye.'

Rosamund watched, tensing her body as Bessie took her coat and hung it to dry over the back of a chair which was facing the fire. The man had thrown another log onto it, making it crackle and throw off orange sparks. She still hadn't spoken a word. Bessie wrapped her in a warm blanket and offered her a cup and a chunk of bread. Rosamund sipped at the weak ale. It tasted different to the beer at home in Kent. She watched as Caleb approached the room's small window and peered outside. It was the second time he'd done so in just a few minutes. He'd lit a long pipe and he was drawing on it then blowing out the nutty-smelling smoke.

'Be dawn soon, must get ye movin' lass,' he said.

'But the coat's still wet, husband,' Bessie pleaded.

'We'll keep it. We c'n find some sacking cloth to wrap around 'er, it won't be long afore she's found.'

Bessie left the room and returned with a sack and Caleb cut it open and wrapped it around Rosamund.

'C'me on lass, come wi' me.'

But Rosamund ran over and grabbed her sodden coat.

'Let the poor mite keep it, Caleb. It's all she 'as in the world.'

Danny put his hand in his pocket. His mother had given him sixpence to bring home a pound of sugar. It wasn't there. He must have dropped it here in the choir stalls, or on the way in. He couldn't understand why he hadn't heard it fall. Maybe the singing or the echo of the boys' chatter as they made their way there had masked the noise.

There'd been a great deal of excitement about the storm and all the talk was that there'd been a wrecking in the bay.

The boys would be allowed to run to the necessary room before making their way back up the stone spiral staircase and into the schoolroom. Danny paused so as to come last. He looked around the stone floor for the little silver coin. As he crouched beside the old carved seats he thought he heard a sniff, and another. He stood, but couldn't see anyone. He kept still, straining to hear. There it was again. Maybe one of the vergers was inside. He peered through the archway into the main nave of the church, its high pillars majestically pointing to the painted wooden beams of the roof. Sniff. He couldn't see anyone. He returned to his task of finding the coin, he would be due back and he needed to listen for the boys returning. As he heard the small door to the school opening and the master's voice calling the boys, he noticed a shiny disc, just under the bench end. He bent to grasp it. It was the sixpence. He puffed out his cheeks with relief. He needed to run up the north aisle and out of the main porch to make it look as though he'd been outside with everyone else.

He stepped down from the quire and was behind the altar when he heard the sniff again. He tiptoed quietly towards the sound and caught sight of a small girl sitting between a pair of the giant pillars. She was staring up at the arch directly across from her. She seemed not to notice as Danny approached. He followed her gaze and saw that her eyes were fixed on a round, carved face, with a large moustache, set into the stone high above.

'Hello,' he said quietly to the girl. She'd turned her head toward Danny and looked back at the face. 'Are you lost?' he asked. He peered around to see if anyone were about, but there was no one. He could hear the dull drumming of the boys scuffling up the stairs and wondered what to do. He looked back at the girl. She was very pale and she was shivering. She had a sack drawn around her shoulders

7

and was clutching a blue coat, which Danny thought was odd. Her head was without a bonnet and her hair was long, limp, and knotted. Her stockings had holes and he noticed there were cuts on her leg beneath and a bruise on her cheek. He couldn't leave her. Although he would get in trouble for being in the church and not outside, Danny ran to fetch help.

Chapter 2

Silence and secrets

Tuesday 12th June 1781

'She hasn't spoken a word since we found her, Mistress Preston,' the Reverend Jackson said. 'We've no idea where she came from. One of the boys found her after choir practice. He shouldn't have been there, but a good job he was.' He studied the little girl, his face puzzled. He hunched his shoulders. 'Sitting on the church's stone floor, it would be so cold, especially in the morning. She could have caught a nasty chill.'

'Aye, Mr Jackson. What a wild night for a child to be out an' about alone. Such a terrible storm, an' the wreckin' in the bay, all souls lost I hear.' Judith Preston shook her head with pity.

'It appears so. I expect that folk are still out there salvaging. There'll be bodies washed ashore no doubt, burials for free,' he tutted. 'I shall leave the child with you and speak with the overseers, hopefully they can find out to whom she belongs.' At that, the Reverend Jackson put on his hat and left.

'Now girl, I'm Mistress Preston an' this is Ann,' Judith looked directly at Rosamund. 'What's your name?'

Rosamund watched the woman. She was tall with a round face and small pug nose. Her teeth exposed by a smile, were uneven. Rosamund said nothing, hugging her coat, her small body trembling, but the woman didn't seem to notice.

'Go along with Ann an' she'll show you to a bed. There's a cloth an' basin to wash your face an' hands, an' we've found somethin' for you to change into. Then come back here an' we'll find you some work.'

Rosamund sat on the edge of a little cot bed and looked around the room. Along the wall ran a row of beds each with a coarse brown cover neatly folded. There was a matching bed on the opposite side. Her own bed was pushed up against the wall and was under a small window. The walls were white washed and the paint was peeling. Although the room was on the second floor of the building there was a musty, damp patch creeping up the wall. There was no one else in the room. She wanted to cry, but the tears wouldn't come. When the man had mentioned the bodies she wanted to scream and run away, but it was as if she'd been pinned to the floor. Rosamund picked up her coat, which was still damp and smelling of salt and seaweed. The normally soft wool felt sticky and held tiny grains of sand which clung to the seams. She turned it inside out to expose the blue silken lining and, running her fingers down the seam from the edge of the left sleeve, she found a short hem which revealed two little black buttons. She undid these, reached her slim fingers inside and lifted out a small, pale brown leather pouch which was closed by a twisted cord drawstring.

'Don't let it out of your possession,' her father's voice

whispered in her mind.

She opened the pouch and took out a locket. It was dry. The leather had protected it. It was oval-shaped and gold-backed. She ran her forefinger gently across the picture painted on the front, her father. He was handsome in his smart red uniform coat decorated with gold braid, its gold buttons fastened over a white waistcoat. He was wearing a short, white wig in the picture, yet his own hair was copper-coloured, just as her own was. Rosamund took a deep breath and listened carefully to make sure that she was alone. She prised open the locket carefully. Inside were two squares of folded paper. Placing the pouch and locket beside her she took one out and gently opened it. On it was a drawing of a face. It was strange, simply drawn, but it had to be a man because he had a large moustache, each side twisted like a skein of wool. The face was oval with wide eyes and a triangle for a mouth. Between the eyes was the bridge of his nose which, at its end, looked more like a snout. Two ears faced forward as if listening. Beneath this were symbols and some pictures of a skull and arrows and other things. Father said it was a cipher and if solved, would lead to a treasure trove that had been hidden for fifty years or more, but none had been able to solve the puzzle. She looked at the face. Her mother had laughed at it, saying it looked like Uncle Sam, though it wasn't him. But Rosamund had seen this face.

She unfurled the other square. It was part printed and part handwritten. She read some of the words.

Promise to pay the bearer the sum of £500 on demand ...

'No one will look for these here, so you must keep them, Rosamund,' father had said, the night before he'd taken her and her mother to the ship at Chatham. She carefully refolded the papers and returned them to the locket. She placed it in the pouch and this time pulled out a watch. It was silver, decorated with a simple design of etched leaves and, in the centre of the back, were the initials RR.

This had been her grandfather's. It had been lost for many years, but was back in the family.

'Keep these hidden in your coat, don't take them out. Speak with no one. You'll meet up with your uncle at Plymouth and he will take you somewhere where you'll be safe,' her father's voice whispered. 'We must never go back to Kent.' Rosamund thought again of the moment when her father had pulled her close to him holding her tightly, kissing her auburn hair. 'Try not to worry. I'll come as soon as I can, it won't be long before we'll all be together again.'

'But this isn't Plymouth, father,' her mind replied. 'What should I do?'

She'd no idea where she was. And mother was missing. And even here they wanted the coat - everyone wanted her coat. Trickles of tears rolled down her bruised cheek. 'I need to keep both the locket and watch safe, hidden away,' she told herself. 'But where can I put them?'

Rosamund wiped her face and, slipping off her dirty dress, she picked up the one that had been left for her. It was woollen. As she pushed her arms into the sleeves she winced at the scratchy, coarse fabric. But it did have large pockets and, after collecting everything together again, she pushed the little leather pouch deep inside. Gathering up the coat and her dress she made her way back down the staircase to find Ann or Mistress Preston.

Danny simply told the truth, he'd lost a coin. It was a lot of money and his mother would have been angry had he gone home with neither sugar nor change.

'And the little mite spoke nothing, Clarke?' Mr Walton said. His voice rasped and he gave a short cough.

'No, sir. All I heard was her sniffling.'

'Well, Reverend Jackson's taken her to the Poor House. He'll need to find out who she is. If she isn't from these parts, they'll have to find her parish and arrange for her return. Did you see anyone else about?'

'No, sir, it was all quiet. But maybe someone came in when we were singing?'

'Aye, that could be the case, we wouldn't see from the quire. Well, let's get back to the school room. Latin's next, can't get behind with your Latin.'

Danny lifted his hand to his mouth to stifle his sigh, lest the schoolmaster should hear. He ran his hand through his wavy, fair hair. He'd much rather be doing science or geography. But even more exciting would be to find out where the girl had come from. Who was she? She was much younger than he was, he hadn't seen her before. If she were from the town, someone must know who she was. If not, how did she come to be in the Priory so early? If she were going to the Poor House, maybe Perinne would be able to find out. He hadn't seen his friend Perinne for months. When they'd met last she'd told him how she had decided to help out there, especially with the younger children. He'd go to the beach after school. He wanted to see the wreck and he might just catch her out riding. If not, he'd have to write her a note.

They made their way up the stone spiral staircase. There were seventy five steps. Danny had counted them many a time. Danny noticed that his teacher seemed reluctant to hold on to the central column. As they neared the schoolroom he could hear the excited chattering of the other boys.

'Silence!' Thomas Walton ordered. He coughed again.

As they passed through the door the boys rose and stood beside their desks. Everyone was watching Danny. He gulped with dread. He could still be punished for not leaving the Priory immediately after choir practice. He'd hate to have punishment in front of the other boys.

'Sit!' Mr Walton strode behind a large, worn wooden table and drew back his chair. Wisps of his dark brown hair were falling from underneath the grey wig he was wearing. The wig wasn't on properly and tilted slightly to one side. Danny thought he must have been in a rush. Not everyone wore them all the time, so why bother to put it on at all. The Reverend Jackson had been the schoolmaster when Danny was here last. Mr Walton had taken over, shortly before Danny's return after Easter.

Danny moved quickly to his desk trying to keep his head down. He may have escaped being in trouble this time. He glanced towards the other doorway across from the one he'd just entered. The storm had brought warmer weather and the door was wedged open. Danny glanced up at the tiny, square window at the top of the stairwell just beyond the door. On the ledge in front of the window was a candle. Danny had heard that it was used as a signal to smugglers out at sea, to tell them it was safe to bring in the goods. He hadn't known much about smuggling until last year when his new friend, Will, had told him of the things which went on in the town. His father wouldn't talk about smuggling, though.

Mr Walton began reciting Latin phrases and the boys were repeating them. Danny didn't see the point but he joined in, he'd already learned this at the other school. The morning dragged on. Following Latin the boys had to practise their handwriting. Mr Walton produced a large sheet of oaten-coloured paper from which the boys were allowed just one small square each. Danny joined some of the boys who were sharpening their quills on the stone of the window case. The light from outside allowed them to check the shape of the nib and to make sure that the split would allow the ink to flow. One boy was re-cutting his with a penknife. The boys set about copying one of the Latin phrases that they'd recited and which Mr Walton had written onto a slate, though his writing wasn't as clear as it usually was. Danny enjoyed the letters he created, he loved it when he made a word that was neat and in a line. He stopped to let the ink dry and let his gaze drift through the windows and out to sea. He could see boats and sunshine glittering off the water; it was hard to imagine it was only hours since the awful storm.

'Clarke!'

'Sir!'

'You have time for day dreaming?'

'I was waiting for the ink...'

'Quiet!'

The room fell silent and all eyes turned towards Danny.

'Clear your things away, everyone, leave your scripts on your desks, the day is done and you can leave.' The boys shuffled from their chairs.

'Not you, Clarke!' The schoolmaster's voice rasped as he pointed his long finger towards Danny.

There was a ripple of mumbles amongst the boys as Danny took a deep breath and remained at his desk. The other boys walked out, some casting glances towards him. He wondered if he were finally to be punished.

'So, Clarke, had to give up boarding, did you?' The teacher was holding a cane in one hand and running it across the palm of his other. 'Sixpence for sugar? Showing off were you?' Mr Walton walked around Danny's desk then sat on the one beside him. Danny breathed in and bit on his lip. 'You should've asked permission to stay behind to look for your coin. You know the punishment.' Mr Walton stood and with his back to Danny, continued. 'I could thrash you for your disobedience. But you have a way out, would you like me to tell you what it is?'

'Y-yes, sir.'

'You seem strong, boy. I have a task and I want you to help me with it. But it is to remain our secret. You must mention it to no one. Can you row a boat?'

'Well, I have done, sir.'

'Good. It's a simple task and you will stay after school tomorrow to assist me. So what is it to be? A thrashing – or help me out and keep a secret?'

Danny couldn't think. A thrashing would soon be over and done with, but what could it be that the schoolmaster needed help with that had to be kept quiet?

'Well, boy, what is it to be?'

'I, er, I'm not sure.'

'I'm not sure, *sir*!' Mr Walton swapped the whip from his right hand to his left and snapped it on the desk with a crack. 'Come on, boy, it's nothing too dangerous. I've heard tell that you're a brave one. Just do the job. Tell no one and that's that.'

Danny was intrigued. 'Should I do it?' he thought.

Chapter 3
Tales of treasure

North Kent, Tuesday 12th June 1781

Josh Blackbourne's stone just missed the clump of grass he'd aimed at, but it made a satisfying plomp into the muddy bank of Conyer creek.

'Josh, what yew adoin'? Come an' have some ale.'

He spun around to see Henry Cotton carrying a tray holding drinks and a loaf of bread. Henry was heading towards his father who was sitting with his friend, Peter Graves, at a stout table on a grassy bank. The sun was hot on his back and a drink was just what he needed. Josh set off at a trot, his bare feet used to the stony ground. As he settled on a small stool his father, Rowland Blackbourn, a blacksmith, ruffled his son's mop of thick, fair hair with his rough hand. They lived on the edge of the creek in a small cottage next to Henry Cotton's little bakery.

His father's friends often gathered like this, though usually at night time. They would occasionally meet up during the day and this time he was with them and he wondered what they would be talking about. Josh knew something had happened, or was about to, because his mother had been cursing. Maybe he would find out now.

The men each took a tankard and lifted them together to a clunk of 'good health'. Josh sipped from his cup of small beer, swishing the liquid around his dry mouth. His belly rumbled as he breathed in the smell of the freshly-baked bread.

Peter Graves was sitting on Josh's right. He was much older than his father and he never seemed to do anything but hang around the boats. Josh liked Peter, he would talk about days gone by and about London and other places that Josh had never been to.

'Hello there!' The shout came from along the lane.

Josh looked around towards the sound of the voice. It was Levi Bird, a skinny-looking man with tanned skin, wrinkled by time and sun. Josh didn't like Levi. He scared him and his father was often in a bad mood after he'd been here.

'So, what be the news on Francis Woolsey?' said Henry.

'Pip followed him to London, but lost him near Blackfriars,' said Levi.

'D'ye think he still be in London?'

'Who knows - until we catch his trail ag'in. He were seen goin' to a bank an' had notes drawn,' he snarled. 'The reward.'

'If that's what it were, Levi,' Henry said. 'We've no proof Woolsey was the informant.'

'Tss! The gang said it were, an' I take their word. My brother could be transported, or worse, could have a rope around his neck. Woolsey's runnin' away, with my brother's blood money!' Levi slammed his fist onto the table.

'Why would Saul want to get involved with that gang. Vicious, they are,' Rowland said. Levi shot him an angry glare.

'What about Woolsey's womenfolk?' Peter Graves asked. He wiped beads of sweat from his bald head with a bright handkerchief and gave Rowland a quick warning shake of the head.

Henry tore a chunk off the loaf ready to push it into his mouth. 'Word we got were the house were shut, belongings gone. Roger Law said they were seen boardin' a sloop at Chatham. They were alone - if 'tis true.' Henry looked at Josh and nodded at the tray. Josh helped himself to some bread.

'Who's Francis Woolsey, father?' Josh asked Rowland.

'A dragoon. A King's man, Josh, through and through.'

'Run and ask Tabitha for some more ale, Josh, will yew?' Henry said. 'And a tankard for Levi.'

'Yes, Mr Cotton.' Josh picked up the tray and ran off to the bake house.

'So,' Henry began. 'Are we still on for that work at Whitstable tomorrow?'

'Aye,' Levi said. 'It's huge. The lander's asked for help an' we'll be paid well. We'll get transport instructions on the night.'

'We'll meet here. Take two carts, Rowland's and yours, Levi.' Henry said. 'Ah, here's Josh.'

Josh set down the tray. He picked up a crust of bread and settled next to Peter.

'I shan't forget 'bout Woolsey, though,' Levi said. 'If I get word, I'll be after him. Saul's stuck in Maidstone gaol. If we c'n get Woolsey, we c'n force him to withdraw his witness, and give back the cipher.'

'What's a cipher?' Josh asked.

'A puzzle, Josh,' Rowland answered. 'Writing and drawings that make a secret message.'

'Levi's brother thought he were about to get his hands on some treasure!' Peter laughed.

'What happened, Mr Graves? What treasure?' Josh asked, brushing crumbs from his lips with the back of his hand.

'The tale goes back many a year, Josh. What an adventure that was!'

The others groaned. They'd heard this tale a hundred

times before. Henry stood and collected the tankards. 'I'd better get back to the bake house or Tabitha will be calling.'

Levi Bird grumbled. 'He can't get away with it!'

'He'll turn up somewhere, Levi,' Henry said. 'We'll get the watch back too and find that treasure, an' we can all live like the rich.'

Rowland Blackbourne stood. 'I've horses needin' shoes,' he said and followed Henry towards the forge and Henry's bakery. 'Yew comin' Josh? I could do with a hand.'

'Leave him be, Rowland, it's too warm an' sunny for a boy to be smithin',' Peter said. 'Come on Josh, let's walk 'long the creek an' I'll tell you the story.'

'You need your boots on, Josh,' his father shouted, a resigned frown across his face.

'All right, father.' Josh ran towards the doorway where his boots were standing. His brown breeches reached down to his knees, where they were unbuttoned, and his grubby white shirt was open at the neck. It was too hot to wear anything more.

The tide was out and the creek was a sweep of mud banks, winding out towards the Swale. The remaining water glistened in the sun, as if it had been sprinkled with sparks from a fire. A few boats were laid up on the banks with their ropes settled into the mud. Josh and Peter made their way down the narrow path that had been worn along the edge of the high bank. Soon, after a gentle climb, they could see the landscape. Heat haze hovered over marshland and out towards the water. Skylarks whistled their cheerful songs and the trill of terns sounded as they swooped over them, down to the mud in search of worms. Peter stopped and, turning, scanned the horizon.

'My family lived inland, Josh. Missed these views they did. Wool were their livin', keepin' sheep and shearin' for the fleeces. For nearly a century owler's have been passin' the wool out o' these creeks an' away without duty bein' paid. My father saw there were more money in avoidin' the taxes and took to the seas. He got in with a gang bringin' in tea and brandy, plus whatever else would make 'em a profit.' He breathed in the air slowly and whistled it back out again. 'An' the adventure? It were a good while back. I'd only be a lad, just like you. How old are you, Josh?'

'Twelve, Mr Graves.'

'Twelve. Hmm..., it were 1747, 'tis 1781, an' I be 46 years of age, so, yes, I were twelve too – just as you be.' He smiled. 'Father'd been away for weeks. But one night, as the autumn was beginnin', he returned home as angry as I'd ever seen him. He'd been on a run, bringin' in tea loaded in Guernsey. A joint venture with a gang from Sussex. They'd agreed a rendezvous in Christchurch Bay but they were caught by a revenue ship. The crew got away, but all the tea they'd aboard, around two tons, plus spirits, were seized. He were furious, their backers were furious too, they wanted their money! Father went to a meetin'. They weren't goin' to let the revenue get away with it and vowed to get the goods back. The only problem was it'd been taken to the Customs House far away at Poole, in Dorsetshire.'

Josh's green eyes were wide with surprise. 'Did they go?'

'Aye they did that. My father and I were with 'em. Mother feared she'd never see us again. Back then punishment for smugglin' were usually transportation to the Americas, but they've made it a capital offence, an' you c'n be sent to the gibbet.'

'Like Mr Bird's brother, Saul,' Josh said.

'Aye.' Peter hung his head, pursing his lips with pity. He took a deep breath. 'We set out with carts and horses, met up with around thirty others Chichester way. Then we headed west, determined to get the goods back. We arrived at Poole, it were on the sixth of October. Men were sent ahead. They came back with news of a navy ship in the harbour, guns pointin' towards the Customs House.

Father thought it mad to try, but the others and the Sussex lot were determined. Father had to go along with it. But what happened were to amaze us all. I were told to stay back as the gang were ready to fight for what belonged to 'em, but they met no opposition at all an', at sea, low tide had laid the ship out of sight. They just went in there. Smashed their way in, loaded up the carts with the tea and left, astonished.'

'And that was it? All over with?' Josh felt let down. He was expecting a huge battle.

'Aye, simple as that.' Peter sat down on a fallen tree trunk and took out a long pipe.

'But what 'bout the watch and the treasure trove, Mr Graves? Where does that fit into it all?'

Peter sucked at his pipe despite it being unlit. Josh sat down beside him. Peter smelled sweaty, but most of the men did. Josh gazed at the cloudless blue sky as Peter continued.

'Well that's the other part o' the tale, Josh. One o' the gang, Thomas Slaughter, was a gambler. He'd no family to worry 'bout back home and had money, more to come with his share of the tea. He told us he'd stay in Poole, catch up with us later. I wanted to stay too, we'd come so far an' I hadn't seen anythin', so my father agreed but only for a short while. We followed Thomas. He seemed to know his way about. He sought out a game, or a fight to bet upon.

We went into an inn. It heaved with people and my ears rang with the noise of the mix of laughter, squeals of women an' the odd growl of an argument brewing. Thomas joined with a group of sailors, just come into the harbour. They'd been at sea months an' had bin paid off an' they got into cards. As the stakes rose people backed off, leavin' it between Thomas an' one man. Thomas Slaughter was winnin' handsomely, but the other fellow wouldn't give up, sure that he could win back the money he'd lost. With everythin' on the table the man offered the coat off his back. Thomas agreed. They settled down, the money an' the coat all rested on the final hand. The place went quiet, people had gathered 'round. At last Thomas showed his hand, it were a winner. The sailor accused him of cheatin', saying he must have slipped cards aside when he'd taken off his coat. They both stood, tippin' up the table. The man took a swing at Thomas, yellin', almost catchin' him square on the jaw. Thomas was furious – an' when he got mad, he could be a fearsome sight. He snatched at the money an' grabbed at the coat. As he did so, somethin' fell out of the pocket.

'Give that to me! I didn't bet that!' The man lunged out. 'Give me the watch, an' you can keep what's inside!'

Thomas grasped the watch to his chest. He opened it an' a piece of paper fell out. 'What is it?' he asked the sailor.

'A cipher.'

'Cipher?' said Thomas.

'It was given to me.' The sailor replied. 'It's the path to a hoard. Gold, silver, jewels! You can keep it, just give me the watch.'

But Thomas made off with the lot! Chased by the sailors he sped to where his horse were tethered an' fled. Father said we'd best move on too, before the sailors came after us. We met up with the rest at Fordingbridge. Thomas was there, gloatin' over his winnin's. He took out the paper an' showed it to everyone. Drawn on it were a face an' curious markings.'

'The cipher!'

'Yes, lad.'

'Why didn't Thomas ever find the treasure?'

Peter tapped his pipe into his palm and stood. 'He never worked out the clues. Not sure where to start, an' nor did anyone else.'

'Did he cheat?' Josh asked.

Peter chuckled. 'Maybe. I didn't spot it, but he certainly

always had money an' cheatin' at cards would be one explanation.'

'So where are the watch and cipher?'

'Last year Thomas became ill. He were an old man. He showed them to Levi's brother, Saul. They'd been in the same gang and he'd watched him grow up. They were close. Said he might have better luck with the cipher. Saul was determined to find out more. Went out to Poole. He made enquiries. It took months, but he found someone who'd been there at the time. He said the sailor who fought with Thomas was called Samuel Pascoe. After our gang had left, Pascoe spoke about the watch belongin' to his father an' precious to him. The cipher, he'd never worked it out either. He said he'd been told to visit Christ's church. 'Which one, though?' Pascoe had said. 'They're all Christ's churches aren't they?'

When Saul returned, Thomas had died, but had left the watch for Saul. One day the revenue men came, helped by some dragoons, including Woolsey. Saul were captured. Levi visited him in gaol an' Saul told him he thought he knew where the treasure was hidden. But when Levi went to get the watch it was missing. Francis Woolsey, no doubt has it.'

'Is that why people are after him?'

'Aye, we were all goin' to go. Try to work out the puzzle, find the hoard and share it between us. But the watch and cipher are only part of it, Josh. There are big rewards if you want to see your neighbours caught for smugglin'. Woolsey seems to have come into some money and Levi's sure it's £500 reward for tellin' the revenue about Saul's smugglin'. Levi's brother could hang.'

Josh gasped. 'But it might not have been him.'

'We don't know for certain if it were Woolsey, but he were definitely there. Trouble is, Josh, Saul's a bad one an' caught up wi' men even worse than he is. Me and yewer father thinks he goes too far, an' Levi does too. C'mon, let's get back. Maybe yer father does need a hand in the forge an' I've kept yew away.'

Chapter 4

Puzzles for Perinne

Tuesday 12th June 1781

Perinne sighed as she gazed across the distance to the Needles of the Isle of Wight. She'd come to love the view from her bedroom window. Along with her parents, Jane and Yves Menniere, Perinne had been staying at Cliff House, home of local landowner, Sir Charles Tarrant, for over a year. She didn't know why they hadn't returned to their home in Rennes, France. Sir Charles was Jane's cousin - though Perinne called him Uncle Charles. A series of raps on the door awoke Perinne from her thoughts.

'Come in,' she said.

'Sorry, miss, but Miss Foster, your tutor's 'ere. It's time for your drawing lesson,' Lucy the maid said.

'Thank you, Lucy.' Perinne looked through the window again, toying with the long, black hair that fell over her shoulder. There was a tree down from last night's storm and a group of men were standing around it.

'Is everything all right, miss? What a wild night it was. There's a wreck in the bay, folks have been out scavenging.'

Perinne turned to her maid. 'Oh, no! That is awful. I can see many boats on the water today, I did wonder why.

What of those on board, were the people saved?'

'Most perished we believe, miss.'

'That is so sad.'

'Yes. Yes, it is,' Lucy said. She looked at Perinne's face. The young girl had seemed lonely lately and she knew she'd been wondering if they would ever go back to France. 'Er, maybe I shouldn't mention this, miss, but the mistress was talking about the new people just moved into Burton Hall. She mentioned that they've a daughter your age and suggested to your mother that you should visit.'

Perinne's face brightened. The new girl could be a friend.

'And Mr Clarke's son is home again, you could meet up with him too.'

'Yes, you are right, Lucy.' It would be good to see Danny. He'd been away for months. 'So, to my lesson and I shall go to help at the Poor House this afternoon.'

A round-faced man was sitting writing at a wide desk when a knock came at the door.

'Enter.'

James Clarke walked into the room, which was a library with a large fireplace, although the fire was unlit.

'Ah, Clarke, you bring news of that ship in the bay, what of survivors?' Sir Charles Tarrant asked, looking up from his work.

'Just the one so far, sir, though I'm afraid he perished. The coast is being watched in case there are others.'

'A tragedy.' Sir Charles shook his bewigged head. 'Did he manage to say anything?'

'Only that it was a navy sloop, the *Anne Marie,* out of Chatham and headed for Plymouth, then on to America.

He said that there were lights. They thought they were near a harbour, so headed for shelter.'

Sir Charles raised his eyebrows in surprise. 'And has the controller arrived from Poole? Do we know what she was carrying?'

'Not certain, sir. The Mayor has asked me to tell you he's sent a message to Kent to find out more.'

'Just keep me informed. Anything of value, unusual cargo, I want to know. Hmm, how long will it be before that elm tree is moved?'

'The men will have it done by the end of tomorrow,' James Clarke replied.

'I see. You may go.'

'Er, there is one other thing.'

'Yes?'

'A young girl was found in the Priory Church this morning. My son, Daniel found her after choir practice. The Reverend Jackson took her to the Poor House.'

'So, what has this to do with me?'

'It's possible that she came from the ship. Her clothes were torn, she had scratches but otherwise unharmed. She was carrying a coat. Good quality, but it had the smell of the sea.'

'The vicar told you this?'

'I was with the mayor when he came in to see him. There was a troupe of actors about last night too. She could've been with them, but unlikely I'd say. Wherever she came from, they'll need to find her parish.'

'Didn't the child say? How old is she?'

'They're not certain. She hasn't spoken a word. Mistress Preston thinks she must be around nine or ten years old, but can't say for certain.'

'It would seem we may have a survivor after all. But little I can do about it.'

As Perrine scampered down the staircase towards the hall she noticed Danny's father leaving the library.

'Mr Clarke!'

'Miss Perinne, how are you today?'

'I am well. I am going to my tutor and I shall go to the Poor House this afternoon.'

'Oh? You're still helping there?'

'Oui, it is what I should do. The children need help. It is not their fault that they are poor.'

'Well, there's a new arrival, a little girl, and no one knows who she is or where she came from. Danny found her, perhaps it's another mystery for the pair of you to solve.' James smiled.

'It would be fun to have another adventure, but we should not get into so much trouble as we did last time, Mr Clarke.'

James's face became serious. 'Yes, we wouldn't want you getting mixed up with smuggling gangs again, would we?'

'I should like to meet with Danny,' Perinne said.

Before James could reply, a woman appeared from a doorway across the hall and beckoned Perinne.

'Pardon, I have to go. Goodbye, Mr Clarke.'

After her lesson, Perinne rode slowly away from Cliff House, her little chestnut Forester pony, Pierre, crunching his hooves on the gravel path. He needed a new shoe and she would leave him with the blacksmith whilst she was at the Poor House. She looked across the fields toward Burton. Cattle were chewing in a buttercup-dotted meadow. In the hedgerows cow parsley, with its white, speckled tops swayed as the breeze blew through the plate-like blooms. Perinne's nose began to tickle. She wondered about the new family who were living at the Hall and what they would be like. No one had mentioned them yet, but it would be good to have a friend.

As she continued toward the town, she could see the tower of the ancient Priory Church, unmistakable against the cloudless, blue sky. Perinne liked the Priory. She loved the old carvings on the seats in the Great Quire. Adam Jackson, the vicar's son, had shown her around. There had been a cathedral in Rennes, but it had collapsed, leaving only the tall, front towers. The warm breeze whispered across her face and she thought about what James Clarke had said about Danny finding a little girl. Surely someone must know who she was. Hopefully she'd discover more at the Poor House.

She rode into the blacksmith's yard. She could hear an argument. A sturdy man with light brown hair and a rugged face was jabbing his finger in the air towards Caleb Brown. Caleb was at least six feet tall and had hulking, broad shoulders. His raven-black hair was tied back under a misshapen felt hat. He wore a leather apron over his dark breeches and his face was red with fury. Perinne knew Caleb and his wife Bessie and they were kind people. What was happening? The little pony carried her quietly towards the scene.

'Why couldn't ye lift it?' The sturdy man growled.

'It were too wet. Couldn't get it off!' Caleb retorted, his face lined with outrage. 'Anyway, who put you in charge of us all? Gettin' the gangs together were meant to make us better.'

'Couldn't bring yerself to do it, could ye? Pah! Ye're soft in the 'ead, Caleb Brown.' The man stood back, as if in defeat. 'So what exactly did ye lift ... .' The men broke off at the sound of Perinne approaching.

'Afternoon, miss,' Caleb said, nodding and tipping his hat. Adam Litty also lifted his hat and bowed his head.

'My pony, he needs a new shoe, Mr Brown,' Perinne

said, jumping down from Pierre.

Caleb took hold of Pierre's reins with his huge, grimy hand. 'Which be it Miss Perinne?'

'It is this one, at the back,' Perinne pointed at the right hoof.

Caleb moved around and lifted the pony's leg. He pulled a hoof pick from his pocket and scraped at the mud and grit. 'I'll see to it straight away, Miss Perinne.'

'I am going to the Poor House, Mr Brown, I shall collect Pierre in two hours' time.' Perinne smiled and walked away towards the high street.

'Do ye think she 'eard us?' Adam Litty said. 'She's a bright one.'

'P'haps.' Caleb hunched his shoulders. 'Doubt it, though, she were too far away, I think.'

Perinne skirted around a row of red-brick cottages until the Poor House came into sight. She wondered what Caleb and the other man were arguing about. She lifted the door latch and walked into the kitchen of the long building. Two young girls were busy there. One was standing by a tub of water kneading at the cloths inside with a thick wooden staff, whilst the other squeezed out the water by twisting the cloth, her arms strong despite her young age. They both wore aprons and caps, once white but now grey with age and washing. Perinne had suggested that given the amount of laundry the girls had to do, that one of the new mangles should be bought. But the overseers hadn't wanted to spend the money.

'Good afternoon, Ann, Martha,' Perinne smiled.

'Good af'noon Miss Perinne,' they answered together, curtseying. Ann added, 'the master an' mistress are in the garden wi' the new girl.'

Perinne walked directly through to the kitchen garden and immediately saw the pair with a young girl who was wearing one of the rough, worsted dresses of the Poor House. Judith Preston greeted Perinne, her face moving from a frown to a smile of acknowledgement. David Preston was leaning on a spade, watching the girl in puzzlement.

'Ah, miss, I'm glad ye're here. We've a new girl, she won't say a word. Maybe she'll speak if ye ask her to,' Judith said, gesturing in the girl's direction.

'Is she the girl found in the Priory, Mistress Preston,' Perinne asked.

Judith chuckled. 'My, my, 'ow did ye know that? The child's been 'ere but a few hours.'

'What will she be doing?' Perinne asked.

'David's showin' 'er the 'erbs, but she's got fine 'ands, not workin' 'ands. I'll prob'ly get 'er mending at first, see if she can knit. T'would help us if she'd talk.'

'Maybe she is frightened, or does not understand. Is there no idea of where she is from?'

'There's talk she may 'ave been wi' the travellin' entertainers. They were out by the Town Hall, an' in the George. Maybe ye'll have better luck in loosenin' 'er tongue, Miss Perinne.'

As Perinne approached, Rosamund turned away, pushing her hands deep into the pockets of her dress.

'Hello, my name is Perinne, what is your name?' Perinne placed her hand upon Rosamund's shoulder. 'Are you all right?'

Rosamund kept her head down, gazing at the stony pathway.

'If you tell me your name, I can try to help you.' Perinne continued. 'Where are your parents?'

Rosamund spun around, her eyes suddenly meeting Perinne's and at first they appeared to plead, but drained into an empty stare.

'I am here to help,' Perinne continued, softly. 'I shall be happy to talk to you when you are ready. If you tell us your name and where you came from, we can arrange for you to go home.' Perinne thought the girl seemed nervous. She felt sorry for her. Who was she? Where had she been? Her hair was matted, but it didn't look dirty. Her skin was fair, though not pale and she had round pink cheeks. She was short, but not small and she looked healthy. In fact, she didn't look anything like the children who usually arrived at the Poor House.

Chapter 5

Malvina Stone

Tuesday 12th June 1781

Malvina Stone stormed to the top of the narrow wooden
staircase leading to the kitchens.

'Maunder! Come to me at once!' she yelled.

Mary Maunder was hauling a coal bucket along the
cellar floor and knew without doubt where all the noise
was coming from. She was wondering where the other
maid was. Apart from herself and Mrs Lane the cook, the
servants were all new and were still getting used to their
roles. Only Mr Benjamin, the Stone's butler, had travelled
with the family. A few servants remained at their country
home in Gloucestershire. She wasn't the least bit surprised
none of the family's servants had wanted to follow them to
Burton Hall, especially having lived under the same roof as
Malvina. It had only been three weeks, but it felt as though
she'd been tied to a demon. It was 'fetch this' and 'bring me
that.' And when you did it was 'the wrong one' or 'too late
you idle child.' Yet Malvina Stone was barely a child herself,
just thirteen years old. Mary thought about Malvina's much
quieter, and far more pleasant older sister, Patience. 'Pah!
patience is what we all need when Malvina's around.'

Mary had worked at Burton Hall since she was ten years old and now she was thirteen, the same age as Malvina. She was a strong girl, strength built from the heavy duties of a maid. When the previous family had moved to Bath, the new owners of the Hall, the Stones, asked if any of the servants would like to work for them. Along with Ann Lane, the cook, Mary'd decided to stay on, so did two other maids, but they soon left and their replacements had only just arrived.

'Maunder!' The voice was clear, and angry.

'What was it she wanted this time?' She put the bucket aside, brushed her dusty hands on her apron, and dashed to the kitchen staircase and up to the bellowing voice.

'How dare you answer my call all filthy,' Malvina scolded. 'Get a clean apron and come to my drawing room, immediately.'

'Yes, Miss Malvina,' the maid replied – '*her* drawing room! Does she think she's the mistress?' she muttered under her breath as she ran to the linen room. When she finally returned Malvina was poking at the fire.

'Coal, Maunder, you were sent to fetch coal!' Malvina's face was almost purple with wrath.

'But, Miss Malvina, that's what I were doin' when ye called.'

'You insolent girl. I shall tell my mother and you'll be dismissed. Then where would you go? Is there a poor house near this place?'

She chose not to answer, it wasn't worth getting deeper into trouble, and she needed the job, as bad as it was with this new family. 'A fire in June,' she thought, 'flaunting their riches.'

Malvina bumped herself into a deep chair by the window and stared out across the field. She grunted, why did they have to come and live here? The new servants were useless, but so were the ones back in Gloucestershire. Father said they needed to be close to the sea for her mother's health, so why live here two miles away from the coast. She'd have to make new friends too. Patience was so boring, always painting or reading or sewing. She preferred to go to the big towns and look around. Have coffee in a coffee shop, visit a jeweller's shop and buy some trinkets and sample scents at the perfumery. Father had given her an allowance, but she knew if she spent more he would simply pay.

Father was home for good. He'd been out in the West Indies where he grew sugar on a plantation. The whole family had lived there for a while but she, Patience and their mother had come home when father bought their house in Gloucestershire. They weren't as rich as many who had made their fortune from sugar, but they had plenty. They were probably richer than the Menniere girl. Perinne, what a silly name, but mother said that she was coming to visit. Malvina sighed. From what she'd seen of Christchurch it was nothing but breweries, stinking the place out, and a few tumbledown shops. A sudden clanking brought her from her thoughts.

'Can't you do that quietly?' Malvina yelled at Mary, who had put down the bucket and was shovelling coals onto the fire. 'You can take some to my mother's room when you've done that.'

'But the mistress doesn't want a fire today, Miss Malvina.'

'Yes, she does. Do as I say!' And at that Malvina lifted herself out of the chair, gathered up her skirts, and stormed out of the room.

After school Danny made his way to the high street to buy the sugar. He pushed to the back of his mind thoughts of what Mr Walton would have him do, he'd said it wasn't dangerous, but maybe he was lying. In any case, he wanted to get back home quickly and go to the beach to see if he could find anything washed ashore from the wreck. He liked June, the days were long and that meant he could spend more time out and about.

It was a warm, sunny afternoon and people were busy picking up provisions. The wetness caused by the storm was giving off a light vapour as it dried from the roofs and roads. Any puddles were quickly drying out and the air smelled dusty. Children were running around chasing one another, their mothers shouting after them lest they get run over by a passing coach, barrel cart or horse rider. Danny spotted a poster pinned to a nearby tree and walked over to read what it said, but it was only about the entertainers who had been in the town at the weekend. He'd been to see the Punch and Judy with his younger sister, Sarah. He remembered how Sarah had laughed, but he thought it was stupid. The girl in the Priory this morning had reminded him of Sarah. They had the same kind of fair face with pink cheeks. The girl's hair had been messy and knotted, but it was copper-coloured like Sarah's. There was talk that she'd been left by the entertainers, though Danny thought that if this was so they wouldn't be far away and she'd soon be returned. He stepped into the general store and searched the dark, wooden shelves.

'Lost something, lad?'

'I need a pound of sugar, please.'

The grocer picked up a bowl and scraper and took the wrapping from a sugar cone set on the counter. He hacked at the sugar, scooped it into the bowl and weighed it on a set of scales. When the scales balanced, he poured the sugar into a paper bag.

'That'll be five pence, farthing, please,' the grocer said.

'So much?' Danny gasped.

'If you want your cakes and sugarplums, lad, then that's

what you have to pay.'

Danny handed the sixpence over the counter. There was a halfpenny and a farthing in return. Danny wrapped the change in his handkerchief and pushed it deep into his pocket, which is what he should have done with the sixpence when his mother had given it to him this morning. But if he hadn't dropped the coin he wouldn't have found the girl. He picked up the bag and, holding it closely, made his way out of the shop. He thought back to what had happened that morning. He'd described everything to Mr Walton and the Reverend Jackson. But he remembered something. He'd told them she was staring up at the arch, but he hadn't mentioned that he thought she was looking at the carved face. Not many people knew about the face, most people went about their work, or their worship, without gazing up at the Priory's beautiful arches. It had been Adam Jackson who'd shown him. They didn't know whose face it was, but it might have been someone who'd helped to build the Priory centuries ago. Maybe the carving had simply caught her eye, it probably wasn't important.

Danny wasn't far down Castle Street when a pony appeared from an alleyway.

'Perinne!'

'Danny, it is you. Hello!' Perinne's broad smile lit up her face, her dark, pretty eyes sparkled. She was wearing a light brown cotton jacket and straw bonnet. Her long, black hair fell over her shoulders. 'I heard that you made a discovery this morning.'

'Yes, a girl, sitting in the Priory all alone. They took her to the Poor House. Is that where you've been?'

'Yes, and I have met her,' Perinne said.

'Did she say where she'd come from? She said nothing to me, or to Reverend Jackson.'

'No. She will not speak, but I think that she must be afraid.'

Pierre snorted and pushed his nose towards the bag of

sugar. Danny stepped smartly back, just in time.

'Everyone was saying she must have been left here by the entertainers, but why would they leave her?' he said. 'Maybe she's from the ship that was wrecked last night!'

'If that is the case, how would she have got from the beach to the Priory?'

'Someone must have brought her, but who?'

The two set off towards their homes, Perinne riding the pony slowly so that Danny could keep up. They were quiet for a while until Perinne broke the silence.

'You have grown taller since I saw you last. You are not at the boarding school anymore?'

'No, thank goodness. I hated it. It wasn't much different from the school here, except for the older boys, who were bullies. And I missed going to the beach. What about you, still living in the same house as Edmund Tarrant?'

'Another bully. I hated what he did to Will.' Perinne breathed in sharply and tried not to get angry remembering how Edmund had behaved towards their poor friend. Will had been driven to leaving everyone behind and sailing to Newfoundland. 'Luckily Edmund has stayed away at school and I do not see him very often.'

'I'm going to the beach later, to look at the wreck, can you come too? We may find signs the girl was there, or interesting things washed ashore. Maybe some gold!'

'I think the idea of the wreck is horrible. All those poor people drowned. But I see that we could look for clues about the girl.'

'Yes there could be something. Let's meet later.'

'All right. I shall come to the beach.' Perinne smiled down at Danny before setting off at a trot into the distance.

Danny stepped up his pace and headed for home. He liked the idea of solving another mystery with Perinne. It was a pity Will wasn't around. Could the girl really have been washed ashore? What clues would they be looking for? Maybe she was simply abandoned in town and found her own way to the Priory. But it had been an awful night. Plus there was the schoolmaster's strange request. He'd go along and see what it was. But he'd keep it to himself - for the time being.

Chapter 6

Missing Will

Tuesday 12th June 1781

Will Gibbs watched in excited hope as the rocky coast of England came into view. Its coffee-brown cliffs and cream-coloured sands lay rich against a glorious azure sky. He'd been away for fourteen months and every day he'd regretted leaving behind his mother Meg and his sister, Beth. Yet it had been an adventure. He wondered whether his friends, Danny and Perinne, would be around to hear about what had happened on his journey to Newfoundland and Boston, and of the things he'd discovered there.

He was standing on the deck of the ship, its sails full to the warm breeze that stroked his face. After weeks aboard he was no longer aware of the smell of the sea. He knew there was still some way to go before they arrived in Poole. Even then he had to catch a wagon. At least he had some money, unlike last year when he had to walk all the way from his Christchurch cottage to the port and away from his tormentor. But he was no longer afraid of Edmund Tarrant, who had treated him so cruelly, especially after what he'd seen in America. For he was coming home, not only to be reunited with his family, but to try to do something about the plight of the African slaves.

Danny approached Muddiford and rolled up his sleeves. The day had become warmer, as if the storm of the night before had sucked away the recent unsettled weather and blown in the summer. As he approached the end of the lane the bay came into view. He could see many small boats scattered across the glistening water, but there wasn't any sign of the wrecked ship. He made his way towards the beach and was amazed by the number of people milling along the shoreline all the way to Chuton Bunny. They were searching the beach, bending down then inspecting what they'd found. Most had sacks. Carts with ponies were waiting patiently under the cliffs, chomping on the sparse grass. Then, on the cliff top, he spotted Perinne riding Pierre. Danny waved and ran towards the path and up to meet them.

'Phew! It's getting hotter,' Danny gasped.

'Let us go into the shade,' Perinne replied, climbing down from her pony and leading him into the shadows of the dark green Holm oaks which grew along the cliff's edge. 'I do not think we shall find any clues on the beach.'

'No. If there were anything, it's probably been picked up by now. Look, Will's mother's there.'

Perinne strained to look. 'And Mistress Brown, the blacksmith's wife.' Perinne pointed towards a woman struggling to carry lengths of wood towards one of the carts, her dark skirts dusting the sands. 'Mr Brown gave Pierre a new shoe this morning. When I took him there he was arguing with a man. They did not hear me at first.'

'What were they quarrelling about?' Danny asked, as he

settled down, using the tree trunk as a back rest.

'The man was shouting at him, why he could not lift something, which is strange, since Mr Brown is so big and strong. Mr Brown replied that whatever it was, it was too wet and that he could not remove it.' Perinne secured the pony to a nearby branch and sat down beside Danny.

'That's an odd thing to say.' Danny wiped his brow with the back of his hand.

'The man said that Mr Brown could not bring himself to do something. He said, 'you are soft in the head, Caleb Brown.' That is all I heard. They saw me and stopped.'

'Are you sure that's all?'

Perinne closed her eyes, lines of concentration appearing on her face. 'I think there was no more - no, I remember, Mr Brown asked the man 'who had put him in charge'.'

'In charge of what?'

'I do not know.'

'I wonder who the other man was. He must have wanted the blacksmith to do something that he was either scared to do, or just didn't think it was right.'

'It could have been anything,' Perinne sighed.

'So, what about the girl?'

'It is strange. I can understand that she will not speak. But she is not like the children who are usually brought to the Poor House, they are thin and the girl looks healthy. Mistress Preston says that she has the hands that are not used to hard work.'

'Well, maybe she'll start to talk soon.'

Danny was interrupted by a sudden shout which bellowed from the beach where a small crowd had gathered. One person waved at two men standing beside a cart that had been set aside from the others. The men made their way down the sands. One of them was carrying something. Danny and Perinne stood to try and see what was happening. The men reached the shoreline and one of them laid out a large sheet of sacking. Next, both men

43

waded into the calm sea almost to waist height. There was something in the water. The first man reached out and caught hold of the object, the second man joined him as they tugged the shape towards the shore. For a few moments nothing could be seen and then the crowd moved aside. The men had laid out a large dark object. It was a body. They wrapped it up, took one end each and carried the corpse up the beach.

Perinne stepped back but Danny leaned forward, curiosity getting the better of him. One of the men pulled over a canvas from the back of the cart to reveal more bodies. They lifted the grim find but as they placed it on top of the others an arm slipped from the sacking. It was white and had long fingers. There was a gash and bone was poking through. The men pushed the arm back, replaced the canvas cover and stood together again as though it was nothing out of the ordinary. Danny felt sick.

'How can you bear to look, Danny.'

'I wish I hadn't,' he replied. 'Come on.'

The pair made their way through the trees and out across a meadow. Bees hummed around the tall grass and a sweet waft of honeysuckle drifted on the air. Perinne was walking, leading her pony with his reins. They eventually reached a fork in the gravel track and stopped.

'So, have we a mystery to solve?' Danny asked.

'I am sure that someone will come to look for the girl,' Perinne answered.

'But who is she? And how did she get to the Priory?'

'Maybe she will be talking the next time I am at the Poor House.'

'And when will that be?'

'I am not sure. Lucy tells me that there are new people in Burton Hall. Have you seen them?'

'No, but mother mentioned it to father. We're not very far away, but they wouldn't want anything to do with us. In any case, it's two girls.'

'Yes, they are called Malvina and Patience. We may visit. Perhaps we can all be friends.'

'Maybe.' Danny hunched his shoulders. Perinne was fun, but most girls were not allowed the freedom Perinne seemed to enjoy.

'So it will be Monday of next week.'

'All right. Shall we agree to meet at the beach?'

'No, let us meet in town. You should come to the Poor House after school.' Perinne took hold of Pierre's saddle. Danny made a stirrup of his hand and Perinne stepped into it.

'Do you miss Will?' Danny said, as he helped to lift his friend onto her pony.

'Yes.' Perinne gazed out to sea, as if Will Gibbs would suddenly appear from the bay. She turned back to Danny. 'Could we solve a mystery without him?' She smiled. 'I shall see you next Monday.'

Danny watched as Perinne trotted away in the direction of Cliff House. 'I'll know Mr Walton's secret by then,' he thought to himself.

Beth Gibbs put down her needle and thread and stood to stretch her legs. It was late evening and the light was fading. She closed her eyes, her pretty face looking tired. She'd been making two mantuas, open-fronted loose gowns, for a lady and her daughter who lived nearby in a village called Hurn. Beth lived with her mother, Meg, in a little cottage close to the riverbank. Their home was looking much brighter these days. When her brother, Will, had left them the year before, they thought that they'd end up in the Poor House. But a gentleman by the name of Sir George Cook had made Will a promise to make sure they were all right and he'd been true to his word. The first thing he did was to arrange for Meg Gibbs to have some eye glasses. She was a stocking maker and had been losing work due to her poor stitching, yet it was a simple matter of having spectacles. He'd also seen to it that Beth had been given tuition in mantua making and, between them, their income had much improved. Beth also worked at the George. She enjoyed the hustle and bustle of the busy coaching inn.

Sir George had also ordered the thatch to be repaired and their neighbour Isaac Hooper, always wishing to gain favour with Meg, had found some whitewash to paint the inside. Where he'd found it from they thought it best not to ask. Will's new friends, Danny and Perinne had also helped. Perinne brought some unwanted curtains from Cliff House that Lady Elizabeth was having sent for pulping and Danny's mother gave them some chickens, so that they would have fresh eggs. 'Yes, things are much improved,' thought Beth, but the best thing of all would be for her brother to come home. The latch on the door lifted and Meg Gibbs appeared.

'Mother!'

Meg stumbled into the tiny room and was holding her arm. Her face was bright red with effort and sweat glistened around her neck. A dog, which had been curled beside Beth, barked as she rushed to catch her mother.

'My arm, our Beth, I've hurt my arm.'

'What happened?' Beth asked. 'Shush, Sam!'

The dog settled down again.

'I fell. I were steppin' aside from a coach. It were about to run a puddle an' I thought I'd get splashed. But I caught a ditch edge an' fell, put me arm out.' She sniffled. 'C'n barely move me fingers, our Beth.'

'I'll run for Dr Quartley.'

'No! We can't afford the doctor. Go fetch Mistress Fyfield she'll know what to do, and find some comfrey. If it's broken, we'll set it ourselves.' Meg held the arm gently to her body and bit her lip. 'Just as we were doin'all right. How will I work if I can't use me hand?'

'Try not to worry, mother. It could be just a sprain. I'll get you a drink and go to fetch help. Then you'll tell me how you really hurt your arm.'

'What do you mean? I've told you.'

'Yes, but the roads are drying out and there's no mud on your skirts.' Beth gave her mother a stern look. 'And I can see sand in your shoes.'

Meg looked at her daughter. She loosened her cap and her grey hair fell down her back. She sighed. There was no point in trying to hide things from Beth.

'I were on the beach, an' so were many others. The collector an' customs men arrived. They'd clubs an' began shouting an' chasing folk. It's not as though the wreck were ashore, it's sunk without trace. That's why they only just arrived. We were checking what the tide brought in, that's all. We'd to run to save us a beating. I slipped on the pebbles by the cliff.'

'I'll get you a cup of water. I fetched some from the pump not long since, it's still nice and cool.' Beth stroked her mother's cheek. 'Try not to worry, you're safely home. I don't think that the collector will bother looking for you here. I'll go for Mistress Fyfield.'

Chapter 7

A mysterious task

Wednesday 13th June 1781

'You're very quiet.' James Clarke was sitting at the table of his Burton cottage studying the *Salisbury and Winchester Journal*. Danny was pulling on his coat.

'It's too hot. It's even hot at school. It's normally freezing in there. Do I have to wear this?'

'Carry it until you get there,' James smiled. 'What's your new schoolmaster like?'

'He's all right.' Danny didn't want to talk about Mr Walton. 'Does the newspaper mention the wreck?'

'It's too soon for that, but there's news of a cricket match.'

'May I read it, father?'

'Of course, but it'll have to be later. Get on your way to school!'

'Yes, father. Oh, and I'll be late home today.'

Hannah Clarke had appeared at the doorway and was standing next to the family's tall clock. Its pendulum tapping out its regular tick-tock.

'And why's that?' she asked.

'Er... a few of us are thinking of playing cricket.' Danny

opened the door.

'Did you ask father if you could?'

'Er... father, may I stay out after school?'

James sighed. 'Yes, but if mother needs you to do any chores, you'll do them as soon as you get home.'

'All right, father, I promise.'

Danny set out on his half-hour walk to the Priory. It was another warm, sunny morning and house martins were twittering in the clear skies above him. Now that he didn't need to go straight home after school, he could help Mr Walton with his task. What could it be? He'd said that it wasn't dangerous. But why would he mention danger at all?

'The girl's showin' herself to be a good needle worker,' Judith Preston said to the group of three men, who were standing beside her in the Poor House herb garden. 'She still 'aint spoken a word, but she understands instructions.'

The men nodded. Rosamund knew they were talking about her but kept her head down and her eyes on the apron she was mending. She listened carefully.

'Wherever the girl's come from her family must be o' some means. Her coat is of good quality.' Judith pointed towards Rosamund's coat, which was spread out to dry across a nearby bush.

Rosamund looked up. The three men were all wearing coats and breeches. One took out a handkerchief and wiped his red face. 'Why did they wear coats when it was so hot?' The men were approaching.

'Good morning, young lady,' the man who appeared the eldest of the group spoke. He was bending towards her and he had a jolly face which made him seem kindly.

His soft voice sounded different to the way people spoke where Rosamund lived with her mother and father. The thought of her mother brought a lump to her throat, but she wouldn't cry. She took a deep breath, drawing in the scent of the herbs around her.

'Please tell us your name.'

Rosamund pursed her lips together. She didn't want to speak with anyone. Her father said to speak only with Uncle Sam. She didn't know who she could trust, not with the secrets she held in her pocket.

'We need your name,' another man said with a sniff. He was tall with a long nose and looked self-important. 'How can we help you if you don't say who you are?' He swung around to face Judith. 'Mistress Preston, we are looking to you to find out her name and where she's from. We'll be back tomorrow.' At that he led the other two out of an archway and away from the Poor House.

Rosamund shuddered, she didn't like the second man and would never speak to him, but she needed someone to confide in, especially after last night.

The night before, Ann, who'd helped her so far, had told the others in the big dormitory that Rosamund had been found alone and that everyone had to watch out for her. It was noisy with voices, some laughing, some squabbling and some just chattering. There must have been sixty women and girls. As they settled down for the night, Rosamund could make out talk of the wreck in the bay and that no one had survived. A group of girls had gathered a few feet away, whispering. One of the women broke up the huddle and sent them to their beds. Their eyes had been on Rosamund. She lay down, pulled a cover over her shoulders and, without making any noise, cried. Then someone sat on her bed and Rosamund felt a finger poke at her shoulder through the thin cloth. She tried to ignore it, but it kept prodding. She peered out with watery eyes to see one of the whispering girls, whose own dark eyes had shadows underneath.

'So, you're Little Miss Lost are you? Won't speak to anyone, well they'll soon beat words from you here, you mind out.'

'Leave her be, Betty.' It was the woman again. 'Molly, you sleep there,' she said, pointing at Rosamund's bed. Rosamund didn't dare move. She was lying on the leather pouch. Betty gave Rosamund one final dig and made her way to her own bed. The tiny girl, Molly, climbed onto the bed and lay down, her head at the bottom and her feet touching Rosamund's legs. No one bothered her for the rest of the night, not even Molly. Rosamund made sure that the leather pouch was close to her until the morning. She tucked it safely in the pocket of her dress.

'We've got to have a name for ye, child.'

It was Mistress Preston. She was standing beside her, hands on her hips, a look of frustration on her face.

Could she trust Mistress Preston, or Master Preston for that matter, Rosamund thought. What about the girl with the French accent, she appeared to be kind-hearted. She hadn't seen her today, maybe she didn't work here. Ann, who seemed to be a maid, had been caring so far, unlike that Betty girl. She worked her needle back into the fabric and made another neat stitch.

The boys had been allowed to take off their coats. Even Mr Walton had removed his own woollen jacket. He wasn't wearing his wig today, instead his brown hair was tied back. After choir practice the schoolmaster had whispered into Danny's ear that he should stay behind at the end of school and his task would be revealed. The sun had moved around towards the west and the room was becoming cooler but it smelled even sweatier than ever. Danny's heart had begun to beat faster as the time neared. At last the desks were tidied and the boys filtered down the stone staircase and away into the Priory grounds.

'Clarke, come with me. Leave your coat, you can collect it later. And remember, not a word to anyone.' The schoolmaster headed from the room and down the south staircase. Danny glanced up at the lamp in front of the tiny window. It had a new candle.

Danny followed his teacher outside and around the walls towards the old mill and quayside. There were people around but Walton moved quickly so he didn't have to stop and chat. Danny followed a few feet behind. Around the back of the mill a small boat was moored. They climbed aboard and the teacher passed him the oars. Danny rolled up his sleeves and undid the top few buttons of his shirt. 'Where could they be going?' he thought. The teacher nodded for him to move off. A welcome cool breeze wafted gently in his face as they slowly made their way from the river Stour and into the harbour. To Danny's right the marshes appeared. Reedmace edged the ponds with its tall green sword-shaped leaves with brown tube tops. To the left Christchurch Head appeared, wrapping its arm around the harbour and pointing to the Run at Muddiford. Surely they weren't going out to sea? Maybe they'd stop on the marsh, or make their way up one of the many creeks or channels. Sea birds swooped overhead and Danny could feel the heat of the sun prickling his bare arms. Thomas Walton rubbed his elbow as Danny tugged on the oars. Danny watched the schoolmaster as he rolled up his shirt sleeves revealing tanned skin and muscular arms. Danny was surprised how strong his teacher looked. On his right arm there was a large bruise. 'That's what it is,' Danny thought. 'He's hurt his arm. That's why he needs me.'

It was obvious that Danny didn't know the harbour very well and Mr Walton looked annoyed, as he occasionally scuffed the silted banks and had to push away using the oars. The water fizzed as the oars dragged hard away. Finally Mr Walton pointed westward and Danny steered the boat towards the northern bank of the Head close to the long sand-spit. Thomas Walton jumped out and stood in the shallow water holding a rope attached to the boat. Another rope was coiled over his shoulder.

'Help me drag the boat.'

Danny made a splash, but the teacher was unconcerned. Once the boat was high on the pebble-spotted beach they made their way over the dunes to the beach on the other side. The tide lapped gently onto the sands.

'Along here. Come on,' the teacher beckoned.

They made their way towards the bottom of the cliff. Here the head faced out towards Christchurch Bay. They began to climb. There was no pathway. Halfway up Walton stopped to let Danny catch up with him. They'd reached a small ledge where Danny could see that there'd been a fire. It had been set deliberately because a small area around it had been cleared, probably to stop nearby plants catching light. Beside the clearing was a large bramble-covered gorse bush, its spring flowers crumpled brown, like burned paper. Mr Walton bent down and reached underneath the shrub. One after the other he pulled out ostler's lamps. Turning, he pulled out a single, strange-looking lamp and a shovel.

'Can you see that rock?' He pointed towards the beach. 'I want you to take the lamps back to the boat, cover them and meet me down there.'

Without a word Danny slipped the handles of the lamps along each of his arms and picked up the odd one by its long metal tube. He wondered what he'd do if he lost his balance on the way down the cliff. He inched down carefully, using his laden arms to balance and crossed the beach to the boat, stowing everything as instructed. He returned to the beach, this time under the cliffs. 'This is all right,' he thought, 'far better than a beating.' The schoolmaster was standing beside the rock where there was a large pile of sand. He was propped up against the shovel.

'Scrape the sand away, carefully,' the teacher ordered.

Danny pulled at the pile. 'What am I looking for?' he asked.

'No questions, Clarke. Just do as I ask and never mention it again. Not to anyone.'

Danny shrugged. As he moved the sand away a dark shape appeared.

'Is this it, Mr Walton?'

'Yes, keep going. There are four bales.'

Danny pulled at the first one. Whatever it was, it was covered in oilskin and was shaped like a drum. The other three were behind the first and he'd soon uncovered them all. As each appeared he felt a prickle of fear rising.

'Help me tie two together then we only have one bundle each to carry to the boat. If you see anyone, put them down and sit on them, hide them as best you can. Hopefully there's still no one about.' Mr Walton glanced around to check the area. 'Lift one onto my shoulder.'

Danny froze. If these were what he thought they were, he'd be in serious trouble.

'Now!' Walton hissed.

Danny lifted the heavy bundle and the teacher wrapped his good arm around it and set off. Danny collected the other bundle. It was heavy and he felt as if he would never carry it as far as the boat. The pair moved in silence, only the sound of the sea and the squawk of gulls could be heard. They loaded the bales, climbed aboard, and set out towards the town. The sun was hot on Danny's chest and he lifted his shirt collar as high as it could go to stop himself from burning. He was sweating, his heart beating hard. These must be smuggled goods. He looked across to his left, where some boys were playing cricket. He would

54

join them as soon as he could, so it meant he hadn't really lied about what he was doing.

Mr Walton told Danny not to return to the quayside but to take a fork from the harbour to follow the beginnings of the River Avon. Danny rowed the little boat past the wharf and towards the eastern end of the Priory.

'Pull over here,' Mr Walton ordered. He caught the overhanging branch of a large tree and pulled into the riverbank. He jumped out holding the rope to tether the boat.

'Quickly Clarke, pass the bales.'

Hidden by the heavy green canopy of the tree, Danny rolled the blackened bundles to his teacher, who was again looking around to check that no one was watching. Between the river and the Priory ran the millstream, Danny feared they would be caught if they were to take the bales across. His stomach lurched. He remembered Will telling him that he should keep clear of smugglers going about their business. And now he'd got himself involved. He was an accomplice. What would his father say if he found out and what would happen to him should they be caught. He should have taken the thrashing.

Walton rolled the bales across the narrow path and they dropped into the Mill Stream then he pushed them to the other side, finding the shelter of overhanging branches. Luckily the water was shallow. It was Danny's turn to cross the stream. The barking of a dog nearby made the pair stop.

'If someone comes, just say you've dropped something. Don't let anyone see these.'

They waited, but no one came. Danny lifted the bales from the water onto the bank and climbed out of the stream.

'Over there,' the teacher pointed, 'by that gate.'

Hidden by shrubs he lifted one of the bales onto his teacher's shoulders as before, and hoisted his. Making sure no one was around they made towards a small door

Danny hadn't seen before. He wondered where it led, but once inside it was easily recognised as the Lady Chapel at the far east of the building. 'Where next?' he thought.

Mr Walton was sweating, and so was Danny. If they were caught he couldn't imagine the punishment that would befall them.

Danny was led down the south aisle and left into another chapel. They entered a narrow spiral staircase, just, like the one to the school room. It was difficult. The bundles were bulky and kept catching on the wall. After what seemed an age they were high above the arches of the ancient church. They tucked the bales away into a corner. There were others there, along with a dark wooden chest. They covered them with sacks. Danny looked down into the church. A sexton appeared and Mr Walton pulled Danny into the shadows and put his hand over Danny's mouth. All Danny could see was the top of the arches. He guessed he would be above the strange carved face that he'd caught the little girl staring at only yesterday. The teacher peered cautiously over the edge and let go of Danny.

'Don't utter a word. Let's get back to the school room for our coats,' he whispered. 'If we're seen we'll say that I kept you behind as a punishment. It wouldn't be a lie, would it, Clarke?'

Chapter 8

A new friend for Perinne?

Friday 15th June 1781

Since the storm of four days ago warm weather had set in. Perinne paced the room in her bare feet as Lucy sorted some lighter clothes from the wardrobe. It was Saturday and she was tidying her books and finding new places for boxes containing some of the items she'd collected over the time she'd been at Cliff House. Her favourite things were the fossils she'd found in the muddy cliffs beyond Chuton Bunny, a green cleft in the landscape where a stream made its way from the forest and down to the sea. She held one up to inspect its spiral form. Mr Brander had visited last summer and Perinne had been fascinated by the story of his own collection, which he'd given to the British Museum some thirty five years before.

Beside the window there was a chair and a small writing table. They'd been brought from her home in Rennes earlier in the year.

'Are you going to put these on, miss?' Lucy was facing Perinne holding up a pair of light, white stockings.

'Yes, I should put my shoes on also, Lucy, but it is so hot today.' Perinne took a piece of brown rag that Lucy had brought to her room earlier and wrapped the shell-like fossil before gently placing it into its box.

The door opened and Jane Menniere appeared. 'Come on Perinne, hurry and get ready. We're due at Burton Hall in half an hour.'

'All right, maman.'

'Why not bring some of your fossils. I'm sure Malvina and Patience would like to see them.'

'Will they? Well I shall bring a few of the smaller ones and some shark teeth.'

'And whilst we're out, Lucy will be able to look out your summer clothes without you interrupting her. Lucy, please help Perinne into her dress,' said Jane as she left the room.

'This one, miss?' Lucy held up a pale yellow cotton dress with lace trims.

'Yes, I suppose so.'

Lucy pulled the garment over Perinne's head and fastened the buttons at the back. She went over to the dresser, rummaged around a drawer and lifted out some ribbon. Perinne sat in the chair.

'We don't have the time to make anything fancy, miss.' Lucy said, brushing Perinne's long, black hair.

'Why is it so important that I have to dress up, Lucy. It is too warm, I shall melt.'

'You have to make a good impression on Mrs Stone, miss and I expect her daughters will also be in good dresses.'

'Pah!'

'There, miss. You look lovely.'

'Thank you, Lucy.' Perinne slipped her feet into a pair of plain, brown shoes with ribbon laces. She picked up the box of fossils and showed Lucy.

'These will be fine to take, do you not think?'

'Erm, I've not met the young ladies, miss.'

'Perinne!' Jane Menniere's voice rose from downstairs.

'Goodbye, Lucy.'

Lucy watched Perinne disappear from the room and wondered how she would be on her return. If the stories told by her friend, Mary Maunder, were true, what was in store for her?

Perinne and her mother were taken the short distance to Burton Hall by John Scott, Lucy's father, who looked after the stables and also worked as a coachman. Perinne could see over the tops of the hedgerows from her seat, a gentle breeze dusting her face. Butterflies were skittering over patches of dark pink clover and in the distance sheep, dotted the fields like tiny white sails on a green sea. Perinne would have preferred to be out riding Pierre, but maybe Malvina and Patience would have ponies and they could all ride together.

She was clutching her box of treasures as they approached Burton Hall. It was close to the road which continued on to Ringwood and eventually to the city of Salisbury. The coach pulled into the driveway. It wasn't as big as Cliff House, but it was just as grand. Perinne tipped her head to see the whole building. It was of red brick and three storeys high and the centre front was built slightly forward from the rest of the building. The doorway was exactly in the middle, at the top of a short flight of steps. It had a stone surround with two small windows on each side. To the right of the house was an orangery with a row of arched windows. Perinne wondered if they would be shown around. There wasn't an orangery at Cliff House. She thought the house was charming and was looking forward to meeting its occupants.

Scott helped them down from the carriage and returned

to his seat to await their departure. Perinne and her mother approached the door. It had a brass knocker. Jane Menniere lifted the handle and gently rapped on the door. The noise of a latch being lifted came sooner than expected and Perinne suspected that whoever would open the door had been watching out for them.

'Good afternoon, ma'am, miss, please come in. The mistress and the Misses Patience and Malvina are waiting in the drawing room.'

The man wore a white wig and had a round face with high cheeks and small eyes. Dressed in a black jacket, breeches to his knees, white stockings and silver-buckled shoes. Standing rigid, his shoulders back, he beckoned to Perinne and her mother. They stepped into a large, bright hallway which had a wide staircase on the left.

'This way, please.'

They followed the servant down the hall, through a door to the left into a narrow passageway, and onwards into a bright drawing room. Perinne looked around. Paper showing flowers so strange that they must have been imagined covered the walls. The fireplace had an ornate marble surround and the floor was covered with a fine woven rug patterned with rich reds, blues and greens. Silver candlesticks were close to strange wooden carvings. The carved chairs were beside a tapestry sofa on which a woman and a girl were sitting. Another girl was seated at a piano which was in the corner towards the back of the room.

'Welcome to Burton Hall, Mrs Menniere.' The woman rose unsteadily and held out her hand. Jane stepped forward, but Perinne stayed still. The woman took Perinne's mother's hand into her own. 'I'm Isobel Stone. And this must be Perinne.'

Perinne smiled, but before she could say anything Mrs Stone spoke again.

'Kelly, you may bring in the tea.' The servant bowed his head, mumbled 'yes ma'am' and left the room. Should

I have addressed you as madame? I apologise for not thinking.'

Jane smiled. 'No. I am English, it's my husband who is French.'

'French? Oh.' Mrs Stone turned her attention back to Perinne.

'Let us take a look at you. Perinne, that's an unusual name.'

Perinne heard a snigger. It was the girl at the piano. Mrs Stone gave the girl a stern look. She held her arm out to the girl beside her. 'This is Patience.' Patience smiled at Perinne. She was about fifteen years old. Her dress was plain, striped blue with a buttoned front. She had a pale, pretty face with big eyes and dark brown hair tied up with a band of tiny flowers. She was rubbing her hands together as if she were nervous.

'By the piano is Malvina,' Mrs Stone continued. 'Come here, dear and meet Perinne.' The girl walked over. She was about the same age as Perinne. She wore a green dress decorated with embroidered white and yellow flowers. Her hair was dark the same as Patience but she had a different face, round with red cheeks. She didn't show any of her sister's timidness.

'What's that?' Malvina pointed to Perinne's box.

'I have brought some fossils for you to see.'

'Fossils? Why would you bring those to tea?'

Perinne wasn't sure what she should say. She was glad when the door opened and Kelly came in with a tray holding a tea pot and some cakes. He placed it on a cupboard, which had already been laid out with cups and saucers.

'Please sit down Mrs Menniere. Let us see your fossils, Perinne.'

Perinne walked over to the sofa and opened the box. Mrs Stone had a strange smell, which wasn't unpleasant, but rather musty.

'Let me see,' Malvina said, pushing her way past her sister. She peered into the box. 'They're not fossils, they're sea shells. Don't you know the difference?'

'Malvina! Let me see, Perinne.' Perinne handed Mrs Stone one of the curled shells.

'You see inside, it is clay. The cliffs are clay and the fossils are found there.'

Patience peered into the box and took something out. 'What is this? This isn't a shell.'

Perinne smiled. 'That is a shark tooth.'

'Oh!' Patience dropped the blackened tooth into the box.

'There are no sharks around here,' Malvina scoffed.

'These are from millions of years ago,' Perinne answered.

Malvina picked up one of the teeth and inspected it. She touched the pointed end and ran it between her fingers. 'Can I have it?'

'Malvina!' Isobel Stone sighed. She was passing a china cup to Jane.

'I can show you where you can find them, Malvina.' Perinne offered. 'Do you have a pony? We could ride there together.'

'No, my horse is at our other home.'

'If you ride, I am sure my Uncle Charles will lend you a horse. Do you think he would, maman?'

'Oh, I don't want to trouble Sir Charles Tarrant,' Isobel Stone cut in quickly.

'I'm sure it would be all right, Mrs Stone. I'll ask on your behalf,' Jane said. 'Perinne, tell Patience and Malvina about your work at the Poor House.'

'Poor House? Where?' Malvina said.

'It is in the town, close to the Priory Church. I go and help with the little ones. There is a school room and I sometimes help to teach them to read.'

'Mother, I shouldn't like to go there,' Patience said.

'Nor me,' Malvina added. 'All those poor people. You

could catch diseases from them.'

'Malvina that is not the way to talk about those unfortunates. Perinne, I think it's very good of you. And I think that Malvina should go along one day.'

'Mother!' Malvina's mouth opened to a wide chasm, showing rows of rotten teeth.

'Could that be arranged Mrs Menniere?'

'I'm sure it can be. Perinne will ask Master Preston if you may visit.'

'Good. Let's have our tea and cakes and I will show you the orangery? We have some interesting specimens that Mr Stone brought back from the West Indies.'

They finished their drinks and Mrs Stone got up. Without being asked Patience reached for a walking stick and handed it to her mother.

'This way,' Mrs Stone said.

Perinne had heard that some people could grow strange fruits so, eager to see what was inside, she walked with Mrs Stone. They were followed by Jane and Patience but Perinne couldn't see Malvina. A few moments later though, the girl had caught up with them.

They made their way across the hall and after passing through another room and down some steps arrived at a window-lined room. It was hot and stuffy and smelled sweet. At the far end was a desk and chair. Some of the plants were standing outside. Inside were unusual-looking plants with long spiny stems which were growing upwards and outwards. Perinne went over to look closely.

'They're pineapple plants,' Malvina said. 'Father's hoping to get some fruit, but they've yet to appear.'

'We had many at the plantation.' Isobel Stone said. 'My husband loves them, but they make my stomach hurt.'

'You grew these on your plantation, Mrs Stone?' Perinne asked.

'Oh no dear, we grew sugar. There's much more money in sugar.'

After the tour they returned to the drawing room for Perinne to collect her box. They said their farewells and Perinne and her mother returned to the waiting carriage.

'Well, Perinne, do you think you could be friends with Malvina and Patience?' her mother asked as they made their journey home.

Perinne shrugged. 'I think that maybe we could be friends.' She wasn't really sure, but would try her best. She made her way up the grand staircase of Cliff House and to her room. She opened the box to return the fossils to her collections. There had been twelve items altogether and there were only ten. She lifted the cloth they were rested on to check if they weren't underneath, but there was no sign of them. One of the shells and one of the shark's teeth were missing.

Chapter 9

A stranger in town

Monday 18th June 1781

Seven days had passed since the storm had blown spring away and the weather had continued hot and sunny. Adam Litty leaned against the wall beside the door of the Eight Bells holding a tankard of ale and watching the road. He'd been surprised that the controllers had taken so long to get to the beach after the wrecking, but that had meant a second chance at finding something decent to salvage. The wreck had sunk and that meant goods could be washed ashore for weeks, months if the weather was good over the summer. It had been a sloop of the Royal Navy on its way to America, only a small crew, or so he'd been told. All he'd found were cases of flour – ruined, and a few barrels of salt beef. Caleb had found some barrels of rum. But two bales of tobacco had washed ashore, and it was certain these weren't from the sunken ship.

As he watched a man appeared from the door of the town hall. He was a stranger. Litty knew a message had been sent over to Kent to ask how many folk were aboard, and who. Word was getting about of the girl who was found in the Priory. People were saying that she may have come from the wreck. If it were true, he couldn't believe she'd survived, no one else had. It simply couldn't be - how would she have found her way from the beach to the town?

The man was approaching. It was Monday, so it was market day and he had to weave his way around the stalls. He was tall and had a broad back. He wore knee-high boots to his breeches and had a waistcoat over his shirt. He carried a tri-cornered hat in his hand that also held a coat hung over his shoulder.

'Good af'noon,' Litty said, raising his tankard and nodding his head.

'An' the same to yew. Does the landlord 'ere keep good ale?' The man was square faced with tanned skin. His clothes were of good quality, but without the frill and fancies of the clothes worn by the gentry.

'Aye, the ale's fine,' Litty answered. The man's dark, wavy hair was to his shoulders, his nose long and his grey eyes piercing though he seemed friendly enough. If he were the messenger, maybe he knew more about what was on board. 'Let me buy you a draught.'

'Well, I thank yew.' The man smiled.

The two men stepped into the stone-floored room and Litty gestured towards a woman already carrying tankards to a table by the window.

'Two o' your finest please, Alice. So, you're not from these parts.'

'No, from Kent. I was sent with details of the *Anne Marie*.'

'Ne'er seen a storm like it, all souls lost too.'

'Yis, though not a full crew. They were pickin' up at Plymouth. But still, a terr'ble business.' The man took a deep breath.

'That's true. Though there's talk of a girl being found.'

The man looked at Adam Litty, his expression serious.

'Adam Litty.' Litty held out his hand.

The stranger shook it. 'An' I'm Roger Law. A girl yew say?'

'Aye, though she could've been with some entertainers. It's anyone's guess. She's at the Poor House. Won't say a word, apparently. I expect they'll find her folk sometime.'

'I'm sure the parish'll look after her 'til they do. So, Adam, what's this town like? Plenty work?'

'Well, as the weather's fair, there's work on the land and fishing. We have a good number of tradesmen here too.'

'An' what of yew, Adam, what's yewer trade?'

'Brewer.'

'An' yew come to an ale'ouse that brews its own?'

Litty laughed. 'Aye.' He waved to Alice to bring more ale. 'So, what were they carrying on the *Anne Marie*?'

A wide grin broke out across Roger Law's whiskery face. 'Well, as she's lyin' at the bottom of the sea, I don't see why yew shouldn't be told.'

James Clarke had also been in the Town Hall when the messenger arrived from Kent. He was back at Cliff House waiting for Sir Charles Tarrant to return from a horse ride around his estate. The news would be of great interest to him.

Mr Walton hadn't spoken about their collecting the bales on the Head. It was as though their little trip across the harbour had never taken place. Danny was relieved. The more he thought about it the more he knew that Mr Walton must be a smuggler and, by helping him, he was an accomplice. He could be in serious trouble. But nothing had happened, so far. As Mr Walton had said, if Danny kept quiet, all would be well. But he was still afraid. Why had his teacher needed him? Were there not other smugglers who could have helped him? What if the Reverend Jackson found out about the goods hidden above the south aisle? The more Danny thought about it all, the worse he felt.

'You're not working, Clarke!'

As Mr Walton's voice boomed across the room, the boys turned to look at him. Danny's face reddened, it was as though the teacher was reading his thoughts. He put his head down and began writing. The classroom was stuffy with the sun high in the south beaming through the windows. He pulled at his shirt neck, his skin felt sticky and his stomach churned. He thought he was going to be sick.

'What is it, boy?'

The teacher left his desk and made his way towards Danny. His arm seemed better than when they were out on the harbour six days ago, he certainly didn't appear to have any problem with his cane. He snapped it onto the palm of his hand and the pupils quickly returned to copying script again, pens scratching away on the coarse paper.

'I feel unwell, sir,' Danny said.

'I think we could all do with a break, this heat is very heavy.' He faced the class. 'Stand!' The boys scrambled from their seats and waited beside them. 'Take a book and go and sit by the school entrance, we will continue our lessons outside.'

Danny joined the line making its way down the stairs. He wasn't sure why he'd suddenly panicked. Mr Walton hadn't said anything further, but that didn't mean he never would.

The sun was high in the sky and the shadow of the north side of the Priory Church was just wide enough for everyone to find a cooler spot for their studies. They milled around with their books waiting for the schoolteacher to join them. As they lingered a figure approached them, it was the Reverend Jackson. The vicar spotted Thomas Walton, who'd just appeared through the doorway, and waved him over.

'Good afternoon, Mr Walton. Giving our students a little fresh air?'

Walton approached him. 'Yes, Mr Jackson, the classroom's hot and stuffy.'

'Well, provided they work just as hard as they would inside. I have something to say, gather them around will you, please?'

Danny wondered what the vicar wanted. He sometimes came into the classroom to speak with them, often to tell them of a service they needed to attend. The boys lined up before the two men. The Reverend Jackson looked around them. He drew a deep breath, his face dour.

'It has come to my notice that boys have been assisting with the bringing into the town of contraband.'

Danny stifled a gasp. His heart began to pound.

'The practice of free trading by any boy from this school will not be tolerated. It is a sin, and you need to be aware that the gangs involved can be most brutal. Punishment by the law is to hang you by your neck until you are dead!'

Danny was shaking. Was Reverend Jackson looking at him? Could the bales hidden in the heights of the church have been found? Is this why he chose to speak to them? He glanced over to Mr Walton, whose face was staring out across the heads of the boys, as if he had no knowledge of such things, but Danny knew better.

The little girl, Molly, had continued sharing Rosamund's bed. It seemed as though the woman who'd kept the bullying Betty away from her was Molly's mother, Sarah. It felt strange to have the little, cold feet knocking her legs at night, but she was getting used to it. Betty hadn't bothered her since that first night, but Rosamund was suspicious of her and worried that she was watching and waiting for a chance to be nasty to her again, or worse, maybe find and steal the pouch. So far she'd managed to keep it secret. She had found a new hiding place. She would check it once she got outside.

It was so hot. The dormitory smelled dreadful, like a sweaty dunghill. She would love a bath, she hadn't had one since a few days before her father had said goodbye to them at Chatham. Soon after arriving she'd plucked some rosemary from the herb garden and kept it in her pockets. There was lavender growing, but it wasn't out yet. She'd collect some fennel instead, it would also keep away some of the awful odours. At the head of her bed was the window. Looking down she could see people walking past. They would have been making their way to the quayside, or maybe to the mill. This place was Christchurch, she'd never heard of it, but it seemed all right. But she wanted her mother and father. Father'd told her to trust no one until they were with Uncle Sam in Devon, but a week had gone by and the only way she'd get away from here was if she told someone who she was and where she was from.

It was a relief to get out into the herb garden, but Rosamund needed shade and made her way to the cool of an oak tree where she would do her stitching. But first she would check the pouch. She looked around and could see the master and mistress beside the door. The French girl was there also. They were speaking with a woman and two girls. They were clearly different from the dowdy clothed inmates. The girls were dressed in dainty cotton dresses and held parasols. One of the girls was keeping close to the woman, but the other, a dark-haired girl with a plump face, was wandering around, picking at the herbs and holding them to her nose. No one else was near. Rosamund reached through a knot of the oak's trunk. Just inside and above the entrance was a small ledge. With her fingertips she felt for the leather and smiled to herself. She was confident that even if someone decided to look into the hole, they wouldn't think to feel just there. Her possessions were safe.

'Girl!' Mistress Preston shouted towards Rosamund, who was now sitting working the cloth. 'Come here.'

Rosamund made her way to the group.

'This is the lost girl who won't speak, Mrs Stone.'

When the end of school came, Danny left as quickly as he could. Mr Walton hadn't even looked at him for the rest of the afternoon but still, Danny didn't want to give him a chance to call him over. Besides, he was meeting Perinne as they'd agreed last week. He passed the tombstones of the graveyard. It was only a short distance to the Poor House. Despite the sun moving lower in the sky it was still hot. As he approached he spotted a woman and some girls coming out of the red-bricked building's door. He didn't recognise them, but saw Perinne who appeared last of the group. A coach pulled up. First the girls climbed on board followed by the woman, who was trying to persuade Perinne to join them, but she was shaking her head. She'd spotted Danny and, at last, as the horses pulled away, she waved. He made his way down the street to meet her, wondering if he should at least tell Perinne of his problem with Mr Walton.

'It is so hot, Danny,' Perinne said.

'Yes, I don't want to do anything but sit,' Danny replied.

'Let us walk to the high street, maybe we can find some small beer. Have you been to school?'

'Yes. And you, have you seen the lost girl today?'

'She is fine, but still will not speak. Though she keeps looking at me and I think that she may soon talk.'

'It is strange. Who were the others at the door?'

'The new people from Burton Hall. Mrs Stone, and the girls are Patience and Malvina.'

'Ah. Did you visit them?'

'Yes, with maman. Patience is very quiet, but Malvina is strange. I think that she took something from me.'

'Oh? What?'

'Nothing of value, just fossils. I took some for her to see from my collection from the cliffs, but two were missing when I returned to Cliff House. Maybe I had just dropped them.'

'Another mystery. A lost girl, maybe from a shipwreck, and missing fossils in Burton!'

The pair arrived at the high street in time to see Reek's wagon arrive. It pulled into the George.

'Shall we see if Beth is there?' Danny asked.

'All right,' Perinne replied.

The streets were still full of people gathered for the market. They turned the corner past the town hall and were met with a sight that stopped them with a jolt. Together they gasped with surprise.

Chapter 10

A surprise party

Monday 18th June 1781

'Will!'

Dashing over the straw-covered street Perinne ran to the tall, handsome figure of Will Gibbs. Danny pushed through the crowd after her and soon they were both hugging their old friend.

'It *is* you!' Danny's eyes were wide with surprise and his face beamed with delight.

Will was fourteen years old and had grown at least a foot taller since Danny had seen him last. Gone were the worn-out shirt and breeches and faded jacket he'd been wearing when he boarded the ship at Poole last year. He was looking neat in a new, crisp shirt. His coat was of good cloth and he wore well-made shoes of shiny leather.

'It's great to see you, Will. We've missed you,' said Danny.

'Yes. It has seemed such a long time,' Perinne said. 'You must tell us all about it.'

Will was about to reply when a shrill scream rang out across the air. It was Will's sister, Beth, who flew at her younger brother, flinging her arms about him knocking his coat to the ground.

'You're back! You're back!' she cried, a glow of delight spread across her pretty face.

'Beth! It's wonderful to see ye.' Will wrapped his sister in his arms. 'Is mother 'ere, is she all right?'

'She's at home. She's fine - we're fine, Will, but so happy you're home at last.'

Danny picked up the coat and he and Perinne stepped back to watch as the brother and sister were reunited. She noticed he had a scar where he had been cut by Edmund Tarrant last year. Most of it had faded, but there was a crescent-shape that ran from his left eye and over his cheekbone. Danny nudged Perinne and nodded towards people who were gathering in the background, pointing and muttering. But it wasn't Will and Beth who were the focus of their attention. Standing beside two large trunks was a black boy. Danny had heard about black boys, but had never seen one. Will, who had been caught up in his excitement, glanced around at the sound of people who had gathered outside the inn. He drew a breath suddenly realising the target of the chattering and beckoned the black boy towards him.

'Everyone, I want ye to meet me good friend, Nathan.' Danny wasn't sure what to do, but Perinne held out her hand. Nathan smiled. Taking the hand gently and, with his other hand held behind his back, he bowed his head. There were gasps from the bystanders.

Beth's mouth fell open as she watched Nathan. Turning back to Will, she began to laugh. 'I'll send the ostler's boy for mother,' she chuckled. 'I can't believe you're here!'

Sir Charles Tarrant paced the library of Cliff House. He rubbed his chin with his hand and pursed his lips together. James Clark held his hands behind his back and waited.

'Gold?'

'Yes, sir. The *Anne Marie* was going out to America taking payments. Then afterwards she would have been on general escort duties, relaying messages and helping stricken vessels and ships of the line.'

'Hmm. What's the depth of the water where the wreck lies?'

'Around ten fathoms, sir.'

'That deep?' Sir Charles sighed. 'Contact Sir George Cook at the Royal Society, explain the situation and invite him down from London. Let's see if the scientists can come up with a solution.'

'Woof! Woof!'

'Sam! Oh Sam I've missed ye!'

A dog with a long, white coat with tan patches made a bounding leap for Will. He was followed by a short woman whose grey hair was just visible under a brown bonnet. Will rubbed the dog's ears and it rolled onto its back ready for its tummy to be tickled.

'Son, son! Oh! It's really you!' Meg Gibbs reached for Will, her eyes glistening with joy. Will pulled his mother into a close embrace and kissed her forehead.

'Aye, mother, I'm back. It's so good to see ye again. Ye're arm's all wrapped up, are ye all right?'

'Aye, it's nothin'. Just look at you! Such fine clothes. Whatever's happened? Come on, back to the house, there's so much to talk about. Let's go an' I can make us somethin' to eat.'

'Oh, I'll stay 'ere t'night, mother, I'll find rooms fer meself an' Nathan.'

Nathan stepped forward. 'Hello Mistis Gibbs.'

Meg's mouth dropped open and her eyebrows rose. She took a step back. Will laughed.

'Come 'ere, Mother. Nathan's me friend. There isn't room at 'ome for 'im an' fer me. An' I've money to pay fer somewhere fer us to rent for a while.'

'But the house has been repaired, Will. That gentleman, Sir George, he had the roof mended an' it's all painted. Are we not good enough for ye?'

'Now, mother, ye know that's not so. It's just...'

'Wi'll come for tonight,' Nathan said, glancing over at Will. 'Mistis Gibbs, I'll manage wherever yu put mi. It'll be all right.'

Will let out a resigned sigh. 'Aye, we'll stay at 'ome.'

'Let's all celebrate!' Meg exclaimed. She touched Nathan's arm, as though she were checking that he was real. She smiled at him.

'I'll buy us all somethin' to eat,' Will offered. 'Danny, Perinne will ye stay?'

Danny and Perinne were standing to one side. Sam had made his way to Perinne and she was stroking him.

'I am sorry, Will, I wish that I could stay. Lucy's father is here to take me home. But it is so good to see you again, we must meet up and you can tell us all about your adventures. Perhaps you and Nathan can come to the beach tomorrow?'

'Aye, of course,' Will replied. He moved towards his two old friends and they grouped into a hug.

'What about ye, Danny? Can ye stay?'

'I ought to go home.'

'We can take you to the Burton road, Danny,' Perinne offered.

Danny looked at Perinne and back at Will, who had a broad smile, his eyes sparkling with joy. A peel of laughter rang from a group of people who had gathered around Meg and Beth. He should go home, he thought, but Will and his curious friend were here. Surely just a half hour wouldn't matter.

'Thank you Perinne, but I think I'll stay for a little while. I'll see you at the beach tomorrow.'

Perinne grinned and made towards the street where a coach was waiting. Will put his arm around Danny's shoulder and led him into the George.

'Ale, Danny?'

'Gold?'

'Aye, that's what he told me. Said it wouldn't matter tellin' me. It were on the seabed, out of reach of any man.' Adam Litty looked around at his gang. They were gathered at the Eight Bells drinking ale.

'But how would a man o' Kent know our seas?' David Preston asked. 'What does Guy Cox say? Has he been on the water to look?'

'Aye. The ship's there all right,' Adam replied. 'But I don't think a man could get far enough down for a chance to poke around.' He shrugged and continued. 'Guy and Henry Lane tried yesterday. Water's calm enough, clear. Henry made it to the bowsprit, masts are gone.'

'Could be anywhere aboard - if it's true,' David said, taking a long drink of ale. He signalled for another draught. 'So, what about tonight, is everything set? What's coming in?'

Adam's voice dropped to a whisper. 'Forty half-ankers o' brandy. Hundred tubs o' geneva an' other spirits, 200 bags o' tea, plus an order for takin' to Bath of casks with figs an' raisins. We'll meet at Muddiford at dusk. We've got lights being set off. One east of Boscomb mouth and another along the cliff top before the Head. If the revenue's out, hopefully it'll put them off our work here, an' if they do realise, we'll be gone afore they can get to us. Spotsman'll signal from the ship at dark. There's barely a moon tonight, so we should see 'im easy. We'll take three boats out from Muddiford and two from 'ere.'

'No baccy with it?' asked Caleb Brown, waving his pipe as though they weren't sure what he meant.

'That's an odd one,' Adam eyed them, slowly moving from one man to the next. 'My contact said a small load had come over last week. I know of none, do any of you?'

The gang shook their heads. After a few moments David Preston spoke. 'We've kept as one gang since last year, Adam. We'd 'ave made money if we'd worked together to bring in that machine. In the end, only Sir Charles Tarrant made any money.'

'Aye, ye right there. David.' Adam took a deep breath. 'Ask Isaac Hooper to check wi' John Hewitt when he sees him t'night. Maybe there's a gang in the Forest we've not found out about. I'm off home. See you all at dusk at Muddiford.'

At that Adam Litty rose and, leaving the old inn, walked away towards the high street. Across the road the George seemed lively. A waggon was waiting and a group of people were making a fuss. He stood outside the town hall and watched the scene. It was the French girl from Cliff House. She was with James Clarke's son. And if it wasn't the Gibbs boy. So, he'd returned. Looked like he'd done well for himself. David Preston was right about that machine and the boy and his friends had made fools of them. But that was in the past, he needed to keep his mind on the night's task. It was a large load and the revenue men could spoil the fun.

Danny was only used to small beer. He was just on his second drink, well he thought that he was, but they were large tankards. His head felt strange, sort of thumping on the top and he was having trouble keeping his eyes open. Every so often a squeal of delight rang out as the merrymaking continued. People had come along to join them. Isaac Hooper, Will's neighbour and friend of his Uncle John was still here, despite saying he'd have to leave soon. In fact, a lot of the men had already gone. It was mainly people he didn't know. Also, word had got around about Nathan and some people had come just to take a look at him. Beth and Meg were sitting on either side of Will, as if guarding him, lest he should try to leave again. Nathan was sitting beside Beth, laughing. Danny looked through the window, it was nearly dusk. It was easy to forget the time on these lighter evenings. He knew he'd be in trouble for not telling his mother where he was, let alone being home this late.

'I think, er, I should go home Will,' he said. He got up, but his legs were unsteady and he wobbled. He raised his voice. 'I'd better go, Will.' The room was stuffy with tobacco smoke and hot with all the people jostling. The noise of the shrieks and laughter made Danny want to get away quickly.

Will finally heard his friend through the hubbub. 'All right, Danny, we'll talk again tomorrow, there's lots to tell.' Will crossed the narrow room. 'Are ye sure ye're all right?'

Nathan had also moved over to Danny and had taken hold of his arm.

'Yes, I'm fine. It's the heat, that's all.' He smiled at

Nathan, thanking him. He stepped outside into Castle Street, where the cooler air swept his face. He felt dizzy and sick for the second time that day.

He tried to concentrate on the road ahead. He thought he was doing fine. He'd almost reached Purewell Cross and the turning for Burton when he spotted a horse and cart waiting. Through the blurred and shadowy light he could make out the face of his Uncle John. What was he doing out and about on the cart at dusk? At first the old man didn't see Danny and Danny wondered if he should hide, but he thought if Uncle John were to take him home he might not be in as much trouble. It was too late, he'd been spotted. He couldn't have run in any case.

'Danny?'

Danny had stopped and was holding on to a nearby fence to keep his balance.

'Uncle Gee-ohn.'

'What in our Lord's name. Have ye been out ale drinking? It were ale, were it Danny?'

'Will's home, Uncle Gee-ohn. We've had a party! And Beth was there and Will's mother and your friend, Isaac and Nathan. Nathan's a black boy, he's Will's friend and he's really funny and ... oh ... .' Danny was clinging to the fencepost. He was going to be sick, he was sure.

Uncle John sighed. He was a landsman tonight, it was a large consignment and there would be a lot to organise, provided Adam Litty had the revenue men fooled. He wouldn't have come this way if he hadn't been meeting Isaac, who should have been here by now. But he couldn't leave his nephew alone like this and the beach wasn't too far away.

'Get up here, I'll take ye to the end o' the lane, but ye must make yer own way. I don't want ye mother an' father to think it were me gettin' ye drunk!' Uncle John held out his hand and Danny took it, pulling himself onto the seat beside his uncle.

The two boats approached through the narrow channel of the Run and joined the other three waiting at Haven Quay. Out in the bay the dim flicker of flint was barely visible, it became a low light and Adam's eagle eyes caught it. He signalled to his men. He jumped aboard one of the boats and the small flotilla left Muddiford along the sand-spit and out to sea. The sky was cloudless and black, splattered by a spray of glittering stars. The sea was calm and little wind meant their progress relied on the strength of the oarsmen. Adam watched the shoreline. The landsmen would soon gather on the beach. It was so different to the wild night when the *Anne Marie* had gone down. Why had she been in the bay? Maybe for shelter. But what lights could the wrecked ship have seen?

There was no sign of any revenue men, though little could be seen of anything. The only exception was the spotting of pale lights from a new house that had been built just a few yards from the beach. He would have to trust the gang to do their part. The tide was high but turning, they'd be on the pebbly shore at low tide, giving more space on the beach to take the carts as near to the boats as possible. Adam breathed in deeply the fresh air that was warm and salty. Things were going well and the gang members should make a fair profit for bringing in this shipment. And once the job was finished, he'd see what could be done about the bounty sitting at the bottom of the bay, but he doubted anything could be reached.

Chapter 11

Danny feels bad

Tuesday 19th June 1781

'Oh. Oh... .'

'Come on, Danny, you have to get up,' Jack Clarke said, gently pushing at his brother's shoulder.

'My head hurts.'

'I think you'll have to put up with that. Mother and father were furious.'

'I can't, I can't.'

'It serves you right. You should have had small beer.'

'I did!'

'I don't think so. Come on, get up. Wash your face and once you've eaten you'll feel better,' Jack said and left the small bedroom they shared in the little cottage.

'No. I don't want anything.'

'Daniel!' A voice boomed from downstairs.

'Oh ... .' Danny lifted his head which felt heavy, as though someone were pushing it back onto his pillow. He swung his legs slowly over the edge of the bed. His stomach churned. He'd been sick before he'd got into bed and didn't want to be ill again. He leaned over to a nearby chair where his clothes had been piled, though he couldn't remember undressing. They were creased and the shirt stained. Holding the edge of the chair he steadied himself and walked over to a chest of drawers where he found a clean shirt. He pulled on his breeches and grabbed a pair of stockings. The bedroom was quite cool, but he felt hot and sticky.

When he reached the bottom of the stairs the clock chimed its half-hour ring for six-thirty. The normally tuneful ting-ting sounded dull and made his face hurt. It also meant he would need to leave for school soon. Jack would walk with him. He was apprenticed to Mr Oake, a watchmaker who had a workshop in town. Danny turned into the kitchen where his mother was standing, her hands on her hips and her blue eyes piercing through the glare on her face. Grandpa was in his chair. Danny looked at him to see if he would wink, as he sometimes did when he'd been in trouble, but he didn't move. It was time to set out for school - too late to do chores, but he knew that he would be chastised over his behaviour later.

'I hear that the Gibbs boy has returned, Clarke,' said Sir Charles Tarrant, striding over the gravel courtyard from the stables of Cliff House.

'Yes, sir. You heard from Miss Perinne, I expect. My son told me about it.'

'He has a black boy with him. Whatever could he have done to come home with a servant?'

'From what Danny told me he's a friend.'

Sir Charles raised his eyebrows. 'Really?'

'That's what he said.' James Clarke didn't want to tell his employer that his son had come home having had too much ale. Besides he didn't know much more because he'd had to come to Cliff House before Danny had woken.

They entered the library which was also Sir Charles's study. Three of the room's walls were lined with books and the fourth held a large fireplace. Sir Charles walked to his desk and lifted a long roll of beige-coloured paper.

'I had this sent over from Poole,' he said, waving it in the air. He unfurled it and, to hold the document flat, placed a glass weight on one edge and a heavy, green-backed book on the other corner. It was a chart. It had a web of criss-cross lines and numbers and showed the coast and Christchurch and Poole Bays. The compass points were drawn neatly in one corner with north pointing inland and drawings of small brown sailing ships and fish were dotted here and there.

'Here, this is the place.' Sir Charles's short, stubby finger pointed at the edge of a line.

James Clarke bent forward, his head leaning to one side. He squinted. 'It's beside the ledge, but surely too deep for a man to get to.'

'That is the problem. Yves and Jane were telling me about a Frenchman, Freminet. He invented a system with a costume and hoses for the diver to breathe in and out.'

'And could a man go to 11 fathoms?'

'Yes, but there was a problem with the device.' Sir Charles Tarrant gave James a dour look and twitched his nose. 'Freminet died using it.'

'Ah.'

'There is Halley's bell machine, though the depth could be a problem. But maybe the idea could be improved upon, after all, it's many years since it was invented. Did you write to Sir George Cook?'

'Yes, the letter went by Post Chaise yesterday morning.'

'Good. Let's see if he can get here and if he has any ideas. We're going to need men too, ones familiar with the bay - but not yet.'

Danny wasn't allowed to see Will again until his father gave him permission. And he had to come home from school direct - no games. His father would speak to him later. He wondered what other punishments he might have. He was eager to see Will again. He wanted to hear all about what had happened in America and to find out more about Nathan. It was very strange. Some people wanted to be near Nathan last night, and they kept touching him. Others shied away, staring and whispering. One woman stroked Nathan's skin and then looked at her hands to see if his colour had rubbed off. At first Danny thought that Nathan seemed not to notice. But he would catch him looking down at the floor and taking in a deep breath, as if he were holding back a burst of protest. Danny had felt like that at times. Times like when he first went to the boarding school. The other boys would prod and poke at him, tease him because he didn't have expensive things like a watch and books and games. They also called him names because his clothes were too big, or worn, but that was just clothes and things. What must Nathan feel like being so different? Danny grabbed his jacket, even at this hour the air was warm, so he flung it over his shoulder and set out to town with Jack.

'What's he like?' Jack said.

'Who?' Danny replied, looking up at his brother as they walked down the lane to join the road into Christchurch. The sweet scent from a bright yellow broom plant swept over Danny's head as they passed by. It made him feel giddy. Whilst the nausea of earlier was passing, he felt very thirsty.

'The black boy,' Jack said.

'Nathan, he's called Nathan.'

'Well, what's he like? Can he talk?'

'Of course he can. He does have a strange way. He speaks English, though he says some words differently. He said Will's party was a jollification,' Danny giggled. 'It was like listening to Perinne when I first met her.'

'And is he Will's servant?'

'No, he's his friend. Why?'

'Well, I heard that black people were not the same as us.'

Danny had had enough he just wanted to walk quietly. 'Well Nathan is. Except his skin is black. And his hair is very dark and thick. His voice sounds a bit odd too. But he's just the same.'

The two boys made their way into the town silently. Seagulls speckled the bright blue sky, soaring lazily. Horses were pulling carts, trundling by slowly, scrunching their hooves into the dry gravel, as if they knew the day would grow hotter and that they should pace themselves. The boys crossed the wooden bridge over the river and over the second ancient bridge. To their left was the old house with its tall, round chimney and beyond this were the castle ruins, high on their mound. And, watching over all of them was the Priory church. Danny broke away from his brother to head for school.

'Hope you feel better soon,' Jack said.

Danny nodded as he crossed the road. Things were buzzing in his mind. Such a lot had happened in the past few days. At that moment he remembered Uncle John. Why had he been sitting on his cart at Purewell? And he didn't call in at home to see mother and father and he'd gone away in the opposite direction to his home at Hinton.

Danny's stomach began to churn. How would he concentrate at school? And what if Mr Walton wanted more from him? He was still terrified someone would find out that he'd helped the school teacher to smuggle contraband – if that's what it was. He needed to speak with his friends. Whilst mother said he wasn't allowed to see Will, she hadn't mentioned Perinne. He would go straight home after school as he'd been told. He'd ask if he could go to the beach. Even if he wasn't allowed to see Will, he couldn't help it if Will happened to be with Perinne.

Malvina Stone grumbled all the way into town. So what if the French girl helped those wretches at the Poor House, why should she? Her sister, Patience, was sitting beside her in the carriage which shook as its wheels skipped and bumped sharply in the dried out ruts of the road.

'We'll be shaken to death,' Malvina said, grabbing hold of the edge of the seat. 'We can't help anyone if it doesn't stop.'

'It's not far, sister,' Patience said, pulling at her gloves. 'But it's too hot. It's not fair that mother should insist that we wear these and keep them on until we return home.'

'Mother says it will stop us catching some dreadful disease. But why we should have to wear these dresses.' Malvina tugged at the sleeve of the dark blue, cotton garment. 'We look like poor people in these.'

'Don't exaggerate, Malvina.' Patience tut-tutted. 'It's sensible that we wear old clothes that can be thrown away, but I'm sure we don't need the gloves.'

'I'm only doing this once,' Malvina sniffed. 'Just to please father. He says we can go to Bath soon. Visit the theatre and look at the shops. He says we can have new dresses if we help today.'

'Yes, I know.' Patience blew out a sigh.

Malvina prodded her sister's arm. 'We're here. Let's get it over and done with.'

The coach pulled up in front of the entrance of the Poor House. Benjamin Kelly, who had grumbled about there not being a coachman to do this job, climbed down from the driver's seat and opened the door, pulling down the steps and holding out his hand to assist the girls.

'Master says I've to come back for you in two hours' time,' Kelly said. Sweat was falling from his brow and he tugged at the black velvet jacket he'd been made to wear. 'I'll wait just here.'

'Thank you, Kelly,' Patience said.

'Don't be late,' Malvina added. 'I don't want to be here any longer than I have to.'

Malvina pulled on a bell chord and, without waiting for an answer, lifted the door latch. The two girls stepped into a narrow, musty hallway. Malvina pinched her nose and Patience took a handkerchief from her pocket and held it to her face. A girl appeared. It was Ann. She was red-faced and had strands of dark brown hair straying from her worn-out cap. She looked Malvina and Patience up and down. 'Misses Stone?'

'Of course we are, girl.' Mavina scoffed. 'Where is Mistress Preston?'

'This way, please.'

The building wasn't very big and Malvina and Patience were shown to a small room overlooking a kitchen garden.

'I shall fetch the mistress.' Ann disappeared through the door and was soon seen through the window talking to Judith Preston.

'Over there, Patience, that's the Poor House Mistress.' Malvina moved towards the window, which was open. She could hear chattering. Beside Judith three small girls were bending, picking at plants and placing pieces in a basket. Judith was leaning over and pointing at something nearby.

'Why doesn't she come immediately? She should be coming in to ... .'

'What should she be, sister?' Patience said, leaning

aside to see what had caught Malvina's attention.

Malvina didn't respond, instead she focused on a figure standing beside a tree. It was the lost girl. 'What was she doing?' she thought. 'That's where she was when we visited with mother.' Malvina watched as the girl's arm seemed to disappear into the tree.

'Malvina, what is it?'

'Hush!'

The girl was looking at something, but Malvina couldn't make anything out. She saw the girl look around and quickly move her arm back into the tree. 'She's hiding something!' Malvina muttered under her breath.

'What did you say, sister?' Patience said moving over to the window. 'What is it?'

'Nothing, nothing at all.' It was none of Patience's business. The Poor House was perhaps more interesting than she'd first thought. She would try to find time to discover what the silent girl's secret was.

Chapter 12

A thief at work

Tuesday 19th June 1781

Judith Preston watched as Malvina Stone walked along the path in the kitchen garden. She hadn't wanted to join her sister helping teach needlework. She seemed to be approaching the lost girl. The girl turned, Malvina was saying something. Maybe she'd decided to try to get her to talk. The girl shrugged her shoulders and set off towards the dairy. Judith sighed. The girl had been at the Poor House for nine days without uttering a word, but she'd done all that had been asked of her. Hopefully soon she would either speak or her family would be found. But she must get on with her own work.

Malvina waited as the girl made her way towards the main building and disappeared inside. She looked around. Small children were still tending to the plants. Ann was busy laying out bedding sheets across the shrubs to dry. There were no men or boys, they'd all been sent out to work on nearby farms. And no sign of Mistress Preston.

She moved towards the tree where she'd seen the girl. She stopped under its shady canopy and fanned her face with her hand, as if she were merely catching the shade on the hot day. She looked around. A delicious shiver ran through her as she stepped up to the thick trunk. There was a hole. This must be where the girl's arm had disappeared. Taking a deep breath, Malvina pushed her gloved hand inside and searched around. It felt damp and dirty. She winced, pulling back with disgust. Nothing. 'There must be something here,' she thought. She flicked grit from the dusty gloves. 'Maybe if I took these off.' She peeled away her gloves and stuffed them into her pocket. Looking around once more, she pushed her hand back into the hole. This time she let her fingers probe the murky hollow. She felt as far back as she could, probing up and down. She was about to give up when something rubbed against the back of her hand. She turned it palm upward and caught a ledge. She pushed her fingers over its edge. There was something there! It felt soft. She could feel her heart beating. What if someone saw her? What if the girl returned? She grasped the object and brought it out. It was a leather pouch. She slipped it quickly into the pocket of her dress. What could be inside?

'Miss Stone.'

The Poor House Mistress was beside the rear door. Had she been seen? It didn't appear so. She pulled on her gloves to disguise her dirty hand. Kelly must have arrived to take her and Patience back to Burton Hall.

'What is wrong, maman?' Perinne entered the drawing room. Aunt Elizabeth, a pale, frail looking woman was standing beside a dresser and her mother was searching through the drawers.

'Ah, Perinne. Aunt Elizabeth has lost her brooch. The one with the picture of a woman with her dogs. It was here yesterday, but she can't find it anywhere.'

Perinne shook her head. 'I am sorry, maman, but I have not seen it.' Perinne could see by the redness of her eyes that her aunt had been crying. 'Is it valuable?'

'The worth is of no concern to me, Perinne,' Aunt Elizabeth said, the lines on her thin face creased with sorrow. 'It was of my mother and it is all I have to remember her by.'

'I will help to find this. It cannot be far if it has been missing only one day.'

'Thank you darling.' Her mother smiled. 'A mystery for you to solve.'

'Please, aunt, you are certain it was here?' Perinne touched the dark oak wood.

'Why, yes, I remember quite plainly.'

'Please tell me. Describe what you did exactly.'

Aunt Elizabeth crossed the room to her chair and, pulling a dark red cushion behind her, she sat. She clasped her hands and resting her chin on them closed her eyes.

'It was yesterday afternoon. Mrs Stone of Burton Hall and her daughters had called to introduce themselves. They brought their maid too. We were in here. The windows were open, just as they are today. It was so hot. I was wearing the brooch but it was heavy on my dress, pulling down the fabric, so I took it off and placed it on the dresser. Yes, on the dresser, there is no doubt in my mind.'

'And this is all?' Perinne said.

'Yes. Lucy came in with drinks. The maid from Burton helped her. They came in, placed a tray on the dresser, served our drinks and left.'

'It could have been one of the girls, or maybe both,' Jane Menniere suggested.

Aunt Elizabeth nodded. 'Yes, I suppose it could have been. It did seem that they knew each other. Well done, Perinne, I will have Joseph question Lucy and send word to Burton Hall.' Aunt Elizabeth reached for a long cord hanging from the ceiling and pulled it. 'I will call Joseph. This has to be the answer. And if it's true, the girl will be dismissed – and her father.'

'Oh, no, aunt. It cannot be Lucy,' Perinne held out her hands and shook her head. 'You are wrong. She would not do such a thing!'

'Perinne!' her mother jumped up, her face red with fury. 'Do not speak to your aunt like that. Go to your room at once!'

Perinne paced her room. It wasn't fair. Lucy would never take things from Aunt Elizabeth. But the worse thing was that it was she who'd raised the suspicions. Joseph had been sent for and asked to fetch Lucy but Perinne hadn't been allowed to stay. In the quiet of her room she cried. She must do something. She crossed to the window and peered out. The white stacks of the Needles sparkled beyond the glittering blue sea. She was supposed to be going to the beach to meet Will and Danny. Nathan would be there too, but how could she go and maybe lose Lucy.

Her small writing desk was beside her and she glanced down at it. She'd been drawing a new relic she'd found recently and was going to send the picture to Mr Brander to ask what it was. She picked it up and twirled it between her fingers, inspecting the tight whorls. Suddenly she let out a gasp. 'I wonder if that is who took the brooch.' Perinne dropped the fossil and ran to the door, pulling it back so hard it banged against the wall. She wiped away her wet face with the back of her hand as she ran down the stairs and burst into the drawing room.

'What if it was not Lucy or her friend who took the brooch!'

'Perinne! What are you doing? You were sent to your room! Go back until I say you may return.'

'But maman, it might not be Lucy, I think it may have been ... .'

'Stop! Apologise to your aunt for coming in like that, Perinne and please leave.'

Perinne took a deep breath and pursed her lips together. She looked around the room and realised Lucy wasn't there.

'Lucy will be spoken to, Perinne,' Aunt Elizabeth said, her bony face stern. 'She will have a chance to explain herself.'

'Yes, aunt. I am sorry that I interrupted.' Everyone was staring at her, it was hopeless. Perinne gave a short curtsey and left. Why would grown ups not listen?

After returning to her room to change shoes and get her bonnet, Perinne made her way down the rear wooden stairway but at the bottom she turned towards the kitchen rather than out to the courtyard.

'Miss Perinne, how are you today.' Susan the cook looked up and wiped her brow. 'Come for some cordial?'

'No Susan, I was looking for Lucy. Have you seen her?

'You as well? Joseph asked the same thing not ten minutes since. As I said to him, she is having a couple of hours off and is visiting her mother then she's collecting some elderflowers for me.'

'I shall go to see her father in that case,' Perinne said.

'Oh, John Scott's gone into town with the cart on an errand.'

Perinne sighed. 'Thank you Susan, maybe I shall find Lucy out in the lanes.'

'Are you all right, miss? You look flushed. The heat I expect, why not stay in the cool of the house.'

'Non, I shall go for a ride. Thank you Susan.'

Ben the stable boy jumped up from dozing in a pile of hay, his hair messy with bits of straw attached. He saddled Perinne's pony, Pierre and she was soon riding out of the gates of Cliff House. She made her way towards Lucy's cottage on the edge of the estate. As she did so she looked across the honeysuckle-covered hedgerows to see if she could spot her. Lucy had been her maid since she'd arrived in Christchurch last year. But she was more than a maid, she was like a friend and she would not let her get into trouble.

Perinne's heart jumped, there she was. She was wearing her maid's green dress and apron and was reaching to break off the creamy blooms from an elder tree, a brown reed basket beside her on the path. Now that she'd found her, what should she say? Would she end up getting Lucy into further trouble? Maybe she didn't know Lucy as well as she thought and she had taken the brooch. Or maybe it was Lucy's friend, Mary Maunder, the maid from Burton Hall, who was the thief and not the person Perinne suspected.

'Pack up your books, boys, we'll finish early today. This heat is not good for studying.'

Danny looked at the teacher and glanced quickly away – he was watching him! The boys shuffled out of the stuffy room and Danny mingled as best he could in an attempt to keep out of his teacher's sight.

'Clarke.'

Danny's heart sank, he wanted to get home quickly, find out his punishment for last night and hopefully meet up with Perinne, Will and Nathan.

'Yes, sir?'

'I heard that you were in the George last night. A friend

returned from a journey. Is that correct?'

Danny's stomach jolted. 'Er, yes, sir.'

'Had a little too much ale I heard.'

'Yes, sir.' There was no point in denying it. His teacher had been told. Danny was already sweating, he could feel it wet on his face, dribbling along his temples. What was his teacher going to say? After all it was out of school time.

'Well, I expect you've learned a lesson from it.'

He nodded. Why was his teacher talking about this?

'I hear you like a game of cricket?'

'Yes, sir.'

'Good. I'm forming a team to play a game against some boys from Ringwood. Would you like to play?'

'If my father will allow it, sir.'

'I can speak with him.' The school teacher took a handkerchief from his pocket and wiped his brow. His eyes pierced Danny's. 'This should get you out after school.'

Danny shifted on his feet. He needed to get home or he'd be in deeper trouble. What did his teacher want? 'May I go, sir?'

'Yes, but say you'll be playing cricket tomorrow, to practise and that I will speak with your father. I'm pleased with you, Clarke. Pleased you've forgotten about the, how should I describe it? Hiding place. I might need just a bit more help, but you can go for now.'

Danny shivered despite the heat. He ran off down the spiral staircase, out of the Priory and away, as fast as he could.

Chapter 13

Perinne hears Will's story

Tuesday 19th June 1781

'Hello! Lucy!'

The girl spun around, saw Perinne and waved. 'Hello, miss, isn't it hot! I see you're wearing your bonnet for once.' Lucy smiled as she broke off another flower head.

'Yes, I do not like the sun on my face, it goes red and burns.'

'I thought you were going to the beach today?'

'Oui. Er yes, yes I am.'

'Then you're going the wrong way!' Lucy laughed.

Perinne took a deep breath. 'Aunt Elizabeth, she is unhappy today.'

'The mistress seemed all right when I served breakfast this morning.'

'She has lost her brooch, the one that shows a lady and her dog.'

Lucy stopped and looked up at Perinne. 'Oh, no! She so loves that. It's her mourning brooch. The lady is her mother. It must be somewhere. She only wears it in the house.'

'So, you have not seen it?'

'No, miss. I shall help to find it when I get back, if it

hasn't already been found. It has to be somewhere.'

'Yes, it must.' Perinne forced a smile. Lucy knew nothing of the affair. 'I heard that there were visitors yesterday, Mrs Stone and her daughters. And they brought a maid.'

Lucy laughed. 'Yes. The maid is Mary Maunder. Mary's family lives close to our cottage, though Mary has lived at Burton Hall for some time. We've been friends for many years. She said ...' Lucy returned to picking the elderflowers.

'What is it that she said?'

'I should hold my tongue, miss. It is wrong of me to talk unfairly about others.'

'Please, tell me. What does Mary say?'

Lucy sighed. 'She says that Miss Malvina is, well, very difficult. She acts as though she's the mistress of the house. She has so much, many fine things, but is never happy, always wanting more.' She paused. 'But Patience is gentle and quiet.'

'Is that so?' Perinne leaned forward and stroked Pierre's main. 'I shall not say anything, Lucy, but maybe you should tell this to Joseph.'

'Why would Joseph want to hear about them?'

'It is important he knows this. I am going to the beach. Will is home and I want to hear all about his travels.' Perinne pulled on the pony's reins and, nudging his haunches with her heels, gently moved off. Her suspicions about the lost brooch were growing.

Perinne reached the cliff top and looked down onto the beach. The tall figure of Will was pointing something out to his friend Nathan, who was nodding his head. Will's dog, Sam, was running in and out of the sea, shaking off the water in sparkling arcs each time he ran onto the sands. Perinne climbed from the pony and led him down the gravel path. She tied his reins to the branch of a holm oak sheltering him from the hard rays of the sun. There was little breeze and the sea lapped the shore gently, broken only by the dog's happy splashes.

'Perinne, it's good to see ye.' Will smiled.

'Hello, Will, Nathan. Danny is not here yet?'

'No, not yet.'

'Perhaps he has been delayed.'

'Maybe. Or 'ad too good a time last evenin'!' Will tilted his head and shrugged.

'Oh? Why would that mean he may not come?'

'We're not sure 'ow 'e'd be feelin' today.'

Perinne looked from one to the other. Nathan was grinning. 'Why? Did something happen to him?'

'A little too much ale, mi tink!' Nathan said.

'Ale? Did he not have small beer?'

'It was only two ales, Miss Perinne.'

Perinne glared at Will, who'd hung his head then glanced away, as if checking on the dog.

'Will, you did that to Danny?'

He held up his hands. 'I'll apologise. We were in such good spirits. It were wrong. 'e'll be fine.'

'It is most likely that he has got into trouble with his father.' She shook her head. 'Let us go and sit in the shade. It is too hot out here.'

The three made their way to the crop of trees. Pierre had shifted as far back as he could and the friends settled down close by under the leafy canopy. They sat quietly, simply taking in the blue of the sea and sky. It was a while before anyone spoke. Nathan broke the silence.

He wiped his brow. 'Is it always warm and sunny here?'

Will laughed. 'No, we don't of'en get weather like this fer long.'

'It is the same in France,' Perinne added. 'Though it can be hot in the south.'

'Why do yu live here, Miss Perinne?' Nathan asked.

'I am not sure. It is something to do with papa's affairs. We have been here since March of last year. That was when I met Will.'

'An' had yu adventure!'

'Yes. That is so. I want to hear what happened after Will left. Tell me, Will what became of the machine? And how did you meet Nathan?'

Sam, who had wandered into the trees, snuffled into Will's hand. Will patted the dog.

'A lot 'appened, Perinne. At first it were 'ard. I were used to the sea, but only 'ere in the bay.' Will nodded towards the calm, blue water. 'D'ye remember Danny tellin' us 'is uncle's tales. About waves as 'igh as Priory Church?'

Perinne smiled. 'Yes, I thought that they were only stories.'

'Well, they're not. The crossin' from Poole to St John's were fearful. Cap'ain Brice locked the boxes in his cabin. He took me under 'is care, began to teach me 'ow a big ship's run. They were going out to bring back salt cod and furs. It were the wrong time o' year for passengers, but people were aboard other than crew. I slept on the floor o' the Cap'ain's cabin, but the others were down below. It stank. The crew were used to the conditions, but the ord'nary folk fell ill. Cap'ain Brice was proud of 'is ship an' kept it as clean as it could be, though there were still a lot o'sickness. As well as salt beef and biscuits we ate soups of vegetables and sometimes fruit. To keep the scurvy away, he said. One spell we 'ad six nights o' violent wind an' crashin' waves. It were frightenin'. Folk were terrified. They were prayin'. One man died, his body were tossed o'erboard as his wife an' children screamed.' Will held his head in his hands, breathed in and looked directly at Perinne. 'Life at sea isn't good, Perinne, but eventually we landed in Newfoundland. The Cap'ain said he'd need to arrange forward passage fer the boxes. The *Majesty* would be in St John's fer three weeks an' afterwards return to Poole. Despite it being May, I didn't relish the return trip an' said I wanted to see the job through an' travel wi' the load. He agreed. So, I went on to Boston.'

'It sounds dreadful.' Perinne looked at her friend, pity in her eyes. 'So, the man who has the machine, can he build it?'

'I don't know, I didn't stay.'

'Why not?'

'Monsieur Dufaut were worried 'bout being wi' me. The French were on side wi' the American army. So I left to find work. I were on me own.'

'You joined with the English soldiers?'

'No. In any case the Americans 'ad won Boston. The war were comin' to an end they said.'

'And when did you meet Nathan?'

Nathan, who was propped against a tree, dozing, opened his eyes at his name. 'I tink it was mi who find Will.'

Will laughed. 'That's a tale for another day. Still no sign of Danny.'

'No. I expect he was in trouble and has to do chores. But it is not like him. He usually finds a way.' Perinne got to her feet. 'I must go. I am worried about Lucy. She may be in trouble also.'

'Who Lucy?' Nathan said.

'She is my maid.'

'Yu have a maid?'

'Yes, what is wrong with that?'

Nathan pulled himself up and looked at Perinne. 'Where do she live?'

'She stays at Cliff House, but her home is not far.'

'And her family, what dey do?'

'Her father is footman and looks after the stables. Why, what is wrong?'

Will had joined them and put his hand on Nathan's shoulder. 'It's not the same as yer family, Nathan. They do their work, but have 'omes an' are free.'

'What do you mean, Will?' Perinne said, as she untied Pierre's reins from the branch.

'Slaves, Perinne. Nathan's family, an' many like 'em, are slaves. Kept no better than animals. They work all day an' live in hovels. Nathan escaped. He were found by a man. He'd been a ship's doctor and 'ad seen the sufferin' an' hated it. He took Nathan in an' taught 'im English.'

'He were a good man. He wrote letters an' tried to tell people 'bout the suffrin'. He died, an' mi were left alone ag'in. Mi will make mi own way in de world an'....' Nathan pressed his lips together and the beginning of a tear glistened in the corner of his wide brown eyes.

'This is why we're back, Perinne.' Will said. 'Things may be changin' in America, but too slowly. We need to stop slavery an' we're goin' to London. We must make the King an' parliament realise that the trade in people from Africa is wrong!' Will slammed his fist into a nearby tree trunk, a flurry of dried leaves raining onto his shoulder. Pierre whinnied.

'I have to go,' Perinne said, her brow lined with worry. 'When will you leave for London?'

Nathan had moved forward and was helping Perinne on to her pony.

'Soon, Perinne. I've the means to keep meself, an' Nathan an' me, we're determined to make people listen.'

As Perinne rode away she glanced back over her shoulder. Will and Nathan were making their way along the beach towards Haven Quay, Sam splashing in the water alongside. So, they were off to London. Will was nearly fifteen, but how could he and Nathan take on such a task. Will had changed, she thought. He had only told her a very small part of what must have gone on whilst he'd been away. Will was not only taller and had some money, but

102

he'd changed and she wondered if he were still interested in her and Danny now he had Nathan for a friend.

It was only a short ride from the beach to Cliff House. The hot sun was still high in the sky. Perinne thought she must have been out at least two hours. Lucy would have taken the elderflowers to Susan. She urged Pierre to speed him up. Why had she let herself stay out so long? She should have returned earlier, but she was sure Lucy was innocent of taking the brooch. It could have been her friend Mary Maunder. Why would either of them steal something so important to Aunt Elizabeth? There were other valuable things in the house that no one would miss. But it was the morning's other visitor to Cliff House she suspected as the culprit, though who'd believe her? As Pierre trotted into the courtyard beside the stables Perinne spotted a coach. It was the Stone's. Someone was here from Burton Hall.

Chapter 14

The stowaway

Tuesday 19th June 1781

Danny left the Priory grounds and set off for home. Mr Walton's last words, that he might need Danny's help again, swirled in his mind. He felt a knot in his stomach, perhaps he should just tell his father, but what would happen if his teacher denied it? He remembered he'd yet to be punished by his father for drinking ale and getting sick. His head spun. The sun was still warm and he stopped at the wooden bridge. He scuttled down the river bank and splashed his face. He had to think of something, he didn't want to get involved with the smugglers.

Danny finally reached the Salisbury Road and turned to make his way to the family's cottage. As he approached he saw that Dr Quartley's horse was tethered against the gatepost. Uncle John's horse and cart was also there. What was going on? Fear rose in his stomach. Instead of going around the back and into the kitchen Danny lifted the front door latch and stepped in. The small parlour was filled with people. His father was holding his mother, who was crying. Aunt Mary was there, she was sitting on a chair and Uncle John had his hand on her shoulder. Sarah, his sister, was sitting on the floor holding her wooden doll, Dilly, looking puzzled. By the fireside was the doctor, turning as Danny appeared.

'What's happened?'

'Come here, Danny,' Hannah Clarke said, beckoning her son.

James Clarke stepped aside to let Danny pass. Danny took his mother's hand.

'It's grandpa, Danny. He's left us.'

Danny looked in turn at his mother and father. 'What?' he said.

'Grandpa Hopkins has died Danny,' his father said, in a soft voice.

Danny didn't move. Images of that morning swam in his head. How could this be? He'd seen grandpa before he'd set out to school. Maybe if he hadn't been feeling sick he would have noticed there was something wrong and if he had, maybe he wouldn't have died. He darted through the room and out of the back, pushing his way past everyone.

'Ye grandfather were an old man, Danny,' Uncle John said.

Danny was sitting in the garden beside the patch where mother grew vegetables. He looked up, his eyes reddened.

'We're all sad, but we all 'ave to go to our maker eventually.'

'But he was all right this morning.'

'He 'adn't been very well an' his time 'ad come, Danny. Come on, let's go inside.'

'I want to stay out here for a while, Uncle John. Is that all right?'

'O' course, take ye time, lad.'

Danny watched as Uncle John went back into the cottage. It was all too much. Danny buried his face in his hands and sobbed.

Conyer, Kent

'So we leave early ev'nin' ... .' That was father.

A gull squawked overhead. Josh looked up, annoyed it made such a loud noise. He couldn't hear anything other than snippets of what was being said.

' ... and we'll be in Christchurch Thursday evenin' ... Roger ... might take a week ... ' Another gull joined in the row. Josh needed to get closer, but there was nowhere else to hide. His father, Peter Graves, Henry Cotton and Levi Bird were going out that evening. That wasn't unusual, but Roger Law had come to tell them of a shipwreck and of a girl that had been found. They thought it was Francis Woolsey's daughter. Roger Law had already set out to the town and he'd send them word. Josh had never heard of Christchurch before. They mentioned treasure and were plotting a journey. If, they were going to Christchurch, he wanted to go too. The men broke up. Rowland headed towards the forge. Once he'd gone inside Josh scrambled from his hiding place and went after his father.

'Are yew going out with Peter and the others t'night, father?' Josh said. Heat from the fire was weaving rivulets of sweat down Rowland's face as he placed another iron on the glowing charcoals. Their horse, Toby, was standing by for his new shoe.

'Why do yew ask?' Rowland said, looking across at his son, standing in the doorway.

'Wondered if I could come too.'

'No yew can't.'

'Why not father? Didn't yew go out with grandfather when yew were twelve?'

'Yewer not coming Josh, and that's final.'

'But father... .'

'No, Josh. I'm not havin' yew get involved. Yewer goin' to learn this trade an' to read an' write an' yew goin' to make somethin' of yewer life.'

It was hopeless. Josh walked up the pathway behind their home, kicking at stones. He reached a grassy bank, sat down and gazed across the creek. The water was creeping back over muddy brown banks that had dried in the summer heat. He watched as the water lapped gently, its earthy smell wafting across the air. It wasn't fair. He knew other boys went out on the luggers. Also, he wanted to see what other places were like. He'd been to Chatham and seen the huge navy ships, Rochester with its tall castle and old cathedral and Faversham with its breweries smelling of malt and hops. But that was all, and this was a chance to see new places. He looked across towards the cottage. The smoke that normally rose from the forge had gone, father was getting ready. It was mother who didn't want him to go. He was sure his father would have allowed it had she not protested. The noisy gull was overhead. The bird was much quieter. Josh let his thoughts drift along as he watched it circling, a free spirit, able to do as it wished. And suddenly he had an idea.

Josh made his way back home. He needed to be careful. The air was soft and warm. He was only wearing his shirt and breeches and that was fine for now, but he needed a coat and shoes if he were to carry out his plan. His father was talking to Henry Cotton. His mother was chatting to Henry's wife, Tabitha, whilst taking in washing that had been drying on the hedge. He saw his mother lift the final garment then follow Tabitha into the rear of the bakery. This was his chance. He made his way into the house, found what he wanted and crept unseen into a nearby field. He waited, hidden by thick bushes, and watched as the sun crept down.

'Josh! Josh, where are yew?' Rowland's voice was muffled by the trees and the cottage. Josh stayed still.

Keeping as low to the ground as he could, silently slipped on his shoes and coat. He edged his way towards the forge and hid behind a large barrel. He could see his father with other members of the Conyer Gang, Henry Cotton, Peter Graves and Levi Bird. There were two carts. Josh leaned aside to gain a better view. His mother and Tabitha were standing watching.

'I can't see 'im, he'll be sulkin' somewhere,' Rowland said and climbed onto the first cart with Peter. Henry and Levi were already settled on the second. 'Sorry Suzy, but we need to leave. We'll be a few days, an' we'll be 'ome. Don't yew worry.' Rowland turned away, took up the reins and gave them a tug. 'Move on.'

Suzannah Blackbourne was looking around. Josh knew she was looking for him.

'Come on, Suzannah.' Tabitha took her neighbour's arm.

Josh watched as his mother was led into their small cottage. The two carts were moving slowly. Dusk was hovering and shadows crept with them along the lane. The wheels were clattering on the dry track. Josh crept as quickly and quietly as he could. Soon he was behind the second cart. Henry and Levi were chattering. Henry lifted his pipe and Josh ducked, thinking he was about to turn around, but Henry simply put it into his mouth. A sudden dip in the lane jolted the cart and Josh knew this was his chance. He jumped onto the back, pulled a piece of sackcloth over him and hid. He would go to Christchurch after all.

Rowland steered the horse to a fork in the road. He could see the shape of a man in the shadow of a large oak. It was here that he, Peter and Henry, would take the eastern route to Whitstable. They'd be collecting goods from the shipment and be making deliveries that would keep them away from home for four, maybe five nights, depending on the success of the mission. Henry's place with Levi was taken by the new man. He was from Saul Bird's gang and would make the journey with Levi to Christchurch.

Rowland, Henry and Peter continued in silence. Rowland glanced back. He was glad to see Levi disappear. He knew why he was taking a cart and not simply riding there – it was to bring back Francis Woolsey, dead or alive. He shuddered. Rowland didn't want anything to do with the capture and torture of any man, even if he were a King's man, especially for treasure that might not even be found.

Plymouth, Devon

Samuel Pascoe was sitting on Plymouth Hoe watching crowds of ships winding in and out of the harbour on the gentle breeze. It was a long time since he was last here. His father, also Samuel Pascoe, was a sailor and would return from his voyages to here or Poole. He cast his mind back to the day his uncle brought him from their home in Sidmouth to meet him. But that was many years ago.

This time he was here to meet his sister and his niece, but there was still no sign of them. His brother-in-law had paid for passage on the *Anne Marie,* which should have reached the port by now. He'd been to the harbour every morning for the past week, but there was no news. It would have been much easier if he were nearer home, he wouldn't have had to travel and have the cost of finding lodgings until they arrived. He breathed in the fresh, salty air. Francis was a brave soldier and he was proud his sister had married such a good man, especially after their father lost the family's fortune. But the letter he'd received from Kent had worried him greatly and he longed for the family to arrive safely.

The weather was set fair, but it had been wild the week

before and he guessed that the ship would have taken shelter, probably at Portsmouth, so delaying it. The sun was still up, and was catching sparks in nearby windows. Yet he knew another day was in its final hours despite its warmth brushing his face. He stood. He wasn't tall. His white-grey hair was combed back over his head and gathered into a pony tail. He lifted his hat and coat from the grassy bank, put on the black hat but carried the coat over his arm and strode off to find an inn. He'd eat some supper and ask around for news.

Samuel made his way past the Citadel and down towards the harbour. It was busy with people out and about. Sailors from the royal navy ships hurried by as though they were late for something. A man on a horse with a dog at its heels trotted past. Across the road a cart was being unloaded into an inn by two men who were each holding an end of a long chest. They were followed by two women struggling to hold large wicker baskets. There was a courtyard beside the inn and Samuel wandered over to take a look at what was happening.

A tall man in a brown shirt was directing the group to a corner of the yard where stacks of straw tied with string had been arranged.

Samuel doffed his cap to the man. 'Good day to you, sir. Are you getting ready for an entertainment?'

'Aye, two nights.'

'Well, I think I'll come along. It'll be good to have a distraction.'

'An' why's that?'

Samuel hunched his shoulders. 'Been here since Wednesday of last week and would like to be back to my own bed.'

'So, what's keepin' ye?'

'I'm here to meet my sister and niece. They're due on the *Anne Marie*. They're late, the bad weather I expect.'

'The *Anne Marie* you say?'

'Yes, do you have news of her?'

The man shifted nervously.

'Sir?'

''Well, er..., we were in Christchurch. There was a violent storm and a ship takin' shelter in the bay was wrecked.'

'And those aboard? Did they get ashore?'

The man took a deep breath. 'No. All hands lost.'

Samuel's grey head bowed and he bit his lips together to fight back his tears.

'But there was a girl,' the tall man said.

'A girl?'

'Someone found a young girl in the Priory Church. Folks thought she were with us and we were abandoning her. There was a rumour she'd been rescued.'

'And where is the girl now?' Samuel's hands were shaking.

'Wouldn't know, the Poor House, I expect. That's where they'd usually take foundlings. Are you all right?' The man touched Samuel's arm gently, his face now drained of all colour. 'Come, sit down here.' The man led Samuel to a nearby bench. 'Lizzie, get a brandy for this gentleman,' he shouted to one of the women who was standing next to the basket.

Samuel sat and buried his face into his hands. 'It cannot be. It cannot be. I must go to Christchurch.'

Chapter 15

Scheming smugglers

Tuesday 19th June 1781

Josh kept as quiet as he could, though it was difficult to keep still. They seemed to have been travelling for hours and the cart had bumped and rattled all the way. They'd stopped a good while back. He imagined it was Henry who'd got off. He'd been right. Someone else had joined Levi and Levi called him Pip. Josh had begun to feel sore from being jolted about. Suddenly the cart stopped. He felt Pip and Levi get down. He curled up as tightly as he could, hoping he wouldn't be caught. He knew that if they hadn't got far, they could turn back.

'Let's rest the horse a-while,' Pip's voice spoke. 'Yew sure 'tis the road?'

'Yis, 'tis the one,' said Levi Bird. 'If we c'n get to Dorking we c'n stop at an inn there. But there's bread and cheese for our journey. Shows for fine weather, so we c'n sleep in the cart or on the ground. Save our money.'

Josh's heart sank. If they did sleep in the cart he'd be discovered. Maybe he could jump off just before they reached the inn and hide somewhere as he'd done at home. The heat of the sun had begun to leak through the sacking covering him. It hadn't been too bad whilst they were moving. He peeked out, and breathed in a little fresh air. He couldn't see anything other than the inside of the cart. He wished he were in father's cart. Then he noticed a hole where a knot of wood had fallen out. He inched towards it and looked through. The two men were sitting by a tree chatting. He couldn't see his father, nor Peter, perhaps they were further ahead. Josh strained to hear what they were talking about. He wanted them to carry on. What if he needed a pee? He was all right at the moment. He hadn't drunk much before they'd left.

'C'me on, let's get a move on,' Pip's voice came louder.

He saw Pip approach. He was tall and his hair was thin. He had green eyes, a long nose and thin lips. There was a scar near to his ear. Josh pulled the cloth fully over him again. What if they checked the back he thought. But the cart tilted, first to one side and then the other.

'Move on,' said Levi.

'So far, so good,' said Pip.

'Yis, Levi, though I'm hopin' it aint a wild goose chase. Is Roger Law sure 'bout the girl?'

Josh gasped. The girl? He thought they were chasing Francis Woolsey and treasure.

'He says 'tis her, and he's watchin' a local gang, in case we need help,' Levi answered. 'Woolsey may not be alone.'

'An' this hoard o' treasure. He's sure 'tis Christchurch?'

'He says a local man told him how the town got its name. It used to be called Twynam but changed when the church was built. Local legend says it were Jesus himself helped to build it!'

Pip scoffed. 'An' why would God's son build a little church in Hampshire?'

''Tisn't a little church. 'Tis as big as Rochester Cathedral!'

'So it might not be an easy job finding the treasure if it be so big.' Pip shook his head.

'First we've got to sort Woolsey. We can get the cipher off him and work out what it means.'

'Won't be easy thing to do, go snoopin' round a church.'

'Roger's let a story go 'round. He wants to take the locals' minds off anythin' we might do whilst he's soundin' them out. He's told them the *Anne Marie* was carrying gold.'

Pip was laughing, his voice scratchy and hoarse. 'An' they believed him?'

'Appears so, e'en the local squire, Tarrant, is gettin' in on it. He's been askin' local men to help, so my contact in Ringwood tells me.'

The men were quiet for a few moments until Levi spoke again. 'So,' he said, 'when we get to Christchurch, we meet up with Roger. Find out where the girl is and lay low. Woolsey will be sure to come for her once he hears she's alive.'

'Yis, that's the plan.'

'How will he find out about the wreckin'?'

Josh strained to hear. What was going on?

'Roger's had people on the lookout for Woolsey, but no one has sin him since London,' Levi said.

'He says that if he put the womenfolk on the ship it would mean they'd be gettin' off somewhere along the south coast. Could be Portsmouth, Poole or maybe Plymouth. He said he'd speak to as many people as he could as he made his way to Christchurch. He'd say he were looking for his brother and needed to tell him 'bout the wreckin' of the *Anne Marie*. Told people to spread the word.'

'There's a chance he'd not hear 'bout it at all,' Pip said.

'But the girl's there. I had a message from Roger late yesterday afternoon. He says people thought she were with entertainers, but they knew nothin' of her. The girl's refusin' to speak. There's no other explanation for her bein' there.' Levi sniffed and checked around. 'The horses need rest, let's stop awhile an' we'll stay near Romsey overnight. After that it'll be an easy trip to Ringwood to see my contact and move on to Christchurch.'

Josh looked through the knot hole. The cart rattled towards the flickering lights of an inn. It was dusk and an orange-red haze bled across the horizon. He felt a lurch in the cart, and before he realised what was happening, a hand pulled on his hair.

'Well what have we here?'

'What be it Pip?' Levi said.

'Better take a look.' Pip's face was full of anger.

Josh stared as Levi twisted on the cart's seat and peered into the back.

'Josh Blackbourne!' If Pip looked angry, Levi's face was red with rage.

Josh pursed his lips. Both men's faces were twisted with lines of fury. Levi's eyes glared with a force that almost pinned Josh down.

'What in the devil's own name are yew doin' here?' Levi hissed.

'Josh began to shake. 'W... w... where's my father?'

'He aint here,' Pip snapped, jumping down from his seat. 'What do we do, Levi?'

''Tis too late to turn back. The stupid brat'll have to come. We went on jobs at his age.'

'Rowland goin' to be mad,' Pip said.

'Rowland's not here. An' Rowland's a coward.'

Josh leapt up. 'No he's not. My father's not a coward!'

'Sit down!' Levi yelled. 'Or I'll give yew a bannockin'!' Levi swung out at Josh, catching his arm and sending him tumbling from the cart and hard onto the gravel track.

Caleb Brown leaned over the small table set beside the open window of the Eight Bells.

'We can't trust 'im,' he hissed.

'I agree,' David Preston added. 'He said he were goin' back to Kent, but he aint gone yet. What's he waitin' fer?'

Adam Litty shook his head. He lifted his tankard of ale to his mouth and drank it empty and waved a hand to have more fetched. 'No idea. We also don't know who's bringin' in the baccy. Maybe this Roger Law of Kent has somethin' to do wi' that.'

'Why would he come all the way from Kent to bring in baccy? They're nearer France, easier there than 'ere surely.' Caleb said. 'An were he telling the truth about the gold? Or were that just to distract us?'

'Even if it were there, it's beyond any man to reach it.' Adam said. 'He must want somethin', or why stick around?'

'Aye.' The men muttered.

'We did a good job the other night. The sea's calm and we have that Geneva comin' over Thursday night. We need to watch the water. Whoever it is, they 'ave to ship it over, offload it and either store it or send it on. We should keep our eyes on everyone and our ears alert.' Adam gave the two men a long look. Caleb Brown and David Preston had belonged to another gang until the two groups got together last summer. Adam wasn't sure he could trust them. But why would they go behind his back? The new group were working well together and the recent landing of the huge consignment had gone without a problem, very smooth in fact, and they'd all done all right out of it.

'Well I 'ave to get back to the forge.' Caleb lifted his heavy black leather apron from the floor. He put it on, wrapping the straps around his large waist and tying them together at the front. 'I'll see what I can get out o' this Roger Law. He's collecting his 'orse later. New shoes.'

'Be careful, Caleb,' David Preston said. 'We don't want

to give anythin' away.'

'Ye know me better than that.' Caleb ducked his head away from a low beam and left the alehouse.

'Caleb's no fool, David,' Adam said.

'But he c'n be soft in the head, Adam,' David said, tapping his temple with his pipe. 'Easily won round for pity.' He let out a breath and gave Adam a strong stare. 'Should we 'ave someone watch this Roger Law?'

'Already 'ave.'

David raised his eyebrows. 'Who be that then?'

'Guy Cox.'

'An' has he seen anthin'?'

Adam shrugged. 'Not much, he says he's been near the Poor House more than anywhere else, 'ave you seen 'im?'

David shook his head. 'No, can't say as I 'ave. Wonder why that is? He doesn't look like he needs 'elp from the Parish. In any case, 'e'd be sent 'ome if 'e did.'

'He seemed interested in that lost girl you 'ave in there.'

'She still aint spoken a word, but the overseers are sending her to Kent. Do ye think he may know her?'

'That's possible I suppose. When's she goin'? 'ow did they find out that's where she came from?'

'Well, they are thinkin' she *was* on the *Anne Marie,* an' it set out from Chatham. They're sendin' 'er up to Ringwood to catch the coach on Friday.'

'So why don't Roger Law just say if he knows the lass? If she's goin' Friday, perhaps Law'll follow her. I'm goin' to speak with him again. Try to befriend him. Find out what 'e wants.'

Roger Law watched as Adam Litty left the Eight Bells. He might need the local smugglers on his side, and it was obvious Litty had a gang. He had no interest in any goods though. Shortly after seeing Adam he saw the Poor House Master leave. He was sure it was the Woolsey girl who'd been found. He could simply turn up at the door and say he was family, but he doubted that would work. Besides, he didn't want the bother of a young girl snapping around his heels. He simply needed to spread the rumour in the right places and wait. Wait for Francis Woolsey to come and claim her. After that he would exact revenge and retrieve the cipher. He'd also sent further word to Levi Bird and hopefully he'd already be on his way. Though he wasn't sure who he'd bring, the Conyer lot wouldn't have the stomach for the task. He'd yet to collect his horse from the blacksmith. He needed it well shod, just in case he had to get away from this town quickly.

Chapter 16

Perinne's suspicions

Wednesday 20th June 1781

Perinne rubbed her eyes. The light crept around the edges of the red curtains which ruffled gently in front of the open window and she knew morning had arrived. Even the fresh air had not helped her to sleep. She simply hadn't been able to get Lucy and her friend, Mary Maunder out of her mind. She was certain they hadn't been responsible for taking the brooch, and it would be most unfair to be dismissed for something that they hadn't done. But the brooch had gone missing. She ran through her mind once more what had happened when she'd returned to Cliff House yesterday afternoon and saw the coach.

She remembered shouting 'Ben!' as she jumped from her pony. The stable boy had arrived and took hold of Pierre's reins. She'd asked who was here.

'It's the lady from Burton Hall, miss and her daughters. Mr Benjamin, their butler was with them, I think he's in the kitchen.' Ben had peered past her, as if he could see into the house. *'They've only just arrived.'* She'd run into the house through the kitchen door. Benjamin Kelly was sitting with Susan the cook. He was drinking a cup of

something, probably ale. *'Miss!'* Susan had shouted.

Perinne scrunched her face as she tried to recall the exact scene and the words and faces came rushing back to her. She'd not answered Susan but had rushed straight through to the drawing room. Aunt Elizabeth was in her chair, cooling her face with a fan, maman was sitting alongside her. Mrs Stone was on the sofa with Patience. But where was Malvina? Hmm, yes, standing close to the dresser. Joseph had his back to me, so I crept in behind him.

' ... *so, madam,'* Joseph had said, *'it appears that Maunder is the culprit. Kelly passed on your message and Miss Stone here went to fetch the maid.'* He'd nodded toward Malvina. *'The brooch was found in Maunder's apron pocket.'*

Aunt Elizabeth looked anxious. *'And Scott, was she part of the theft?'*

Mrs Stone had answered. *'Maunder denies everything, Lady Elizabeth. Of course, she's been dismissed. I trust you'll deal with Scott in the same manner. We cannot give servants any second chance or they'll take advantage.'*

Recalling what she'd done next, Perinne banged her fists into the bed. If only she'd waited, but she hadn't been able to stop herself pushing past Joseph.

'But Lucy hasn't done anything!'

'Perinne! Quiet,' maman was furious.

She'd said it in a low, hard voice. Was Malvina smirking? She was facing away from everyone else in the room.

'I do not want you to think that my household cannot be trusted, Lady Elizabeth, that is why I insisted on returning the brooch myself.'

'I am very grateful, Mrs Stone.'

Aunt Elizabeth was brushing her finger over the enamelled picture. Malvina spoke. *'It was most definitely the maids, I can remember, they were standing just where I am now, whispering to each other. It was a conspiracy.'*

Why had no one tried to stop her?

'That's quite enough, Malvina. You made it clear to me at home what you'd seen. See, Lady Elizabeth, there is no doubt about the matter. We will take your leave and return to Burton Hall. Please do visit us soon.'

Mrs Stone had gone into the hall followed by Patience and Malvina. Malvina had given a sly sideways glance. Joseph left through the other door to tell Kelly to fetch the coach to the front drive.

Perinne rolled over on her bed as she thought hard, it was only yesterday. Then, as if a bolt of lightning had run through her, she realised that when Aunt Elizabeth had described what had happened, she'd said that it was Malvina who'd been standing by the dresser. Lucy and Mary Maunder had simply set down the tray and served drinks. It had to be Malvina who had taken the brooch. But who would believe her?

The door opened. It was the scullery maid, who normally came in to help with the fires and laundry.

'I been told to bring ye this drink, miss, an' see if ye need 'elp dressin',' she said.

Perinne thought she looked like a house mouse. The maid's eyes were flitting around, trying to avoid looking directly at her. Her light brown hair was lost under her cap and she was shaking. Perinne shrugged.

'Put it on my desk, and I need no help today.'

'Yes, miss,' the girl said, setting down a wooden tray holding a cup. 'And the mistress asks if you'd like to do sewin',' she added, curtseying. Holding her head down, she left the room with a shuffle.

Perinne jumped off her bed. 'So, no Lucy this morning. I need to prove it was Malvina, but how? I need to think.' Perinne quickly pulled on her dress and stretched to reach the buttons behind her neck. She didn't want to sit with needlework, so instead she'd go to the Poor House. She'd say she'd promised to help today and that would give her time to work out what to do and maybe speak with Will and Danny.

Rosamund joined the queue for a drink and bread. The girls were giving her long looks.

'Ye can still scream,' Betty's spiteful voice hissed. 'Ye kept us all awake. Bad enough wi' the heat and smell without all that noise from ye.'

There was a mumble of low voices from the others. Rosamund wanted to cry. She inched along the queue and took her food, making her way to the corner of the long room where she could see the woman, Sarah and little Molly.

'You all right?' Sarah asked.

Rosamund nodded.

'It were a bad dream, that's all. Take no notice o' Betty, other girls 'ave nightmares.'

'Sarah,' Mistress Preston's voice cried over the chatter of the room. 'Send the girl to the hallway, the overseer's here to see her.'

Sarah nodded at Rosamund who made her way down the room, past the other girls to where Judith Preston was standing by the doorway. The hallway was cool and dark, the only light leaked through a small window above the door. Inside wasn't the jolly-looking man but the tall one whom Rosamund hadn't liked. He looked down at her, his breath smelled like rotten cabbage.

'Now, girl, the mistress here tells me you've yet to say where your parish is. Rumours have been spread that you came on the ship that was wrecked, is that true?'

Rosamund pursed her lips. 'Speak with no one,' her father's voice whispered.

'Your coat smelled of the sea,' the man waited for a reaction but Rosamund stared, as if frozen.

'We've no idea of how you got to town, but it's the only answer. So, we'll be sending you back to Chatham, where the ship set sail. They can deal with you there. You leave Friday. Have her ready mistress.' Turning, the man opened the door to the street and left without further word.

Judith Preston bent her knees and took hold of Rosamund, staring directly in her face. 'Say where ye're from, girl. If it ain't Kent, then tell us!'

Rosamund felt dizzy. 'We must never go back to Kent,' father had said. She wanted to scream, 'NO!' but nothing would come out.

Judith tutted, holding up her hands with dismay. 'Get yer sewing. If yer not from Kent, ye'd better tell me afore it's too late.' At that Judith strutted off.

Rosamund tried to think. Perhaps she could run away. Or tell Mistress Preston she was from Plymouth and she should be sent there. But she knew no one in Plymouth, Uncle Sam was only meeting them there. Them. She suddenly remembered her mother and softly sobbed. She sat down on the bottom step of the nearby staircase. If she were leaving in two days' time, she would need to get the pouch, she'd check and maybe take it today in case she didn't get another chance. She rubbed her face with her hands and went to the laundry room to collect the garments that needed stitching. No one would be concerned if she sat under the tree to do her work as she'd done before.

Rosamund reached the tree. There was no one around. Rays of sunlight shone through the branches which were thick with leaves and were casting a green hue. A sudden flash of red in the tree made her start, but it was only a squirrel. She reached into the hole and ran her hand up to the ledge. Her fingers stretched and searched, she lifted herself as high as her toes would take her. Her fingertip caught the inside of the trunk. A hard gulp ran down her throat and her heart bumped in her chest. The pouch wasn't there.

Perinne's head was buzzing. If only Danny were around, she could speak with him, tell him what had happened, but he'd be in school by now. She could go to Will's house and ask him what he thought. She wondered if he'd be interested, but she'd try. If Will wasn't there she could wait for Danny later when he was returning home. Pierre's hooves grated on the gravel track and soon clopped onto the hard dirt of the road through Purewell. She reached the edge of the town and crossed over the first bridge. The River Avon was low. She peered over the edge and could see fish basking in the shallow water. Passing the town hall she entered the high street. People were out and about, the ladies in bright dresses and fancy hats. Some were holding parasols. Windows were opened and on one side she could see shopkeepers sitting inside to keep out of the heat. On the other side of the street they were sitting outside in the shade. Eventually she arrived at the top of the narrow lane where the Gibbs' cottage was found. There was a mounting block near to where the Bargate had been and she used it to dismount and walk Pierre down the last few yards. She knocked on the door. The cottage looked much better with its repaired roof. It had been almost falling down last year. There was no answer, not even a bark from Sam. A head appeared in the door of the next cottage.

'They're out,' the man said. Perinne recognised Isaac Hooper. He was a strange old man who knew Danny's Uncle John. 'C'n I 'elp?'

'Do you know where they are?' Perinne asked.

Isaac shook his head.

'Then you cannot help me.' Perinne sighed. She was hot. She made her way slowly towards the Poor House, took Pierre to the stable and went into the room that Master and Mistress Preston used to keep records and do their paperwork.

'Ah, Miss Perinne, just the person I need. Could ye have one last try at getting the girl to speak? She's goin' to be leavin' the day after tomorrow,' Judith Preston told her. 'She's been havin' nightmares. Screamed out last night, so she sure 'as a voice. She went as pale as a new cotton sheet when the overseer told her she were goin' back to Kent. I just wish she'd say somethin'.'

Perinne crossed the kitchen garden to the girl who seemed to be just staring into the air.

'Hello, are you all right? Mistress Preston tells me you are going home soon.'

Rosamund looked up. Perinne noticed her eyes were red and streaks of tear tracks lined her face. She'd got thinner since Perinne had first seen her. She sat down next to the girl.

'You are upset. What is wrong? You can tell me, I promise I will not say anything if you do not wish me to.'

Rosamund's mouth opened slightly and Perinne thought she was about to speak, but she closed it again. They sat quietly. Birds were twittering above and it was cool under the canopy of the tree. A sudden rustling noise caught Perinne's attention. It was coming from the undergrowth a short distance away. She watched as a creature appeared.

'Look,' Perinne whispered. 'Can you see it?' This time she pointed. A fox cub was just visible in the tall grass. His long nose was searching the ground and his thick orange tail swishing to and fro. At first it didn't notice the two girls. It sniffed, looked up and darted back into nearby brambles.

Perinne laughed. 'How sweet! I expect it was lost and looking for its mother.'

A deep gasp sucked into Rosamund's lungs. She turned. Her eyes were wide and full of sorrow. Throwing her arms around Perinne, finally, and broken by sobs, she spoke. 'Help me, please, help me.'

Chapter 17

Rosamund's story

Wednesday 20th June 1781

'It's sad for all of us, Danny,' James Clarke was sitting next to his son, his head down and his hands cupped together.

Danny looked across the room. Grandpa's body lay in a wooden coffin, which was set above the stone floor on blocks. It was at the back of the parlour, the coldest place in the house and shaded from the small window. Danny couldn't see grandpa, for he was wrapped in a light woollen shroud and had a square of pale linen covering his face. But there was a faint odour that he knew to be death.

A beam of light from the small window cast a ghostly hue across the centre of the room. Danny gazed at the specks of dust dancing inside it. He'd been to many funerals before. He had to sing at some with the choir at the Priory, but he'd never been to one of someone he loved. He was hot. Like his father, he was wearing only his shirt and breeches. Another tear trickled down his reddened cheek and fell onto his shirt leaving a grey blot.

'It was grandpa's time, son,' his father said. 'He wouldn't want you to be sad.'

Danny rubbed his eyes with the heels of his hands and

nodded with a sniff.

'Look, I have to go to Cliff House for a while. Why not go to the cricket practice this afternoon? Mr Walton was fine about you not going to school, but he seemed very keen to have you on his team. I'm sure he'll be pleased to see you.'

Danny jumped up, knocking his chair back. 'No!'

'It's all right, Danny,' his father said, pulling the chair back on to its legs. He sighed. 'It was only an idea. It would do you good to get out for a while, I thought you enjoyed cricket.'

'I don't like Mr Walton. I don't want to go. I'm going outside to mother.'

Danny walked through the door towards the kitchen and out into the garden. His mother was sitting in the shade. Aunt Mary was also there. They were making favours of ribbon and sprigs of rosemary ready for the funeral. Both were wearing black dresses. Sarah was weaving a daisy chain and humming. 'Why wasn't she sad?' Danny thought.

'Danny, come and sit in the shade,' Hannah Clarke said.

'Why has Jack gone to work?'

'He had to go, Danny, and afterwards he's collecting the gloves we've bought for tomorrow.'

'Why do we have to wear gloves? It's so hot.'

'We must show our respect to grandpa,' his mother said.

'Are you not sad?'

'Yes, of course I am. Grandpa was my father.'

'And he were mine too, Danny,' Aunt Mary said. 'But we must mourn the proper way an' we must hold a good funeral for him.'

'Have all the neighbours been to see him?' Danny's mother rose, lifting the reed basket which held bunches of the favours.

'I think so, father will know.'

'Well, let's go and ask him. These can go in the front

room beside grandpa. And then I need to start baking.'

'I think I'll stay out here,' Danny said. 'Will Uncle John be here soon?'

'He'll be over in the mornin' Danny, well before the journey to church,' Aunt Mary said. 'Why don't you go and pick some flowers?' she added, following her sister into the cottage. Sarah picked up her daisy chain and left too.

Danny kicked at the grass. His bare feet were dirty and dusty. He'd go and pick flowers. At least that way his father wouldn't mention the cricket. And he wouldn't go tomorrow. He'd say he had to help after the funeral. Hopefully after that his teacher would have found someone else to help him smuggle his bales and that would be the end of it.

Josh watched the countryside disappearing from view and more appearing as the cart moved along. He was sitting up. His shoulder hurt where he'd landed on it. Pip had helped him to his feet but had backed away as Levi screamed to leave him. Since then Pip and Levi had barely spoken. He'd never liked Levi and Pip seemed just the same.

Last night they'd eaten supper and slept by the cart as planned, but there wasn't as much food now that they had another mouth to feed. Before they'd set out Pip had said the weather was on their side and they should make good time. The day was warming and Josh breathed in the scents from the hedgerows as they drove, but it wasn't enough to kill the smell of sweat from the two men. What should he do? They were going to call into a place called Ringwood. Levi needed to see someone there and he'd ask if they knew of somewhere that Josh could be left as they did their work in Christchurch. As he watched the road, Josh wondered if he ran, whether he could find his way home. But a part of him wanted to see if there really was treasure trove to be found. He could claim a share for his mother and father.

It took most of the day to get to Winchester. Josh saw that like Rochester, it too had a cathedral, busy high street and castle. Were all big cities like this? They'd said that Christchurch was only a small town, but with a large church. He could always go to Christchurch on his own. But he didn't like the thought of being all alone.

Samuel Pascoe watched the rolling hills of the Dorsetshire countryside pass by as the coach journeyed on. He'd left home in Sidmouth the day before and had stayed overnight in Exeter. It was midday. The sun was high above them, though the heat wasn't as bad whilst they were moving along. He leaned out of the window but pulled back again to avoid the dust being thrown up by the four horses, fresh after a change at Bridport. He hadn't travelled this far before. He'd heard about the dangers and feared the highwaymen. He felt down to check his purse, deep in his breeches pocket. This was all the money he had for his trip. They would reach Poole by late afternoon when he would have to find a coach that would take him on to Christchurch. If the girl were Rosamund she must be afraid. He hoped his young niece would recognise him. He had little to show that her mother and he were brother and sister. And where was Francis? He should have reached Sidmouth by now.

'My name is Rosamund.'

'That is pretty,' said Perinne. 'How old are you?'

'Ten.'

'How did you get here? Did you come from the wreck?'

'Yes, a man lifted me from the sea and put me on his cart. His wife was there, they took me to their cottage. I heard them say it was dangerous for them to let people know they'd helped me.' Rosamund looked down, she was wringing the apron she'd been sewing. 'I hoped that m-mother had also been found.'

'I am sorry.'

'The people, they left me in the church and a boy found me.'

'That was my friend, Danny,' Perinne said. 'And where do you live?'

'We lived in Faversham. We had to leave. Father has enemies. He put,' Rosamund hesitated. 'Mm- mother and me on the *Anne Marie* at Chatham...,' she sniffled '... and we were going to Plymouth where my Uncle Sam was to meet us. Father sold our home and many of our things were also on the ship.'

Perinne took Rosamund's hand. 'So, why not tell Mistress Preston that and you will be sent there instead.'

'Uncle Sam does not live at Plymouth. I'm not certain where he lives. Mother knew.' Rosamund bit her lips together as more teardrops fell down her pale cheeks.

Perinne put her arm around Rosamund's shoulders. 'Where is your father?'

'All I know is that some bad men were trying to find him. He is trying to lose them so that they can never find us.'

'Why?'

'Something about smugglers. He's a dragoon captain. Smugglers shot and killed three of his men. They shot him too and he's hurt his arm. Are there smugglers here in Christchurch?'

'Yes, there are. And I know how bad they can be.'

'Do you? How?' Rosamund looked hard at Perinne, she hoped she wasn't being tricked into saying too much. She wouldn't mention the cipher – yet.

'Last year Danny and I with another friend, Will, helped to solve a mystery. A machine was smuggled and two gangs had different parts. They fought each other to get them. One day I was snatched and taken to an old cottage. The man pointed a pistol at us and it was Danny and Will who rescued me. And we solved the mystery and found all the machine's parts.'

Rosamund's face changed to a look of surprise.

'And I will try to help you find your father.'

The girl's shoulders fell and her sad look returned.

'What is it?' Perinne asked. 'You would not be pleased to see your father again?'

'I've let him down.'

'How? It is not your fault that there was a bad storm and your ship was wrecked.'

'It's not that.'

'Then what is it? What is wrong?'

Rosamund began to cry again. 'Father gave me a pouch to look after. Mother sewed it into my coat to keep it hidden. It had a watch and a locket. The watch belonged to my great grandfather. It had been lost for many years, but father had just found it. The locket had some money inside. The pouch has gone.'

'Do you mean you lost it in the sea?'

'No. Everyone wanted my coat. Someone on the beach, even the man who rescued me and here at the Poor House. They all wanted my coat, so I took out the pouch and hid it.'

'Where?'

'Here, in this tree. It has a hole and just inside is a small ledge. I'd put it there.' Rosamund pointed.

Perinne lifted herself on her toes and inspected the hole. It wasn't very high. 'Maybe it's only fallen.' Perinne felt around, but there was nothing.

'It's no good. It's gone.'

'And you told no one?'

Rosamund shook her head.

'It is certain that someone must have seen you.'

'I sit here to do the mending, no one bothers me.' Rosamund paused. 'Except yesterday.'

'What happened?'

'A girl in a pretty dress came to me. She said they needed me in the dairy, but when I got there it was only Betty. Betty has been bullying me. I thought it must be one of her tricks.'

'Pretty dress? Here?'

'Yes, she was here before. You were there. Two days ago.'

'What did she look like?'

'Her hair was dark. Her cheeks were red and her teeth were rotten.'

'Malvina Stone!' Perinne hissed.

'Do you think it was she who took the pouch, Perinne?'

'It would not surprise me if she had.'

Chapter 18

A plea from Will

Wednesday 20th June 1781

Malvina Stone sat at her writing table and opened the pouch. The first item she found was a watch. It was gold with engraved letters. She held it in her palm. She stroked it around the edge, finally flipping it open. Its face was marked with Roman numbers. It had stopped and the hands were stuck at two thirty. She set it aside. Picking up the locket she stared at the face of the man whose picture was painted on the front. He was handsome and had deep auburn hair. She popped the clasp. Two pieces of paper toppled out onto the red leather desk top. She opened the first and sat back as she saw it was a banknote for a large amount of money. Next she took the other piece and unfolded it, expecting more money. Instead it had curious markings, a face, some arrows and Roman numbers. Malvina opened a small drawer in the writing table and pulled it fully out of its hole. She reached inside and pressed a small button. A hidden drawer popped out at the side. Inside was a mixture of rings, chains and other jewellery. A black shark's tooth looked odd sitting on a ribbon and next to this the whorl of a fossil was visible. Malvina stuffed the watch, locket and papers back into the pouch, pushed it into the little drawer and closed it. She then replaced the first drawer. She'd had to return the brooch, but she'd make sure she kept her latest finds.

She made her way down the broad staircase and into the wide and bright hall. It was cool here and she sat beside the table which was set in the middle. Her father would be arriving soon. He'd been away in the West Indies and she wondered what gifts he'd bring her this time.

'This way, please boys,' James Clarke showed Will and Nathan into the book-lined room. It was stuffy and dusty. Sir Charles was sitting behind a large, untidy desk. Books and scrolls of paper were stacked at each side. He wasn't wearing his usual wig and his head was almost bald. No jacket, simply a shirt and breeches.

'So, Will, you're home and I see you have brought a friend with you.'

'Aye, sir.'

'And you have a request to make?' Sir Charles looked at James Clarke, signalling him to stay in the room.

'Aye, sir. This is me friend, Nathan. Nathan doesn't 'ave a surname. His father didn't either.'

Sir Charles raised his eyebrows and gave a faint cough.

Will continued. 'Nathan were born on a sugar plantation. There are many people like 'im. The people are taken from their 'omes in Africa an' lucky to survive the hard sea crossing to the West Indies. They're sold an' kept as slaves, treated no better than animals. It's our countrymen doin' this, Sir Charles. It's a vile trade an' if we are to be a civilised society, it 'as to stop.'

Sir Charles shifted in his seat. 'Strong words. And what

is it that you want to ask of me. I have no part in this slavery.' He looked at Nathan, who had been silent beside Will.

'I were hoping you'd 'elp me gather support against the trade an' fight to free these people.'

Sir Charles laughed. 'Help you? What can a mere boy do?'

'I c'n travel to London. Go to Parli'ment. Petition the King.' Will kept his voice as calm as he could. 'Nathan'll be wi' me. He c'n give a first 'and account o' the cruelty.'

'Do you not think the King has more to think about? Surely you know that England is at war in America?'

'Will ye 'elp?'

'I don't see that it has anything to do with me.'

'I think ye owe me some support at the least.'

Sir Charles Tarrant's face was turning redder. 'Owe you? And how's that?'

Will gave a mocking laugh. 'When I took that machine to America I left me 'ome an' family, not only to 'elp you, but to get away from that bullyin' son of yers.' Will ran his finger along the scar above his cheek.

Sir Charles leapt to his feet. 'How dare you come into my home and make such accusations. Get out. And don't come here again. See them off my land, Clarke.' He grunted. 'Then come back here.'

James Clarke gave Will a scowl and tilted his head towards the door. Will kept still.

'Come on, Will. Wi'll find other ways,' Nathan spoke, taking Will's elbow.

Will stormed out. Nathan kept still. 'I thank yu, sir jus for lettin' us ask.' He gave a short bow of his head then calmly followed Will.

James Clarke led the two boys to the rear door, passing the kitchen.

'Well if it aint young Will,' Susan said.

James shook his head at her and the three left the house

in silence. At the gate James stopped and put his hand on Will's shoulder. Will, still reeling from Sir Charles' reaction, took a deep breath. He expected to get a telling off for letting Danny get drunk. But what he heard was surprising.

'Don't give up Will, this is a noble cause.'

'Ye feel the same as me, Mr Clarke?'

'Yes, Will. And I have an idea, but I can't do anything just yet. My father-in-law, Danny's grandfather has died. It's the funeral tomorrow. I hope you'll come, Nathan too. After this, give me a few days. I have an idea as to who might be willing to help.'

Will's dark eyes lit up and a smile crossed his handsome face, but dropped again. 'I'm sorry 'bout Mr Hopkins. Danny must be upset. We'll call in on 'im. He'll be at 'ome, will 'e?'

'Yes, he's home and he'll be pleased to see you both.'

James watched Will and his friend pass through the gates then made his way to see what else Sir Charles wanted. When he reached the library Sir Charles was standing by the opened window.

'The cheek of that boy,' he seethed.

James didn't reply but waited to see what else his employer needed. He didn't want to be away from his family longer than necessary.

'When do we expect Sir George?'

'Friday afternoon, sir.'

'At last. We'll see what he thinks, maybe it's time to get help. Though I'm worried it will come to nothing.'

'Yes, sir.'

'I expect you want to get to your family. The funeral's tomorrow?'

James nodded.

'That fits fine. Go on, see to your family, Clarke, and we'll send the coach to the inn to wait for him. I've kept Scott on despite the problem with his daughter.' He sighed.

'And I thought she was a good child.'

James gave a short bow and left. As he made his way out of the house he called into the kitchen. Susan was sitting with a drink, a row of pastries on the table ready for serving at dinner. Joseph was cleaning pans and returning them to the racks on the walls.

'Mr Clarke,' Joseph said, nodding.

James looked seriously at them. 'Is it certain it was Lucy Scott who took Lady Elizabeth's brooch?'

Joseph and Susan shot each other looks and Joseph shook his head.

'I can't believe she'd do such a thing, Mr Clarke,' Joseph said.

'Nor me,' Susan added. 'She's a good girl.'

'And the girl from Burton Hall, Mary Maunder?' James said.

'She's Jed Maunder's girl, a decent family, Mr Clarke. Hard workers. They struggle like everyone.' Joseph answered.

'Well, it's a mystery to me why these girls took the notion to steal something when they were sure to get caught. I must go. If you can get away, it would be good to see you tomorrow at my father-in-law's funeral.'

Joseph shook James's hand. 'We'll try our best.'

'I think that we should tell Mistress Preston you have no one in Kent,' Perinne said.

Rosamund's pretty face was etched with worry lines.

'The overseers will have to make enquiries and it will give us more time to find the pouch.'

'You think it can be found?' Rosamund's face brightened.

'We must try. Think hard, have you seen anyone else around here?'

Rosamund leaned back against the tree and closed her eyes. Perinne couldn't think what else to ask. Suddenly, Rosamund sat upright.

'A man. Tall with dark hair and a black hat. His eyes were staring. I have seen him by the wall - the one beside the road that crosses to the church. He's been looking into the garden, but has never been inside the Poor House. Master Preston mentioned him to Ann. He asked if she knew who he was and she said 'no'.'

'Has he spoken to you?'

'No.'

'It is not someone that you know?'

'There is no one here, Perinne.'

Perinne helped Rosamund to her feet.

'I must go. Do you want to tell Mistress Preston about your pouch? She looked across the garden a few minutes ago, so she will have seen us talking. What do you want me to say?'

'My father said to trust no one. What should I do? Maybe I should go to Devon. Uncle Sam is there, somewhere, but we had to keep it secret.'

'All right, we shall not mention that yet.'

'You can mention my pouch, maybe the house will be searched. Please say I am not from Kent.'

After speaking with Judith Preston Perinne put on her bonnet and left to find Pierre at the stables and made her way home. The boys should be leaving school, so she'd catch up with Danny and ask him what he thought about it all, especially Malvina. She looked across the graveyard. A few boys were outside. She led the pony by his reins and entered the church grounds. Danny's mop of curly fair hair usually marked him out from the other boys, especially as he was taller, but Perinne couldn't spot him. Adam Jackson was away at school and she didn't recognise any of the others. A short, pale boy was approaching.

'Pardon,' Perinne said, 'is Danny Clarke here?'

'He's not been at school today, miss,' the boy said. 'His grandfer's died. He were needed at 'ome.'

Perinne gulped. Poor Danny, she thought. 'Thank you, I will call.' She continued on towards the high street, passing the Eight Bells where two men were talking. One she knew as Adam Litty, a smuggler, the other she didn't know, but he was like the man Rosamund had just described. She noticed Litty glancing sideways as she passed by. She looked straight ahead but listened as hard as she could in case they said something. She could hear the tall man talking. His voice was different from the local men. Was he the man who'd been watching Rosamund?

She reached the large house at the top of the street and used its low wall to climb onto Pierre. She would call in on Danny and offer her sympathy to his family. There was so much to talk to him about too. There was Rosamund's speaking at last and the mystery of her missing pouch. She couldn't prove it was Malvina who'd stolen it, or for that matter Aunt Elizabeth's brooch, or even the fossils that had gone missing. But Malvina was present each time. Why would someone as wealthy as Malvina Stone need to steal things? The pouch could have been taken by the girl, Betty, after all, Rosamund did say she'd been bullying her. She might well have seen her hiding the pouch. There was a lot to do. After she'd seen Danny she needed to get back to Cliff House as there was still the problem of Lucy and Mary Maunder. She could not believe Lucy would steal. Perhaps she should go to Burton Hall and confront Malvina.

Chapter 19

Danny stays away

Wednesday 20th June 1781

Danny sat amongst the bright buttercups holding a stem. He tilted the shiny yellow petals alongside his wrist and looked at the reflection it made on his skin. Grandpa said if it did that, it meant you liked butter. He gazed across the meadow. It was high with grasses and splattered with pink, white and yellow. He didn't think any of his friends would see him picking flowers, but he didn't care, these were for Grandpa Hopkins and he wanted to do his best. He couldn't believe he'd never read to him again. He felt the tears welling and his throat tensing.

He lay down. The warmth of the afternoon sun and the low hum from the bees dipping from flower to flower in search of nectar, made Danny sleepy. Above him wisps of cloud floated by. He let his mind drift with them and conjured up pictures from their shapes. He could make out a ship. He'd never been on a big ship. He'd like to see what it was like, especially one like the *Majesty* that Will had sailed on his journey to Newfoundland. Will had been on more since. What would people do without ships? They took people to and from countries overseas. They brought

141

food and clothes, strange-looking animals and birds from far-away places. Ships were used by the smugglers to carry the goods they brought onto the beaches or into the harbour and up the river. But ships can sink, like the one in the bay nine days ago, with everyone aboard. Dead. But it would be worth the risk, not every boat sank. It would be great to get away, especially from school, and Thomas Walton.

Perrine arrived at the Clarke's cottage. It had been lovely riding along, it made a cool breeze across her face and she'd had time to think. She would tell Danny all that had happened. He must be feeling very sad and perhaps the mystery would take his mind off things. She reached the gate of the small cottage and slid down from her saddle. There was a nearby water trough and she walked Pierre over and tied him close enough for him to be able to drink.

The windows of the cottage were all wide open. Perinne opened the gate and knocked on the door. There was no answer so she poked her head through the window into the small room. It was empty, save for the coffin. She wondered if she were intruding. She heard a squeal and thought it must be Danny's sister Sarah. Perinne followed the path at the side to the garden at the rear.

'Ah, Miss Perinne, it is good to see you,' Hannah Clarke said.

'Hello Mistress Clarke, Mistress Hewitt. I am sorry that Mr Hopkins has died.'

'It is good of you to call. Did you want to see grandpa?'

'It is Danny I have come to see. I have not seen him for a few days and I thought that he would be sad and like to talk.'

'That's a lovely idea, thank you, but he isn't here,' Hannah said.

'But we are!'

Perinne looked around to see Will Gibbs and Nathan coming from the back of the cottage carrying drinks.'

Hannah smiled. 'Will and his friend also called to see Danny.'

'Hello, Miss Perinne,' Nathan said, bowing his head. 'It's good to see yu again.'

Will had gone back into the house and returned with another cup. 'We went to Cliff 'ouse, we thought we might see ye there,' he said, handing it to Perinne. 'But they said ye were at the Poor 'ouse.'

'Yes, I go there to help.' Perinne took a sip from the cup, it was weak tea.

'That's very good of ye, miss,' Aunt Mary said, taking a cup from the tray. 'Those poor souls wi' nothin' in the world.'

'Aye, Danny told us, 'e said there were a girl an' he'd found 'er in the Priory.'

'Yes, it is true, Will. Where is Danny, Mistress Clarke?'

'He went to gather some flowers ready for tomorrow. It's the funeral,' Hannah's eyes closed for a few moments. 'We go from here at noon to the church at Sopley.'

'I will see if maman will let me come. Papa is not here.'

'You would be most welcome, Miss Perinne.'

'I have to go. Will, Nathan, could you help me onto Pierre, please?'

The two boys nodded and the three went out into the lane. There was still no sign of Danny.

'I am pleased that you are here, Will, and you also, Nathan. I called at your cottage this morning to talk about a problem. The problem has got worse since then.' Perinne stroked Pierre's long nose.

'Oh? An' what's that?' Will said.

'My maid, Lucy and her friend, Mary Maunder, from

Burton Hall are in trouble. A brooch, very precious to Aunt Elizabeth, was stolen. I tried to help by having my aunt think about when it went missing. It was during a visit by Mrs Stone and her two daughters, Malvina and Patience who are living at Burton Hall. She said it was on the dresser where Mary and Lucy had placed the tea tray. Mother and Aunt Elizabeth said it could have been them and asked Joseph to find Lucy and get a message to Burton Hall. I saw Lucy afterwards and she knew nothing of it. But Lucy has been sent home and Mary has been dismissed. Yesterday, Mrs Stone brought the brooch to Cliff House and said it had been found in Mary's pocket.'

Will hunched his shoulders, not knowing what to say. Perinne continued.

'Maman and I were invited to visit Mrs Stone, Malvina and Patience. I took some fossils and when I returned home two were missing.'

'P'rhaps it were just the Burton maid,' Will said. 'It seems so.'

'But Mary does not work at the Poor House.'

'What dat have to do wid it?' Nathan asked.

'The girl who was found, Rosamund, has spoken to me. She had a pouch that her father gave her to look after. She hid it. It had a watch and money. The pouch has also gone missing, just after Malvina and Patience were at the Poor House. They wouldn't have visited if I hadn't told Mrs Stone I went there to help sometimes. I am certain it is Malvina who is taking these things. I was going to see her after calling here.'

'Why'd she do that?' Will scratched his head.

'This is the problem. The family seems very rich. They have another big house in Gloucestershire and a sugar plantation in the West Indies.'

Will frowned. He shot a glance at Nathan. Perinne was surprised, so far Nathan had been full of smiles, but his face was angry, his bright eyes scowling.

'What is it? What have I said?' Perinne asked.

'Slaves, Perinne. Have you 'eard 'bout slaves?'

'Yes, but I do not know very much about it.'

'The slaves are people, Perinne, but kept like animals by the plantation owners. They're owned, just like ye own Pierre an' kept no better. They live in wooden shacks wi' bare floors where they 'ave to sleep. They're made to work as soon as the sun rises 'til it goes down again. They're bought an' sold, just like at markets, an' kept in chains. Hundreds of slaves are moved by ships from this country. Liverpool, Bristol. Many die on the journey. They are whipped, worse than beasts, an' worked 'ard until they die. An' so more slaves are bought.' Will stamped his foot into the ground and a pall of dust rose. 'People like the Stones are rich through the pain an' sufferin' o' the slaves. They've no shame.'

Perinne wasn't sure what to say. She looked at Nathan.

'Some of us is freed,' Nathan said. 'Others manage to get away, but it ain't easy. I was born on a plantation. Mi mama and daddy were part of a group dat tried to work together, to make our lives easier. We'd food, but not much, so mama and others got together to grow food and wi shared it. But daddy got ill and died. Mama got work, cookin' in de big house but she dropped some dishes and was beaten. De massa said dat he would sell mi to make up for de loss and mama flew into a rage. She was whipped and sent back to work the fields. I was tied up, but mi mama came in de night and set me free. 'Run, Nathan, run and keep running. Go north cross the seas and go to America.' Nathan bit on his lip and looked down taking a deep breath. Will put his hand on his friend's shoulder.

'How did you get away?'

'Mi ran. There are people in America who is a-fighting against the trade in people, and slavery. I thought that I could help. But I was only thirteen. Africans is a-fighting in de war. De Americans want freedom from de King. Slaves want freedom for their lives.'

'You fought in the war?'

'No, but mi ran errands. I worked mi way north, to Boston. A man, William James took mi in. He'd bin a preacher and a ship's doctor. Seen the cruelty and was trying to muster others. He taught mi English. That's where mi met Will.'

'And you told Will your story?'

Nathan nodded. 'He is angry 'bout the way our people are treated. The word needs to pass to people here in England, and in other countries, like France and Spain and Portugal.'

'That's why we were at Cliff 'ouse,' Will said. 'There've been millions o' people like Nathan an' 'is family. We want to get this country to stop the wicked trade.'

'And what did Uncle Charles say?'

'Puh! Nothin'. He won't 'elp. But at least Danny's father will. Says there's someone we c'n talk to.'

'And I will help also, if I can. It is terrible. I will speak with my maman. And papa too, when he returns. Maybe they can get Uncle Charles to change his mind.'

'Thanks,' Will smiled.

'Yes, thanks, Perinne,' Nathan added, wiping the wet from under his eyes with the backs of his fingers.

'I must go. I want to see Malvina,' Perinne said.

'No, not yet,' Will said cupping his hands to help Perinne onto Pierre. 'If she is the thief, maybe we c'n use that knowledge to our advantage.'

'How?'

'I'm not sure yet – maybe blackmail!'

146

Danny could see Perinne in the distance, close to his home and talking with Will and Nathan. He didn't think they'd hear if he shouted and didn't want to run lest he drop the flowers he'd collected. He held them gently in his arms. The perfume from the honeysuckle brought back memories of walks in the lanes with grandpa, who'd pointed out the different flowers and trees to him. The scents from the flowers would make the parlour smell sweet and would brighten it ready for the funeral tomorrow. He saw Will helping Perinne onto her pony and saw her ride away. Will and Nathan also set out down the lane that led to Purewell. He expected she was telling Will about the lost girl. He wished she hadn't turned up at the Priory, or at least it hadn't been him who'd found her, for then he wouldn't have been in so much trouble.

Chapter 20

Smugglers at work

Wednesday 20th June 1781

John Hewitt drove his cart over the old bridge. It was late and the sun was down. Candles flickered in nearby windows and an oil torch burned outside the George. As he passed the castle he spotted Isaac Hooper standing by the town hall.

'Was sorry t'ear 'bout old Mr 'opkins, John,' Isaac said, jumping onto the cart. He smelled of ale, but was sober.

'Aye, thanks.' John steered left towards the shadowy tower of the Priory Church, and right again following the twists and turns towards the town quay. 'Funeral's tomorrow. Will ye be comin'?'

Isaac nodded. 'Aye.'

'Could o' done wi'out 'avin' to fetch this load t'night.'

'It's only a small one, John. Soon be done with. Anyhow, it'll make a change goin' out on the water.'

'It will that, Isaac. Did Adam tell ye why they were short o' men?'

'Caleb's struck wi' a bad stomach an' David Preston's dealin' wi the overseers. That girl they found. She's talkin' at last.'

'Is she?'

'Aye. The French girl got her speakin'. She were bein' sent back to Kent Friday.'

'What's she said? Were she on the wreck?'

'Seems so.'

John whistled.

The *Solomon* was barely moving on the water as John pulled up the cart and tethered the horse.

'Ready fer some 'ard work t'night, Isaac?' Adam Litty said as the skinny old man approached.

'Not unless I need to, Adam.' Isaac shook his head as John joined them. 'They need rowers, John.'

'You need some young blood, Adam,' John said. 'Old folk like me an' Isaac can't do all this 'eavy work. Don't mind running carts and being spotsman, but rowin'?'

'It's just fer tonight and it might not come to it, there's a bit of a breeze.'

'Dark enough, Adam,' John said. 'What we bringin' in?'

'Only tubs, brandy, geneva,' Adam said. 'Guy Cox is already aboard and Moses Pilgrim and Henry Lane are comin', plus me, so we'll take most o' the pull if we have to. Isaac, you can steer, ye know the harbour as good as any man. John, ye'll be our eyes. We heard somethin's comin' in and it's not ours.' Adam handed him a spyglass. 'Here, take this. There'll be a sliver o' light from the moon t'night. Just keep a look out for other boats.'

'And the King's men!' Moses and Henry approached.

'We're all 'ere. Come, let's get going,' Adam said as he jumped aboard.

Standing in the shadows of the nearby ancient tide mill, Roger Law watched the *Solomon* leaving the quayside. After the boat and men had disappeared, he made his way through the dark graveyard towards the Eight Bells. The others should be arriving tomorrow, and, with luck, word would soon reach Francis Woolsey about the wreck and the girl. If their scheme worked all they need to do was to wait. Levi Bird could do what he liked. He was only interested in the treasure. If Woolsey didn't appear, he'd offer to take the girl back home to Kent.

Law looked up at the high, square tower of the church and grunted. Woolsey has to have the cipher, he thought. Maybe these locals could help with the symbols - for a small reward. He wondered how much the trove could be worth. If the story Thomas Slaughter told all those years back were true, it could be a very large amount indeed.

'Well, jist one more night an' we'll be there,' Pip said.

The two men were sitting at a low table in the shadowy corner of a small alehouse. They'd reached Winchester an hour since and were resting the horses before moving on to Romsey.

'How long will it take to get to Christchurch, Mr Bird?' Josh asked. He was sitting on a settle, across from the others. The room was smoky and filled with men, chattering and drinking.

'Yewer not comin' to Christchurch, so it's no concern of yewers,' Levi snapped.

'We don't want yew anywhere near us,' Pip said.

Josh's shoulders dropped, his bottom lip pouting outwards. 'I want to help to find the treasure. I c'n read an' I might be able to solve the cipher. It's not fair, I c'n run fast an', an' I c'n be a look out an'... '

Levi leaned directly into Josh. 'I'm saying yewer not coming. An' don't even think to try to follow us. Do yew understand me Josh Blackbourne?'

Levi's scrawny face was seared with a hateful look and his tobacco-laden breath smelt foul. Josh trembled. His eyes prickled and a snuffle filled his nose, but he didn't want Levi to see him cry. He got out of his seat and ran off towards the cart.

'We should've left the brat when we found him.' Levi returned to his seat, picked up his ale and swigged it in one gulp.

'Are yew sure this contact of yewers'll take him in?'

Levi shook his head. 'He wun't, but he'll have someone under his control who'll do as he bids. We need Wolsey an' I don't want anythin' gettin' in our way. I want justice for Saul.'

'Yew want blood, not justice! There may be no need for violence,' Pip said, his voice rising above the hubbub of the alehouse. 'Do yew want all of us to end up at Tyburn?'

Voices in the inn went quiet and people stared.

'Stay calm,' Levi said. 'C'me on. Let's get to Romsey while there's still enough light. We c'n sleep outside again and set out to Ringwood at first light. Once there, the road goes south into Christchurch. We'll reach Sopley by noon. We'll stop there an' rest until dusk after that, go down an' find Roger. He wrote to go to a place called the Eight Bells an' he'd find us there. We won't know any more 'til then. Let's move.'

'Here he comes!' John Hewitt, took the spyglass from his eye. 'Pass the lantern.' Moses set his oar aside and leaned forward.

'Is it still alight?' Adam called from the back of the boat.

'Aye.' John took the handle and waved the lamp from side to side. Lifting the glass back to his eye a flash of blue light appeared ahead. 'They've got us. Row!'

'Ahoy! Who be ye there?' A gruff voice spoke from the deck of a slender cutter.

'The *Solomon,*' Adam called back.

'Heave to, come alongside. We're ready for ye.'

The men pulled on the oars and Isaac deftly steered the small boat until it met the side of the ship. Soon ropes tied around tubs began to descend. Between the ship and the boat the sea slopped about, but not enough to wet anything. The men worked with speed and in silence, Moses taking the barrels and passing them to Henry to untie. Henry passed them on to Adam and Guy to store in the hold.

John Hewitt looked around. The moon cast a faint silver line along the water, but not enough to see much. Behind them, in the distance, the coast was barely visible. Only speckles of candlelight from houses along the beach gave signs of life. He glanced over to the Head and stopped. Lights. He held the spyglass to his eye and scanned the waves. Nothing, he looked again.

'Isaac, come 'ere.'

Isaac picked his way past the others, 'What is it?'

'Look, over by the Head.'

Isaac took the spyglass. 'It's a boat, they're offloading!'

'Do ye recognise the boat?'

'Nah. Too dark. Too far away.'

'What is it?' Adam Litty shouted across.

'Over by the Head,' John said. 'Another gang. It must be where the baccy's comin' in.'

'We're nearly done 'ere. We'll row over to them.'

Isaac shook his head. 'Too far, Adam, we need to get back before the tide turns or we won't get into the harbour.'

'In that case we come out again tomorrow night and try an' catch 'em. Takin' our business they are.'

'But maman, I am sure that the thief is Malvina. Lucy would never steal.'

'Oh, darling, why would Malvina take things? You've seen that she has everything. And Lucy has yet to be dismissed, she's only been sent home. Go to sleep. I shall come with you tomorrow if you're determined to go to Danny's grandfather's funeral. It is a kind thing to want to support your friend.'

'You will meet Nathan. I like him, he makes me smile.'

'Perinne, I don't think that you should be talking to a black boy.'

'Why not? He is a friend of Will.'

Jane Menniere sighed. 'I was hoping that you and Malvina would become friends. You need friends Perinne, not poor town boys and ladies' maids and working in Poor Houses.'

'Do you know about the slaves maman?'

'What do you mean?'

'That people are stolen from their homes and taken to America and sold.'

'You need not worry about things like that, Perinne.'

'But it is true, maman. Nathan's parents were slaves and Nathan escaped and ...'

'Go to sleep. I'll hear no more about this or we shan't go tomorrow. Goodnight Perinne.'

'Bonne nuit, maman.'

For the second night in a row, Perinne couldn't get to sleep. She got out of bed and wandered over to the window. There was a quarter moon, but it was too dark. All she could make out were tiny lights at sea, but they could be anything. She sighed. Perhaps maman was right. She didn't have any friends. Danny and Will were boys and she hadn't seen them until recently. Will didn't seemed interested at all about the missing things or Lucy. Perinne wondered about Will and Nathan. She'd learned little of what had happened and how they'd met. She hadn't heard so much about slaves before and thought it sounded very cruel. Will was right to try to help the slaves.

'Are you awake, Jack?' Danny lay on his bed, it was dark in the bedroom but still warm and he lay on the top of his covers.

'Yes, but I want to go to sleep.'

'I'm worried.'

'About what?'

'Tomorrow, grandpa's funeral.'

'Why? You've been to funerals before.'

'Yes, but this is Grandpa Hopkins.'

'It'll be fine, Danny, try to get some sleep.'

Danny curled up on his bed, pulled a cool sheet over his shoulder and soon his pillow was filled with quiet sobs.

Thomas Walton waited by the water's edge. A light, salty breeze rippled through his hair, the night was too balmy for a hat, but he held one in his hand. Beside him a lantern gave off a low, yellow glimmer in the darkness. He put the hat in front of the long spout and away again, three times. It was difficult to see, but the swish of oars on the water told him that the rowing boat was getting near.

'Who's ashore?' a voice shouted from the dark.

'Who's asking?' Walton responded.

'Crew from the *Zeus*.'

'I'm alone, it's safe to land.'

A splash from the feet of a stocky man in a felt hat and leather breeches broke the gentle lapping of the sea.

'Three bales and a trunk, is that all?'

'Yes, that's all,' Walton said. 'Can you help me carry them to my boat? It's not far, just across the sand, harbour-side.'

A second man passed the goods over and got out, pulling the little boat onto the sand. The two each heaved a bale onto their shoulder.

'This way,' Walton said, carrying the trunk.

They were soon back and the two men pushed out the boat and scrambled aboard. Walton watched them row away and noticed out at sea the shape of a ship and dots from lamps. 'I'm not the only one out working tonight,' he thought. He lifted the last bale, and the lamp, and made his way back across the sand spit. This wasn't as easy as Philip Stone said it would be. He could have been drowned landing the first lot during that storm. This was his second load and he'd have to deal with it himself. How he'd get the goods from the Priory and up to Burton Hall, he wasn't sure. The Clarke boy was getting nervous. He'd seen this before in boys. It was time to stop, or he'd squeal like a pig – he'd have to make certain that didn't happen.

Chapter 21

The strange, pale man

Thursday 21st June 1781

Thomas Walton made his way up the stony lane on foot. In the field to his right heads of golden wheat shimmered in the gentle breeze. On his left was the flat expanse of the Avon valley, the river though, was too far away to see. Walton was glad the dark wooden chest he was carrying wasn't heavy. Despite this, he stopped for a moment to give his arms a rest. A grey horse pulling a cart approached driven by a man wearing a straw hat, his eyes shaded from the morning's bright sunshine.

The man nodded. 'Good day.'

Walton touched his hat, which had only a small brim, and he squinted to see if he might recognise who it was. He didn't.

'And to you, a fine one it is again.'

The cart rolled by. It was carrying two large milk churns. Walton imagined it was heading for town. He knew very few people here in Christchurch, despite having arrived six months ago, just after Christmastime. But it was what Philip Stone wanted. He wished he were back in Bristol. He could still go back. He had friends there. The city bustled, it had grown and continued to do so with the new industries and he could get any work. But Stone was paying him good money.

He gazed across the watermeadow towards the town. He was about a mile away, though the Priory Church was clear, towering above the low rooftops and scattered trees. Christchurch was such a small place, but not as innocent as it first appeared. He knew the town was well known for smuggling, in fact that's why he was here. He'd soon found out who the town's smugglers were, and they seemed to work as one gang. Stone's new friend, Meekwick Ginn, said it would be easy to set up a new gang, but he didn't think so. If Stone's new venture were to be successful, it wouldn't be from the town, he'd soon discovered that.

He turned up a dusty cart track and reached the Salisbury road following it to Burton Hall. Benjamin Kelly was waiting for him by the stables.

'Ah, you're here, the master's waiting for you. He's in the orangery. Come, this way.'

The dour-faced man led Walton through the stables and out to the rear of the grand house. The garden sloped down towards an ornamental pond which seemed to mark the edge of the property. Walton breathed in the scents from a nearby flower bed.

Philip Stone was standing outside the doorway clipping a strange-looking plant. Walton knew he'd had species brought back from the West Indies, but had never seen any of them before. Stone wasn't wearing a wig and had a light shirt over loose breeches. Turning his tubby frame, his square face held a welcoming smile.

'Ah, Thomas, is the job working out?'

'The teaching or our other matter?' Walton asked, handing the chest over to Kelly.

'Both. You make a good teacher. You were doing well back in Bristol and it's excellent cover for, how shall we put it, other activities.'

'The school's fine. They're not bad boys, in fact some are quite bright - though they don't have the gumption of lads in Bristol.'

'So, what news of our goods?'

'They're still in the Priory, Mr Stone. I need help to get them out.'

'Hmph. I thought you said you'd managed to get help.'

'Not really.' Walton didn't want to mention Danny. He'd have to explain he'd been a bad choice. 'The local gangs work together, we'd have to share goods - or pay them.'

'No, that won't do at all,' Stone said, waving a hand that still held a pair of clippers. 'Ginn said it'd be easy, few preventatives here. So, what do you suggest? We won't make money if we don't sell the tobacco on.'

'I thought perhaps Kelly here could help.'

Benjamin Kelly spluttered, his face covered in shock. 'I don't think, sir, that I could lift such weights.'

'They're not that heavy,' Walton said before Kelly could make further excuses. 'They're baled to make lifting easy.'

'Good idea, Thomas.'

'But ...'

'When should he come?' Philip Stone looked directly at Walton, ignoring any protest from his butler.

'Tonight. If he brings your cart to the back of the church, he can help me carry the bales down the stairs and we can store them here in the stables. There shouldn't be any problem.'

'Yes, that could work,' Stone said, nodding.

'Sir, I think the mistress will want me to ...' Kelly tried to hide the scowl on his face by forcing a smile.

'We can take them out to the place your Mr Ginn spoke of,' Walton continued.

'Ridley Wood, I believe,' Stone said. 'Though he's yet to confirm that we can have a place to trade there. So, what time should Kelly be there tonight?'

'Just after dusk.'

'Excellent. Kelly you may do the mistress's tasks.' He motioned his hand in the direction of the main house and turned back to Walton. 'We'll get these first bales sold and decide what we do next. Would you care to look at my plants?'

'Yes, but I must go soon. There's a funeral at Sopley village today, a student's grandfather. I heard the riding officer was going. I'll go too. Show my respects and find out if he's about tonight.'

Hidden by a tree beside the lake, Malvina Stone watched as her father and the visitor moved into the orangery.

Josh's head rested on the side of the cart. It was only half-past seven but they'd been on the road since five. He was tired. He'd lain awake wondering what to do. It wasn't the first time he'd thought about running away, but it was hopeless. Their next stop was Ringwood to visit a man with a strange name, Meekwick Ginn, maybe he'd find out more there. And whilst Pip had seemed less hostile towards him, he'd prefer to keep away from Levi, he scared him. Josh hadn't liked the way Levi had pushed the horse. Its head hung down as the cart reached the crest of a hill. All around them was an expanse of heather-covered land. Levi said it was the New Forest and they hadn't far to go to the next stop. The poor animal pulled the cart to the top of the rise and Josh could see the road slope down again. At the bottom was a town, its square-towered church rising through the middle of green trees.

'Ringwood,' Levi said. 'We pull off here an' Ginn's place isn't far.'

Josh wasn't sure what to expect. The cart pulled into a short driveway with a large thatched cottage at its end.

Beside it was a stable and close by a trough. Levi pulled alongside it and the tired horse pushed its nose inside and drank.

'Stay there,' Levi ordered, his eyes stern.

Josh watched as Levi and Pip approached the house. The door opened and he caught sight of a short man leaning on a stick. He had the palest face Josh had ever seen, framed by white hair and long white whiskers. The two men went inside and the door closed. Josh climbed down from the cart and went to the stable. Inside was a small coach, painted black. There were two stalls each with a horse inside, one chestnut-coloured and the other dapple grey. He grabbed some hay and went outside to give it to the cart horse. It must have been around ten in the morning and the sun was climbing steadily blasting down strong rays. Josh took off his hat and fanned his face. Across the yard the windows of the cottage were open and he could hear voices. He crept up close to the side of the house and listened.

'... the boy will be fine with Stephen. He'll have to work for his keep though. Just say I sent you.'

'So can we trust anyone in Christchurch?' Pip asked.

'No.' A low, shaky voice replied. Josh thought it had to be the pale man, who must be Meekwick Ginn. He was still speaking. 'I had some men working Christchurch until last year. They joined together with another mob.'

'We've got Roger Law checkin' out the local gangs.'

'Yes. He's been in touch. Says to meet him at the Eight Bells,' Ginn said. 'I do have someone just outside the town. Philip Stone, he's new. Sold his plantation in the West Indies and has a place in Gloucestershire.' Ginn huffed. 'Just bought a place at Burton and wants to turn his hand to venturing.'

'Should we go to him?' Levi was speaking.

'No. I'll get in touch with him, send a message, or maybe ride down there myself. The new schoolteacher, Thomas

Walton, is working for him and is hoping to set up a gang. He's a free trader from Bristol way. He could help, if you mention my name.'

'Did Roger say anythin' 'bout the girl?' Levi said.

'Nothing other than he's sure it's Francis Woolsey's daughter. A miracle she survived, it was the wildest night, trees down everywhere, thatches blown off.' Ginn said. 'I've done my bit and spread the word. What'll you do if you catch him?'

Pip looked at Levi, who took a breath. 'I could kill him, but that's no use. We'll tie him up an' take him back to Kent an'...' he cast a sly glance at Pip, '*persuade* him it'd be a good idea to say my brother Saul wasn't involved in the killings.'

Outside Josh's eyes widened. Killings? He'd thought Saul had just been caught with contraband. He stretched to take a peek through the window. They had a drink. He'd not been given a drink. He was thirsty, like the horse. Pip and Levi cared about neither of them. He knew they hated him, he hated them, but the horse had to take them back to Kent. He pulled away, but continued to listen.

'And this treasure, how do you know he'll have the cipher?'

'We won't, that's just an extra,' Pip said. 'That's if we c'n work out the cipher.'

'Thomas Slaughter may not have been telling the truth about how he got that.' Ginn grinned.

'Yew knew him?' Levi had surprise in his voice.

'He was with a friend, Ben Perkins. Ben told me what really happened.'

'And?' Pip asked.

Ginn chuckled. 'It's over thirty years ago, who cares. But if you can't solve it, leave it with me. In fact I'll buy it from you. That's if Woolsey has it with him - if he comes.'

'Time to get goin' again, the horse has had his rest. We'll stop at Sopley to drop off the brat with this shepherd. We'll stay there an' go into Christchurch in the evening. Thanks for the ale.'

Josh heard a chair scrape. He slipped back towards the cart and began to stroke the horse's nose. The men came out into the sun, putting on their hats. The door closed behind them but Josh didn't see Ginn again.

'Get on the cart. I told yew not to move.'

''Tis too hot, Mr Bird. I went to the shade.'

'Went to the stable as well, didn't yew?' Pip said. Josh's heart skipped a beat. Had they seen him by the cottage? Pip laughed. 'Feedin' the nag Mr Ginn's hay!'

Levi climbed on the cart. 'C'me on, let's get to Sopley.'

Chapter 22

Danny's sad day

Thursday 21st June 1781

'Quiet!' The Reverend Jackson glared around the schoolroom. There were a few boys missing. He knew Daniel Clarke would be absent. Perhaps other boys were attending his grandfather's funeral. The new schoolmaster, Thomas Walton, had also requested a day's leave of absence to attend. He said he'd been invited by the boy's father. This meant he'd have to teach the boys himself today.

He wasn't sure about Walton. He'd prefer a clergyman to do the job, though he seemed committed enough, often staying late to prepare for classes. His references from the school in Gloucestershire had been glowing but there was something odd about the man, though he didn't know why he felt that way. The noise of seats being moved and desks closed quietened as the boys settled. Now that he was here and had the boys' attention, he'd take the opportunity to talk to them about the evils of free trading. After that, he might let them out of school early. His son, Adam was due home from boarding school today and he was looking forward to seeing him again.

Danny lay on his bed, not wanting to move. He had slept, but not very well. His eyes felt itchy and heavy. He glanced around the little bedroom. Jack was still asleep. Through the window the sky was a vivid blue, like some of the beautiful hues in the stained glass of the Priory. It was as if someone had taken a paint brush and coloured in the panes. In one way he was pleased it would be another sunny day. Bright and cheerful, like grandpa. But it also meant it would be hot again and yet he'd still have to wear a coat and hat and gloves.

It would be later in the morning before they'd set out for the church. It was over two miles and it would take about an hour to get there. A long, slow walk in the heat. But he had to do it – he would do it, for grandpa and he wouldn't cry. Boys shouldn't cry.

'Jack! Danny!' It was father. 'Get up, we need help.'

Danny couldn't think what they might need to do. He swung his legs over the edge of the bed, leaned over to where Jack was lying and gave his brother a nudge.

'What?'

'We have to get up, Jack.'

James Clarke's head appeared around the door. 'Come on, boys.'

'Do we have to get ready now, father?' Danny said.

'Not yet, just put on some old things. I need you to help Uncle John. You can put your best clothes on later.'

When Danny came down the stairs there was a strange smell. He knew what it was. It was the body. But there was also the smell of the honeysuckle he'd picked and the dried lavender that Aunt Mary had brought. He could hear his aunt talking with mother somewhere. Uncle John appeared.

'Ah, it's Danny,' Uncle John said, ruffling Danny's hair.

Uncle John was dressed in black. His shirt was dark, too. His coat and hat were laid across a chair.

'Do you want to help get the cart ready?' he asked.

'All right. What do we do?'

'Come with me.'

Danny, Jack and their uncle went out to the front of the house. Instead of Uncle John's trap, outside was a large cart, the kind the farmers used to carry hay and milk churns.

'Climb up and you can sweep it out.'

Danny scrambled up and his uncle passed him a broom.

'How many people will be coming?' Danny asked, as he pushed dust and mud off the back of the cart into the road.

'Not sure, lad. We've gloves for twenty, but that's only family. Cousin Betsy's comin' from Burley. Your uncles and aunts and those cousins are travellin' from Ringwood and Wimborne. Then there are friends an' neighbours, we 'ave ribbon an' favours for those.'

Dust was swirling and getting into Danny's eyes and throat. He coughed.

'Aint you done yet?' Aunt Mary appeared.

'Nearly.' Danny checked his work, he was pleased. The farmer would think it was new. He jumped down.

'That's a good job, our Danny, I'll fetch the ribbon.' Aunt Mary disappeared returning this time with a basket of black fabric.

Danny's mother also appeared. The two women set to work draping the ribbon along and around the cart's sides, fastening it with wide bows. Jack had been set the task of brushing the carthorse, a large black beast with wide haunches. Danny and Uncle John were making sure the brasses shone. Finally, a plume of black feathers was attached to the horse's head. When they'd finished, the cart looked completely different.

'See, Mary, Hannah, I told ye we could make it look as good as any undertaker could.'

'It's a grand job.' James appeared, putting his arm around his wife's shoulder and hugging her. 'Come on, boys. Go and get washed and into your clothes. Mother's left them in your room.'

Danny went with Jack through to the garden where a large tub containing water had been set out. The boys undressed and washed themselves and went inside. On each bed lay a pair of black breeches, black stockings and their usual white shirts. Their jackets had been brushed and cleaned and the new black hats were in a box on the dresser. By the time they were downstairs again, people had begun to arrive.

There was a hum of chatter and the small parlour was getting crowded. Danny recognised his Aunt Ann and Uncle Richard, who lived at Ringwood and sometimes visited them. The others he wasn't sure about.

Grandpa's coffin was closed. The table, normally in the centre of the room, had been pushed against the wall. Mother had set out plates covered with cloths and Danny lifted one to see what was underneath. Biscuits. Through the open door he could see his mother. She was holding Sarah and standing with Aunt Mary. Danny went outside. People were going up to them and hugging them or shaking their hands. Father was giving out gloves. If they didn't get gloves the women were given the rosemary and ribbon favours to wear, the men had black silk to put around their hats, others came with white muslin weepers tied around their cuffs.

'Here boys,' father said, handing them each a pair of black gloves.

'It's time, James,' Uncle John said. He was with three other men, each dressed in black, from the village. Two looked alike. One was slightly taller than the other but both had fair hair and handsome faces. Danny thought they must be brothers. The third man was stocky with brown hair and a red face. The four lifted the coffin and carried it outside. People stood aside and the men took off their hats. Gently the coffin was placed onto the cart. The stocky man and the shorter brother climbed on to the seat.

Danny, Jack and their cousin, Betsy stood behind their parents. Behind them were other aunts, uncles and cousins. Danny peered back. There were also people from the village. Someone waved to him. It was Will. Nathan was also there. Further back, coming along the lane with her mother, he spotted Perinne. She was wearing a dark dress and black bonnet. She was some way behind the queue of people.

'Walk on!' The man on the cart said. The big horse pulled away and the mourners began their journey, led by the taller brother. The only sounds were the scrunch on the gravel of the hooves and cart wheels and of people's steps.

The sun had climbed high in the cloudless blue sky. Danny had to keep wiping his face with a handkerchief and he could see sweat falling down his father's neck.

They reached a bend in the road which took them passed Burton Hall. A flight of crows took off from nearby trees, cawing as they rose. Danny watched them and wondered what the procession looked like from the sky. He imagined it would be like a giant, black snake, winding its way, silently. And those who did not know it would watch, but keep their respectful distance. It was going to be a long, hot and sad journey and they were barely halfway there.

Malvina Stone watched from the parlour window as the funeral procession passed by. She scoffed.

'Patience, do come and see.'

'I don't want to. Why would I want to look on someone's sorrow?' Patience said.

'It's an old farm cart, look the coffin's on an old cart.' Malvina let out a laugh. 'And only the chief mourners have gloves!'

'If it's people from the village, they may not be able to afford them,' Patience said.

'It can't cost that much. There can only be around forty people.'

'That's a good amount. It must be someone lots of people knew.'

'I can't believe my eyes. Come, sister, you must see this. It's the French girl, it's Perille, look.' Malvina pointed.

Patience set down her sewing and joined her sister. 'It's Perinne, not Perille.'

'It's still a stupid name. And there's a black boy! I wonder whose pet he is? What joy, I didn't think a funeral procession could be this amusing.'

Patience stretched to see the tail end of the procession as it disappeared around the side of the house.

'Has that Walton person left yet?' Malvina said, turning to Patience.

'I heard the door several minutes ago.'

'Good. We'll finally find out what gifts father has brought us. I can't think why he had to see that man before he spoke to us. Come on, let's go to the orangery.'

The road straightened again, green farmland stretched on either side with sheep scattered around, nibbling on the multi-coloured meadow. Close to the edge of the road, two rams with black faces looked up briefly before returning to their grass. Danny peered ahead. He could see a group of people standing at the top of the lane that came up from Christchurch at the west of the village.

'Looks like more joining here, Hannah,' James said. Hannah nodded, shifting Sarah on to her other arm.

'Here, let me take her for a while,' Aunt Mary said.

Danny could make out some of the people. Will's neighbour, Isaac was there, he recognised his skinny frame. He was with other men from town whom Danny had seen around. The big blacksmith was unmistakable, towering beside the others.

'How did they know grandpa, father?' Danny asked.

'Lots of people knew him, Danny, he lived off the sea, like many others around here.'

Danny took another look behind and saw the long column of people. The church at Sopley was only small and he wondered how everyone would fit inside. He couldn't spot Perinne, nor Will and Nathan, but he was pleased they'd come. Turning back he stopped with a jolt.

'Danny!' Jack almost stumbled over him.

Danny froze, as if an invisible wall was stopping him moving forwards. It was Mr Walton! What was his teacher doing here?

Chapter 23

Things get worse for Danny

Thursday 21st June 1781

'Not far, boys,' James Clarke said, turning to face his sons.

'Danny doesn't look well, father,' Jack said.

'Danny? What's wrong?'

'I'm ... I'm too hot,' Danny replied. He didn't want to cause any problems but, in truth, after seeing his teacher was here, he felt sick.

The road was sloping gently. To the left the river sparkled in the sunlit valley. The big horse kept up its gentle clip-clop as the sad line of people followed his course.

'Look, Danny, the church,' Jack said. 'We'll soon be there. It'll be cool inside.'

At last they reached Sopley. Danny looked over towards the Woolpack Inn. People were outside. There were two men sitting away from the others in the shade, drinking ale. A thin, fair-haired boy was with them. Danny thought he looked the same age as him. The man standing next to him was an older man, skinny with a tanned face and Danny wondered if he were the boy's grandfather. He felt a pang of envy. As the procession passed people stopped what they were doing, respectfully removing their hats and holding them to their chests, but the two men with the boy stayed seated.

Finally, the cart turned into the lane and climbed the hill to the church, pulling to a halt at the bottom of the path leading to the entrance. The vicar was waiting for them. He was a short man with a thin, wrinkled face. He wore a wig and was dressed in a black cassock. He was carrying a prayer book.

The stocky man stayed where he was, keeping the horse steady after his long walk. The two brothers came to the back and began to slide the coffin from the cart. The shorter brother was at the end, keeping the coffin from sliding and falling to the ground. James, Uncle John and Danny's two other uncles stepped forward and the coffin was lifted on to their shoulders. The church bell began to toll.

Walking in front of the coffin, the vicar led the mourners up the hilly path saying:

'I AM the resurrection and the life, saith the Lord: he that believeth in me, though he were dead, yet shall he live: and whosoever liveth and believeth in me shall never die.'

Danny's mother and Aunt Mary were wiping their eyes. Danny took hold of Sarah's hand, Jack took her other and they followed the coffin through the narrow porch and into the church. There was an eerie chill inside. The coffin was set down on two stone blocks and Danny and his family took their places. Danny tried to concentrate on the service. There were psalms and prayers. When all was quiet again the vicar climbed into the wooden pulpit and began his sermon.

'We have come here today to lay to rest the mortal remains of Benjamin Daniel Hopkins.'

Danny knew he'd been given his own name from his grandpa, but it was strange hearing it spoken.

'It is a testament to Benjamin's goodness that so many people have joined the family today.'

Danny glanced back. The pews were filled and people were also sitting in the transepts. He spotted Perinne and her mother, Perinne saw him too and gave a gentle smile. Will and Nathan were at the back, standing close to where the bells were rung. As he turned to face the front again he spotted Walton, standing in the shadow of an arch of the north aisle staring at him. Danny gasped and looked down at his feet.

'Are you all right?' Jack whispered. Danny nodded. The vicar was still speaking.

'Benjamin was a hard-working man, making his living from the sea. His four sons and two daughters were brought up as god-fearing people and as decent and honest as their father. Two sons, Roger and Andrew began working as merchant seamen, trading from Poole to Newfoundland, bringing back skins and salt cod, and paying their duties as any honest citizen should. It is a sad reflection of our times that the sea is filled with ships of war and ships of illegal trading. Visit our country's larger towns and cities and you will see soldiers and sailors are as common as tradesmen. And visit the quieter parts and the free traders will ply, not the trade routes, but the coast where they will not be caught evading duty.'

A low mumble passed through the congregation.

'What's all this got to do with grandpa?' Danny wondered.

'Today, we bury the mortal remains of Benjamin Daniel Hopkins, his spirit in heaven with the righteous. And so deserved. But any man, or boy, who goes against God and the King, by illegal works and handling of smuggled goods, shall be assured a place in hell!'

The vicar banged his fist onto the edge of the pulpit and eyed the congregation, moving his glance around so everyone caught his glare. It seemed to end in Danny's face and a cold shiver ran down the whole of his body and he began to feel dizzy.

The vicar stepped down and continued the service, though Danny couldn't hear, his mind was resonating with the thought of hell. He stared at the coffin. Without a word his father and uncles rose, moved forwards and lifted it onto their shoulders for the last time. The bell tolled again. They walked on, led by the vicar, through the door at the side of the chancel and out into the graveyard. The grave was waiting, and the smell of the freshly-dug earth clung around the edges of the mound. In the background the sound of the waterwheel of the nearby mill splashed steadily in sympathy with the bell. The vicar went to the head of the grave.

'Man that is born of a woman hath but a short time to live, and is full of misery ... '

The vicar continued as the coffin was lowered. Father was holding Sarah and had his arm around Danny's mother. Danny was beside her with Jack, tears falling again. They each took some earth and threw it onto the coffin.

'Forasmuch as it hath pleased Almighty God of his great mercy to take unto himself the soul of our dear brother here departed: we therefore commit his body to the ground; earth to earth, ashes to ashes, dust to dust... '.

Danny's neck felt strange, as if someone's eyes were burning it with their glares. He knew Mr Walton was staring, he just knew.

'It's a lovely view, Danny,' Uncle John said, coming up behind him and giving him a hug. 'Grandpa would approve. An' ye can come and talk with him anytime. It's not far, is it?'

Danny shook his head. Should he tell Uncle John about his teacher?

'Father!' Cousin Betsy called over. 'We're going back to Aunt Hannah's.'

'Come on, Danny, let's go.' Uncle John strode off.

Danny looked around for Will and saw he was already going down the path with Nathan. He dashed across the graveyard to try to catch up with them. They'd listen. As he passed the east end of the church, he noticed Thomas Walton standing by the entrance chatting with his father. He wondered what they were talking about, though he knew it wouldn't be about the bales in the Priory.

'Will, Nathan, wait!'

When Danny got to the end of the path he saw there was a coach waiting. It was the Tarrant's and must have come to collect Perinne and her mother. Jane Menniere was speaking with Hannah and Aunt Mary and Perinne was chatting with Will and Nathan.

'Hello, Danny, it is a sad day, are you all right?' Perinne said. Danny shrugged. He didn't know what to say. 'Perhaps we can all meet up at the beach tomorrow?' she added, stepping into the coach.

'Yes,' Danny said. 'I'd like that.' At least if he didn't get a chance today, he could tell his friends about Walton then.

Jane stepped aside and, to Danny's surprise, Aunt Mary and his mother, carrying Sarah who was sound asleep, also got into the coach.

'Your mother is tired Danny, we'll drop them off at your cottage as we go back to Cliff House,' Jane said.

With all aboard, John Scott, in full green Tarrant livery, climbed into the driver's seat and pulled the reins of the two horses.

'Your aunts and uncles will return on the cart, Danny. We'll walk. Come on,' James Clarke said. 'I've been speaking with your teacher. He tells me he's pleased with your progress and especially the work you've done for him so far. I'm very proud to hear that.'

Danny felt a gulp catch in his throat. If only father knew what those tasks were he wouldn't be so proud. Nor that his teacher wanted more from him.

'You can take off your things,' his father added. 'Put them on the cart, you'll be cooler.'

Danny took off his jacket, hat and gloves. Where

was Will? Most of the villagers had already set out. He spotted Will and Nathan walking ahead with Isaac and the blacksmith, who he had heard being called Caleb. Father was walking ahead with Jack.

'Daniel.'

Danny froze. Walton. What did he want?

'I understand why you are unable to help me again today.'

Danny kept quiet. If he didn't speak, he couldn't get into any further trouble. He started to walk as quickly as he could, but Walton easily kept up with him. They walked in silence. It was a beautiful, sunny afternoon. Any other time he'd be at the beach or playing with his friends after school. But it had been grandpa's funeral and Walton had spoiled everything. He hated him.

They'd passed through the village of Winkton and would reach Burton soon. Danny hoped he hadn't much longer to keep quiet. With luck, his teacher would turn down the lane where he'd joined the procession earlier. At least he'd stopped talking. But, Walton broke the calm.

'I'm pleased you haven't spoken to anyone about our little task.'

Danny gritted his teeth.

'The vicar was most firm with his views in the sermon. Don't you agree?'

Concentrate on catching up with Will, Danny told himself, if he was with them, maybe Walton will stop trying to talk.

'Do you read the newspapers, Daniel? People are keen to give information these days, especially about free traders. The latest rewards can reach five-hundred pounds if a ship's captured or gang exposed.' Walton paused. 'That's a mighty big temptation to the poor, or a teacher, to tell tales.'

Danny wanted to say he'd tell them about Walton, but his teacher would only accuse him of being an accomplice, which he couldn't deny although he had been tricked into helping. He looked down the lane. His father and Jack were some way ahead. Will and Nathan were getting onto a cart with Isaac and Caleb.

Without warning, Walton grabbed Danny by the shirt sleeve, dragged him behind some shrubs and pushed his face into Danny's. 'I want you to listen, and listen very carefully,' he hissed. 'You do not mention to anyone what we did or anything about the goods.'

Danny reeled as the words hit him in a spray of spittle. He was shaking, he couldn't see anyone around. There was no one to help him.

'In any case,' the teacher went on. 'Who'd believe you? I'm a respectable school teacher.' Walton pushed Danny to the ground and leaned towards him pointing his finger almost into his eyes. 'No one will believe you. But I'm telling you, if you breathe a single word of what we've done, to anyone, I'll make sure the hangman doesn't get you, because I'll get you first. Do you understand, Daniel Clarke?'

Danny was leaning back on his elbows, terrified. He nodded.

'Good.' At that Walton stormed off.

Danny sat, unable to move, a wave of despair crashing through his body. When he dared to stand his legs were unsteady. He looked down the lane. There was no sign of father and Jack, Will and Nathan had gone too. His shirt was stained with soil and a bramble had pulled a hole in the sleeve. He couldn't keep this to himself, but he had to. Walton would kill him. He didn't want to go home. They'd realise something was wrong and start to ask questions. Danny turned his back on the village of Burton and fled down the lane back towards Sopley.

Chapter 24

Danny hears a tale

Thursday 21st June 1781

'Don't fret, Hannah,' James Clarke said.

'But he should have come home with the rest of us, James, where can he be?'

'The beach, or maybe he chased after Will an' he's in the George,' Uncle John said.

'Don't joke about it,' Hannah snapped.

'Sorry, Hannah.'

'Time for us to get back, John,' Aunt Mary said, giving him a stern look. 'And I agree with James, Hannah. Danny won't be far away. Losing his grandpa has hit the lad hard. That much was clear at the funeral.'

'All the more that he needs be at home,' Hannah said, lines of worry crossing her brow.

Uncle John and Aunt Mary climbed onto the large cart. The ribbons had gone and it looked bare.

'Goodbye, we'll call again next week,' Uncle John said, as the big horse set off down the lane for his final job of the day.

'It must be close to seven o'clock, James,' Hannah said. Shall we send Jack out to look?'

'Let's give him another hour, it's not dusk yet. He'll have lost track of time. Come on, let's go inside.'

James and Hannah went indoors. The smell of honeysuckle still hung in the air, but it had wilted and its pollen peppered the table. They began to clear the small parlour and return the furniture to its usual places. Grandpa's chair, normally set beside the fireside lay empty in the corner.

'No,' Hannah said, as James lifted it. 'Leave it there.' She burst into tears.

'Come on, let's have a drink,' James said holding his wife and wiping her face with his hand. 'Then I'll go out with Jack and see if we can find Danny.'

'Sorry, sir, Reek's wagon left for Christchurch a half-hour ago.' The old ostler at the Antelope Inn said, rubbing his grey whiskers.

Samuel Pascoe's shoulders sank. 'Are there no others?'

The ostler shook his head. 'Not from here. Doubt you'd get anything at this time. You could hire one. Or there might be a boat.' He pointed down the high street towards the quay.

'Thank you, ostler. Could I leave my trunk whilst I go to look?'

'Aye, it'll be safe with me.'

Samuel set out. If he were the kind to curse, he would have done so. But what use was it. He couldn't change the journey he'd just had. He couldn't fix the wheel that had come loose near Dorchester.

He made his way down to the harbour's edge. He wasn't sure how long it would take to get to Christchurch by sea. They said it wasn't far. But it was getting late and he doubted anyone would be going out until the morning.

He was surprised at the number of ships and boats on the water. The masts looked like a giant spider's web across the dusky sky, trying to catch the gulls on their final squawking flight before roosting for the night. Whilst such ships were nothing new to him, it was the sheer numbers that surprised him. There were plenty of people about and some ships were being loaded. He imagined they'd be for the high seas and not coasting vessels, which would be the kind that would take him to Christchurch. A tall man in a tricorn hat and long coat was approaching, Samuel doffed his hat.

'Good evening, sir. May I ask if you're from these parts?'

'I am that, may I be of help?' the man said.

'I wondered where the coasting vessels depart.'

'Why, just along here,' the man said, pointing. 'Where are you going?'

'I hope to go to Christchurch.'

The man shook his head. 'My business is rope making, we deliver to Bucklers Hard on a Friday, but don't stop at Christchurch.' He saw Samuel's face drop. 'If you can't get a boat, there's possibly a package coach, otherwise it's a good three or four hours walk. Come this way. Let's see if someone can help.' The man smiled.

The two walked on. But there were no boats leaving for Christchurch that evening. Samuel decided to go back to the Antelope and ask for a bed for the night. Besides his stomach was rumbling, he was hungry. He thanked the stranger and made his way back up the high street.

Josh watched as Levi and Pip left in the cart to find Roger Law in Christchurch. Levi'd threatened to kill him so many times Josh no longer believed him. They'd come back for him when the job was done. Josh wondered if his father had got home and if he'd come to find him, after all, he knew where Levi was going. He wanted to go to Christchurch, that's where his father would look for him.

He joined the shepherd, Stephen, who was sitting outside his small cottage. It wasn't far from the Woolpack Inn. Stephen was wearing an old smock and breeches. On his head was a battered straw hat and he was smoking a long, white pipe.

'Sheep are out in the fields, Josh. Shearin's underway an' ye can help wi' the roundin' up, to earn food an' drink.'

Josh nodded. Stephen seemed all right. 'C'n I have a look 'round, please?'

'Aye, but no goin' far. Stay 'round here, keep the inn in view till ye get familiar with the place.'

'I will, thanks.' Josh relaxed. He was glad he was away from Levi. Stephen seemed a kindly person, but he wouldn't tell him his plan to go to Christchurch.

'An' be back afore dusk,' Stephen shouted, 'I don't want to have to come lookin' for ye.'

Josh set out towards the Woolpack. He'd noticed there was a river close by and he'd go there to see what it was like.

Danny left the churchyard. He'd returned to talk to grandpa, like Uncle John had suggested. When he'd got there, the gravediggers had been and covered the coffin. He'd sat beside it on the grass. The vicar had seen him and brought him a drink. He'd told him grandpa was in heaven. Danny didn't dare tell the vicar why he hadn't gone home. In any case, like Walton said, who'd have believed him?

Now he was walking alongside the river Avon. It was still warm, so he wasn't missing his coat. He couldn't make up his mind what to do. He didn't want to go home, he was afraid. He reached the water's edge, there was no one around, not even a boat. He crouched down and cupped some water in his hand and splashed his face. The water looked clean, but father said not to drink river water, only from a spring, or a well. His mind went back over what Walton had done and said. He'd tell Will. He'd know what to do. But should he go, or wait? If he waited he'd have to find somewhere to sleep. Walton might see him in Christchurch. He'd go to the beach tomorrow. A rustling noise made him jump. He leapt to his feet.

'Hello.'

Danny looked at the boy in front of him. It was the boy who'd been at the Woolpack when the funeral had passed.

'I be sorry 'bout whoever died,' Josh said, pushing his hands into his breeches pockets.

'It was my grandpa,' Danny said. 'I saw you at the inn. Were you with your grandpa?'

'T'were ... er, some people my father knows.'

'You're not from around here, are you?'

'No.'

'What are you doing here?' Danny sat down on the grassy bank.

Josh pursed his lips, he wasn't sure he should say much.

'It's all right if you don't want to tell me.' Danny knew about keeping secrets and it was obvious that the boy didn't want to share his.

'How did yew rip yewer shirt?'

Danny stared at the ground.

'Look, a sharn bug.'

Danny looked at the boy, puzzled. The boy pointed at a stag beetle.

'What be Christchurch like, what be there?'

Danny shrugged. 'It's only small, but it's all right.

There's a castle and an old house and the Priory Church.

'Father said there were a church.'

'It's as big as a cathedral. I've been to Salisbury. There's a cathedral there. The Priory's as big as that.' Danny smiled. 'But it's not as tall and doesn't have a big spire like Salisbury.'

'There's a cathedral an' a castle at Rochester,' Josh said. He gulped, he hadn't meant to mention places.

'Is that where you're from? Where's that?'

''Tis in Kent, but I don't live there, I jist go there sometimes.' Josh sat down next to Danny. 'I'd like to go to Christchurch, but I've to stay here.'

'It's not far,' Danny said. 'I could take you.'

'I'd have to be careful. I could get into trouble, but I'd love to go.'

'What's the problem?'

'I c'n't say.' Josh held out his hands in frustration.

Danny was pleased he wasn't the only boy who had to keep secrets.

'I'll have to go soon,' Josh said. 'The shepherd said I'd to git back by dusk. The sun's startin' to go down. Will we meet t'morrow?'

'Maybe, not sure,' Danny said. 'I don't live here. I'll have to go home, but I'm meeting my friends at the beach tomorrow.'

'I'd like to go to the beach, but I'm not sure I'll be able to get away. What's yewer name?'

'Danny.'

'I'm Josh.' Josh took a deep breath. He shouldn't mention this, but had to ask.

'Have yew heard of hidden treasure in the Church?'

Danny looked at the fair-haired boy. 'Yes, why?'

'Yew have?'

'It's an old story. Nothing's ever been found. How do you know about it?'

'Someone has a cipher, to show where it were hidden.'

'A cipher?'

'I haven't sin it. It's a piece of paper or somethin'. It's got drawings on it but yew can't tell what they mean. They think it's hidden at Christchurch.'

'It's lucky it's lasted. It would be over 300 years old.'

''Tis not that old,' Josh said, puzzled by Danny's words.

'Prior Draper's treasure. It's said he hid precious things belonging to the Priory before King Henry destroyed the Priory buildings.'

'No, this be different.'

'Maybe I could help you find it,' Danny said. Danny remembered Walton. But Josh spoke again.

'Well, there be a problem.'

'What's that?'

'I don't have the cipher.'

'Then it's pointless!' Danny grunted and got to his feet. 'I thought you needed to get back?'

'But I know who has it,' Josh put in, fearing Danny'd think him stupid. 'All we need to do is get it back.'

'Is that why you're here?'

Josh blushed. He should have kept quiet. He'd only just met Danny. He shrugged.

'Look, Josh. I'm in trouble and I don't want to get into any more.' Danny sighed.

'What, with yewer father?'

'No. Someone else.'

'Like me. I hid in a cart to get here, thinking my father was coming too. By the time I realised, it was too late. The men I came with are angry and one hit me. Tell yewer father 'bout the trouble.'

'I can't.'

'Why not? I wish my father were here to talk to.'

Danny couldn't really answer. Surely his own father would believe him that he'd been tricked into helping Walton. And father worked for Sir Charles Tarrant, he was a magistrate. Besides maybe he only needed to keep quiet about the bales as Walton demanded. Perhaps things weren't as bad as he thought. But he did worry that Walton might still ask for more from him.

'C'n I go to the beach with yew tomorrow?' Josh asked.

'If you want.'

'Where do I go?'

'The road we came up this morning, you need to go that way. Carry on walking, don't turn off. You go past a big, red manor house. You come to a stone cross in the road. I'll meet you there about three o'clock.'

'Great!' Josh's face had a wide smile, which faded into a sigh. 'Maybe I won't be allowed, but I'll try my best! See yew tomorrow.' Josh ran back towards the church and away.

Danny looked across the valley. The blue sky was turning redder as as the sun dipped into the horizon. He'd thought about sleeping in the church. But he'd been cheered by Josh, should he go home?

Chapter 25

Who has the cipher?

Thursday 21st June 1781

'John not comin' to town t'night, Isaac?' Guy Cox asked, tipping his tankard and taking another drink. A sliver of sticky, brown ale trickled down his chin and dropped onto his shirt.

'No, we shan't see 'im 'til the next job,' Isaac said, rocking back on the stool set beside the entrance to the George. 'How long's this hot weather goin' to go on?'

'Sky's glowin' a good red, probably keep on,' Guy said. 'Adam's here. We'll find out what he wants. 'Nother job, no doubt.'

'Good evening, Guy, Isaac,' Adam Litty said, nodding. He was wearing his hat, despite the heat, but only a pale shirt and dark breeches, no stockings and old black leather shoes. 'I'll just see if Beth's about and order ale.'

As Adam disappeared through the coach entrance Caleb appeared. 'Everyone here?'

'Just us, Caleb,' Guy said. 'What does Adam want to tell us?'

'Somethin' to do wi' that Roger Law o' Kent,' Caleb said, remaining standing and looking across the street.

'Found out any more about him?' Guy asked. 'I've had no luck.'

Caleb shrugged. 'Not sure. Adam said he were goin' to try to befriend 'im. Find out why he's 'ere. I gave his 'orse new shoes yesterday, but 'e said nothin' to me other than he expects to be 'ere a few more days.'

'Ah, here's the lovely Beth,' Isaac said. 'How's ye mother?'

'Mr Litty will be with you shortly, gents,' Beth said, setting ale on the table by the men and ignoring Isaac. 'He's just speakin' with Mr Martin.'

Isaac drank his ale and passed the empty tankard to Beth, who left through the cobbled courtyard. He lifted his long, white pipe to his mouth, sucked and blew out a stream of smoke. A sound turned his head. It was a cart and two men. One was driving and the other was walking beside the horse. Isaac nudged Guy, who looked over his shoulder at the scene. Caleb also watched as the cart made its way passed the George, steered left and disappeared around the town hall and into Church Street.

'Seems to be a lot o' strangers lately,' Isaac said.

'An' they may have somethin' to tell us,' Adam Litty appeared behind them with Joseph Martin, who was wearing a dark apron that smelled of ale.

'You know them, Adam?' Guy said.

'Not exactly. They're a gang from Kent. And we may be able to help them find somethin' they've lost.' Adam raised his eyebrows and gave a wry smile.

'Well, tell us, Adam,' Caleb said.

'I'll let them do that. Come on, we're meeting them at the Eight Bells.'

Joseph shrugged. 'I'll leave you to it. I'm too busy here. Tell me what happens.'

The men sat for a while and finished their drinks. Before long they set out in the same direction as the cart.

'Here 'tis.' Levi Bird said, pointing to the small frontage of the Eight Bells.

'Where do we leave the cart?' Pip asked.

Levi shrugged. 'Roger'll know. I'll take a look, see if he's inside.'

Levi Bird, who'd been walking alongside the cart since they'd arrived at the edge of the town, went into the alehouse. It was a tiny place. He looked around, but there was no sign of Roger.

'Can I get you anything, sir?' A woman in a long, cream-coloured skirt and blouse, covered by a white apron approached him.

'Not at present,' Levi answered and stepped back into the narrow street. He shook his head at his friend.

'Not quite as grand as Rochester, but as long, easily,' Pip said pointing to the Priory.

'Rochester's a cathedral, this is just a church. When Roger said a church, I wasn't expecting somethin' this size.'

'I hope the cipher's not too difficult to solve, else 'tis a lost cause an' we've come all this way for nothin'.'

Levi was standing beside the cart again. 'We c'n still get Woolsey,' he scowled.

'D'yu think massa Clarke can help?' Nathan said.

The boys were standing at the quayside. Nathan picked up a stone and tossed it into the water. The splash sent a wading bird swishing into the dusk. Will breathed in the air, the tide was low, and the river flow shallow. There was a muddy smell.

'If 'e c'n, he will. I trust 'im,' Will said. 'But I fear it'll take some time. We need to show too many people what's goin' on. I'm sure they just don't understand what an evil slavery is.' He shook his head.

'Yu all right?' Nathan asked.

Will hunched. 'Aye. Well ...'

'What? What is it?'

'Things don't feel the same as when I left.' Will faced his friend. 'It were just along 'ere, beside that boat.' He pointed. 'It were only last year as I met Danny. We seemed the same, we were easy friends, but now, I'm not so sure. I 'aven't 'ad a chance to talk with 'im because of 'is grandfer dying. But, 'e looked so ... .' Will took a few moments to think. 'Well ... 'e weren't just sad yesterday, 'e'd a curious look about 'im .'

Nathan sniffed.

'What?'

'Mi seen sadness, Will. Mi seen people mourn and cry out pitiful wi' grief. Anyone who live on a plantation has. Danny yesterday was different.'

'Different? How?'

'Him face, Will. It was full of somethin' else dat mi seen a-plenty.'

'And what's that?'

'Fear, Will. Danny, him scared.'

'Men!' The sturdy, square-shouldered figure of Roger Law appeared from around a wall where the path led to the church.

'At last,' Pip said.

'Yew c'n leave the cart there,' Roger said. 'We're meetin' with the local gang.'

'Yew trust them?' Levi Bird said.

'Possibly. Where's Rowland?' Roger stretched to look around.

'He's on a job with Peter by Whitstable,' Pip answered.

Roger was about to speak, when Levi cut in. 'We're best off wi'out him, Roger, the man's a coward.'

'It's not like that, Levi and yew know it,' Pip said.

Roger scowled. 'Fightin'? Yew've been fightin'?'

'Josh Blackbourne stowed aboard the cart, Roger,' Pip said. 'By the time we found him it were too late to turn back. We couldn't bring him here.'

'Where is he?'

'At Sopley. With a shepherd, someone Meekwick Ginn told us about,' Pip said.

'It's Peter Graves's fault,' Levi spat on the floor. 'Fillin' the lad's head wi' tales.'

'That's enough,' Roger snapped. 'Look, they're here.'

A group of men appeared approaching through the dusk, Adam Litty, Isaac Hooper, Caleb Brown and Guy Cox. Adam nodded at Roger Law.

'Let's get ale and go and sit under the trees in Priory grounds,' Adam said. 'The inn's too small for all of us.'

Guy Cox went to the door and made a signal to someone inside. 'Kate'll bring the ale.'

The men settled on a grassy bank close to tombstones standing along the ground, casting shadows. The final glow from the sun highlighted the golden hues of the tall tower of the church against a darkening sky. Adam spoke first.

'Roger and I have been talkin' and we've agreed to put a plan to you all.'

''Bout what, Adam?' Isaac said.

'Listen. Roger's goin' to explain why his gang are here. Then we'll have a show of hands. If we agree with what he offers, we go on with the plan. If not, we leave Roger and his men to get on with their job and say nothin'.'

The men muttered and nodded in agreement and Roger stepped forward.

'The story I put out about the gold on the *Anne Marie*, bain't true. I wanted to watch what happened, find the local gang.' Roger scanned the men. 'The true story be that someone, we don't know who, hid a rich treasure trove in a church. Whoever that was made a sketch on a paper. It has strange symbols and pictures, a cipher to lead him back to his bounty. We believe it was hidden in yewer church here,' Roger lifted his hand in the direction of the building.

'There's a legend o' treasure, but no one's ever found it,' Isaac said.

'I've told Roger about Draper's treasure, Isaac. It's not the same.'

Roger nodded. ''Twas over sixty years ago, a long time but not long enough to be yewer treasure. A generation back a friend o' Levi's family, Thomas Slaughter, was in Poole. He got into a card game with a sailor just into port. Thomas won an' won well, even the coat off his opponent's back. A watch fell out o' the coat. The sailor said that wasn't part o' the bet though hidden inside was a cipher, Thomas could keep that, but he wanted his watch back. As he pleaded, he told Thomas that the puzzle, when solved, would lead to treasure worth a king's fortune. Thomas took the lot!'

Levi and Pip laughed. 'That was Thomas all over,' Levi said.

'The thing is,' Roger continued, 'Thomas never could work out where the treasure could be. He died last year an' the watch was passed on to Levi's brother, Saul. Saul decided to go to Poole. There he spoke to people an' found someone who was at the card game. He couldn't believe his luck. The sailor, Samuel Pascoe, had told this man that the only clue he'd been given was that it was hidden in Christ's church, which is pretty much all of 'em. He checked Canterbury an' after that went to London, Oxford an' other places on his travels, but never worked it out. Then I came here on our other matter. I met an old man, sittin' here in this churchyard. We got chattin'. He knew a lot 'bout this old town o' yours. It used to be called Twynham?'

'Aye, we all know that,' Caleb said.

'Well, he told me the legend, how it became Christ's Church an' hence the name of the town. We think this be the church where the treasure is hidden.'

'So, let's look at the cipher,' Guy said, looking around the men for agreement, none came. 'Maybe it'll be easier than we think,' he shrugged.

'Wait, Guy, there's more,' Adam said.

'Saul got caught up in a raid by dragoons an' the revenue men. There was a man with them, Captain Francis Woolsey. He saw the watch, claimed it belonged to his wife's family. He took it, an' the pouch. So he has the cipher.'

'So ye don't have the thing!' Guy sneered.

Roger held up his palm towards Guy and carried on. 'Saul was taken away. He's waitin' for his trial, he'll probably hang. It was the second raid in a month. We believe Woolsey was responsible for namin' the gang an' takin' the reward. He's not afraid to use his pistol, nor his rank.'

'Where's this Woolsey?' Isaac asked.

Levi scoffed. 'If only we knew.'

'Well, what's the point?'

'We're hopin' he's on his way here to Christchurch,' Roger said.

'Why'd he come 'ere?'

'Fer the girl.'

Caleb looked around at his friends. 'The one from the wreck?'

'Yis. We think she's Woolsey's daughter. Word's bin

spread 'bout the wreck o' the *Anne Marie* an' that a girl was rescued. It may even get into news sheets. He's goin' to hear soon an' he'll come fer her.'

'And how can ye be certain he'll have the cipher with him?' Guy asked.

'They've shut their house, sold up. They were movin' away, he's bound to have it,' Levi put in.

'So, why do you need us?' Caleb asked.

'First, we want Woolsey captured. We want to take him back to Kent, get him to say Saul wasn't part o' the gang. With local men on our side we're less likely to be caught an' in trouble ourselves.'

Isaac shrugged. 'Makes sense.'

'Also, time's not on our side,' Roger said. 'Your friend, the Poor House Master, told Adam here that the girl's bein' sent back to Kent tomorrow. We need to make sure she don't go.'

Chapter 26

Another gang at work

Thursday 21st June 1781

The night fell over the town and stars speckled the purple sky. Fresh, crisp air wafted from the river. Will and Nathan sat watching the darkening water. Nathan broke the silence.

'Wi agreed to meet at de beach. Danny seemed keen. Wi can ask him if somethin's wrong den. I'm hungry. Let's get somethin' to eat.'

Will nodded. 'Aye, come on, we shan't be able to see where we're goin' soon.'

The two boys walked past the old water mill, it was in darkness, the miller having closed for the day. The sounds of the stream gushed. There were candle lights flickering from nearby buildings. Will stopped.

'Look, there's a light in the Priory.'

'Is dat unusual?' Nathan asked.

'On the ground floor, no, but see, above. Will pointed. 'It's said it were used by smugglers years ago, but not as long as I've known.'

'Maybe it bein' used again,' Nathan said. 'Yu been away some time.'

Will shrugged. 'P'rhaps.'

They passed through a gate in the wall and walked towards the Poor House.

'We can cut through the graveyard. Beth's at the George t'night. We'll eat there,' Will said.

In the distance the lamps of Church Street glimmered. Nathan stopped.

'What?' Will said.

'Shhh ... see across dere. A gang o' men.'

All that could be seen were the shadows between thick yew trees. Some of the men were sitting, others standing. Pipes were being smoked as the odd fleck of burning tobacco gave off a split-second glow.

'Maybe dem waitin' for whoever's in de Priory.'

'Well, let's see if we c'n find out what's goin' on.' Will crept around the tombstones towards the men. Nathan followed crouching low.

'So,' Roger Law said, 'We say Pip and Levi were sent by the girl's father to check if 'tis her. We say 'tis her an' we'll send word. We wait two more days for Woolsey, but if he ain't arrived we take her back to Kent.'

'An' then what?' Caleb asked. 'What'll ye do wi' a young girl? It's a crazy plan.'

'It shouldn't come to that,' Levi Bird said.

'But it might. An' this has nothin' to do with us.' Caleb walked away from them.

'Caleb, come back,' Adam Litty said. 'There's the treasure, we could make some real money here.'

'That depends on the father turning up.' He threw up his huge hands. 'An' what if he don't have the cipher with him? What then?'

'He's right,' Guy Cox said. 'It could all be for nothin'. But at least they're not the gang that's bringin' in the baccy.'

'We don't know anythin' 'bout baccy an' we don't need yew,' Levi hissed.

'If Woolsey comes wi' others we will, Levi,' Roger Law said. 'What do yew think, Pip?'

'We c'n handle Woolsey. He won't have his dragoons here. But I'm not hurtin' no girl.'

'Not you too.' Levi kicked at a nearby shrub and petals fell, littering the dark path. 'The girl won't be harmed.'

'Look,' Roger said. 'We just need help from the Poor House Master. Pity he 'aint here. Can't yew fetch him, Adam? There's a candle lit in his window, he must be there.' He tilted his head in the direction of the red building.

Adam strolled off, Caleb sighed.

'Yew a soft one, blacksmith,' Levi grunted. 'Seems to be the way wi' blacksmiths. Is this yewer Poor House Master comin'?'

Adam Litty and David Preston appeared.

'Tell 'em what you just told me, David,' Adam said.

'The girl has a pouch, with a watch.'

'That's it!' Pip pitched in. 'The cipher should be with it!'

Adam and David looked at each other.

'What?' Levi said.

'The pouch and the watch are missing,' David answered.

Will nudged Nathan and the two boys crept back towards the path, making their way along it as normal. The chattering came to an abrupt halt at the sound of Will and Nathan's approaching footsteps.

'Another fine evenin',' Will said as he strolled past. He

spotted Isaac first and Guy and recognised Caleb. They'd not said anything about any meetings when they were travelling back from the funeral this afternoon.

'Evenin' Will,' Guy Cox said. 'Expect you're pleased not to be mendin' nets anymore.'

Will stopped. 'Aye, that's true, Guy.'

'So, how did you come into your fortune?'

'That's a long story, Guy an' we're too 'ungry to linger an' talk about it. Aren't we Nathan?'

Nathan smiled. 'Yes, let's go, Will.'

The two boys continued along the path. 'Did yu know all of dem?' Nathan asked.

Will shook his head. 'No. Isaac an' Guy, Caleb an'Adam Litty are all townsmen, but 'aven't seen the others.'

'Sounds like dem plotting, mi wonder what dat treasure is all about?'

Will smiled, 'Maybe the same as 'appened to us, eh? I don't like the sound of 'em using the girl. Perinne mentioned 'er. The other thing is they're the Christchurch gang, so it weren't them in the Priory.'

They crossed the road and went into the George. Beth spotted them and came across the yard.

'What's the landlord got cookin', Beth?' Will asked his sister.

'We've some lovely salmon, poached, with peas and potatoes.'

We'll 'ave some o' that. An' can we 'ave small beer too?' Will asked. 'We'll sit outside at the front.'

They sat at the table occupied earlier by Isaac and Guy. People were strolling out in the warm evening, some carrying lanterns. Rushlights, set into iron holders, gave off a dim light not only outside the George but along the street. The town hall was in darkness but a group of young boys were chatting in the arches underneath.

'Here you are.' Beth set two metal plates in front of the pair who began to tuck in.

'Dat look good, Beth,' Nathan said.

They ate their meal. Beth had returned to clear the table when the rattle of a cart broke the quiet. It approached the George, turning into Castle Street. Two men were on the seat, one covered in black. Its driver stared ahead. He was coatless. It was difficult to tell the colour of his hair, but the man's face was visible lit in the stony gloom cast by the rush lights.

''e were at the funeral. Do ye remember, Nathan?' Will said, wiping his mouth.

'Yes. Im didn't speak to anyone. Im was standing at de side, under de archway. I can't remember seein' im on de way back.'

'Who is 'e? D'ye know, Beth? Will looked up at his sister.

'It looked like the new schoolmaster,' Beth said.

'He don't look like a priest,' Will said.

'I don't think he is. Why not ask Danny. How is he?'

'He didn't look good, Beth. But we're seeing 'im tomorrow.'

'Well tell him we're thinking about him.' Beth lifted the empty plates.

'Dat cart looked full. Wonder what a schoolteacher was a-carrying 'bout at dis time?' Nathan asked.

'Looks like 'e's goin' about in the shades, but the town's gang's in the graveyard.'

'He's no lamps, perhaps he don't want to be seen.'

'Come on, let's follow 'im',' Will said, handing coins to his sister for the meal.

'No, it's been a long day. Mi tired. Let's ask Danny tomorrow, im might know somethin'.'

Danny had been sitting on the verge not far from his cottage for about an hour. One or two people saw him and came over to say they were sorry. Danny had simply nodded. He was thinking what to tell his parents about where he'd been and why he hadn't come home with everyone else. He could say he'd been in town with Will and Nathan, but that lie could be found out. He could mention the boy, say he was lost and he'd helped him find his way back to the shepherd's cottage where he said he was staying. That would work. In the end he decided to say as near to the truth as he could. He'd been upset and gone to talk with grandpa. And that he'd met the boy on the way back. Sudden cries rose from the twilight.

'Danny!'

'Dan!'

It was father and Jack. In the distance there was a tinge of bluey yellow from the fat of a rush light. He set out to meet them.

'Here you are,' James Clarke said. 'Mother's been fretting.'

'Sorry, father.'

'Just look at your shirt. Where have you been, it's hours?' James pressed his hand on his son's shoulder. 'Let's get home.'

'It's time you were in your rooms,' Isobel Stone said, folding a bolt of silk, wrapping it in tissue and returning it into the chest on the floor with other fabric.

'Where will we find a seamstress, mother?' Patience asked.

'I'll ask Jane Menniere, I'm sure she can advise us.'

'Where's father?' Malvina said, peering out of the window.

'He's got business to do.'

'Is it that Walton man again?'

'That's of no concern to you, Malvina,' Isobel said. 'Go to your beds, you'll have to help each other undress until we find another maid.'

'What about the other girl? She should help.'

'She's not here. We allowed her the day to go to that funeral and visit her family. And the way you spoke to her this morning, I suspect we'll be lucky if she returns.'

Patience's eyes looked up in dismay. She gave her sister a push on the arm.

'Leave me alone. Did you see Patience hit me, mother?'

'No, she didn't, now go. Or I'll tell father of your behaviour and we shan't take you to Bath next week.'

Malvina and Patience left the drawing room and climbed up the broad staircase of Burton Hall. After helping each other undress, the girls split into their rooms, which were at the front of the house and adjacent, joined by a door.

Malvina went to her desk. Kelly had lit a candle and the beeswax smell hung around in the air. She wanted to get the pouch and take another look at the strange message. A chill went through her shoulders. She went over to the window, which had been left open. As she closed it a cart pulled into the drive and stopped beside the stables. Her father appeared followed by a man with a bent back who was leaning on a stick. A dark shape got down from the cart, it was Kelly. He opened the stable door. The cart driver had got off and was at the back. He was lifting large bundles and passing them to Kelly as her father and the bent man watched. She counted eight. Kelly unhitched the horse. Malvina squinted through the dim light. It was one of her father's horses and it was led into the stable. Next the cart was stored in a space beside the coach and the doors closed. The shadowy figure peered around.

'It's that Walton person,' Malvina thought. 'What does father have him do?'

Conyer, Kent

The cart turned the final corner and the forge at Conyer creek came into view. Rowland was surprised to see Susannah running towards him. Her normally neatly-combed hair messy and straggling down her shoulders.

'Is Josh with yew, Rowland?' she said. Her fair face strained with lines of worry.

'No, why would he be? Is everythin' alright, Suzy?' Rowland jumped down, handing the reins to Peter. Henry climbed out of the back.

'When yew left, he ne'er came home.'

'Not e'en to eat?'

'No, we called and called. Some o' the boatmen went out searching the marshes. He's nowhere to be found.' She was sobbing. Rowland took his wife into his arms, hugging her. He looked up, biting on his lip.

Peter approached. 'Missin'? Josh?'

Rowland nodded. 'No one's seen him, but I think I know what might have happened.'

'What be that?'

'He followed us.'

'Why would he do that?'

'He thought we were goin' to Christchurch. He wanted to go. I said no.'

'That's because we weren't.' Peter's face went pale.

'I'm sorry, Peter, but I 'spect this is down to yewer romancing 'bout that treasure. I 'spect Josh sneaked onto Levi's cart. Looks like yew an' I'll have to go to Christchurch after all.'

Henry approached. 'But if that's where he be, Rowland, he's also with that awful Levi Bird an' his crony.'

Chapter 27

Samuel finds a way

Friday 22nd June 1781

Samuel could hear noises outside his window. The light was already funnelling through a gap in the thick cloth curtains. He got out of the bed and dressed. It was Friday and he had to get to Christchurch, even if it meant walking. He shuddered at that thought. He went down the narrow staircase to find the landlord, who was sweeping the floor of the front parlour.

'Ah, good mornin', sir. I trust ye slept well?'

'Aye, I did that, landlord, quite soundly. I was most tired after my journey. Too much for an old man I think.'

'It's good that yer rested. Sit down and I'll bring ye a bite to eat.'

'Will there be a coach today to your neighbouring town?'

'Not as I'm aware, not from 'ere, sir, but ask Jim, the ostler. He'll tell you if there's somethin' goin' o'er there.'

'Thank you. Could some bread and cheese be wrapped for my journey?'

'I'll 'ave that done for ye.'

After paying the landlord, Samuel left to find Jim. A stable boy was carrying dusty straw bales and piling them into a corner. The yard smelled of manure. He spotted the ostler speaking with a man by the gate. Outside the air was much fresher and there was a salty bite to the morning.

'Good morning. ostler, am I all right to leave my small trunk again?'

'Aye, sir, that's fine.'

'I still seek passage to Christchurch, do you know of anything?'

'As a matter o' fact I do,' he said. Samuel's face lit up. 'There's a package coach leaving at five this af'ernoon. The road's rough an' it'll take a good two hours, but bein' summer you'll at least arrive in daylight.'

'I see. That's good news, but I think I'll go to the harbour again. Check for a boat in case I can get there any earlier. Otherwise I shall return and make arrangements.'

Jim nodded and returned to the yard.

Instead of the high street Samuel took the nearest route to make his way to the quay. It wasn't far and he was surprised to spot the King's Customs House. He stopped and studied the building. Before he died his father had told him that this was the place where smugglers, who had travelled from Kent, had attacked the building and snatched goods taken from them by the revenue men. His father believed it was one of their number who had stolen his fortune. He sighed and continued beside the harbour. The place was already bustling. He thought that it must be around six o'clock. Men were wheeling carts and tall ships were raising their sails ready to start their journeys. He imagined they might travel to faraway places that his father had spoken of like Africa, the Americas, India and the Far East. He walked along to where he'd been the previous night.

'Good morning, sir,' he called to a sailor who was passing crates to his mate aboard a small boat. 'Are you aware of anyone visiting Christchurch today?'

The man shook his head. 'Try Coopers,' he said, pointing to another craft further along the dockside.

Samuel strode towards a small cutter and asked again. He was almost taken aback.

'Aye, sir. We're takin' some cargo out to Christchurch.'

'Would you take a passenger?'

The man shrugged. 'I'll ask.' He disappeared into the hold, then appeared again, sticking his head through the hatch. 'Master says he'll take ye for a shillin'.'

'Fine, when do you sail?'

'We have to make the tide at Christchurch, so we leave at noon. Does that suit?'

'And the journey time?'

'If the sea's kind, mid-afternoon.'

'Splendid.'

The door to Perinne's room opened and she was surprised to see her mother and not the mousey maid. Perinne sat up and rubbed her eyes.

'Maman? What is it?'

'Ma petite,' Jane Menniere said, her face serious. 'You'll take breakfast with Aunt Elizabeth and me. She wishes to talk with you. Please dress and we'll see you soon.'

Before Perinne could speak, her mother left, pulling the door closed behind her. Perinne couldn't think what it was her aunt wanted to say. Perhaps she was beginning to believe her about Lucy not taking the brooch. She used a cloth by the bowl on the dresser to wipe her face and hands and reached into the wardrobe, choosing a cool, blue dress. From the top of the stairs she noticed Danny's father talking to Joseph before leaving him to go into Uncle Charles's study. She crept down to the bottom of the stairs.

'... and after all there's no large amount of gold, but there is somewhere some treasure in the ... '

The door closed.

'Treasure?' she thought.

Breakfast was being served in the small dining room. Here was a round table, unlike the large long table in the main dining room. It was laid out with breads, cheeses, some ham and fruit. Aunt Elizabeth was standing by the window watching the garden. There was no sign of maman.

'Ah, Perinne, you're here,' Aunt Elizabeth said. She moved over to the table. 'Sit down please, dear.'

Perinne's mother appeared from the doorway opposite and joined them. Aunt Elizabeth spoke first.

'I'll come straight to the point. You are thirteen years old and it is important that you spend time learning how to run a home and of manners and how things should be – you ride without proper clothing! It won't be too long and your parents will be looking to find a suitor for you.'

Perinne's face dropped. Was she being sent away?

'Miss Foster tells us that you are a good and diligent student. A fine hand at painting and that you have a quick mind. It is important that we nurture this and encourage you to meet with young ladies more to our type.'

Perinne was puzzled. She wasn't sure what her aunt was saying.

'You have far too much contact with the poor of this town and it is best that it stops. We will make enquiries as to other young ladies with whom you would be far better mixing, rather than servants and town boys.'

Jane Menniere looked down. She was clasping her hands and running her thumb over her knuckles.

'I received word that your mother and yourself attended the funeral yesterday of a man living in Burton village. He had no connection to you. In fact, the deceased was the family of one of our servants.'

Perinne looked at her mother. She was surprised that her mother hadn't mentioned Danny's grandfather.

'But Danny is my friend, Aunt Elizabeth.'

'Exactly dear. I see that you were well-meaning and that they are not bad people, but you should not be friends with common boys from nearby villages. This has to change. Your mother and I will be looking to find you new friends in much better circumstances.'

Perinne didn't know what to say. Her mind was swirling. She couldn't think quickly enough. She was meeting with Will and Danny later. She didn't understand why they shouldn't remain friends.

'May I still help at the Poor House?' Perinne asked.

'That has to stop also. We have the poor on the estate we must look to, you may help with this.'

'I promised Mistress Preston that I would go today. The lost girl has started to talk, but only to me. If this is the final thing I do there, please let it be so, aunt.'

'Just in this instance, I will allow it, but there will be no more visits after today, Perinne.'

Perinne's mother nodded. They ate breakfast in silence after which Perinne left for her last visit to the Poor House.

Danny had heard his father leave shortly after he'd woken. His parents seemed so relieved to see him last night that they weren't concerned as to why he'd stayed away after the funeral. They'd also agreed that he needn't go to school, so he wouldn't have to face Walton until church on Sunday. That would give him a chance to talk things through with Will. He felt so much better and had slept soundly. He stretched on his bed. Jack had left for work and he could hear his mother playing with Sarah downstairs. He wasn't meeting Will, Nathan and Perinne until later. He'd go back to Sopley to see if he could find Josh. He'd like to learn more about the treasure.

'Well who's a gentleman, receivin' post,' Meg Gibbs teased.

Will was pleased with himself. Learning to read whilst on his travels was the best thing he'd done. He was sitting in the cottage in just his breeches. His skin was tanned. There was no sign of Nathan, or Sam the dog, who was enjoying the attention of so many under the small roof. He looked at the letter. The signature on the seal was clear, it was from Sir Charles Tarrant.

'Well, are ye goin' to open it?' Meg said.

Will picked at the red wax and opened out the paper. It didn't say much.

It would be appreciated if you would attend Cliff House, Monday, at noon. I have a matter to discuss which may be of interest. Sir Charles Tarrant ...

'Wonder what he wants?' Meg asked.

'Maybe somethin' t' do wi a question I asked of 'im yesterday. But 'e was set against it,' Will said, shrugging. He leaned over the chair and reached for a clean shirt from his trunk.

'Nathan an' I can't stay 'ere much longer, mother. We need rooms.'

'I know, I know.'

'We'll stay in Christchurch fer now, but I think me work's in London.'

'Your work? What work be that?'

'Stoppin' slavery, mother? Do ye know how the sugar gets 'ere?'

Meg shook her head.

'Well it's evil. People like Nathan's family were treated worse than cattle an' they do all the work an' the plantation

206

owners get rich. Me an' Nathan want to try an' stop it, an' we can't do it 'ere. I'm hopin' Sir Charles Tarrant will 'elp.' He pulled on his shirt and slipped into his shoes. 'Did ye see where Nathan went?'

'Just by the river, I think, Will.'

Will pulled his mother towards him and hugged her. 'Y've no need to worry 'bout me, mother. I've money an' c'n look after ye, an' Beth, but I 'ave to do this work.'

Meg smiled up at Will's dark, sparkling eyes. 'I'm proud o' ye son an' ye father would be too. Ye must do what's right.'

Nathan wasn't far away. He was by the river bank throwing sticks into the water and Sam was leaping in after them. He waved as he saw Will approach.

'We've been asked to Cliff House. Monday, not sure why. Maybe 'e's had a change o' heart.'

'Only one way to find dat out,' Nathan smiled.

'Look!' Will said. 'Father's old boat, like a trip onto the 'arbour?'

Nathan gave a broad smile. 'Dat'd be good?'

Perinne left Cliff House with a heavy heart. Why did life have to have so many rules? Why couldn't she have friends like Danny, and Lucy for that matter? She had so much to do. She would first visit Rosamund. It was sad that it would be her last visit to the Poor House. It was early, but that didn't matter and it was cooler than it would be at midday. Pierre had been saddled by Ben. She would return later and afterwards go to the beach and meet with Will, Danny and Nathan. Whilst it was difficult to think of not helping the poor children, it was even harder to imagine not seeing her friends anymore.

She was soon at the Poor House and rode to the back where she could tether Pierre. There weren't many people about. The grownups would have been sent out to the farms. Perinne walked through the herb garden and past the dairy house. As she did a girl came out carrying a large jug and nearly walked into Perinne.

'Sorry, miss.'

'It was an accident, do not worry.' Perinne hadn't seen her before. 'Are you new here?'

'Yes, miss, came yesterday with me family.'

'You do not have a father to look after you?'

'He's been ill. He's 'ere too. My wages were all we 'ad.'

'Were? What did you do?'

'Maid at Burton Hall. Were there three years.'

Perinne sucked in air, shocked. 'Are you Lucy Scott's friend, Mary Maunder?'

'That be me.' Mary's head bent down as she blushed.

'And you know who I am?'

'Yes, miss. You're Miss Perinne.'

'Look at me Mary and tell me the truth. Did you take my aunt's brooch?'

'No, miss. I swear. I didn't see it at all until ...'

'Until what?'

Her gloomy eyes were ringed with shadows. 'Miss Malvina found it in me apron pocket. I swear, I've no idea 'ow it got there.'

'Carry on with your work, Mary.'

Mary curtseyed and went into the kitchen. Perinne felt rage that a family was in the Poor House and she was certain it was Malvina Stone's actions that had put them there. She looked around for either Mistress or Master Preston. If Rosamund's pouch hadn't showed up, she was sure that she knew where it could be found.

Chapter 28

Rosamund in danger

Friday 22nd June 1781

Perinne found Judith Preston in the small office with a man. He had his back to her. It didn't look like the stranger, he wasn't as tall.

'Speak, child, we know you can!' The voice was angry.

Perinne could see Judith Preston biting on her lip. 'Come on Rosamund. See, we 'ave yer name. The overseers 'ave arranged that ye go to get the London coach at Ringwood, then onw'rds to Kent. But Miss Perinne says ye told her ye weren't from Kent.'

Perinne moved closer. Rosamund was sitting on a chair. She had a dress on that Perinne thought must be the one she was wearing when she arrived. She was holding a blue coat and staring ahead.

'Keep her here, Preston,' the overseer said. He spun around to face Perinne.

'Oh. Are you the child she spoke with yesterday?'

'Yes, sir.'

'Did she say she was from Kent?'

Perinne had to think quickly. 'She said she was on her way to meet with her uncle.'

Rosamund shot Perinne a glance.

'And where was that?'

'She wasn't sure where he lives. Her mother was with her on the ship, she knew, so Rosamund didn't need to.' Perinne felt pleased with herself, she hadn't lied, yet she hadn't broken her promise to Rosamund.

The man shook his head. 'I'll return later Mistress Preston. I need to speak with the others. I'll be at the town hall.'

He approached the door. Judith Preston put her hands either side of her head, her hair was falling from her cotton bonnet.

'What a day. And we've 'ad a letter from Cliff House to say ye can't come 'ere any more Miss Perinne.'

Perinne hunched her shoulders. 'It is sad, but I have to do what my aunt says.'

Judith sighed. 'Take Rosamund into the garden, please, I'll come an' tell ye what's 'appenin' shortly.'

Perinne held out her hand and Rosamund took hold of it. Just as they began to walk along the hall there was a rap at the door. The overseer moved aside as Judith went to answer it. She opened the door to the face of the tall, dark-haired man.

'I've come on behalf of Francis Woolsey, we believe his daughter, Rosamund is here.'

Danny felt a lot better today. He wasn't in school, so didn't have to face Thomas Walton. He would be seeing Will, Nathan and Perinne later and he'd made up his mind to tell them all that had happened. But first he was going to Sopley again. Josh had to know more about the cipher and treasure.

He decided rather than follow the road, he'd cross the fields. It would be quicker. Josh had said he was helping with shearing. Danny wasn't sure where, but he thought that he might see the sheep being rounded up. He would follow the Salisbury Road to the Hall and take the footpath to Holfleet. There was an inn there, the Lamb, and there he should be able to see across towards Sopley.

The morning was bright and sunny and there was a hum of bees from the sweet-smelling hedgerows. Burton Hall wasn't far and it was easy to spot towering above the few homes around it. He knew there were new people, but hadn't seen anyone yet. As he neared he saw a coach with two chestnut horses standing on the short gravel drive. He lifted his head to see over the wall. A man with a white wig was helping a woman into the coach and another man, dressed in a fine crisp white shirt and brown jacket and breeches was waiting behind. Once the woman was inside the gentleman followed. Footsteps came up behind him. It was a thatcher, he was carrying a bundle of wheat straw.

'The new people, the Stones,' he said, and continued on towards a cottage nearby where others were working on the roof. The man with the wig moved to the front and climbed onto the seat. He took hold of the reins, gave them a tug and the coach set out. 'They mustn't have a coachman,' thought Danny. He could see two girls looking out of a window of the Hall's second floor.

He reached the entrance to the footpath. Walking along he enjoyed the shade of trees, it was cool. The song of blackbirds cheered him. He pulled at the heads of grasses at the side, stripping them of their seeds and tossing them into the air. Soon the smell of hops told him he was nearing the Lamb. He waved at the brewer on his way past. In the distance, he could see a flock of sheep, huddled like a snowdrift at the far point of the field. The grass was dry under his feet, there had been no rain since the storm and the hot sun had dried the ground. He could see men moving about and spotted the fair-haired Josh. Danny waved. Josh saw him and beckoned to him.

'Yew can help if yew like. I have to carry the fleeces to the shed o'er there,' he pointed to a wooden shack. They're heavy.'

Danny smiled. 'All right.'

The two boys worked in the sun. They'd taken off their shirts and had been given aprons. The fleeces were soft but smelled bad. Stephen the shepherd told them he'd put off the task, but had to do it, it was far too hot for the sheep. Those that had been sheared were kept penned under trees to prevent the sun burning their skin.

A girl came out with a tray of drinks. The boys took theirs. Josh swigged his, but Danny hesitated.

'What's wrong?' Josh said.

'It's ale.'

'Yis, 'tis good,' Josh smiled.

'Not sure I want it,' Danny said, the smell brought back memories of drinking ale the night Will came home and he didn't want to repeat that experience.

'Taste it.'

Danny sipped at the ale. It wasn't strong and it had been kept somewhere cool.

'What time will we finish?' Danny said.

'Stephen said he'd only do as many as the pen would hold. There don't seem to be many left.'

'So will you be able to come to the beach? We can get there early.'

'Yis, I asked at breakfast. I'm free once these next ones are done.'

Before long the two boys were setting out across the fields. When they reached the Lamb they scrambled down to the stream to wash away the smell of the fleeces. The water was cool and refreshing and they splashed each other. They put on their shirts and set out for the beach.

'It's the stranger,' Rosamund whispered. Her face had gone pale and her eyes were wide and fearful.

Perinne heard Judith Preston speaking, but not what she was saying. She strained to listen.

'She needs to be back with her family in Kent,' the stranger's voice said.

Rosamund was shaking her head, her face drained of colour and full of horror. Perinne pulled the girl and they ran to the back of the building.

'Hurry!' Perinne said, speaking softly. They reached the barn and disappeared inside. 'Can you ride?' Perinne asked.

'Y... yes.'

'I want you to take my pony. Go up the street towards the town, the one where you can see the top of the old castle. Turn left towards the high street then right past the town hall. Keep on that road. You will go over two bridges. Carry on and you will reach a cross roads. There is a coppice nearby. Ride into there, deep, so that no one can see you.' Perinne removed her cotton jacket. 'Put this on and hide your hair in my bonnet.' She passed them to Rosamund. 'Give me your coat.' Rosamund hesitated. 'You have to trust me,' Perinne assured her.

Rosamund slipped into the clothes. Perinne pulled the blue coat around her shoulders and led Rosamund to the side of the barn where Pierre was tethered. She helped the girl into the saddle.

'Keep your head down. Go! Do not stop!'

Perinne watched as the girl and pony left the barn and rode away from the Poor House. She crept into the garden. Mary Maunder was there. Perinne put her finger to her mouth. 'Mary, if Mistress Preston asks if you have seen me, tell her the girl was by the tree and you think I may have gone back to Cliff House, but you are not sure. Can you do that?'

Mary nodded. 'Yes, miss.'

'Rosamund is in danger. I have to go, but when this is over, I will try to help you.'

Perinne ran back to the barn. She didn't like asking Mary to say things that weren't true, but she had no choice. She slipped out of the rear door and ran to the nearby woodland. Once there she took off the coat, rolling it as small as she could make it. After tucking it under her arm, she made her way to the high street. There were plenty of people about, either walking or riding. Anyone who knew her would see she was alone. Then she spotted David Preston. He'd seen her too. She held the coat behind her back.

'Ah, Miss Perinne, 'ave ye been to the Poor House yet?'

'Yes, Master Preston.'

'It's a shame ye can't visit anymore.'

'Yes, it is.'

'Was the overseer there?'

'Yes.'

'Has Rosamund left yet?'

'No.' Perinne wished he'd stop asking questions. He might also wonder why she didn't have her pony once he got back.

'Thank you for all yer 'elp. I 'ave to get back.' He lifted his hat, gave a gently bow and walked off.

Perinne set off too. As fast as she could walk she passed by the George and followed the road over the first bridge. When she reached the second bridge she spotted two boys on the water in a boat.

'Will! Nathan!'

The boys looked up. Perinne beckoned them and they rowed nearer to the bridge.

'I need help, come to the coppice, as quickly as you

can.' She looked over her shoulder and ran on.

The day was so hot, her hair was becoming wet, but soon she reached Purewell and sought out the crop of trees where Danny and Will used to meet. Leaving the road she trod over weeds and shrubs and was soon inside the cool of the trees. Rosamund had hidden herself well, for there was no sign of her. Perinne began to worry that she'd gone the wrong way or, worse, been caught.

Chapter 29

Danny tells all

Friday 22nd June 1781

Many years had passed since Samuel had been on a boat. Despite the relative calm of the harbour, the motion of the vessel made him feel queasy. He hoped he either felt better soon or the sea was just as calm. Whatever happened, he needed to get to Christchurch. The thought of his dear niece not only having lost her mother, but being placed in a Poor House for nearly two weeks, made him tearful. He sat on his trunk on the deck letting the fresh, salt air fill his lungs. It had been a long journey but in only a few hours' time he would finally see Rosamund.

Two horses were waiting outside the smithy at Conyer Creek. Peter Graves was sitting on his, a sturdy grey mare with a long, white mane. The other, a handsome brown stallion, was still tethered to the hitching post. The horses had been hired at Sittingbourne, but the cost was of no consequence, the important thing was finding Josh safe and well.

'We'll reach Christchurch Sunday, Suzy, he'll be fine. Levi Bird wouldn't dare hurt him.' Rowland Blackbourne was hugging his wife. He looked up at the cloudless sky, lest she saw the lines of worry etched on his face.

Susannah let go of Rowland and wiped her eyes using her apron. Rowland marched over to the horse, undid the reins, slung the saddle bag over the beast and mounted him, slipping his feet into the stirrups. He nudged the haunches with his heels and the horse set out at a trot, Peter followed and soon dust clouds rose along the lane in their wake.

'An' she were by the tree?' David Preston asked Mary Maunder.

Mary nodded. Her legs were shaking, but she didn't want to let down Perinne. Lucy had told her how kind she was - completely the opposite to Malvina Stone and Mary was sure if Perinne said she'd help her she would do so.

David looked around. There was no sign of the little girl. Judith said she'd asked Perinne to take her into the garden. Mary said Perinne had gone home, though she didn't have her pony when he'd seen her on the high street, but at the same time she'd been alone. The girl must have wandered off. Roger Law's face had been furious when they couldn't bring her to the door. David didn't like it. Nor did he like the other men from Kent with their talk of treasure in the Priory and wanting revenge on a dragoon officer. Why should they help? They had their own revenue officers to contend with. He wished Adam hadn't got them involved. He returned to the kitchen, Judith was waiting. He shook his head.

'The men an' boys are all out in the fields,' he said. 'We need to find the child, but there's no one to 'elp.'

'Why on earth would she take off like that?' Judith said. 'Oh, what a day.'

'She can't be far, where would she go? She don't know a soul.'

'I'll send Ann and Martha to look for her. They'll be behind with their work, but we've got the overseers wanting to put her on the coach and now this Roger Law sayin' he's here to take her home. Don't like the look of him. How can we be sure he's tellin' the truth?'

David knew the answer. His wife was right. As soon as the girl was found he'd take her to the town hall and make sure she got away to meet the London coach at Ringwood.

Perinne's feet crunched on the dried-up brown leaves carpeting the coppice. What had she done? Had she made things worse for Rosamund? She didn't want to call out. She didn't want anyone to hear. Suddenly she heard the snort of a pony – Pierre! Following the sound she spotted Rosamund in the thicket. She was down from the saddle and stroking the pony's nose.

'You are here, you are safe until we work out what to do,' Perinne said.

Rosamund handed over the reins. 'Thank you, Perinne, but what will we do?'

'My friend Will is on his way. He will know.'

Rosamund started to cry. Perinne looked at her. The girl had been very brave. She was young and had lost everything.

'I think the important thing is to keep you away from

218

that man and try to find your Uncle Sam,' Perinne said.

'What about my pouch? Do you think it was the girls who visited?'

'I think it was one of them. Her name is Malvina Stone. I think that she stole some things from me also and from my aunt.'

'Can it be returned? It has money in a locket and the watch and ...' Rosamund stopped.

'There is something else?' Perinne said.

Rosamund thought it was time to tell Perinne about the cipher. She was about to speak when the crack of a breaking branch broke the silence. She looked up. Two boys were approaching. One was tall and handsome, the other a black boy. She grabbed Perinne.

'It is all right, they are my friends,' Perinne said, holding Rosamund's hand.

'What's goin' on? We've just seen Danny an' another boy. They're on their way.'

'This is Rosamund. She came from the wreck and has been in the Poor House since.'

'Yes, we've 'eard about 'er. Why's she 'ere?' Will said.

'There are some men. Rosamund says they are smugglers, bad ones and they tried to kill her father. They are here in Christchurch and want to take her,' Perinne said, the words rushing from her mouth.

Will squatted beside Rosamund and looked directly at her. 'Ye're sure it's them?'

Rosamund looked up at Perinne, who nodded. 'There's been a man watching. He came today. The overseer was sending me to Kent and the man said my father had sent him. This can't be true.'

Perinne smiled at her. 'You can trust Will. Tell him everything that you know.'

'The smugglers were in a fight. They killed some soldiers and my father was injured. Some of the smugglers were caught and because father can give testimony, they want to kill him. But he's determined they should not get away with what they'd done. He said that if we stayed in Faversham, we would always be under threat, so he wrote to my Uncle Sam and told him we were going to move to Devon. It's where my mother's from. Father got a reward, £500, and this was to pay for everything.'

Nathan had stepped forward and was next to Perinne. Rosamund had a blank stare, as if seeing her family's story move across her mind in pictures.

'Our house and most of our things were sold by friends and mother and I were to sail on the *Anne Marie* to Plymouth where Uncle Sam would meet us. Father was to go to London to deal with our money and travel on to Devon. He said he might take longer, as he was sure the gang would follow him. He said I was to speak with no one. Trust no one.' Rosamund's wide eyes looked directly at Will.

'It's all right.' He took her small hand and gave it a gentle squeeze. 'We'll 'elp ye find Uncle Sam and ye father. I'm sure, once he reaches Devon and 'ears about the wreck, 'e'll come lookin for ye.'

'Maybe im find out before den,' Nathan said.

Rosamund clung harder to Perinne as two other boys approached. Each had fair hair and were younger than the first two.

'Hello!' Danny shouted, 'This is Josh, he's staying at Sopley.'

Josh nodded.

'Who's this?' Danny asked.

'It is Rosamund, the lost girl. Some bad men are here and they want to take her away,' Perinne said.

Josh let out a loud gasp.

'What is it Josh?' Danny said.

'She 'as to be somewhere,' Judith said, 'didn't anyone see 'er at all?'

'A woman saw a girl in a blue coat in the trees at the back of the high street, but nothing since,' David said. He scratched his head.

'Whatever could have made her run like that?'

'I think I know.'

'Well, what be it, David?'

'When the man who came sayin' the girl's father'd sent him, were Rosamund still here?'

'I think so. I'd just asked Miss Perinne to take 'er into the garden. Why?'

David sat down, putting his head in his hands.

'David? What be it?'

'He's wi' others, from Kent. They're chasin' the girl's father. She's afraid, Judith, that's why she ran. An' our gang's got mixed up wi' it all.'

'They're called Roger Law and Levi Bird and the other man's Pip.' Josh was being held against the tree by Will. 'They're bad. Levi said he'd kill me if I followed them to Christchurch.'

'They want the girl. You've seen she's with us,' Will shouted.

'I won't say anythin'. They think I'm with the shepherd.'

'Let him go, Will. He's all right,' Danny said.

'I swayer, I won't say anythin', to anyone.'

Will stepped back. 'If they're bad, why did ye come to Christchurch with 'em?'

'I thought my father was comin'.'

'An' is he bad too?'

'No! My father's a good man. He doesn't like Levi. An' I'm good too, I'll keep yewer secret.'

Perinne stepped forwards. 'What are we going to do?'

'We need to 'ide Rosamund somewhere 'til we sort this out,' Will said. 'Christchurch's no good, what about Cliff 'ouse?'

'I do not think Aunt Elizabeth will allow it,' Perinne said.

'Danny, what about you?'

'Not at home. Perhaps Uncle John and Aunt Mary would help, but they're out at Hinton.'

Josh fidgeted. 'What 'bout the big church. Could yew hide her there?'

'Maybe Josh shouldn't hear where wi hide her. If de men find Josh they might squeeze it out o' 'im.' Nathan said. The others mumbled in agreement.

Will scratched his head. 'In any case, we said not in town.'

'But the treasure's bin hidden there fer a long time an' no one has found it,' Josh said.

'Treasure?' Perinne wondered if it were the same as that her uncle had been speaking of.

'There's a cipher. Rosamund's father has it. It leads to some treasure an' Levi an' the others think it's in yewer church. That's why I came. I wanted to help solve the cipher an' find the treasure.'

'I think, Josh, ye should go back to Sopley. Danny, take 'im back,' Will said.

Danny looked at Josh and then to Will. 'But I wanted to talk to you about something.'

'Is it about Rosamund?'

'No, something else.'

Nathan pulled Will to one side. 'Yu said dat he wasn't 'imself. Mi said he was afraid. Maybe he want to tell yu somethin'. Give 'im a chance.'

'Can ye tell us all?'

Danny pursed his lips and looked up to the tops of the trees. He had to say something. These were his friends and Josh would know what it was like. 'My teacher, Thomas Walton, he tricked me into helping him smuggle in some tobacco. I helped him hide it in the Priory. He's threatened me. Just like Levi has threatened Josh.' There, it was out. Danny slumped to the ground.

Will shook his head. 'If ye were tricked, why didn't ye tell yer father?'

Danny hunched his shoulders. 'I was afraid. I thought I'd be sent to prison, or hung.'

Nathan knelt down and pressed Danny's shoulders. 'Yu be fine. People in town've been tryin' to find out who did dat. It's yu teacher who in trouble, not yu.'

'Thomas Walton?' Josh said. 'Meekwick Ginn mentioned his name.'

'Meekwick Ginn?' Danny gasped. 'We might have guessed he'd be involved.'

'Yew've heard of him?' Josh said.

'Yes, he was behind a gang who tried to hurt Perinne last year.'

'We need to find somewhere to 'ide Rosamund. Soon as possible,' Will said.

Chapter 30

A shock for Malvina

Friday 22nd June 1781

'They're a bad lot, Caleb, why did Adam think we should get in with 'em?'

'That treasure, David, that's what - if it be there at all. They don't e'en 'ave the cipher.'

'Let's get the gang t'gether tonight. Get it sorted. Run 'em out of town if needs be.'

'What do we do now?' Levi hissed.

The three men from Kent were sitting by the riverside. The river was high. Here that meant the tide was also high. Pip was throwing stones to the other bank.

Roger Law rubbed the claw end of his pistol with a cloth until the grain of the wood shone through. 'We wait.'

'Not good enough, Roger, 'tis costin' us money sittin' around waitin'. The girl's missin', so what's the point?'

'She can't be far. Where could she go to?'

Pip spat on the floor. 'Locals are a waste o' time.'

'Be patient,' Roger said, pushing the pistol into his belt and taking out his other one. 'She'll turn up.'

The boat eased through the entrance of Poole Harbour into the open sea and set a course eastwards. To Samuel's right waves were breaking. He guessed there was a sandbank, but he set his hope on the captain, who would know the waters well. They were moving slowly along the coast line, the sails barely moving. Mile upon mile of sandy beach edged the landscape. Cliffs and clefts in the land would make good landings for the free traders, he thought. It must be a hard job for the revenue men here.

'See that headland?' The sailor, who first spoke to Samuel, was pointing. 'That's Christchurch Head. The harbour entrance is beyond that. If we're there for the incoming tide, we should make it to Christchurch quay by four.'

'Thank you,' Samuel said.

It was a beautiful day, hot and sunny again. The sea sparkled as if the stars themselves had fallen from the sky and were littering the water. Sea birds swirled and squawked and the bay was dotted with boats. Further out tall ships with white sails skirted the horizon. The gentle breeze whispered against his face. He felt calm. He knew he would soon be there.

Over to the right there were white cliffs and a set of stacks. He'd heard of the Isle of Wight, but had never been there. It looked so close. They neared the Head. The boat suddenly lurched, dipping up and down. The waters were swirling and Samuel clung to the side of the boat. The crew looked unconcerned and soon they reached a long sand spit and made a left turn. There was a quayside with black and white buildings. On the landside of the sand spit was a large harbour and, in the distance the tower of Christchurch Priory was clear for all to see.

The journey across the harbour was soon completed. Samuel could feel his heart beating hard in his chest. After all he'd been through he was here. The boat pulled up along the quayside and was tethered. Samuel lifted his trunk.

'Do you know where I can find the town Poor House?' Samuel asked the sailor.

The man laughed. 'For you?'

Samuel knew he was making a jest and smiled.

'See that red building just through those trees? That's the Poor House.'

Even better, it was close by. His trunk wasn't very big, but he wouldn't want to carry it far. He made his way passed a crop of cottages. The Priory church was to his right. At last he was here. The door was directly onto the road and he lifted the knocker.

'Yes, may I 'elp, Sir?' The woman looked harassed, her round face and stubby nose red.

'Is the Poor House Master here?' Samuel asked.

'He's out, but I be the Mistress,' Judith Preston replied.

'My name is Samuel Pascoe. I believe you have been taking care of my niece, Rosamund Woolsey. I've come to take her home.'

Judith gasped. 'Oh no, come in, Mr Pascoe. I'm afraid I've bad news.'

Samuel's heart sank. What now?

'Gone missing? How? Where could she be?' Samuel was sitting in the office. A drink had been brought for him. Judith paced the room. David Preston had returned and was on a chair across from Samuel.

'We simply have no idea, Mr Pascoe. Rosamund wouldn't speak. She said nothing of who she were. At first it weren't certain that she were from the ship, the beach is two miles away.'

'Yes, I saw that today.'

'The overseers decided that she should be sent back to Chatham, from where the ship had sailed. At last she spoke, to a girl, the niece of a local squire. She was adamant she weren't from Kent.'

Samuel felt a mix of fear yet pride.

'Her father said to trust no one. He is a brave man and the family were to start a new life in a new place. Rosamund would do as her father asked.'

'We're going to get people out to look for 'er, Mr Pascoe,' David said. 'They're all out in the fields or at sea, but the nights are light an' we c'n get 'elp we're sure.'

'Yes, thank you Master Preston. Is there an inn where I could stay?'

'I'll take ye to the George. The Landlord, Joseph Martin's a friend. He'll look after ye.'

Rosamund stepped forward. 'What about my pouch. It's still missing. Can you help me find it?'

'I think I know who took it,' Perinne said. 'Malvina Stone.'

'Ye mentioned 'er before. That she'd taken a brooch from yer aunt an' some things from ye when ye visited.'

'Yes, Will, and I am sure that it was Malvina who stole the pouch. Rosamund had hidden it. Malvina must have seen her taking it out of the hiding place. They searched the Poor House but it was not there. It has to be her.'

'Is that the new girl in Burton Hall?' Danny asked.

'Yes.'

'So, why don't you go and ask her. It looked as though

her parents went out. A butler was driving the coach. I saw two girls watching from the window.'

'It would not be unusual for me to call,' Perinne said. 'They have no maids. I saw Mary today, all her family are in the Poor House because of Malvina.'

Will looked at Josh who was standing behind Danny. He'd had an idea and didn't want him to hear his plan for Rosamund. Maybe he wouldn't say anything, but Nathan was right, if those men were as bad as Josh said, they might force him to tell them.

'Leave Rosamund wi' me an' Perinne. We'll find somewhere safe fer 'er. Let's all meet at the beach tomorrow an' work out what t' do next.'

'All right,' Danny said. He felt much better now that he'd told Will about Walton and tomorrow they could all meet and it would be like it was before. 'Come on, Josh, let's go.'

The two boys made their way through the thicket and disappeared.

'All right,' Will said. 'This is what I think we should do.'

Perinne and Rosamund stopped beside a large thatched cottage. Pierre had his nose down and was nibbling on the grass. Will and Nathan were ahead, close to the wall of Burton Hall. Will waved. It was the signal that Mr and Mrs Stone were still out. Perinne and Rosamund joined the boys and after tethering the pony to a hook by the stables, the four walked up to the front door and knocked.

All was quiet. Nathan looked through the narrow window at the side. He shook his head.

'Come on, let's go 'round the back,' Will said.

The house was tall, but not too wide and they followed a path to reach the garden. Sitting at a table under a tree were two girls.

'Keep back, everyone,' Will said. 'Ready Perinne?'

Perinne had taken back her jacket and bonnet from Rosamund. 'Hello,' she called, walking across the lawn.

'What are you doing here?' Malvina hissed.

'I have come to visit you.'

'But we didn't invite you. Go away.'

'Malvina, that is unkind. Come Perinne, join us, please,' Patience said.

Perinne moved to the table, but there were only two chairs.

'You're dirty,' Malvina said.

'I have been busy. I have been at the Poor House.'

'Euch. Keep away from me.' Mavina screwed up her face showing her rotten teeth.

'That is a horrid thing to say,' Perinne said.

Patience looked first at her sister then at Perinne, opened her mouth and closed it again.

'What do you want?' Malvina asked.

'As I have said, I have come to visit you. I met someone that you know at the Poor House this morning.'

'No you didn't. How would I know anyone there.'

'What about Mary Maunder then?'

'She's a servant, she doesn't count.'

'She's there because of my aunt's brooch. She has no job and she was the one who fed her family. They are all at the Poor House.'

'So what, serves her right. Thief.'

'But she is not the thief, Malvina. It is you who are the thief.'

'How dare you. Get off our land.'

Perinne kept still. 'Non. My aunt has her brooch back, but you have other things that do not belong to you. I am certain of this and I am going to tell my uncle. He is a

229

magistrate and he will send you to prison. Your family will be shamed.'

Patience gasped and began to fan her face. Malvina's face was red with fury.

'You talk nonsense Perille Menni ... whatever, I am no thief. You cannot prove this.'

'My name is Perinne and I can. You were seen.' Perinne knew what she was about to say was a guess. She could only hope that she was right. 'You were seen taking the pouch belonging to the lost girl from its hiding place.'

Malvina's face was as white as a sugar cone. She sat down.

Perinne gave her a few moments to take in what she'd said. The good thing was that Malvina hadn't denied it. 'Do you still have the pouch?'

Malvina nodded.

'And my fossils?'

Another nod.

'In that case you will return them and I shall speak with my uncle, ask if he will be lenient towards you.'

'No! Don't tell him. My father will be furious. He'll stop my allowance and ...'

'Then you will do as I ask.' Perinne had to hold back a smile. It was working. She turned and waved. Will, Nathan and Rosamund approached.

'It's a black boy,' Patience said.

'It's the girl from the Poor House,' Malvina said.

'Yes, and I want you to return her pouch and take care of her. She is in danger. You have plenty of space. She can stay in Mary's room. You must not mention this to your parents. You must give her water to wash with, some food and some clean clothing that will fit her. I will call again tomorrow.'

'But ... .'

'But first,' Will stepped forward. 'Ye'll bring the pouch.'

Chapter 31

The lost girl

Friday 22nd June 1781

Patience followed Malvina into the house. Will, Perinne and Nathan joined hands, smiling.

'It's working. If we can keep Ros'mund here until we find out 'bout her uncle or daddy, den dat would be great,' Nathan said.

There was a sniff. Rosamund was in tears. 'I don't like that girl,' she said.

'She will not hurt you. I am sure Patience will take care of you. Malvina is scared,' Perinne said.

'Look, 'ere's Patience. She's brought us all drinks. She wouldn't do that if she were 'orrid like 'er sister,' Will said.

Patience set the tray on the table. It looked like lemon water. 'Please, have a drink, it is so hot.'

'Patience,' Nathan spoke. 'Will you take care of Ros'mund? Shi's frightened. Such a lot has happened to her and wi need to be sure shi's safe.'

Patience gave Nathan a hard look. He returned her stare with his bright smile.

'Yes, I'll make sure Rosamund doesn't come to any harm. I'm used to Malvina's ways.'

'Dat's good. Ah, here shi is.'

Malvina put the pouch on the table. 'What's that strange piece of paper inside the locket?' she said.

Rosamund took hold of the pouch. 'It's something that's been missing from my family for many years, that, and the watch.' She opened the leather strap and tipped the contents into her hand. The watch and locket were undamaged. She slipped the watch back and opened the locket. There were two pieces of paper as before, the money bill and the cipher. She dabbed her eyes. 'Now they're returned. My father will be pleased.'

'Is that your father on the locket?' Perinne asked.

'Yes, that is my father, Francis Woolsey.'

Will, Nathan and Perinne left the same way as they'd entered. At the stables, Perinne mounted Pierre. 'I shall visit in the morning. I am allowed to come here, but it is sad. My aunt says that I can no longer meet with you and Danny, nor go to the Poor House.'

'That's a shame Perinne, maybe she'll change 'er mind,' Will said. 'What 'bout the cipher. Shall we 'elp Rosamund solve it?'

'That would be fun. Imagine hidden treasure in the Priory. We will still meet at the beach. I will ask Rosamund if she will allow me to bring the cipher.' Perinne nudged Pierre and trotted down the lane.

'Look,' Nathan said. 'Is dat de cart wi saw last night?'

'Could be,' Will said.

The boys slipped into the stables. There were four stalls, all were empty. At the back of the first stall something was stacked and covered in sacking.

Will lifted the corner. 'Oilskins, so this is where the other gang are hiding the baccy.'

'Is Ros'mund goin' to be safe here?'

'So long as it's only Malvina an' Patience who know she's 'ere. Let's get back to town an' get somethin' to eat.'

'David wants us to join the search for the girl,' Adam Litty said. The men were in the George.

'Do the Kentish know?' Guy Cox asked.

'Yes. But not about her uncle.'

'Uncle?' Caleb looked at Adam then saw Beth and waved for ale.

David Preston appeared. 'He arrived this afternoon at the quay. He's staying 'ere.'

'So, we're pulling out of the deal?' Guy asked.

'Aye. Let 'em find their own treasure,' David scoffed. 'If it exists.'

'Can't ye get rid of 'em?'

'They'll go as soon as this business with the girl's sorted,' Adam put in.

The men nodded in agreement. Beth appeared and set down a tray of tankards. 'Has the girl been found yet, Master Preston?'

'Not yet, Beth, we're setting out to look, just waiting for a few others.'

'More important to us is who's bringing in that baccy.' Guy took a drink. 'Heard there were some comin' over tomorrow night.'

Isaac took his pipe from his mouth. 'Those lights Wednesday night, that were 'em. We need to hide on the Head, Adam.'

'Whoever it is, they're using the harbour to move on the goods.'

'We don't know how many there'll be, do you know, Isaac?' Guy asked.

'Can't be too many or we'd know about it. In any case, it were too dark to see what kind of boat they had.'

'We'll meet on the quomps. Keep a watch out, are we all in?' Adam said. 'If it's only a few, then it won't matter, will it? We need to be prepared.'

Caleb tipped his drink back in one. 'Let's get looking for the girl or we'll lose the light.'

Beth watched as the men joined a group of people under the town hall arches. The overseers were there, the tall man and the kindly man. The tall man was pointing and sending people in different directions. She wondered where Will could be, she hadn't seen him all day. He'd be good at looking for someone. He knew every nook in this town.

In the room above the George's entrance Samuel Pascoe wondered about joining the search, but he'd been here only a few hours and knew nothing of the town and its geography. How could he trust a town that lost a foundling in such a way, but he'd no choice. They were no doubt making every effort to find his niece.

He looked around the room. It had a low ceiling and the bed was beside the wall. His trunk had been brought up and there was fresh water in a jug beside the basin. The plate of meats and vegetables that the girl had fetched were sitting, uneaten on the low table, and the tankard of ale still to be drunk. What had begun as a joyous day was as bad as it could get.

Francis Woolsey's arm hung limply at his side, lost in his dark coat sleeve. His one good hand steered his horse towards the smoke rising from the chimney that had first alerted him to the inn. Its nutty wood smell made it look an ordinary place and hopefully somewhere where no one would know of him. His arm was a giveaway to his pursuers, but he prayed that they would never find him. He wanted nothing more than this journey seeing the end of his troubles and the start of a new life in a new home with his wife, Amelia and daughter Rosamund. His horse was weary and they both needed to rest. He decided to stay here for the night and made his way into a courtyard where a boy wearing just breeches ran towards him. It was still light outside despite the late hour.

'Is the master of the house around, lad?'

'Aye, sir, I'll fetch 'im.' The boy ran off towards a door as Woolsey climbed from his mount. He'd been on the road for nearly two weeks. His whole journey from Kent to Devon could take more than a month, avoiding the turnpikes and taking a roundabout route. Since leaving his old home for good, he'd first called to see a friend in London. Now he wasn't far north of Marlborough.

'Good ev'nin', sir.' A short, plump man with a white wig and wearing a long apron appeared.

'Do you have a bed for the night, landlord?'

'Aye, we have that.' The landlord spotted the lifeless arm. 'Shall I have the lad take those?' he said, pointing to a pair of saddlebags.

'If he'd be so good, I'd be grateful.'

'Tom! Come and get the horse and take the bags up to the room at the front. Go, sir, and sit in the parlour, I'll fetch ye some ale.'

Francis made his way into the small room. It was twilight and candles had been lit and were gently flickering. There was a group of men sitting around a table chatting. They nodded to him and he docked his hat and took it off. He went over to a small window, opened to let in the cooler evening air. There was a bench with red cushions and he sat down. He scanned the view. The inn wasn't very far from the turnpike which continued towards Salisbury and south towards the port of Poole. But this wouldn't be the way he would go. If his enemies had somehow worked out his plans they would expect him to use that route. Instead he would cross to Wells and on through Somerset to his final destination. He drank the ale and retired to his room asking the landlord to serve him supper there.

'Let's find somewhere to stop here,' Rowland said.

Peter nodded. They'd arrived in Winchester and the city was busy, people making last minute purchases from a street market. There were pavements and a man was lighting oil lamps.

'Probably expensive in the centre,' Peter said. 'Let's walk on a bit.'

'Yis, but not too far, the beasts are tired.'

They followed the road through the town. There were new houses and, at the top of the hill a castle. They reached the outskirts of the city and spotted an inn. As they dismounted, an ostler came forward.

'We need a room an' stablin', plus some supper,' Rowland said.

'Good job we made good money on that last job,' Peter chuckled.

The horses were led away and they went inside. There were a few people about, sitting eating or just drinking. The two men settled down.

'So, in the mornin' we head for the New Forest,' Rowland said. 'It cuts across directly to Christchurch.'

'Popular place it seems,' said an elderly man with a whiskery face. He was sitting at the next table.

'Oh, why be that?' Peter asked.

'Two men and a boy, two nights' since, they were going to Christchurch. That's what the lad was sayin'.'

'What was he like, the boy?' Rowland said, sitting up.

The man took his long, white pipe from his mouth and pushed out his bottom lip. 'Hmmm. Eleven, maybe twelve, skinny, fair hair - I think.'

Peter nodded at Rowland, whose face had lit up in the dimness of the room.

'Friends of yours?' the man said.

'Pah. Not any more. Let me buy yew ale, old man. An' yew c'n think on what they were talking 'bout.'

Will and Nathan turned into Purewell. There were plenty of people about, in fact there seemed to be a buzz about town.

'What's 'appenin'?' he asked a short woman who was with a boy around eight years old.

'It's the lost girl, she's,' the woman paused, 'well, she's lost!'

Will wanted to laugh, but knew it would look bad.

'The overseers have organised a search, look everywhere they say. Lots of townsfolk are out helpin'.'

'Hmm, we'll see what we c'n do,' Will said, giving Nathan a sideways glance. The woman and boy turned off the road into a side street and began to look under bushes and behind walls.

'Shall we say anything?' Nathan asked.

'We should be able to trust the overseers, but who knows in this town.'

Chapter 32

Perinne sees the cipher

Saturday 23rd June 1781

Francis Woolsey woke early the next morning feeling rested. He would eat breakfast and make a start on the next part of his long journey. He made his way down a narrow staircase, he'd ask the boy to bring his bags. He sat in the same place as the night before. This time a woman appeared. She looked almost the same as the landlord, short, plump and pleasant.

'Mornin' sir, trust ye slept well?'

'Yes. Thank you.'

'It's another fine day. It's been a sight better 'ere since the storms. Did you get them where you were?'

'Just a thunderstorm, nothing of note.' He wasn't sure he wanted to talk, but the woman was only being friendly. She left and returned with a plate of buttered, toasted bread with some slices of meat and a cup of tea.

'They had it bad on the coast,' the woman said. 'A ship sunk in Christchurch Bay, all souls lost by all accounts.'

'Really?' Francis's heart began to pound in his chest. 'Do you know which ship?'

'Oh, now, what was it? John!' she shouted. The plump

man appeared. 'What did that gentleman say the name of the ship lost at Christchurch was?'

'Why, it was called the *Anne Marie*, on her way to the West Indies. You all right, sir?'

All the colour had drained from Francis's face. He was silent for a minute or more before jumping to his feet. 'I'll thank you to get the lad to saddle my horse and hurry with my bags, landlady. I have to leave, at once.'

Despite the dangers, Francis Woolsey headed out to find the turnpike and a way to the coast and to Christchurch. In this heat, he'd take more than a day, or it would kill the horse.

Perinne was out of bed and dressed when the house-mouse maid brought in her drink. The girl tried, but it wasn't the same as having Lucy around.

'Breakfast's in the small dining room again, miss,' she said. 'The mistress and Madame Menniere are already there.'

'Thank you,' Perinne said.

'Did you want me to brush your hair, miss?'

Perinne didn't want her to, but had begun to feel sorry for her. 'All right.'

The maid fetched Perinne's brushes from her dressing table and began to work through her hair.

'Wonder if they found the girl, miss?'

'I have not heard. I am sure that she will be found soon.' Perinne was surprised at how gentle the girl was.

'Shall I put in some ribbon?'

'If you wish to.'

'There, that looks pretty.'

It was the first time Perinne had seen the girl smile.

They left the room together, the maid continued along the corridor to the back staircase and Perinne went to the large one which took her to the hall. As she was coming down the stairs she could hear voices. Someone was arguing. It sounded like her maman and Aunt Elizabeth. As she neared, she caught a few words.

'She is a free spirit. I would not wish her to be ... .'

Perinne appeared at the door.

'Good morning, Perinne. Come and have some breakfast,' Aunt Elizabeth said. She had a small plate in front of her and on it some morsels of cheese. Maman had an egg. 'I believe you made your last visit to the Poor House yesterday. I am so pleased.'

Perinne's mother's face went red, she was holding her breath.

'We have some good news, don't we Jane.'

Jane Menniere relaxed and smiled. 'Yes, yes we do. Perinne, papa should be arriving in the next few days.'

'C'est merveilleux!' Perinne said, jumping from her seat and dancing around the room.

'Sit down,' Aunt Elizabeth said. 'This is exactly the thing I mean, it is not becoming for a young lady to squeal and shout so. She needs a governess, Jane.'

Jane nodded to Perinne who took her seat again and chose some fruit to eat.

'What will you do today,' Aunt Elizabeth asked.

'I thought that I would visit Malvina and Patience at Burton Hall.'

'That's much better. I shall leave you with your mother. I shall be in the drawing room.'

Jane followed her with her eyes until she'd left. She leaned over to Perinne. 'I have some other news.'

'What is it maman?'

'We shall be moving out of Cliff House.'

Rowland and Peter looked at the horse.

'I can't ride him like this,' Rowland said, looking at the stallion, which was holding its back hoof off the ground.

'Take mine, I'll get it looked at an' catch up.'

'I need yew with me, Peter. We'll take him to a smithy, it looks like a stone or somethin's cut him. We'll rest them today. We've pushed them too hard in this weather. We'll get there Sunday.'

It had been only two days since the funeral, but it seemed longer. Danny had just finished collecting eggs. He heard a cart arrive as he returned to the cottage. It was Uncle John and Aunt Mary. Danny's mother and his aunt were going to sort out grandpa's things. Danny didn't think he had much to sort.

'It's Danny, how are ye, boy? Feelin' better?' Uncle John asked.

'A bit.'

'It were good of yer friends to come and pay their respects, especially Miss Perinne.'

'An' it were good of Mistress Menniere to take me and your mother home,' Aunt Mary added.

'Never hear the last o' that,' Uncle John laughed. 'Ridin' in a fancy coach!'

'Shall we start, Mary?' Danny's mother had come into the room. 'Sarah's having a sleep, we can get it done.'

Aunt Mary climbed the stairs. Uncle John sat down in

grandpa's old chair and began to rock it gently.

'He were a grand old man, yer grandpa, Danny.'

Danny nodded, he wanted to ask Uncle John a question, but didn't want him to wonder why he was asking. But he remembered what Will had said at the coppice yesterday.

'Do smugglers go to hell, Uncle John?'

Uncle John laughed. 'Why on this earth would you ask that?'

'The vicar, at grandpa's funeral, he said about free traders that they'd go to hell.'

'He weren't talking about grandpa, Danny.'

'But do they, go to hell?'

Uncle John rubbed the grey whiskers on his chin. 'I expect some will, but others won't.'

'Why?'

''Cos for some it's a matter of fillin' the bellies o' their family, they do no harm. But for others it's big business and they'll stop at nothin'.'

'So, if someone smuggles by, er, mistake, they're all right?'

'Why ever d'ye ask that?'

'Just wondered.'

'If it were a mistake, then how can it be a sin? The Lord's supposed to forgive us, isn't he?'

His uncle's words made Danny feel strange. He smiled, yet he felt that he was going to cry. His shoulders fell and he let out a long sigh. Uncle John got out of grandpa's chair and hugged him.

'Do yu think Sir Charles Tarrant has changed him mind, Will?' Nathan said as the boys left the small cottage. Sam the dog was sniffing down by the river's edge. He kept turning to watch the boys moving up the lane.

'It'd be a good thing if 'e did, but why the sudden change o' 'eart if that's what it is?'

Nathan shrugged. 'Conscience?'

Will laughed out loud. 'Conscience, Sir Charles Tarrant? We'll go to Cliff 'ouse on Monday as we've bin asked. Let's make our way to London. We c'n find others who'll 'elp stop the wicked trade.'

'Well, dere's certainly a lot goin' on here to keep us busy until den.'

'Aye. I want that teacher to pay for using Danny like 'e did. He's usually so cheerful.'

'And de two gangs, we can't take dem all on.'

'That's true, we 'ave to get the local gang to see that the Kentish men are bad.'

'But dey is too keen on dat treasure.'

'Hmm.... We know where the cipher is, with Rosamund, so we need to make sure she's safe too.'

'Danny's tormentor, Walton, is smuggling for de massa at Burton Hall. Do we need to move Ros'mund?'

'Let's go to the beach. We're meetin' Perinne an' Danny, we c'n work somethin' out.'

'Shall wi call an' see Beth first? Get a drink?' Nathan said.

'Aye, why not,' Will replied. 'Sam! Come on, boy!'

Perinne set out for Burton Hall. She would have to speak with Mrs Stone. She didn't like her but it couldn't be helped. She hoped that Rosamund had been looked after and that she would be able to speak with her alone.

She passed close to Danny's cottage. There was a cart outside. It was Danny's Uncle John's.

She arrived at the Hall and rode into the drive. Kelly, the butler was near the stables. The brew house was close by and that's where he was heading.

'Good morning, miss. Can I help?'

'I have come to visit the Misses Malvina and Patience.'

'I'm sure they'll be pleased to see you. I'll tie your pony in the stable, there's hay and water.'

Perinne dismounted and, after Kelly had settled Pierre, she followed him. He first took her into the drawing room, the same room she had been in when she'd visited with her maman.

'It's Miss Perinne, mistress.'

'Ah, Perinne, how delightful to see you. You have come to see my daughters?'

'Yes, Mrs Stone. Aunt Elizabeth wishes that I make friends.'

'Well, Patience is around, but Malvina has taken a strange turn. She's been in her room since last afternoon. We're not sure what is wrong. She doesn't seem ill.'

'That is a shame. But it would be good to see Patience in any case.'

'Of course. Kelly take Miss Perinne to Patience, she's in the library.'

'Yes, mistress. This way, miss.' Kelly beckoned with his hand and Perinne followed him across the wide hallway.

'Perinne,' Patience said. She put her book onto the table next to her. 'Thank you Kelly.'

Kelly sniffed and left the room. Patience moved over and closed the door.

'I've done as you asked. Rosamund is fine. When we see Kelly outside, I shall take you to her.'

Perinne thought Patience had brightened. Her face had more colour and she seemed less shy.

'It's been so exciting.'

'Your mother says Malvina is unwell,' Perinne said.

Patience smiled. 'I'm pleased you caught her out, Perinne. My sister can be most unpleasant at times. Look, there he is. Come on, up the stairs. Mother and father were late home last night it has been easy to bring things.'

The staircase was wide and bright and Perinne followed Patience to the top floor to what seemed like the attic. They went into a small room and sitting on the bed was Rosamund. Her face lit up when she saw Perinne. Perinne was surprised. Rosamund looked well. Patience had kept her promise and more. Rosamund's hair had been washed, brushed and tied in a ribbon. She wore a pale blue dress which although it was too big for her, had been tied with a white sash and bow to make it fit. The small table beside the bed had an empty plate and glass.

'Hello, Rosamund. How are you today?' Perinne said.

'I am well. Patience has been very kind.'

'Yes, I can see that is true.' Perinne touched Patience's arm. 'Thank you.'

Patience replied with a broad smile.

'Will you stay here while Will tries to find your uncle and father?' Perinne said. Rosamund nodded. 'Can you do that, Patience?'

'Yes, I am sure. Father left this morning until Sunday, and mother never comes up here.'

'That is good. Is it possible for me to have a drink?'

'Yes, I'll bring some cordial.' Patience left the room and Perinne sat next to Rosamund on the bed.

'Can I see the cipher Rosamund?' Perinne asked.

Rosamund leaned to the top of the bed, reached under her pillow and found the pouch. She took out the locket, unclasped it and gave one of the papers to Perinne. Perinne unfolded it. It showed a simple drawing of a face followed by small sketches, words and other figures.

'The face, I have seen it,' Rosamund said. 'Father

said it looked like Uncle Sam. He said if we find the Face of Sam, we can find the treasure.'

'Where did you see the Face of Sam, Rosamund?'

'In the church, where the big man left me.'

Chapter 33

Should the friends tell?

Saturday 23rd June 1781

Glistening sea washed foamy, white bubbles gently onto the soft sands of the beach. Sam ran in and out of the water fetching the stub of a branch that Nathan had picked up on the way.

'Wi're here first, Will,' Nathan smiled, 'and with another piece of dis puzzle.'

'Yes, Beth said it were bein' kept secret, so the Kent gang don't find out.'

'Samuel Pascoe needs to be told dat his niece is all right. We'll have to tell him when we get back into town, Will.'

'Aye,' Will's face creased with worry. 'We'll 'ave to think 'bout what to do if Danny brings Josh.'

'Yes, it's awkward. I doubt he'd talk.'

'Not willin'ly per'aps, but like ye said, they could force it out of 'im.'

'Well, we don't need to worry, look, on the cliff.'

Perinne was sitting on Pierre, Danny leading the pony by its reins. Perinne waved. Sam spotted Danny and bounded across the beach, his stick forgotten.

'C'm'on, let's find some shade,' Will said.

'It is a long time since we sat together like this,' Perinne said.

'So much has happened and just like before, we have a mystery to solve,' Danny sat on a fallen tree trunk next to Perinne.

'We 'ave more than one puzzle, Danny,' Will leant against a tree. 'There's such a lot 'appenin' at once, but they all seem to be connected to the gang from Kent.'

'Has Josh said anythin' more to yu, Danny, since wi all met at de coppice?' Nathan asked.

'He's scared of Levi but he'd like to help find the treasure.'

'He heard that it does not belong to Levi, but to Rosamund and her family,' Perinne put in.

'He told me his father's friend, Peter, said it was won in a card game,' Danny said. 'There was the story of some men coming from Kent to Poole to get back smuggled tea and other things from the Customs House.'

'That sounds unlikely.'

'I thought that too, Will. I could ask Uncle John if he's heard about it, he's at our cottage.'

'Or maybe I could ask Isaac.'

'So, the cipher could belong to Levi?' Perinne asked.

'It's possible. We only 'ave Rosamund's word,' Will replied. 'She might not 'ave been told the truth.'

'So how do we find out who it truly belongs to?' Danny said. 'Rosamund's father?'

'It doesn't really matter who it belongs to if we c'n't find it,' Will looked towards the beach. Sam had wandered back to the sea and was digging by the shoreline.

'I have seen the cipher,' Perinne said. 'Rosamund showed me this morning. At the top it has a face and she said she'd seen it in the Priory.'

'Yes!' Danny jumped up. 'I remember. When I found her she was looking up at the arches. There's a carved face there. Adam Jackson showed me. I hadn't noticed it before.'

'What else is on de cipher?' Nathan asked.

'There are other pictures and marks. Rosamund did not want me to bring it.'

'Well, if it possible to work out de clues, de treasure could be found – if it still dere.' Nathan hunched his shoulders.

'So, what do we do?' Danny sat again.

Will gave Nathan a long look.

'What is it, Will?'

'Rosamund's uncle's in Christchurch. He's stayin' at the George. But David Preston said it were bein' kept secret hopin' the Kent gang don't find out.'

'So he will think Rosamund has gone missing, we must get word to him that she is safe,' Perinne said.

'Maybe he knows more about the cipher and who it really belongs to.' Danny's face lit up.

'We'll tell him Ros'mund is safe and ask im 'bout it,' Nathan suggested.

They all nodded in agreement.

'The next thing to decide is what to do 'bout Thomas Walton,' Will said.

'Nothing!' Danny shouted. 'He'll know it was me if anything's said.'

'I think there's another way an' I've 'ad an idea.'

'What's that?'

'When we took Rosamund to Burton Hall we saw bales of tobacco 'idden at the back o' the stable. Josh said that 'e'd heard Levi speakin' with Meekwick Ginn 'bout another gang. It's not a gang it's Walton. We saw 'im with another man in a cart on Thursday night an' there were lights in the Priory 'igh up.'

'That's where we hid the bales,' Danny put in.

'It 'as to be 'im. I'm sure that Sir Charles Tarrant would be very interested in agreein' the arrest. We don't need to mention ye at all Danny.'

Danny gave a weak smile. 'Are you sure?'

'Don't worry. But it would be better to catch 'im in the act,' Will said. 'An' only ye know where 'e's landin' the goods.'

'We get the last lot tonight in one load. Ginn's arranged some help for you. Three men, they're here from Kent on some other business, he didn't say what,' Benjamin Kelly said.

'And you'll be waiting on the marsh?' Thomas Walton leaned against the wall of the stables at Burton Hall.

'Yes, we can't risk the Priory again. Have you been to the spot?'

Walton nodded. 'I took the boat there on my way. Left it moored on the bank and walked here. I know the route, and should be all right.'

'Good. You'll meet me and another man from Sopley way. We'll bring the stuff here then Ginn will arrange sales at Ridley Wood.'

'And when will I get paid for my troubles?'

'Soon, the master's back tomorrow.'

Roger Law leaned on one of the arches of the town hall and watched the round-faced man leave the George. He'd seen him arrive on the quayside the day before and go straight to the Poor House. He'd asked the skipper of the coasting vessel who his passenger was, and was intrigued to hear he'd come from Poole and was desperate to get to Christchurch. It was no use asking any of the Christchurch gang, they'd gone blank on him. He didn't care. Levi'd gone to Ringwood to see Ginn. They'd been hired for a job tonight and Levi was getting details and to call at Sopley. At least it'd relieve the boredom. All he really cared about was capturing Francis Woolsey and getting the cipher. Suddenly the doorway to the upstairs of the hall opened. Law recognised the tall overseer.

'Any news o' the missing girl?' Roger asked.

'None,' he replied. 'Are you the man who said her father had sent you?'

'Yis. That's right.'

'Well, the girl's uncle has also arrived. He's staying at the George.'

'Why, that is good news, I'll go to see him, thank yew.'

'It's not good news that the girl's missing though, is it?' The overseer sniffed and walked off.

Roger made his way to the wharf. They'd found an old boat and had been sleeping there. The weather had been on their side. Behind them the church tower pointed high into the blue sky, sea birds were settled on the calm river, dotted around like lilies on a pond.

'Is Levi back yet?'

'No,' Pip replied. 'Has somethin' happened?'

'The girl's uncle's turned up.'

'Here?'

'He's staying at the George Inn,' Roger sucked on the stem of his pipe.

'What shall we do?'

'Wait. Even if Woolsey doesn't hear about the wreckin' on his journey, he's sure to find out when he reaches its end. He'll come.'

'How much longer, Roger?'

Roger hunched his shoulders. 'At least we'll have a bit of money after tonight.'

'But the girl's still missing,' Pip kicked at a wooden board set into the riverbank.

'That's a mystery even the townsfolk can't solve, but that don't concern us anymore,' Roger replied, spitting on the gravel. 'We want Woolsey, not the girl. She's just the worm for the bird.'

Samuel Pascoe entered the porch of the Priory church. The cool of the building was a welcome break from the heat of the day. He pushed open the door and gasped. The nave was bright with sunshine through the windows above the high arches. Over this was a wooden roof, its trusses painted. There was no one about. He walked down the centre aisle. Ahead was an altar, in front of a stone carved screen. Beyond this he imagined was the quire. It was like a cathedral, not a parish church. There were a few pews ahead and he sat down. This was where Rosamund had been left by someone who must have brought her from the beach. He'd saved her life, but where was she? Sam bent, set his elbows on his knees and rested his forehead on his clasped hands. He prayed.

'I think we should tell someone,' Danny said. 'It's too dangerous. We could have been shot last year when we got involved. You told me yourself that smugglers carry pistols.'

'Ye're right,' Will said. 'Perh'ps we should tell yer father.'

Danny's face went pale.

'Your father will not be angry, Danny. You were tricked. You should not have been punished for helping Rosamund that morning.' Perinne put her arm around Danny's shoulder.

'Perinne's right, Danny, Walton's de one who should be punished,' Nathan said.

'Where's ye father, Danny?' Will asked.

'At Cliff House, I think. He's not at home.'

'If we go to Cliff House, I will not be allowed to help anymore,' Perinne said. Her large dark eyes scanned across her friends' faces.

'Let's go into Christchurch an' speak wi' Ros'mund's uncle,' Nathan said. 'Wi can tell 'im Ros'mund is safe an' ask im about de cipher.'

'I agree. We've no idea when Walton'll be bringin' in the next load. Once we do, we can speak wi' Danny's father.'

'How will we find out?' Danny asked.

'I'll ask Guy Cox if he's 'eard anythin'.'

Perinne rose, dusting leaves from the bottom of her dress. Nathan helped her on to Pierre and the friends set out. They walked to the harbour's edge.

'Over there, on the sea side of the sandbank,' Danny pointed. 'That's where we were. The bales had been hidden. I had to bring lamps from the cliffs too.'

'Lamps?'

'Yes, coach lamps, or the kind the ostlers use. I can't remember.'

''ow many?'

Danny puffed out his cheeks. 'Hmm... five, six. I hung them on my arms. There was another lamp with a long tube coming out of it.'

'A spout lamp,' Will said. He drew in his breath and his face wrinkled.

'What is it?' Danny asked.

'Did 'e say when they were landed?'

'No.'

'Try t' think Danny, when did Walton ask ye?'

'The morning I found Rosamund. It was because I'd stayed after choir practice instead of going out. The morning after the storm.'

Will swung his arm and clicked his fingers. 'He were usin' the lamps to signal.'

'But dat' would be normal, Will, wouldn't it?' Nathan asked.

'Wi' a spout lamp, aye. But puttin' lamps on the side o' the cliff.' He shook his head.

'What is wrong, Will? You look so angry,' Perinne said.

'Can't say, I need to think. But if I'm right, Walton could be 'anged for what 'e's done.'

Chapter 34

Walton unmasked

Saturday 23rd June 1781

Will, Nathan, Danny and Perinne followed the lane towards Purewell in silence. The boys were all in shirts and breeches. Danny was wearing a hat, but Will and Nathan's heads were bare. Some new houses had been built, but the harbour and the marsh were still visible. They reached the well and stopped for a drink.

'Is this safe?' Perinne asked, climbing down from Pierre.

'There's an alehouse not far down de lane,' Nathan pointed.

Will pulled at the rope and raised a bucket. He cupped his hands and drank. 'Why d'ye think it's called Purewell?'

The others laughed and took their turn sipping at the cool, clear water. After taking her drink, Perinne led her pony to the water's edge where she let him take a few sips.

'Look! Come quickly!' Danny called, keeping his voice low. He was standing by the road. The others ran to join him.

'What is it?' Nathan asked.

'Thomas Walton. He's just turned off the track. He's going on the marsh,' Danny said. 'Let's follow him.'

'There's not enough places to hide, 'e'll see us,' Will said.

'What is he doing?' Perrine had joined them again.

'My guess is findin' somewhere t' land his goods. He needs a new place. Ye know 'bout the Priory.'

'He'll easily spot mi, and Danny can't do it,' Nathan said. 'Why don't you and Perinne follow him? He'll think you a couple out for a walk.'

Will blushed. 'Perinne, are ye all right t' do that?'

'Yes, we can walk past him. He will not think anything of it.'

'Come on,' Will took Pierre's reins. 'If we take Pierre and Walton chases us, we c'n both get away quickly.'

'We'll meet you at the coppice,' Danny said.

'Is it really awful for the slaves?' Danny asked Nathan. They'd reached the coppice and settled in the shady canopy.

'Yes.'

'Are the plantation owners bullies?'

Nathan looked at Danny. 'More dan dat, Danny.'

'What happens?'

'On de plantations?'

'How do they get there?'

'Dey trapped in de villages and taken to ports in Africa and put onto ships. Many die crossing de ocean. Dey crammed into de hold, chained and poorly fed. There's disease and much sufferin'. De people dat survive dey taken to market and sold, like de goats and cattle. Den dey treated with great cruelty.' Nathan drew a deep breath. 'But some people are seein' it for what it be.'

'Like the man who took you in?'

'Massa James, he were a good man. Educated me best he could. Said I could be a great man. But he was old. He got ill an' died an' I was on mi own again. Dat's when I met Will.'

'So, are you really going to London?'

'Yes. Will's sure wi can do somethin'.'

'What do you think, Nathan? Can you do something?'

'Mi think it'll take a long, long time.'

A rustling noise made the boys look up. It was Will and Perinne.

'He had a boat tied up,' Perinne said.

'It were as I thought, he's been lookin' for a landin' place,' Will said.

'I think that I should go home,' Perinne glanced at the ground anxiously. 'I will be in trouble if I am seen with you all in Christchurch.'

'Can you go to Burton Hall again in the morning?' Danny asked.

'Yes. We need to move Rosamund. Malvina and Patience's father comes home tomorrow. But I may have to go to church also.'

'Do yu have to go to church, Danny?' Nathan asked.

'Yes, I'm in the choir. Maybe Malvina and Patience have to attend? Will and Nathan could go to Burton Hall for Rosamund.'

'Per'haps, if it's safe. If it's not, we need to think o' somewhere else to take her,' Will said. 'Come on, let's get to town.'

'Prayer can open one's eyes to things hidden by the trials we endure in life, sir,' Samuel Pascoe said.

'Indeed, Mr Pascoe, indeed,' said the mayor. 'Your

niece had to have help and Miss Perinne seems to be the only person she would trust. And you're correct in your thoughts that a young girl would be too afraid to run off on her own.'

'Unless something truly had frightened her.'

'I think it had to be a mixture of both. I've sent for the Poor House Master. Let's see what he has to say about it all.'

Samuel looked around him. The town hall was a single room, set on arches and he was on the first floor. There were windows on all sides and the high street and others surrounding it could be watched. He should have visited the mayor immediately after discovering Rosamund had gone missing, but he was in shock. After resting and having time to think in the quiet of the church, he'd come to his senses and decided to act.

John Cook, Mayor of Christchurch moved to the window at the north of the room and peered out. The sash was up, allowing a light breeze cross the room. 'Here he is.'

The sound of footsteps drummed on the wooden staircase and David Preston entered the room. He took off his hat. 'Mr Mayor.' He paused as he saw Samuel. 'Mr Pascoe.'

'There is still no sign of young Rosamund?'

'No, Mr Mayor.'

'Has Miss Perinne attended the Poor House today?'

'No. We 'ad word from Cliff House that she weren't allowed to come any more.'

'But she was at the Poor House yesterday?'

'She were, but only for a short while.'

'Did she come by coach?'

David shook his head. 'No. She came on her pony.'

'Did you see her leave?'

'I were busy. She'd been seen in the garden.' He paused. 'I saw her on the high street. Rosamund weren't with her... .'

'What is it?' Samuel urged. 'What have you remembered?'

'She didn't have her pony with her. Maybe she gave it to the girl. Can she ride?'

'I believe so,' Samuel said.

'Then we need to speak with Miss Perinne,' the mayor said. 'I'll send a message to Cliff House. Thank you, Preston.'

'Mr Pascoe left some time back,' Beth whispered.

'We'll 'ave to call back later,' Will walked away.

'Where to next?' Nathan asked as the three boys left the George.

'The quay, let's see if the *Solomon*'s there and if Guy Cox is around.'

They cut through the Priory graveyard and across to the mill. The grinding sound of the wheel broke the peace of the afternoon. There were few boats tied up. The others would be out at sea, making the most of the fine weather. A young boy with bare feet and a dark cap was sitting on the quayside, mending a net. Danny nudged Will.

''ello, is the *Solomon* out?'

'Aye,' the boy said.

'Was Guy Cox aboard?'

'Guy's over there.' The boy pointed to a group of men sitting in the shade of a large chestnut tree.

'Will, lad,' Isaac Hooper saw him first. He was with Guy and Adam Litty.

Guy took his pipe from his mouth. 'What c'n we do for ye?'

'It's 'bout what we c'n do for ye,' Will said, raising his

eyebrows and grinning.

'Oh, an' what be that?' Litty asked.

'We've information ye might find very interestin'.'

'Go on, tell us.'

'We know who's bringin' in the baccy.'

'What baccy?' Guy huffed.

'Ye know.'

'Who?' Litty stepped forward.

'Afore we tell ye, we want ye to promise to 'elp us.'

'Tell me more first.'

'That gang from Kent.'

'What've they got to do with ye? It's not them bringin' in the stuff.'

'No, but they want the lost girl, an' 'er father.'

The men laughed. 'You boys!' Isaac said.

'How did ye find this out?' Guy asked.

'That's not important. We want ye to catch the person bringin' in the baccy an' give 'im over to the revenue officer.'

'What? 'elp them?' Isaac gasped.

'An' we may need 'elp with the Kent gang.'

'Who are ye to make demands on us?' Litty asked.

'Up to ye, 'elp, or we don't tell ye who's makin' money that ye should be makin'.' Will swung around, as if to walk away. Nathan and Danny turned too.

'Wait!' Litty shouted, 'we'll listen.'

Will told the men about Walton. That he'd tricked a boy from the town into helping him and that he was working for the new owner at Burton Hall.

'The stuff's comin' in tonight,' Adam said.

'Do ye know where he's landin' it?' Guy asked.

'Yes, at the end of the Head. He'll bring it 'arbour side. So far, 'e's stowed it in the Priory, but we think 'e's goin' to take it to the marsh this time, an' on from there.'

'How d'ye know this?' Guy glanced at Adam, puzzled.

'It don't matter. It's true.'

'Can we get a crew ready for tonight?' Isaac asked.

'If Walton's been working alone, we only need three or four, there can't be many landing such a small amount that one man can handle.'

'I can come,' Guy offered.

'And me,' Isaac said.

Adam faced Guy and Isaac. 'I'll see if Caleb's around, or Henry Lane. We'll meet here at dusk.'

'No need to get them. I'm comin' too,' Will said.

'Will, no.' Nathan protested.

'I'm goin'. I want to make sure Walton pays for what 'e did.'

'Why, who is it he's wronged?' Guy asked. Danny shifted his feet and faced away from them.

'That's my business.'

'You're a boy, Will. This is man's work,' Isaac said.

'I'm fourteen an' I've been 'alfway 'round the world on me own. I'm comin'.'

'I'm tired,' Danny complained.

'Me too,' Nathan said. 'Are yu sure about a-goin' tonight, Will?'

The boys were sitting in the old castle. The sun was moving down the sky and leaving a pale, yellow shadow. Swifts were squealing and diving overhead. A smell of roasting meat floated from a nearby building.

'Yes.'

'Then I'm goin' too.'

'What about telling Rosamund's uncle she's safe?' Danny asked.

'Hmm, we need to do dat. Shall wi go to de George?' Nathan said.

'Tis only fair, 'e should know,' Will replied. 'An' we c'n ask 'im 'bout Rosamund's father.'

'I'm going home. What will happen next?' Danny asked.

''opefully Walton'll be dealt with by the mornin'. We'll 'ave to find a way to get Rosamund to 'er uncle an' we c'n all get back to normal.'

'And the treasure?' Danny said.

'That depends upon what Samuel Pascoe 'as to say.'

Chapter 35

Danny fears for Will

Saturday 23rd June 1781

'Who's there?'

'I'm Will Gibbs, Master Pascoe. Me sister Beth, works 'ere.' Will was outside the dark, wooden door of an upstairs room in the George, Nathan behind him. 'I need to talk to ye.'

'Talk to me? About what?'

'Rosamund, sir.'

The sound of a key turning in the lock was followed by the latch lifting and a round-faced man with small, prominent eyes and grey hair appeared.

'My niece, you have news of her?'

'She's safe.'

'Come in, Will, tell me more.' Samuel opened the door, stopping suddenly on seeing Nathan.

'This is Nathan, he's me friend.'

Nathan smiled. 'Sorry we untidy, Massa Pascoe. Wi've bin out all day and we wanted to see yu before yu retired for de night.'

Samuel closed the door and sat on the bed. 'Now, boys, tell me, where is Rosamund?'

'She's at Burton Hall. She's bein' looked after by one of the daughters of the owner,' Will said.

'And tell me how and why she was taken there and not left at the Poor House.'

'Dere are some men here in town, sir,' Nathan said. 'Dey from Kent and dey here to attack Ros'mund's father. One of dem went to de Poor House, sayin' her father'd sent im. Ros'mund was scared. Our friend, Perinne, saw de danger and sent Ros'mund away on her pony.'

'Perinne. That was the name of the girl the mayor spoke about. A message has been sent to her home, but I'm sure it wasn't Burton Hall.'

'No, it weren't,' Will said. 'Perinne lives at Cliff House with Sir Charles Tarrant. He owns a lot o' the land 'round 'ere.'

'Well, I expect that the mayor will also find out this information,' Samuel said. 'I should soon be reunited with her, this is good news.'

'But the men're still 'ere. We think ye may also be in danger.'

'Surely the mayor should be told of this. Have the men arrested. Do you not have a constable or soldiers?'

'We 'ave no proof, an' they've done nothin' wrong 'ere.'

'Dey also seek some treasure, sir,' Nathan said. 'Dey say dat Ros'mund's father stole a cipher from dem. Dey said it belonged to a friend who won it playin' a card game with a sailor in Poole, years ago.'

'That's not true.'

'Ye know 'bout it?' Will asked, surprised.

'Yes, I do. That sailor was also called Samuel Pascoe. He was my father.'

264

'Enter!'

Joseph had the message on a silver salver. Inside the library Sir Charles Tarrant was sitting across from a man with thin, greying hair. Standing beside the large desk James Clarke beckoned to Joseph and took the paper. Joseph nodded and left.

'Whose seal?' Sir Charles asked.

'The mayor,' James said.

'Open it. Read it out.'

James broke the red wax seal, catching its crumbs, and unfolded the letter.

'Dear Sir Charles

You will be aware of the young girl found in the Priory Church some twelve days past who has been under the care of the Parish Poor House. There has been some issue as to her origins, but her Uncle, a Mr Samuel Pascoe, has arrived in town to claim her and to take her home. Unfortunately, sometime yesterday afternoon, the child absconded. A search was undertaken to no avail. This is, of course, somewhat of an embarrassment for our town that we cannot hold a young girl safe in our keeping. I come to the matter of my correspondence. The girl was, until the day before yesterday, mute. However, she has spoken but only to your niece, Miss Perinne Menniere. We now understand the girl to be Rosamund Woolsey, formerly of Faversham, Kent. I would make a request that you speak with your niece. It appears that she was the last person to be seen with Rosamund and might be questioned as to whether she knows anything of the disappearance.

Yours sincerely
John Cook,
Mayor

'Ask her mother to bring her here immediately, Clarke.'

'Yes, Sir Charles.'

'Where've you been all day, Danny,' Hannah Clarke asked.

'At the beach,' Danny said, diving into a plate of food.

'Well, you seem brighter today. You need to have a good wash. It's church in the morning.'

'Yes, mother.'

After eating some fish and vegetables Danny went into the garden. The first stars of the night were winking through the purple dusk. His mother was right, he did feel better. He wished he could watch what happened at the Head tonight. He wanted nothing more than to see the last of Thomas Walton, but he worried about Will going out with the smugglers. He might have travelled a long way and had adventures, but it was still dangerous.

'Pssst... Danny.'

Danny scanned the garden. There was a shadowy figure by the fence. 'Who's that?' he said.

''Tis me, Josh.'

Danny walked across the grass. 'What are you doing here?' he whispered.

'I've bin working all day. I went to the stream to wash, so I thought I'd call.'

'It's late.'

'Yis, sin a flittermouse or two, but I had to come.'

'Why?'

'Levi came to Sopley today an' I thought yew'd want to know why he was there.'

'What did he want?'

'Levi, Pip an' Roger Law are helpin' bring in some tobacco t'night. Levi came to the farm. He'd bin to Ringwood to see Meekwick Ginn. Levi needed someone to help, he said on the marsh. Do yew know that place?'

'Yes.'

'One of the shepherds is to go to Burton Hall. The others are leavin' with the teacher - from somewhere called the wharf.'

'We have to tell Will and Nathan, they think Walton's working alone.'

'How?'

'I'll go indoors. Say I'm going to bed then sneak back downstairs. We'll have to go and find Will.'

'Me go too? But what if they've set out? They're dangerous, Danny. No one said 'bout them killin' the soldiers until Rosamund told us.'

'Hmmm... .' Danny slumped onto the grass.

'Tell yewer father, that's what Will said to do.'

'But father'll have the revenue men out and Will could get into trouble.'

'Where's Will goin'?'

'To the Head.'

'So, tell yewer father 'bout the marsh, they'll catch Walton there.'

'But that doesn't solve the problem of the Kent gang.'

'Yew need to tell yewer father everythin'.'

'Yes, I think you're right. Come on, let's go.'

'He isn't here?'

'No, he's at Cliff House. Let's run!'

'It seems young Perinne still enjoys her adventures, Charles,' Sir George Cook said with a smile.

'She acts more like a boy than a girl,' Sir Charles said.

'She's young.'

'She's old enough to act like a young lady. My wife is insisting, but Jane wishes her to be free of rules. They're

267

moving out. I think because they can't agree on the matter.'

'And they will stay in Christchurch?'

'Perhaps, it suits Yves. He can be in France soon from here, and secretly if necessary.'

A rapping broke the conversation. Jane Menniere stepped into the library closely followed by Perinne in her nightdress, her black hair loose around her shoulders.

Sir Charles came forward. He bent and looked directly at Perinne. 'This is important, a child is missing and the mayor seems to think you, Perinne, might know where she is.'

A candle flickered on the low table and an umber glow settled on the dusty boards of the room. Will wondered what the old man was going to tell them.

'Rosamund has a pouch containing a watch. It was given to my father as a reward for saving the life of a rich gentleman. My father was cheated of it, more than thirty years ago, and not far from here, over at Poole.'

Without further thought, Samuel Pascoe spilled out his family story.

'We lived at Plymouth, a place not unlike your town, but much larger, especially the port. We were four children. I am the eldest, my sister the youngest and there are two brothers in between. We lived off what father could bring in from working at the docks. He decided we needed better. Once my brothers were able to work, father joined a merchant ship and headed for the West Indies. He would be away months at a time, but when he came back there was money, though we were never rich. Mother didn't like it, though. Our brothers left home leaving myself and Amelia, Rosamund's mother. Mother wanted father to stay at home. He agreed, but only after one last voyage. He left in the spring of 1747 and returned home, penniless, in the October with a tale of lost fortune. He said that he'd been given a reward for an act of great bravery.'

'What did he do?' Will said.

'He was at sea. The ship was carrying passengers back home to England. They hit a storm. Not unusual I believe. The ship was caught by a giant wave and people were washed overboard, including my father. He helped as many as he could and managed to keep one man afloat, risking his own life. He finally got them both back aboard, though the man was in a bad way, too bad that the ship's surgeon could not save him. Before he died, the man, Richard Redcliffe, gave my father a watch, a sum of money and the cipher. The reward would see our family live a comfortable life.'

'Wi've both been at sea, wi seen how bad storms can be,' Nathan said.

'And one has taken my beloved sister,' Samuel lowered his head and bit on his lips.

'Wi very sorry,' Nathan said.

'So 'ow were the fortune lost?' Will asked.

'It was stolen from him. His ship returned to Poole. He played cards and got into a game. He was winning, handsomely. The man accused him of cheating and grabbed father's coat to look for hidden cards. There were none, of course, but the watch and money which were in a pouch, dropped from the pocket. The man grabbed it and the money from the table and ran. All father's money and the cipher were gone. The theft broke him, just months later he caught a fever and died. We were as poor as ever.' Samuel's voice had begun to quiver.

'So, how is it that Rosamund has the watch and cipher?' Will asked.

'My sister met Francis Woolsey, a captain in the dragoons, when she worked in a house used as lodgings by officers. He was visiting Plymouth from Kent. They fell in love. She married him and moved away. They lived at Faversham. Amelia told Francis about the family's loss. Francis knew about a raid made by a gang from Kent on the Customs House at Poole and he guessed that the man could be from that gang. It turns out he was. That man was Thomas Slaughter who swore that he'd won the items fair and square. But it wasn't the truth.'

'Dat quite a tale, sir, and what of Francis Woolsey? Why were Ros'mund and her mama on the ship?' Nathan had been listening intently.

'Francis vowed to get the watch back and return it to us. He was still a King's man and smuggling is against the law. Thomas Slaughter was an old man, but still funding smuggling. Francis heard of a venture between him and a gang led by a Saul Bird. He plotted to catch them red-handed with their contraband and implicate the fellow. But the gang was ready for trouble. There was shooting and three of Francis's men were killed. Francis was hit in the arm. But the soldiers and the revenue men won out and the rest of the gang was arrested. Saul Bird was taken to Maidstone gaol and could hang. He will face trial and Francis has sworn witness to his deeds. This is why the men are chasing him. Francis decided to make a clean break – to move away and leave no trace of where he might be. He sold their house and put Amelia and Rosamund on a ship, the *Anne Marie*. I was to meet them off the ship in Plymouth and now the ship is at the bottom of your bay.' Tears welled in the man's eyes. He took a handkerchief from his pocket and blew his nose.

Will looked at Nathan who scratched his head. He wasn't sure what to say, he knew how people depended upon smuggling, but also knew some gangs were violent.

'Please, if you know where Rosamund is, take me to her.'

Chapter 36

Call out the dragoons!

Saturday 23rd June 1781

'Wi sorry Master Pascoe, we don't have horses. We were going to bring Ros'mund to yu in de mornin',' Nathan said.

'An' the men may still seize 'er if they find 'er,' Will said.

'But the mayor should be able to help, surely?'

Will looked at Nathan. 'Thing is, Master Pascoe, Rosamund's safe an' ... .'

'She'll be safe with me,' Samuel stamped his foot. 'Where is this place? I'll borrow a lamp from the ostler and go for her myself.'

'It's at least a 'alf-'our's walk, Master Pascoe,' Will said. 'An' ye may get lost.'

'You shall come with me.'

'We can't, there's somethin' we 'ave to do.'

'Then tell me the way. I'm going, however long it takes me.'

Will sighed. 'All right ... .'

Even with the ostler's lamp Samuel found the track difficult to follow. But soon he was on a road where there were several cottages with candlelight winking through the windows. Ahead, he saw the ground floor of a grand house lit by rushlight. It was a tall building, rising high into the darkness of the sky. To the side he saw a small stable block from where he could hear sounds.

He knocked on the stable door. 'Good evening.'

'Who's that?' a nervous-sounding voice called out.

'Pardon my interruption at this hour, but I believe my niece is here?'

'Niece, what's her name?' Benjamin Kelly asked.

'Rosamund.'

'I fear I'll disappoint you. We have no girl with that name here.'

'She was brought here for her safety.'

'No. The master's away or I'd ask him if he knew of such a girl, but the family is new here. They've met few people as yet.'

'I apologise I have made a mistake,' Samuel said. He walked away, his head bowed. Surely there were no other such houses in this village. He couldn't have come to the wrong place. The lamp's light was dimming. He could see no alehouse or shelter. He would have to make his way back to town.

'Now, Perinne,' Sir Charles said. He was sitting on a chair by the empty fireplace. 'I want you to tell me everything you know about the girl found in the Priory. She is missing and her uncle, who has arrived to take her home, is most upset. The mayor thinks you're involved in her disappearance.'

Perinne was in her bare feet. The warmth of the daytime had seeped away and the room was chilly. She looked up at her maman who nodded.

'She is not lost and she is safe. Will and Nathan have gone to tell her uncle so that he does not worry.'

'And you had something to do with this?'

Perinne took a deep breath. She wasn't sure how much to say. They were going to tell Danny's father, but not until they knew when Danny's teacher could be caught. James Clarke was standing at the back of the room by the large desk. There was another man sitting opposite Sir Charles. She recognised him. It was Sir George Cook, who had helped Will last year.

'Well, Perinne,' Jane Menniere said, giving her daughter a stern look.

'There are some men in Christchurch. They are chasing Rosamund's father. The overseers were sending her back to Kent, but she did not want to go. One of the men came to the Poor House. He said Rosamund's father had sent him. We knew this could not be true, so I put her on my pony and told her to ride away. I told her where she should go to hide, then I left a different way.'

'So, where is the girl?'

'She is at Burton Hall. Patience is looking after her.'

'Why did you take her there?' Jane asked. 'Why not here?'

Perinne hesitated.

'Why not, Perinne, we would have helped the child?' Sir Charles said.

'Malvina is a thief. She visited the Poor House and stole something belonging to Rosamund. I said that if she did not look after Rosamund I would tell Uncle Charles about this and that she had stolen Aunt Elizabeth's brooch.'

'Is this true?' Sir Charles said.

'Yes, it was not Lucy. And Mary from Burton Hall is in the Poor House because of Malvina's lies.'

'But you could have told us this, Perinne.'

'I tried to tell you she was a thief, maman. No one would listen to me. Also I was afraid that Aunt Elizabeth would be cross with me for being with boys and Poor House children.'

Jane coughed.

'Hmm ... and Will has gone to let her uncle know her whereabouts?' Sir Charles asked.

'Yes.'

'We must send a note back to the mayor, Clarke. Tell him what Miss Perinne has just told us. It's a simple matter of reuniting this family. It's a miracle the child survived the sinking, but to have a fear of being taken by strangers.'

'Yes, what about these men, Charles,' Sir George said. 'Could they be a danger still?'

'What did the girl say about the men, Perinne?'

'Rosamund told me her father was a dragoon captain and that the men were smugglers and had shot him, hurting his arm. They had killed three of his soldiers. One of them had been caught and was in gaol. They want to make Rosamund's father say he had made a mistake and that the wrong man was in gaol, I think.'

'Smugglers again, Perinne. Did you not learn from last year to avoid them?' Sir George put in.

'Yes, this is why I got Rosamund away. And they have ... .' There was a sudden rap on the door.

'Yes?'

Joseph came in. 'I'm sorry, sir, but Master Clarke's son is here with a young friend. He says he needs to speak with his father as a matter of urgency.'

Sir Charles waved his hand at James Clarke who followed Joseph out of the room. In the kitchen Danny was sitting at a long table next to a fair-haired boy James hadn't seen before. Susan had given them each a drink.

'What are you doing here? And who's this?' James said.

Danny leapt up. 'Father, Will is in danger. Some smugglers from Kent are going to the beach to help Mr Walton and Will doesn't know, he thinks it's just a few and he's got the other smugglers from Christchurch and ... .'

'Stop! What smugglers? Mr Walton? What have you been up to?'

Danny's face reddened.

'Tell him Danny, remember what Will and Perinne said,' Josh urged.

'Perinne's involved? James ran his fingers through his hair. 'You'd better come with me. Sir Charles needs to hear this also.'

'And who are you and where do you live?' Sir Charles said, inspecting Josh. The three children were standing in a row in front of him.

'He's called...' Danny started.

'I was asking the boy.'

Josh was trembling. He'd never been in such a grand house before and there were two men in front of him in smart clothes, they must be important. 'I'm Josh Blackbourne, sir. I live at Conyer.'

'That's north Kent, is it not?' Sir George said.

'Yes, sir,' Josh's voice quivered.

'So how is it you're here in Christchurch?' Sir Charles asked.

Josh told the story of how he ended up on the cart with Levi and Pip and that he'd been left with the shepherd at Sopley.

I jist wanted to help find the treasure. I met Danny at Sopley an' asked him 'bout it.'

'Treasure?' Sir Charles said.

'Ah! first gold and now treasure. I suppose that's another fancy,' Sir George said.

'Well, there is a story about treasure in the Priory.'

'It's different treasure,' Danny said. 'But it's Will we're worried about, he's in danger.'

'And how is that?' Perinne said.

'There's been another gang bringing in tobacco and Will is helping some men catch them tonight,' Danny said.

'Young Will, involved in smuggling?' Sir George said.

'It's because ... .' Danny realised it was time to say what had happened. His legs started to shake. He closed his eyes.

'Tell them, Danny,' Josh urged.

James moved to his son and took hold of his shoulders. He knelt. 'Come on, Danny, what's happened?'

'When I found the girl in the Priory, I got into trouble with Mr Walton for not leaving after choir with the others. He said I could do a job for him instead of being whipped. I said yes. He made me sail to the Head. There were lamps and bales of tobacco hidden. We put them in the boat and took them to the Priory. We hid them high up near the roof. He wanted me to do more, but grandpa died.'

'Yes, Walton was at the funeral,' James said, anger rising.

'He yelled at me. He said if I told anyone the hangman would have me for smuggling, or if not, he would kill me.'

'Why didn't you say something, is that why you didn't come home after the funeral?'

Danny sniffed and nodded. Perinne took hold of his hand.

'And how is he connected with the Kent people?' Sir Charles asked.

'The men are here because o' Rosamund,' Josh said. 'They're Roger Law, Levi Bird an' another man, Pip. They say her father'll come for her an' they want to torture him an' take him back to Maidstone gaol and free Levi's brother.'

'Roger Law? Isn't that the messenger who came after the sinking?'

'Don't forget to tell uncle about Meekwick Ginn, Josh,' Perinne said.

'How's he involved in all this?' Sir Charles asked.

'We stopped at his cottage on the way,' Josh said. 'I overheard him tell Levi an' Pip that he was helpin' someone in Burton to start venturin'. I've heard father

276

mention venturers. They buy the boats an' have the money to buy the goods, don't they?'

Sir Charles shifted in his seat. 'The only place that's been sold in Burton recently is the Hall.'

'We know where they're landing the tobacco tonight,' Danny said. 'The Head, then on to the marsh.'

'Tell Scott to saddle our horses and he can get the cart out and take the boys home, Clarke.' Sir Charles stormed to the hall. 'Perinne, go to your room. You should have come to us earlier. I fear it's too late to get anyone to the Head, though it's possible to have someone on the marsh and capture this load. We'll rouse the revenue officer and see if there are any dragoons about.'

Chapter 37

Caught red-handed

Saturday 23rd June 1781

'But Uncle Charles, if Malvina and Patience's father is part of the new smuggling gang, Rosamund is still in danger!' Perinne held out her arms, pleading.

'She's right, Charles,' Jane said.

'Oh, so much going on. Clarke!' Sir Charles dashed out of the hall, through the back of the house and into the courtyard. Perinne and her mother ran after him, followed by Danny and Josh. A wind had begun to pick up and the rush lamps were giving off sparks. Dogs were barking. 'Clarke!'

John Scott appeared from the stable leading a horse towards the cart. 'Mr Clarke's bringin' the other horses out, sir.'

'Get the coach, Scott.'

James Clarke appeared, two horses saddled for riders. 'Sir?'

'I think we should get the girl from Burton Hall. Scott can take the coach. He can leave Daniel and the other boy at your home and continue on, Jane will go with you. We must get to town!'

Perinne appeared at his side, rubbing her shoulders against the cold. 'But Mrs Stone does not know about Rosamund. I should go with them.'

'You can't go, look, you're ready for bed,' Sir Charles shouted.

'We'll get cloaks,' Jane said.

'Still no sign of him,' Isaac said.

Guy Cox shrugged. 'Perhaps it's not tonight.'

'Nah, some's coming in by the Island,' Adam sucked on his pipe, the smoke drifting into the night air. 'It could be they think Walton's with us. Word's out that Christchurch is just one gang.'

'Maybe he's gone from the Avon,' Isaac suggested.

'Hmm, it's possible. All right, let's go. You still with us, Will?'

'Aye.'

'All right, men, keep alert. Watch for the slightest spark.'

The first cloud to cover Christchurch since the storm of twelve days ago darkened the night. The three men, followed by Will and Nathan, ran from under the dense cover of chestnut trees clustered on the quomp and climbed into a long, open boat. Adam pushed out the boat and jumped on board. Isaac sat at the tiller. He'd been sailing the harbour for over five decades and knew it well. The water would be above the causeway and they'd be at the sandbank in less than half an hour. In the boat were shovels, a lamp – unlit, ropes and a pile covered by a black oilskin. Nathan nudged Will and nodded towards Adam whose coat had opened. The hilts of two pistols were poking from his belt.

'Where did Danny say they landed?' Isaac asked Will.

'Just by the point, where ye c'n see across.'

'We'll take her to the east of that an' crawl.'

'But there be no shelter,' Adam objected.

'The dunes'll cover us. It's too late to dig in.'

'Look,' Nathan pointed. 'Walton's boat.'

The hooves of Sir Charles Tarrant's stallion crunched into the gravel as he rode away, followed by James Clarke.

'Come on,' Jane Menniere said, 'let's get on our way.'

Scott drew up the steps, closed the door and climbed into the driver's seat.

'Will the shepherd have missed you, Josh,' Jane asked as she sat next to him.

Josh shrugged. 'He's been away since this morning, says he's in the eastern fields and will stay there.'

'We need to keep you away from these men. Would you stay with Danny tonight? If I speak with your mother, Danny, would she mind?'

Josh was looking out of the coach. He'd only ever been on a cart before and the cushioned seats were comfortable. He felt sleepy after his long day.

'Josh?' Jane touched his arm.

'Sorry, mistress. Yis, if it's all right with Danny.' He watched through the window just as a cart went by. 'The shepherd! It was the shepherd on that cart!' he shouted.

'That confirms it,' Jane said. 'Let's get you boys home. Perinne and I must fetch the girl as soon as we can.'

'Open up! Open up!' Sir Charles banged hard on the door of the Chief Riding Officer's cottage.

A candle light flickered in the window and a face appeared. 'Come on, Stevens, answer the door.'

'Sir Charles, what is it?' A red-faced man appeared. He wore a powdered wig and a woollen coat.

'There's a landing tonight, there could be trouble. Come on, we need help!'

'Where?' Joshua Stevens asked stepping into the street.

'They're landing on the Head and in through the marsh.'

'We'll never get men to the Head in time, it'll have to be the marsh.'

'Can we raise the dragoons from their billets?'

'Yes, we'll round them up.'

'We'll watch the marsh. Come on James, let's make a start.' Sir Charles looked across towards the river and harbour. 'It's very dark, we'll be lucky to spot them.'

'It is kind of you to take care of Josh,' Jane Menniere said to Hannah Clarke as she returned to the coach. 'We'll arrange for him to be taken home to Kent as soon as possible.'

'Thanks,' Josh called, as the horses took off.

'Are you boys coming inside?' Hannah said. 'It looks as though we might get some rain. It will be welcome, the plants need it.'

'Can we stay out for a while?'

'It's dark and it's late. Come on in. Why didn't you tell me you were going to Cliff House, Danny?'

'Sorry, mother.' Josh was standing with his head bowed and his shoulders slumped. 'What is it, Josh? Aren't you pleased you're safe from those men?'

'I'll not get a chance to look for the treasure,' Josh said.

281

He looked at his friend. 'Are you all right?'

'No. I'm worried about Will. Perinne's mother said they were getting the dragoons out. And what if they don't catch Walton? He'll know it was me who told and come after me.'

'There's no one about,' Jane said, looking up at Burton Hall. It was in darkness.

'Patience and Malvina must be here.' Perinne pulled her cloak tightly around her shoulders.

'They have a butler, Kelly wasn't it?'

Perinne nodded. 'He could be helping Mr Walton.'

Jane rapped with the door knocker, its sound echoing in the hall behind it.

'There has to be someone here. Knock again, maman.'

Jane brought the metal down as hard as she could.

'Someone is coming down the stairs,' Perinne said, her nose pressed hard against the glass of the window beside the door. 'I can see a candle.'

'Who's there?'

'It's Jane Menniere, please, open the door.'

A key turned and Isobel Stone's hard face, yellowed by the candlelight, glared at Jane. Her eyes widened when she saw Perinne.

'What do you want? Have you seen the hour?'

'Yes, Mrs Stone. But there's a girl here and we need to take her to Cliff House.'

'A girl? Here?'

'Yes, Patience has been looking after her,' Perinne said. 'She helped us, the girl was in danger.'

'Nonsense. I would have known about this.'

'She is upstairs in Mary Maunder's room. I saw her just

282

this morning.' Perinne pointed up the wide staircase.

'It is true, mother.' Patience appeared. 'I helped Perinne.'

'Why did you not tell me about this?'

Patience held her head down.

'Well, girl?'

'Could we come inside, please, Mrs Stone, it's cold standing here,' Jane said,

'Fetch the girl, Patience, now.' Isabel snapped.

Patience ran up the stairs.

'How long has she been here?'

'We brought her here only yesterday, Mrs Stone,' Perinne said. 'Some bad men were trying to take her away.'

'What did you bring her here for?'

'Because we needed somewhere safe, where no one would think of looking.'

'And how did you get my daughters to agree to this?'

Perinne looked up at her mother.

'Well, shall I have an answer?'

'Mrs Stone, I'm sorry,' Jane said, 'but it appears that it is Malvina who took Lady Elizabeth's brooch. Perinne told her she would tell her uncle if she didn't help.'

'How dare you.'

'But it is true,' Perinne stepped forward. 'Malvina took Rosamund's pouch, and when I visited you last week, she took some of the fossils I brought to show you.'

'Mother.' Patience had returned and was holding Rosamund's hand.

'Is this the place?' Stephen asked Benjamin Kelly.

'It's where Walton told me to wait. Keep to the track, he said, it's a marsh. We don't want to get stuck.'

'Can't see a thing, dare we light a lamp?'

'Later, Walton's going to signal from the boat as he nears. We just need to sit and wait.'

'Dere, under de cliff,' Nathan whispered.

''e's not alone. Who's that with 'im?' Will craned his neck to try to see through the gloomy damp.

'We need to get closer,' Adam Litty said.

Guy crawled next to him. 'But there's nothing to hide behind, it's flat beach from here.'

'Dere's three altogether, look.'

Adam rolled onto his back. 'We're lost, Guy, two boys, a useless old man and just you and me against how many? Any sign of a ship?'

'One of 'em's lighting a spout lamp,' Isaac said. 'And I'm not useless.'

'Look, there be a boat comin',' Will pointed. 'It's not much bigger than yours, Adam.'

'All right,' said Adam. 'This is what we do.'

'It's best to watch the harbour from the marsh if not the Head, Stevens.' Captain Palmer was riding a tall chestnut horse. The gold of his uniform dimmed in the dark of the evening. Spots of rain were falling.

'Send some men to watch the quay for landings there in case our informers are wrong, but we'll go to the marsh, Sir Charles has gone on ahead. Come on!'

Two soldiers headed towards the town. Captain Palmer and the remainder, along with the revenue officer, set off at a gallop towards Purewell. Walkers, huddled against the cold, wet breeze pulled into doorways to escape the drum of hooves thundering down the street. The riders soon caught sight of the Ship in Distress where Sir Charles and James were waiting. Rush lights glowed at its entrance and the hum of people grew louder as they neared. Slowing, they turned onto the field that led to the marsh.

'There's only two o' 'em in the boat,' Isaac raising his voice above the sound of rain drumming on the sands. 'That's five against five. Let's take 'em.'

Crack! Adam's pistol split the night apart. Waves were crashing onto the shore. Adam and Isaac ran along the water's edge where the sand was hardest and made for the boat. Will and Nathan sped to the cliff, the rain lashing into their faces.

Guy stepped back, pistol aimed towards the harbour.

'Stop, or we'll shoot,' Adam shouted.

One of the men was standing in the water, whilst the other passed bales from the boat. His head and face were covered by a large hat. He spotted them and reached towards his belt.

Crack! Guy's pistol blasted as the face of Roger Law appeared. Law fled back towards the harbour, shouting.

'They're runnin'!' Will yelled. 'After 'em!' They dashed over the damp dunes in time to see Walton, Roger Law and Pip jump into their boat and push off into the harbour.

'They're gettin' away,' Will cried. 'Come on, Adam!'

Adam kept the gun pointing at the man in the hat. 'Keep the rest. And don't try to land anything here again,' he shouted against the sound of the pounding waves.

'We been landin' here years,' the man shouted.

Isaac stepped forward. 'Well I'll be, it's George Carter.'

'Put the pistol away,' the man replied. 'That's Isaac Hooper. We're not enemies.'

'What's 'appenin'?' Will appeared. 'They're gettin' away. What be it Isaac?'

'This man's a friend, we've worked together many a time.'

'We thought Walton was with your gang, Isaac. Aren't you all working together these days?'

'Walton's on his own. Those men are from Kent.' Adam tucked his pistol away. 'Not sure how he got in with them.'

'We only started last week. The night of the storm was the first drop.'

'Ye were 'ere that night?' Will pushed in front of Isaac.

'Yes, lad, why?'

'What did Walton do to signal?'

'Why, the fool lit the cliffs like a manor house.'

'An' did ye see the *Anne Marie* go down?'

'We did. The sea was mad. It were all we could do to save ourselves.'

'You could help no one?'

'That's the thing, a miracle it was. We pulled out six men. They caught the side o' the boat'

'What 'appened to 'em?'

'Spent a day recovering, then they made their way to Portsmouth.'

'Just six?' Will sighed.

'There was another.'

'Oh?'

'Lucky the moon poked through, it were near full an' we just spotted someone. A woman. We pulled her out of the water and took her back to the Island. She's been in a fever these past two weeks. Didn't think she'd survive. All she's said is, 'my Rosa, my Rosa' and 'don't tell anyone I'm here'. She's been ill since.'

'It's got to be Rosamund's mother!' Will said.

'You know her?'

'A girl was also saved that night. Rosamund.'

'Is the woman well enough to be moved?' Adam asked.

'M'ybe.'

'Bring her t'the quay at Christchurch tomorrow. She'll see her Rosa again.'

'Seize them!' Captain Palmer ordered the soldiers who were chasing Kelly and the shepherd.

'Keep a watch on the water, they'll have to land along here,' Joshua Stevens kept his voice as low as he could. 'Come on, men.'

'There's a boat coming,' James Clarke pointed.

'Get to ground! Muskets ready! As they land, grab them!'

Chapter 38

Fathers learn the truth

Sunday 24th June 1781

Rowland and Peter found the road that would take them on to the New Forest. They'd never been there before, but the old man at the inn had told them the best way to go, especially when they explained the reason for their journey.

'Looks an easy route, Peter, hopefully be there quickly.'

'Yis. We'll have to decide what we're goin' to do.'

'Oh, that's an easy one. We go straight to the constable, if there be one.'

'Isn't that a risk, Rowland? What if Levi an' Pip have the help o' others?'

'We're talking about Josh, Peter, my boy's in danger.'

Francis Woolsey could see the square grey tower of a church on the horizon, so he wasn't far from the town. He'd heard of Christchurch, but had never been there.

Now he was here, a darkness clouded his thoughts. If all hands had been lost on the *Anne Marie*, so had his wife and daughter. But he had to go. He had to be sure. And, maybe their bodies were found and he could visit their graves.

He'd seen death before, cruel death, but this cut his heart in two. It had been made even worse, because they were to begin a new life. He'd served the king well enough, including nearly losing his life, but it was only the use of his arm that he'd lost. He'd decided it was time to restore the family's fortunes, build back what had been stolen from his wife's father more that three decades ago. And it all lay at the bottom of the sea. He hung his head. Maybe he shouldn't go. But he had to say his goodbyes.

Once in town he'd find the mayor, or someone who could tell him what had happened. He noticed a wide river valley to his right. The land was flat and golden brown with a shimmering heat haze hovering above the ground. He came to a bend in the road. The wider way went left, but the narrow track looked the more direct route and he wondered what to do. Maybe the track ended, or joined the other. He decided to continue on the main road. There were more dwellings here, it was perhaps a village. There were some men putting a new thatch on a cottage.

'Good day,' Francis said. 'What is this place?'

'It's Burton, sir.'

'Is this the correct road for Christchurch?'

'Aye,' another man said. 'Ye could've gone straight down, but continue on, you reach Purewell. Go right and the road goes into town.'

'Thank you.'

Before long he reached a crossroad. 'This must be where I turn,' he thought. To his left two horses were approaching. They were good horses. He could ask again. He stopped, hoping to call them over when a sharp shock ran through his body.

''Tis Francis Woolsey!' the older of the two men shouted. The other pulled up his horse. He was a strong-looking man.

Francis recognised the accent, they were Kentish, but he hadn't seen them before. One of the men reached for his pistol.

'Stop!' Francis cried. 'I am defenceless!' He pushed his limp arm with his good hand showing he was holding only the reins of his horse. 'Who are you, why would you wish me harm?'

'Put the pistol away, Peter, we're not here for Woolsey,' Rowland Blackbourne yelled.

'Take pity on me, sirs, for I have lost my wife and child in the waters here.'

'An' I've lost my son,' Rowland said. 'An' I fear fer his life also. But yew are known to us as a man who happily condemns others to death an' takes the rewards.'

'How's that?'

'Saul Bird. He's facin the gallows an' it's yew who'll be sending him there,' Peter said.

'Saul Bird? But he and his gang killed three of my men in cold blood. They'd fallen from their horses and could not defend themselves, but those men killed them anyway.'

Rowland and Peter exchanged looks, eyes opened wide.

'I could've been dead also, but I got away. One shot caught my arm, it's useless.' He looked down at the lifeless limb.

'This is not the story we were told,' Peter said, his face cross.

'It is the truth. They're a bad lot, this generation and the last.'

'His brother's out fer revenge,' Rowland said.

'Yes, I know this. But I have only one arm, I'm of no use to the king. I want no more of fighting.'

'Well yew'd best be aware,' Rowland said. 'Levi Bird

be here an' he's waitin' for yew.'

'Why would he think I'd come here?'

Peter and Rowland looked at each other. 'Yew don't know, do yew?' Rowland said.

Francis shook his head.

'Yewer daughter, she survived the wreckin' of the *Anne Marie*,' Peter said. 'She's here, kept in the Poor House, or so we're told.'

Francis's mouth opened. He felt as if he were dreaming. Could this be true?

'Why do you tell me this? Are you not with Levi Bird in your hatred for me?' Francis gasped.

'He's not our kind,' Peter said. 'We're no murderers.'

'An' he has somethin' of mine,' Rowland said.

'What's that?' Francis asked.

'My son, an' I want him back, like yew want yewer girl, Francis Woolsey.'

Samuel Pascoe was standing by the door of the George. It was Sunday. He'd go to church. He didn't know what to think of this town anymore. First they find his niece and lose her again, next those boys telling him where she was for it not to be so and being kept awake by the noise of dragoons celebrating something. Last night's wasted journey to claim Rosamund had tired him, but still he hadn't slept. It was early but people were bustling about. The sun was out again, drying the roofs from last night's rain. A cart approached and pulled up outside. The ostler appeared.

'Hello, John, sunny once more, but we needed that rain.'

'Aye. Sir Charles has asked me to fetch a Master Pascoe, is he here?'

291

'I am he,' Samuel stepped forward. 'Is that the gentleman the mayor sent a message to yesterday?'

'Just been asked to fetch ye, sir.'

'Yewer the one used to catchin' smugglers, what should we do first?' Peter said.

'First we go to the Poor House to see my daughter. After that we find whoever keeps the peace around these parts. I guess there're revenue officers, if anything. A coastal town like this is bound to need them.'

'What about finding my Josh,' Rowland said.

'If Levi Bird and his cronies have your son we'll need help. I'm no use. Peter doesn't look like he can run more than a few paces.'

'Hey!' Peter shouted.

''Tis true, Peter,' Rowland said.

'Let's ask someone.' Francis led his horse to a nearby wooden bridge, the others following him. There was a boat on the water and a man was sitting fishing.

'Hello there,' Peter called down. 'Be there a constable in this town or a mayor?'

'There's a mayor, sir, and the revenue officer's cottage just over there.' The man pointed. 'Is there trouble?'

'There might be, sir,' Peter said.

'Thought they'd caught 'em all last night,' the man said, casting his line again.

Francis pulled on the reins. 'Let's go.'

'Dat was quite a night,' Nathan said, biting into a chunk of fresh bread.

'Aye. Though I need t'see Sir Charles Tarrant afore Walton's sent to Winchester. I didn't get a chance last night, though I spoke wi' Danny's father.'

'Wi going to Cliff House?'

'Aye, unless Sir Charles comes into town.'

'Wi could do with a horse each, Will, with all dis a-walkin'!'

'We'll go to the ridin' officer's place, see where the prisoners are.'

'You boys off out again?' Beth said, coming down the narrow steps from the roof space where she slept with her mother.

'Yes, Beth,' Nathan smiled.

'We've barely seen you since you came home.'

'Sorry, sister.' Will went to a drawer and took out a bone comb, ran it through his long, dark hair and tied it back.

'So, those men are caught and you 'elped. That's a good deed done, Will. And you too, Nathan.'

'Aye, but we've a bigger fight on our hands. We're goin' to London, Beth.'

'London? Can't you stay a bit longer?'

Will kissed his sister's forehead. 'M'ybe, but only fer a while. Are ye ready, Nathan? Let's get goin'.'

A cart pulled away from the George as Will and Nathan left the high street.

'That's Scott wi' Master Pascoe,' Will said. 'He'll finally get to see Rosamund.'

'Yes. Mi feel bad 'bout last night. Him must have been turned away if Ros'mund's at Cliff House.'

'Look, someone else's visitin' Mr Stevens.'

'It can't be long since im went to bed,' Nathan laughed.

'I think you're late for the fray, gentlemen,' Joshua Stevens said. 'The men you speak of are held at the back

293

here, waiting transport to Winchester.'

'Was there a boy?' Rowland asked, his face pale and fear set in his eyes.

Stevens shook his head. 'No, just the two Kentish men and the teacher. The girl were missing, haven't heard what happened there. Ah, here's young Will Gibbs, he were there last night, he'll tell ye.'

Will raised his hat. 'Can I 'elp?'

'I'm Francis Woolsey, these men are Rowland Blackbourne and Peter Graves of Kent.'

Nathan smiled. 'Yu Josh's father?'

'Yew know o' Josh?' Rowland said, leaping from his mount and staring at Nathan. Peter joined him.

'Aye, an' Rosamund, they're both safe,' Will said.

'Well, where are they?' Francis asked.

'Rosamund is at Cliff House. We've just seen Master Pascoe leaving the George wi' the Tarrant's coachman. He must be on his way to fetch 'er.'

'Sam's here?'

'Aye.'

'Where's Josh?'

'He's stayin' at our friend, Danny's 'ouse.'

Francis, Rowland and Peter whooped with joy.

'Where is this place, I want to go to my son,' Rowland said.

'Not far, but Danny'll be comin' into town. It's Sunday and he's in the choir. Josh may be with him.'

'And Cliff House? Where's that?' Francis asked.

'About two, three miles along this road, but there's ... .'

Francis Woolsey pulled on his reins and, before Will could speak further, he rode off at speed.

'There's what? What were you about to say?'

'I'm goin' to Cliff House.' His eyes met Rowland's. 'C'n I borrow your 'orse? Tell 'em, Nathan.' Will leapt on the stallion and galloped away.

'Dere were three men from Kent, each wantin' to capture

Francis Woolsey,' Nathan said. 'Two are 'ere with yu, Massa Stevens, but de third is still free and still a danger. Wi don't know where im is.'

'Who's that? Peter Graves asked.

'Im called Levi Bird.'

'Where will we go? Back to France?' Perinne asked.

'I'm not certain, Perinne. Papa has got work here in England, but it's difficult for him in both countries. It will be England, but where I'm not sure.' Jane fastened the final clip into Perinne's hair.

'Will we have a maid?'

Jane laughed. 'I expect so.'

'Please maman, can it be Lucy?'

'I'm not sure.'

'Please, maman, Lucy is not a thief, it was Malvina who stole Aunt Elizabeth's brooch.'

'Yes, that's true.'

'And Mary Maunder could work for Aunt Elizabeth, she would get away from the Poor House. But ... .'

'What?'

'I should miss Christchurch.'

'Mistress.' It was the mouse-like maid. Her name was Clara.

'You should knock on the door first.'

'Sorry, mistress. The gentleman's here for Miss Rosamund.'

'And did Perinne's old dress fit her?'

'Yes, mistress.'

'Come on, maman, let us go and see him.'

Francis Woolsey slid from his horse. His face ran with sweat and his hair straggled from the ribbon that tied it back. 'I'm Rosamund's father, please, take me to her.'

'Why, of course, Master Woolsey. She's with her uncle, he arrived not fifteen minutes since. She was all ready to go to church with Miss Perinne.'

'Will, are you coming in too?'

'I wish to speak with Sir Charles, Joseph.'

'Please come, both of you. Wait in the library, Will.'

Rosamund was kneeling on the rug next to her Uncle Sam in the drawing room. She suited the pretty yellow dress that had once been Perinne's. Bright sunlight shone through the windows onto the walls. She kept looking at him. He really did look like the man on the cipher. Father was right, she would have known him from the face. Sir Charles was sitting in a chair beside Aunt Elizabeth. Sir George Cook was there, standing by the fireplace.

Perinne was next to her maman, smiling. 'So we can all go to the church this morning and afterwards Uncle Charles will try to find your father, will you not, uncle?'

'Yes, of course. You'll go on to Devon, Master Pascoe?'

'Yes, I'll take Rosamund home, I'm sure we'll see Francis soon.'

'Sooner than you think.' A voice came from the opened door.

'Father!' Rosamund leapt to her feet. Everyone's gaze fell on the handsome man with the copper-coloured hair.

Francis knelt and folded his arm around Rosamund, kissing her face, tears of joy wetting their cheeks.

Joseph crossed the room to Sir Charles and whispered to him. Sir Charles stood.

'If you would excuse me.'

'What is it? Why are you here?'

'I'm sorry, Sir Charles, but it's important.' Will stood firm.

'Well? Surely Clarke told you what had happened when he spoke last night?'

'Yes, sir, but I didn't get a chance to tell 'im somethin', an' the information could send Thomas Walton to Tyburn.'

'So, tell me.'

'When Danny told us 'bout what Walton'd made 'im do, 'e mentioned there were lots o' lamps. Last night, when we spoke wi' the Islanders we found out the first landin' was the night of the storm.'

'Go on.'

'I asked what lights Walton'd used to call 'em to shore. They called Walton a fool, saying 'e used many.'

'Are you saying what I think you are, Will?'

'When ye're out at sea, lights on the shore tell ye things. Lots of lamps'd look like buildin's. I think the captain o' the *Anne Marie* thought 'e were near a 'arbour, Poole maybe - 'e were too close an' struck the rocks. It's Walton's fault the ship went down. Walton's not only a smuggler, but 'e's to blame for the deaths o' all who drowned that night.'

Chapter 39

The Face of Sam

Sunday 24th June 1781

'Walton's more a fool than we first thought. I remember. The sailor who was found said they thought they were near the shore. I'll see to it that he pays for what he's done, Will.' Sir Charles Tarrant was dressed ready for church in black breeches and a crisp, white shirt, though he'd yet to put on his jacket. The window of the library was open and a gentle breeze ruffled the long curtains.

'Thank ye, sir. I were angry at 'ow 'e'd treated Danny.'

'You've done well for yourself, boy. It was a hard thing that you did to leave everything behind and risk the troubles in America.'

Will shifted on his feet. Was Sir Charles about to apologise for the way his son Edmund had bullied him last year?

'I've given some thought to what you had to say to me last week, about the trade in African slaves. At first I was thinking it was a foolish notion, but I've discussed it with Sir George and he's in agreement with you. There are groups of people, in America and here in England. He'll put you in contact with them, though they're in London.'

'That's all right, sir. Nathan an' me, we're goin' there to gain suport.'

'Indeed, you said that much.'

'But we need more to join us, people with power.'

'Hmm, I'll speak with our Member of Parliament and ask him what you need to do. Sir George will be your contact in London, I'm sure. I must get back to the others.' He made his way to the door.

'Sir, one more thing, I want to speak wi' Rosamund's family.'

'Why?'

'I've some more good news for 'em.'

Sir Charles raised an eyebrow.

'Somethin' else we were told on the beach last night.'

'Thanks for lendin' me some clean clothes,' Josh said.

'Sunday best!' Danny laughed.

'Yewer all right now that Walton's bin caught,' Josh said.

'And you're going to be taken home.'

'Yis, but wi'out the treasure,' he smiled weakly and hunched his shoulders.

'Can you write?'

'A bit.'

'Then we'll keep in touch.'

Just as they turned into Purewell, Nathan approached, walking in front of two men, one on horseback.

'Josh!'

'Father! Mr Graves!'

'She's alive? Alive!' Rosamund, Samuel and Francis fell
into an embrace, relief and happiness lighting up their
faces.

'How did you find out, Will?' Perinne asked.

'On the beach. There were men from the Island, they
picked 'er up from the sea, took 'er 'ome an' 'ave cared fer
'er. They're bringin' 'er over to the quay today.

Francis looked up. 'Oh, Sir Charles, I can't thank you
enough.'

'It's Will and Perinne you have to thank, and Daniel,
the son of James Clarke who works for me, but isn't here
today. They're the ones you should thank.'

'When shall we see mother?' Rosamund asked.

'I'll watch the quay. If you go into town, I'll come fer
ye. They didn't give a time.'

'Come to church with us. Will can find you there.'

High above the nave of the Priory Church, Levi Bird
watched as people came in for the Sunday morning
service. 'There be the Poor House Master an' his wife. No
sign of Adam Litty or Guy Cox, keepin' their heads down
I suspect. Oh, what be this? It's Peter Graves an' Rowland
Blackbourne, what they be doin' here. They're with the
black boy. Josh Blackbourne's with them too, why isn't
he at Sopley? How did they find him? Hmph, here come
the squire an' his family. That French girl too. An' there's
Pascoe. He's with the girl an'...who's this? Well, well, if it

300

isn't Francis Woolsey,' he muttered to himself. He felt for his pistols.

Danny scanned the congregation. Josh and Rosamund both had wide smiles. Rosamund was sitting between her father and her Uncle Sam. Josh was with his father and the other man. Perinne and her mother were behind Sir Charles and Lady Tarrant, who were in their stall with Sir George Cook. Danny hadn't seen him since last year when he'd last had an adventure with Will and Perinne. This time had been different, this time he'd feared for his very life. His mother and father were with Jack and Sarah. Grandpa hadn't been able to go to church for some time. He still couldn't believe he'd gone for ever. He felt foolish for not having told his family about Mr Walton. There was no sign yet of Will. Maybe he wouldn't come. Nathan was there though, Adam Jackson, too. He hadn't seen him since last year.

Danny looked up at the arches of the church. He spotted the Saxon face. He smiled. It did look a lot like Rosamund's Uncle Sam. The choirmaster tapped a stick. As Danny started to sing, he thought he caught sight of something else, a shadow moving high in the space above the arches, near to where he'd been with Walton. He shuddered. It'd be a bird, or maybe one of Josh's flittermice. He smiled and began to sing.

The service was over, but there was no sign of Will. Danny walked down the aisle to Perinne, she was standing with her maman speaking with Rosamund. Rosamund glanced round as he approached.

'Father, this is the boy who found me.'

'I have to thank you. What is your name?'

'I'm Danny, sir.'

'We're most grateful that you found Rosamund and took her to safety.'

'She was sitting just over there,' Danny pointed to the spot where he'd first seen Rosamund.

Rosamund followed their gaze. Suddenly, as if all the sadness of the past two weeks that had clouded her mind had floated away, she remembered something.

'And father, we've found Uncle Sam's face, the one on the cipher, look!' Rosamund pointed to the face of Sam.

'Well, so it is!'

'Well, bless my soul,' Samuel said. He laughed out loud. 'He does look like me, doesn't he!'

'Can we help you to find the treasure Mr Woolsey?' Danny asked.

'Oh, yes, please, could we?' Perinne joined in. 'But what about Will and Nathan. They would like to help I am sure.'

Danny looked around, Nathan had left. 'I'll ask my brother, Jack. He's over there with mother and father. He can go to the quay and wait for the boat and ask Will and Nathan to come and help.'

Francis smiled. 'Why not, whilst we wait for the boat to arrive.' He took the pouch from his jacket and handed it to Rosamund, who opened it.

Perinne watched as Rosamund unfolded the paper, but Danny was looking at the back of the church.

'I think there's someone else who'd like to help,' he said.

Rosamund held up the cipher and the others crowded around. Will and Nathan were approaching.

'The trail must begin here with Sam's face.' Rosamund looked up at the carving on the tall Norman arch.

'The next clue 'tis strange,' Josh said, eager to play his part. ''Tis like two letter 'm's pushed t'gether.'

'Look, over there, on the wall.' Danny pointed to a set of decorative arches directly ahead.

Nathan went into the aisle. 'Dey're all along here, which one will it be?'

The others joined him and all six were standing in the south aisle. It was bright, but smelled dusty. Perinne sneezed.

'That mark underneath, it's like an arrow, p'haps it means we go this way.' Will pointed down the long walkway.

'Shall we try that? What is next Rosamund?' Perinne asked.

'It looks like two dragons.'

'Let me see,' Danny leaned across and peered at the paper. 'They're faint, but yes they're dragons. He closed his eyes. 'I've seen these. Follow me.' He ran down to the broad transept and stopped at the foot of a wide column. On the corner of the base of each was a carved dragon. Pride beamed across his face.

'That's it, Danny,' Will said. 'But we've lots more to work out. There's another arrow, I think we carry on down 'ere.'

'What comes after de arrow Ros'mund?'

'I'm not sure what it is.'

'They're Roman,' Danny said. 'VIII means eight.'

'Could dey be steps?' Nathan held his head to one side and then the other, trying to work out the shape underneath the numbers.

Josh had gone on ahead. 'There be some steps here,' he shouted disappearing out of sight. 'Eight!'

They were all standing in the quire. Nathan was looking at the carvings on the seats. 'Could de clues be in dese, Danny?'

'There is a cross after the steps,' Perinne said. 'Maybe that means we should not come this way.'

'But why put it there?' Danny asked. 'Let me look at the next bit, Rosamund.' Rosamund handed Danny the paper. His smile was even wider. 'I know this too! Come on!' He sped back down the steps, quickly followed by the others.

He looked at the floor.

'See. This tombstone has all these, a skull, crossbones and these arrows.'

''Tis a place where a pirate might hide his treasure,' Josh said, excitement in his voice. 'Twill be hard to lift.'

'It c'n't be 'ere, there be more clues. An' maybe we follow those arrows. What's that church drawin'?'

'It's over the door of that chantry.' Danny pointed. 'It's what the Priory looked like a long time ago. The man who saved the Priory from King Henry is buried here, Josh.'

'Maybe he has the treasure after all,' Josh beamed.

'No, we go left next,' Danny said. 'I think that's supposed to be the beam that sticks out of the wall.' He handed back the cipher to Rosamund.

They went left and ahead was the Lady Chapel. Danny pointed up to a large wooden beam jutting from a space high above them.

'That was supposed to be put there by Jesus himself.'

Nathan scratched his head.

'Make a wish, Nathan.'

Nathan closed his eyes and smiled. Danny glanced into the chapel. It was only days since he'd brought the tobacco bales in through the small door on the right, but that was all over. He was brought from his thoughts by Rosamund's voice.

'Turn left again, look for Roman seven and a face.'

Danny stopped by a small wooden door. 'It goes up to the school. There's another to the outside as well as the stairs.' He tried the door, but it was locked.

'Have you seen anything like the faces around here?' Perinne called to the boys who'd straggled behind in case they could see the schoolroom.

'Let me see.' He shook his head. 'No. Let's look around.'

Rosamund was standing on tiptoes trying to see into one of the chantries. Danny joined her. 'What are these, Danny?'

'They're little chapels, but no one uses them anymore.'

'Look!' Josh called out. Danny and Rosamund stepped back to see what he'd found.

'Yewer hidin' them! Are there seven?'

Along the wall of the chantry was a row of carved faces. 'Seven!' Josh beamed.

'Nearly there,' Will said, looking over Rosamund's shoulder. 'One arrow, a picture an' some words.'

'There is another chantry, maybe that is it.'

'What de next picture? What wi lookin' for?'

'I can't tell. It looks like an angel, but it's got feathers.'

'This is easy, there they are,' Danny looked up at yet more beautiful carvings. 'What does the cipher say next?'

Rosamund looked at the words. They were faded and difficult to read.

'I think it says, *See not the priest, nor he spy thee.*'

'What does it mean? Perinne asked, a puzzled look on her face.

The group peered at the chantry. This was where the clues on the cipher ended, but was it where the treasure was hidden?

Chapter 40

Treasure!

Sunday 24th June 1781

'Any luck?' Francis Woolsey appeared with Rowland and Peter followed by Jane Menniere and Danny's mother.

'We have not found it.' Perinne shrugged.

'We can't work out what this last part means,' Rosamund said, handing the cipher to her father.

'We could ask Adam if he knows,' Danny suggested.

Everyone nodded in agreement and Danny disappeared into the church.

The grown-ups left the children to their task. They continued looking in nooks and crannies. Nathan and Will went down into a nearby crypt, but came back shaking their heads. Danny returned.

'Where is Adam?' Perinne asked.

'He can't come, but he said that a long time ago priests in the chantries could look out, or others could look in through squint holes.'

'What are those?' Rosamund asked.

Danny looked around the sides of the chantry with the angel-like carvings and pointed out a small hole on the corner of the left-hand side. 'He says there are lots of squint holes in the Priory, it's where the monks used to look through to check things out.' He peered into the small room.

'Come an' see this,' Will said.

At the opposite end, around the edge, was a small wooden board. It had an angel painted on the front. The paint was fading.

'Looks like there were a 'ole 'ere too. The picture's wedged inside.' He tried to pull out the board, but it wouldn't budge.

'What is on the other side?' Perinne asked.

Danny pushed open the chantry door and went inside. 'It's another piece of wood.'

'Will it come out?' Rosamund asked.

'It looks stuck.'

'Den try to prise it out, Danny.'

'I don't have a pen knife with me, do you?'

Will dug into his breeches' pocket and pulled out a small knife. He passed it through the window.

Danny slipped the point in between the stone and the wood. The edge scraped against the stone and a small chip came off the block.

'It's no good it's stuck.'

'Try again,' Josh urged.

Danny took a deep breath. He leaned into the hilt of the knife and pushed as hard as he could. 'It's moving!' And, with a last scrape, dust rose in a cloud around his face. The wood fell away and clattered onto the floor.

'There's something here!'

Everyone had their faces pushed to the windows to see what was happening. Danny reached into the hole and pulled out a dark leather sack and, with a wide smile on his face, shook it.

With excited squeals they ran into the nave and towards the west door, where everyone had gathered. Francis Woolsey stepped forward and took the sack from

Rosamund. Rosamund passed the cipher to Uncle Sam, who looked at it and laughed again. Francis pulled with his teeth at the lace that was tying the pouch. He gently tipped some of the contents into Rosamund's hand. A shaft of sunlight lit up a glitter of whites, reds and blues. Francis moved to a nearby table and to a chorus of 'ahhs' he emptied the rest of the treasure onto a white linen cloth that lay on a small table. There were diamonds, rubies, emeralds and at least a fistful of gold and silver coins.

'Why, 'tis a king's ransom,' Peter said. There were mutters of agreement.

'And it is returned to our family.' Francis looked at Rosamund. 'But there are things even more precious.' He reached to the table and selected five gold coins. 'Danny, Perinne, Will, Nathan and Josh, I want you to have these.' He handed each of them one of the coins. 'I have you all to thank not only for finding the treasure, but for looking after Rosamund and keeping her safe. I cannot think what you have all been through and how you have watched the plot unfold. Perinne, who found out who stole the pouch from Rosamund and Danny, Will and Nathan, putting yourselves in mortal danger. You are all to be commended.'

As Perinne took her coin she noticed that Rosamund's face looked sad and wondered if it were because her father hadn't given her a coin. But surely she would want for nothing now that the treasure – and the money that had been hidden in the locket, had been returned to her family.

'What is wrong, Rosamund? Are you not happy?'

'I don't want treasure, I want my mother,' said Rosamund.

'We'll get back to the quay,' Will said. 'They must be arrivin' soon, c'me on, Nathan, let's go.'

They left by the open door where the Reverend Jackson was bidding farewell to Sir Charles and Lady Elizabeth. James Clarke and Hannah had also made their way outside and were chatting to Rowland and Peter. Perinne, Danny and Josh held their coins, watching as Uncle Sam gathered the treasure back into the sack and drew tight the laces.

'Soon, we'll see her soon, Rosa,' Francis Woolsey said, stroking his daughter's hair.

A sudden crash echoed off the thick stone walls.

'I'll have that!' Levi Bird glared at Francis Woolsey, his face twisted like a snarling hound and his sly eyes scanning the church.

'Maman!' Perinne cried out.

Josh grabbed Danny's arm and hid behind him. Levi lurched forwards and grabbed Rosamund pointing his pistol at her head. She screamed a piercing cry that filled the huge building with her fear.

'Stop!' Francis shouted. 'Don't you dare harm her!' He stepped forward.

'Then give me what be mine,' Levi snarled.

'It isn't yours,' Francis shouted.

'It was won by a friend.'

'It was stolen!' Samuel put in.

'Stop it. Let her go, Levi Bird. She's done you no harm.'

Danny looked at Josh, Josh nodded and they sped away.

'Help! Help!' They rushed through the door and out into the sunshine, the bright light making them blink. They each ran to their fathers.

'Come, quickly, Levi's holding a pistol to Rosamund's head,' Danny screamed.

'What?' It was Will. He was with Caleb.

'Come here, boys.' Danny and Josh ran to Danny's father. 'Stay here. Jack, run for help.'

James, Rowland and Peter ran into the church, the vicar followed them.

'There's a door,' Will whispered to Nathan and Caleb. They disappeared around the back of the building.

'Put down the pistol!' James Clarke demanded.

'This is a house of God!' The vicar pushed himself in front. 'Let the child go.'

'Give me the treasure.' Levi snarled as he held onto Rosamund tightly.

'Give it to him, Francis,' Samuel pleaded.

'Father!' Rosamund cried.

Before anyone could speak again a brown hand swiftly grabbed the pistol and two huge arms surrounded the skinny Levi, pulling him to the floor. Caleb held Levi down and Will and Nathan used their belts to tie his hands and feet.

Rosamund collapsed to the floor. Caleb bent and scooped her up into his arms for the second time.

'It's you. You saved me, that night on the beach. It was you who brought me here.'

The Reverend Jackson ordered drinks to be fetched.

'Is my wife here yet?' Francis asked.

'Almost, sir,' Will said. 'The tide's changed an' they'll be in the 'arbour soon.'

'With these men out of the way and my family together again, we can begin our new life in peace. Thank you everyone.'

The gathering made its way down to the quayside. Except for Sir Charles Tarrant and James Clarke, who waited until the constable and Joshua Stevens arrived to take away Levi Bird.

'So, sir, Philip Stone was setting up a gang with the help of Meekwick Ginn.'

'Hmmph, we'll soon put a stop to that. Draft a summons and send it to Burton Hall ordering Stone to attend the assizes, and the daughter, Malvina is it? No doubt they'll buy themselves out of trouble, but it'll shock the girl out of her ill behaviour and hopefully see the family leave Christchurch for the shame of it all.'

Rosamund, Francis and Samuel were waiting at the water's edge, the others a short distance away.

'Do yew always have adventures?' Josh asked. 'I don't have friends like yew in Conyer to have adventures with.'

Danny, Will and Perinne laughed.

'It seems that way,' Will said. 'But it c'd be our last.'

'You're going to London?' Danny asked.

'Yes. We're goin' to meet some people who are also tryin' to stop the slave trade.'

Nathan nodded.

'And Perinne's aunt says she can't see us anymore,' Danny said.

'Aunt Elizabeth will not be able to give orders to me soon.'

'Why?'

'We are moving out of Cliff House.'

'Where to?'

'I do not know.' Perinne looked sad.

'Look,' Nathan said.

A small boat with a single white sail appeared on the calm of the water. It passed by the reed beds and approached the wooden pier. A man with a wide brimmed hat jumped on to the quayside and tied up the boat. He held out his hand. A small, slim woman with a blue cloak and an old faded bonnet stepped off. She scanned the riverbank. Rosamund let go of her father's hand and ran leaping with joy into her mother's arms.

About *The Face of Sam*

The carved face 'Sam'

The 'Face of Sam', and indeed all the carvings described in the cipher, can be found in Christchurch Priory Church. The 'face' is high above the nave and was given the name 'Sam' by author Eric Cockain, who has examined the Saxon origins of the Priory Church.

We will never know who he was, but he inspired this book.

Raid on the Customs House, Poole

The raid on the Customs House at Poole was a true event. It was a joint venture between a smuggling gang from Sussex and the Hawkshurst gang from Kent, to smuggle in a large quantity of tea and other items. They were caught in Christchurch Bay, all their goods seized and taken to Poole. They vowed to get their goods back and staged a daring raid. On arriving in Poole it is said they found no defence other than a navy ship on the harbour with its guns pointing at the Customs House. However, these were rendered useless at low tide and the gang took their chance. They met with no opposition and regained their goods.

On the return journey some of the men were recognised by friends, but they were to pay for this as they were taken and tortured. Smuggling was big business and things often got nasty.

The Treasure

There is a legend of treasure being hidden somewhere in Christchurch Priory Church. Not the treasure in the story, but that mentioned by some of the characters as Prior Draper's treasure, a term I invented for the book. John Draper was Prior at Christchurch at the time of the dissolution. It was he who persuaded Henry VIII to give the church to the people of Christchurch as a parish church, rather than have it demolished like many other religious buildings, due to the King's fall out with the Pope and Rome. It is said that some of the treasures of the Priory were secreted away before the monastic buildings were destroyed. They could be somewhere!

The Funeral

18th-century funerals were, especially for the wealthy, grand affairs and processions of mourners could reach a mile long. The horses would wear black feathers, more associated with the Victorians. The family of the deceased would provide gloves and other such favours to the mourners.

Glossary

Ankers – Small barrels, usually carrying spirits, such as gin or brandy.

Baccy – tobacco

Bannocking – A beating

Cordial – a drink, though not like the cordials we have today. The first reference to cordial I can find is in a 1747 cookery book and is for cordial poppy water. Most drinks were brewed to kill bacteria from unclean water.

Collector – Person who collected duties at ports.

Controller – The Controller of Customs was in charge of collecting payments of dues at ports and was in charge of the collectors.

Flittermouse – A bat

Free Trading – Another term for smuggling

Geneva – Gin – the name comes from the French word, genévrier, meaning juniper, an ingredient of gin.

Islanders – In the book, this refers to people from the Isle of Wight, another place popular with smugglers.

Owlers – Wool smugglers

Landers – Once contraband had reached the shores, smuggled goods became the responsibility of the lander. The lander organised the transport onward, arranging for ponies and carts and for men to carry the goods ashore.

Spotsmen –The man on board ship responsible for ensuring the vessel reached the correct point on the shore to land.

Mantua making – Mantuas were a type of ladies' coat or garment for over a dress. In 18th-century Christchurch many young girls undertook apprenticeships in mantua making.

Fossils – Barton Cliffs are well known for the fossils

encased in the clay cliffs. It is also possible to find fossilised sharks teeth along the shoreline. [The cliffs can be dangerous as the mud can be wet and people do get stuck.]

Gustavus Brander – Gustavus Brander was a resident of Christchurch. He collected and catalogued fossils he found at Barton on Sea and presented his collection to the British Museum.

Ostler – The person in charge of the stables at an inn.

Overseers – Overseers were appointed to look after the needs of the poor in the parish, to find them work and provide a poor house.

Poor House – or workhouse – A place for people who were unable to look after themselves

Preventatives – Waterguards stationed around the coast

Quomp – The word is believed to describe a wet, boggy area.

Scurvy – A disease caused by lack of vitamin C. Sailors in the 18th century and before who made long journeys often caught scurvy.

Side saddle riding – Perinne would have ridden her pony side-saddle and would have had a special ladies' saddle for this purpose.

Places in Christchurch

Here are places in Christchurch mentioned in *The Face of Sam* that you can still visit (v) or see:

Christchurch Priory & St Michael's Loft (School room) (v)
    (Note: the cipher is made up of actual carvings and can be
    followed in the Priory Church)
The Red House Museum (Poor House) (v)
Place Mill (v)
The Castle (v)
The Old House (the Constable's House) (v)
The George public house (v)
The Eight Bells shop (v)
The Ship public house (v)
The Ship in Distress public house (v)
The Marshes (Stanpit Marsh) (v)
Mudeford (v)
Quomps (v)
Sopley Church (v)

Dr Quartley's house still stands but is a private residence.
Burton Hall is now private residences
There remain some old cottages in Burton similar to the one
    Danny would have lived in.
Will's old cottage would have stood near to the by-pass where
    a car park now stands.
There was no such place as Cliff House. There was a building
    called High Cliff and this was replaced in the early 19th
    century by Highcliffe Castle.
The Bargate was destroyed in 1744 but there is a road,
    Bargates, in the town centre
Poole is an ancient port and the Customs House of the story
    was replaced with the current Customs House.
Bournemouth did not exist in 1781 but Kinson, Throop and
    Holdenhurst were villages at this time.

Bibliography

Local

Beamish, Dockerill, Hillier – The Pride of Poole 16881851 –
Borough of Poole / Poole Historical Trust -1974
Christchurch Priory - Guidebook
Cockain, E – The Saxon Face of Christchurch Priory – Natula
Publications 2004
Newman, Sue – The Christchurch and Bournemouth Union
Workhouse – S Newman 2000

General

Day, Malcolm – Voices from the world of Jane Austen – David &
Charles 2007
E Russell Oakley – The Legends of the Miraculous Beam and The
Buried Treasure at Christchurch Priory Church as recorded by
writers in the 18th Century and later– E Russell Oakley 1944
Olsen, Kirsten – Daily life in 18th-Century England – Greenwood
Press 1999
Picard L, Dr Johnson's London – Weidenfeld & Nicholson 2000
Platt R, Smuggling in the British Isles – Tempus - 2007 Quennel
M & CHB
Smith, Graham, Hampshire and Dorset Shipwrecks – Countryside
Books 1995

Other sources

Christchurch Priory Church
Christchurch History Society
The Red House Museum and Gardens

The internet

www.thepirateking.com
www.localhistories.org
www.bl.uk
www.timetravelbritain.com
Rootsweb at www.ancestry.com
www.kentresources.co.uk/smug.htm
www.discoveringbristol.com
http://blog.mikerendell.com/
www.ukagriculture.com/livestock/sheep_wool_production.cfm
www.kentarchaeology.ac/

The Author

J. A. Ratcliffe

Married with three adult sons and two grandchildren, Julie Ratcliffe is an honours graduate of the Open University (1988). She studied British social history and literature from 16th to 19th centuries, including comparative work between Britain and Europe and Britain and America.

Julie has enjoyed writing from childhood. She began writing children's stories when working for Bolton Public Libraries, and often read her work to visiting school children. However, she never attempted to have the stories published. She continued to invent stories for her three boys, but it is only now that she has decided to publish her work.

Although born and raised in the north west of England, Julie has lived in Christchurch, Dorset since 1980. Here she has become fascinated with the history of this ancient town with its medieval relics, beautiful, cathedral-sized Priory Church, two rivers and quays. The town's development has been well-documented throughout the ages; Christchurch can trace its Mayors back to the 12th century.

Julie is a member of the Society of Authors and the Society of Women Writers and Journalists. She is a member of the Christchurch History Society and attends meetings of the Village Writers, who gather monthly in the New Forest. *The Face of Sam* is her second children's novel.

www.julieratcliffe.co.uk

Domini Deane

Domini Deane is a popular Dorset artist whose work has been featured on numerous book covers, prints and greeting cards, and in various publications, including ImagineFX magazine. Most of Domini's illustrations are in watercolour, and her art is noted for vibrant use of colours and exquisite detail.

Domini is currently designing a Chinese zodiac collection and a series of multi-cultural angels. She recently created three of the popular lion sculptures in the Pride of Bournemouth exhibit. Domini also loves illustrating children's books and plans to write her own someday.

Born in the Rocky Mountains of Colorado, Domini has spent most of her life in England. She and her husband (a graphic designer) live and work in south Dorset.

For more information, please visit:

www.dominideane.com

By the same author

The Thirteenth Box

'Nearly everyone in Christchurch is a smuggler, or at least takes in the spoils,' Will Gibbs tells his new friend. 'But somethin' different's goin' on.'

It's March 1780. Smuggling along England's coast is rife, and dangerous ... Boxes holding parts of a mysterious machine have been smuggled into a small, south coast town and the chase is on to capture them, especially the all-important thirteenth box.

In this thrilling story of mystery and adventure, three young friends put themselves in great danger whilst trying to find out what's going on in their seemingly ordinary town. Who does the machine belong to? And amongst the strange characters they encounter, just who can they trust?

The Thirteenth Box, is the first in the series *Smugglers' Town Mysteries. S*et in 18th-century England, it is action-packed and full of colourful characters. With a historically correct setting and using real places which families can still visit, it gives a fascinating insight into life at the time.

National Self-published Book of the Year Award – Runner up

Organised by *Writing Magazine* and the David St John Thomas Charitable Trust

'Magnificently produced'
'Fantastic attention to details.'

What the press says

'A cracking good adventure story ... nothing interferes with a story led plot perfect for around 10-12s...'
The School Librarian

'The pace never lulls in this intriguing adventure that throws light on times past.' ★ ★ ★ ★
Bournemouth Daily Echo

'...an exciting children's story of smuggling ... the well thought out plot moves along quickly ...'
Town and Village Times

What readers say

"I really enjoyed this book. It was really exciting and the best book I have ever read. My favourite character is Perinne. I think the author is a really good writer. I like the way it is based in a real place."
Nicola, age 9

"I really liked your book, The Thirteenth Box. My favourite character was Perinne."
Isabel, age 10

"I found her reading your book very late at night when she should have been asleep!"
Rob, Isabel's Dad

"As for the book, "The Thirteenth Box", although it's aimed at Youngsters and I am not far off 81 it is one of the most enjoyable "unputtable down" quality books I have ever read.

The author has the talented secret in her writing which is that her characters come alive from the pages. One can see and hear in imagination the sounds and detect the smells even! Well I can anyway!"
Lee